LAUREN HANEY

FLESH OF THE GOD

A MYSTERY OF ANCIENT EGYPT

AVON BOOKS

An Imprint of HarperCollinsPublishers

This is a work of fiction. Names, characters, places, and incidents are products of the author's imagination or are used fictitiously and are not to be construed as real. Any resemblance to actual events, locales, organizations, or persons, living or dead, is entirely coincidental.

AVON BOOKS
An Imprint of HarperCollins*Publishers*
10 East 53rd Street
New York, New York 10022-5299

Copyright © 2002 by Betty J. Winkelman
ISBN: 0-06-052189-9
www.avonmystery.com

First Avon Books paperback printing: February 2003

Avon Trademark Reg. U.S. Pat. Off. and in Other Countries, Marca Registrada, Hecho en U.S.A.
HarperCollins® is a registered trademark of HarperCollins Publishers Inc.

Printed in the U.S.A.

10 9 8 7 6 5 4 3 2 1

Acknowledgments

I wish to thank Dennis Forbes, editor of *KMT: A Modern Journal of Ancient Egypt,* for reading this novel when I first completed it and for never giving up hope that it would one day be published. I also owe thanks to all those who, through the years, have urged its publication.

Cast of Characters

At the Fortress of Buhen

Officer Bak — Egyptian officer in charge of a company of Medjay police, formerly a chariotry lieutenant in the regiment of Amon

Sergeant Imsiba — Bak's second-in-command, a Medjay

Hori — Youthful police scribe

Pashenuro
Kasaya — Medjay policemen
Ruru
and others

Commandant Nakht — Officer in charge of the garrison of Buhen

Azzia — Nakht's foreign wife

Lupaki — Nakht's devoted servant

Nofery — Proprietress of a house of pleasure in Buhen

Lieutenant Nebwa — Infantry officer, senior officer in the garrison, and second in importance to Commandant Nakht

Lieutenant Paser — Caravan officer, responsible for transporting gold from the mines

Lieutenant Mery	Watch officer, responsible for the security of the garrison
Harmose	An archer friend of Azzia
Tetynefer	Chief steward at Buhen
Iry	Tetynefer's wife
Kames	Chief scribe
Neferperet	Chief goldsmith
Heby	A surly goldsmith
Wadjet-Renput	Overseer of the gold mine known as the Mountain of Re
Roy	Scribe at the mine

Plus various and sundry soldiers, scribes, townspeople, miners, and tribesmen

Those who walk in the corridors of power at Kemet

Maatkare Hatshepsut	Sovereign of the land of Kemet
Menkheperre Thutmose	The queen's nephew and step-son, who ostensibly shares the throne with his aunt
Commander Maiherperi	Head of the guards of the royal house

The Gods and Goddesses

Amon	The primary god during much of ancient Egyptian history, especially the early 18th Dynasty, the time of this story; takes the form of a human being
Maat	Goddess of truth and order; represented as a feather
Horus of Buhen	A local version of the falcon god

Re	The sun god; gold was considered the flesh of this god
Khepre	The rising sun
Thoth	Patron god of scribes; usually shown with the head of an ibis
Montu	The god of war; represented as a falcon
Khonsu	The moon god
Hapi	The river god

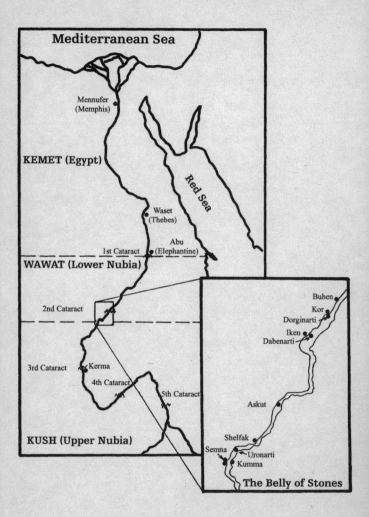

Mediterranean Sea

Mennufer
(Memphis)

KEMET (Egypt)

Red Sea

Waset
(Thebes)

Abu
(Elephantine)

1st Cataract

WAWAT (Lower Nubia)

2nd Cataract

3rd Cataract   Kerma

4th Cataract

5th Cataract

KUSH (Upper Nubia)

Buhen

Kor

Dorginarti

Iken

Dabenarti

Askut

Shelfak

Semna   Uronarti

Kumma

The Belly of Stones

FLESH OF THE GOD

A MYSTERY OF ANCIENT EGYPT

Chapter One

"All men who err must suffer the consequences. If you'd offended the gods to the extent some men have . . ." Commandant Nakht must have realized how harsh his voice had become, for he clamped his mouth shut, focused on Bak, and smiled. "Forgive me. I've no wish to burden you with the wrongs of others."

Bak uttered a sharp, bitter laugh. "Is that not why I've been sent to Buhen?"

Nakht, commandant of the fortress of Buhen, eyed him thoughtfully, shook his head. "No. Some burdens are mine alone." He turned away, closing the subject, and began to climb the long series of ladders that led to the battlements. "Come, Officer Bak, let me show you your new home."

Bak wondered if he should press further, but Nakht's rigid back forbade him. He climbed after him, his thoughts returning to the dull and dreary life he faced in the grim, uninviting fortress.

The interior of the tower was dimly lit, the mudbrick walls too thick to admit much light through the narrow loopholes placed at regular intervals so archers could rain arrows down on the enemy. Except, Bak thought dismally, the last uprising in this foul land of Wawat had been smashed twenty-six years before. The battles now were little more than skirmishes with tribesmen who swooped down on the caravans, stole whatever they could, and slipped away in the desert.

The two men climbed to the uppermost landing, passed through the open portal, and stepped onto the sunstruck walkway atop the massive white mudbrick wall surrounding the city. The hot breath of the lord Re, the sun god, enveloped them. Rivulets of sweat trickled down Bak's face, chest, and legs. Even skirmishes, he thought, would be better than the loathsome task he had been given.

"I'm an officer," he said, "a man trained in the art of war. Give me a company of spearmen or archers. I'd at least be doing what I best know how to do."

"No, Bak." Nakht's voice carried a note of sympathy, but was firm nonetheless. "Commander Maiherperi sent you here to police this city. That you will do."

As if to stress the finality of his words, he strode up the walkway. Wide enough for four men abreast, the path connected the regularly spaced towers projecting from the outer face of the battlemented wall. Bak walked beside him, half-blinded by the glare. A warm northerly breeze stirred the air, vying with the heat to dry the moisture seeping from his body. A dog's mournful howl sounded in the distance. The faint odors of fish, cooking oil, and animal waste mingled with a dust so fine he could feel it between his fingers but not see it.

Far below the breastwork lining the walkway, the white rooftops of the buildings within the citadel lay spread out like a map. Block after block of interconnected structures filled the almost square fortification, each block separated from the others by narrow lanes and streets. The heat rose in waves from the roofs. Air-shafts and courtyards, flimsy pavilions erected for shade, and the people who walked the lanes seemed to shimmer in the slight breeze. A second, outer wall enclosed a much larger rectangular area spreading north and west and south of the citadel, its stark white towers appearing to melt into the pale sandhills rising behind Buhen.

Bak eyed the city with distaste. "I've been torn from my regiment and my companions. Another officer leads my men. My horses grow fat and lazy at my father's home and my chariot grows dusty. Is that not punishment enough?"

Nakht stopped in the shade of a tower and silenced the plea with a reproving scowl. "You were a lieutenant of high merit, I've been told. Yet you felled a man of noble birth and you, with the men in your company beside you, laid waste to a house of pleasure frequented by the highest men of our land. What do you expect from me? A reward for your lack of wisdom?"

Bak smarted at the repetition of his offense. "Not a man in that house used honest throwsticks. They won all my archer's implements of war and mocked his loss. They thought the rest of us too lowly, too meek to speak up for what was ours."

"There are many ways to right a wrong, Bak, but few so rash they draw the eye of our sovereign, Maatkare Hatshepsut herself. You should be grateful you're here and still an officer. Instead you plea for a task I cannot grant you."

Bak studied the commandant, searching for a crack in his will. He found none. A hint of compassion maybe, but an unbreakable resolve to follow the instructions he had been given, instructions sent by Maiherperi, commander of the palace guard in the capital city of Waset.

Maiherperi had called Nakht an exemplary officer, a man without peer. So he seemed, in bearing more than appearance. He was of medium height, a hand's breadth shorter than Bak, and probably fifty years old, more than twice Bak's age. Where Bak's shoulders were broad and his muscles clearly defined, the commandant was slender, his well-formed body more graceful. His dark curly hair, gray at the temples, was clipped short and followed the curve of his head. Bak's hair was thick and straight, bobbed below his earlobes in the military fashion. Both men were tanned a deep bronze. Both wore thigh-length white kilts with a sheathed dagger hanging from a narrow belt. Only the commandant wore jewelry, a turquoise scarab ring and a broad collar made of red and blue beads. And only he carried a baton of office. Bak had not yet been given a new baton denoting his altered status.

"I'll do as you command," Bak said, bowing his head to acknowledge Nakht's authority.

Nakht could have reminded him he had no choice. Instead, he glanced toward the sun as if checking the time, then walked to the nearest crenel, rested his hands on the base of the opening, and looked out at the distant horizon.

"To be an officer in charge of a company of Medjays is an honor many men would envy," he said. "Those who guard the palace and those who police the mightiest cities of Kemet are highly esteemed for their courage and honesty."

"That I know," Bak admitted. "During the voyage from Waset, I learned to like and respect the men I brought with me, especially my sergeant, Imsiba. But to stay within these walls, to punish men who pilfer and cheat, to break up drunken brawls . . ." He paused, unwilling to confess he thought the task degrading.

Nakht swung around so Bak could see his wry smile. "The punishment suits the offense, does it not?"

Bak's face grew hot with embarrassment.

The smile vanished and Nakht leaned back, elbows resting on the base of the crenel. "You think your task unimportant and not worthy of your skills. In that you err. True, you'll not have your chariot and horses, but you'll use your other skills. And your wits as well."

Bak was offended. Surely the commandant knew he had led the first rank of chariots, the premier company of charioteers in the regiment of Amon. Was he implying such a task required no thought or planning?

Nakht raised his baton to acknowledge a passing sentry, a muscular, square-faced man wearing a kilt like Bak's, carrying a white cowhide shield and a spear taller than he was. The sun, high overhead, touched the bronze spearpoint, making it glitter more like gold than the baser metal.

If the commandant was aware of Bak's indignation, he gave no hint. "Since the great king Akheperkare Thutmose took back this land from the rebels, we've rebuilt the city within these walls. Now, the time has come to hone its rough edges, to make it more a place for living and less a garrison. The soldiers, the traders who come and go, the prisoner-miners who pass through, and the camp followers who serve their base needs—all must learn to behave as they would in any city of Kemet. That is why I asked Maiherperi to send a company of Medjay police. They, with you at their head, will go far toward making that happen."

"Will we bring order to Buhen?" Bak asked in a dry voice, "or will we be the center of a storm?"

"You surprise me," Nakht said, eyeing him with approval. "How did you guess so soon?"

"Wawat is the birthplace of my Medjays. Their grandfathers fought the soldiers of Kemet, hoping to free their land of intruders, and many lives were lost on both sides. Their fathers rebelled and again men died. Their brothers live here still and some of them raid our caravans, taking lives each time. Even though my men grew to manhood in Kemet and think of it as their homeland, I know—as do they—that they'll not easily be accepted or trusted by men who think of Medjays as the enemy. I said as much to Maiherperi."

"And he said?"

Bak had to smile. " 'To face a challenge and win is far more satisfying than to win by default.' "

Nakht chuckled. "Yes, he would say such a thing. He spouts wisdom with the ease of a priest."

They laughed together.

Nakht sobered, gave Bak a speculative look. "I think you have the wit to do any task set before you, the stubbornness to see it through to the end, and the pride to do it well. You'll need those traits and more to assimilate your Medjays into this garrison. Do you think you can curb your rashness and swallow your resentment at being sent here long enough to prove your worth and theirs?"

Bak took the question as a challenge, one his pride would not allow him to resist. "Last evening when our ship docked at the quay and we entered this fortress, few men we passed greeted us with a smile. I can make no promises, for men's thoughts are difficult to change. But I hope, when I sail back to Kemet, that I'll see my

Medjays standing beside those same men as trusted companions."

Nakht nodded his satisfaction. "I can ask no more."

He stepped aside, making additional space at the crenel so they both could look beyond the wall. Bak frowned at what he considered the most forbidding land he had ever seen. Below, along the terraced base of the fortress, the brownish waters of the river that gave life to this land flowed wide and deep, north to Kemet, where he longed to be. Three long stone quays projected into the water in front of two towered gates and a broader pylon gate. Two sturdy cargo ships and four smaller, lighter trading vessels were moored alongside. A line of men plodded along the quay between the gate on which they stood and the larger of the two cargo vessels, their backs bent low beneath heavy copper ingots bound for workshops in Kemet.

Farther out, a dozen fishermen's skiffs tacked diagonally across the water, their sails appearing in the distance like the wings of birds. Across the river, a long stretch of green, a fertile oasis in a land of rocks and sand, looked dusty and indistinct in the sweltering haze. Nothing lay beyond but sandhills bleached almost white by the unforgiving sun.

The faint honking of geese drew both men's gaze to the pallid sky above. A flock of thirty or more birds flew south, too high for arrows to reach, too wily to rest and feed near an oasis inhabited by man. Bak watched them fade from sight, envying them their freedom to go where they wished.

Nakht, who must have noticed the wistful look on his face, gave him an understanding smile. "I lived in the land of Hatti for many years, a place as rich in its own way as the valley of this river. As I grew older, I yearned to return to Kemet, the land of my birth. I thought to spend the remainder of my life with my feet on its rich black soil, walking through fields of grain and fruits and vegetables." His smile gave way to a cynical chuckle. "When finally I did return, I was sent here to the southern frontier."

"You dislike Buhen, as I do?"

Nakht's smile dissolved. "The fortress, no. It's much like any other garrison. And dislike is too pale a word; I was afraid." He held out his hand as if making an offering of the view across the river. "It was the land itself I feared, this dry, barren land of Wawat, this desert which surrounds us. I thought it an empty and brutal place where no man could walk without thirst or hunger, heat or poisonous creatures. However, in the year I've been here . . ." He paused and his smile this time contained no irony, no cynicism. "I cannot say I've grown to love the desert, but I respect it and think it a place of great beauty."

Bak could think of nothing to say; he was too surprised the commandant would utter such personal thoughts to a man he had met less than an hour before.

Nakht laughed—at himself, Bak thought. "I've said enough, perhaps too much. I hope one day you'll come to like Buhen and be as proud to serve this garrison as I am to command it."

Bak swallowed a denial. He was convinced he would never like this vile city or the onerous task of policing it.

The commandant seemed not to expect a hasty and insincere promise. He once again glanced toward the sun, and his voice became crisp, purposeful. "You must, within the next few days, impress on the men in this garrison that I mean to have order here. They must see you and your Medjays in action and me standing behind you with the scales of justice. Sweep the market for false weights or . . . ?" His expectant look left no doubt he wanted a suggestion which could be expanded to a plan.

Bak stared at the sunbaked land across the river, mulling over various ways of introducing a police force in a place where none had ever been. The most obvious idea was the least appealing, for it was born of his own past behavior.

"I've heard the monthly rations were given out today," he said. "Many men will visit houses of pleasure this night. Name for me the foulest of the lot, one with many patrons, a place louder and more unruly than all the others. My men and I will come upon them in the dark and take them like fish in a net."

He felt like a traitor, plotting the downfall of men no better than he.

Bak raced around the corner with six armed Medjay policemen close on his heels. In the flickering light of the torch he carried, he saw twenty-five or more men scuffling in the gloomy moonlit lane. The hard-packed sand beneath their bodies was slick and wet, the air thick with the stench of sweat, stale beer, and vomit. A far-off chorus of barking dogs mingled with garbled, drunken taunts and the thud of fist striking flesh.

A pottery jar flew through the air, spewing beer from its open mouth. Bak spotted the missile, ducked. The jar whipped past his head and smashed into the wall beside him, splattering its sticky contents over his bare torso and fresh white kilt. Muttered curses echoed his own and he guessed several of his men had also been caught in the shower.

He raised his torch high. The lane, three cubits wide, broad enough for three men abreast, ran arrow straight between two rows of connected single-story mudbrick houses, their doors shut tight. It ended at a broad path which ran along the base of the massive wall enclosing the fortress. A torch at the far end told him Sergeant Imsiba and six additional Medjays were there to bag the prey he meant to sweep into their hands.

In the middle, trapped between the two forces, were the brawlers: soldiers alleviating the boredom of frontier duty, sailors relieving the tedium of a long voyage, prisoner-miners celebrating the completion of their sentences before going home to Kemet. Their shadows flitted across the facades of the houses as they pummeled each other, rolled over broken jars and puddles of beer, tried to creep away only to be caught up and drawn back into the fray. A dozen or more heads peered down from above, residents who had complained long and loud, so Nakht had said, about the frequent brawls outside their homes.

The focus of the battle was a place of business midway along the lane, the house of pleasure of the old woman Nofery. Her bulk, planted in the doorway, cut off much of the light streaming from within. She stood, crossed arms resting on her mammoth belly, braying like an ass to goad the fighters on. She would sing a different song later, Bak thought, would whine like a starving cur at what he had in mind for her.

He turned to the men behind him. "Ready?"

The way they hefted their spotted cowhide shields and heavy, head-high wooden staffs told him they were. The way their teeth flashed in their dark-skinned faces told him how much they were looking forward to the skirmish. He raised his torch and waved it back and forth. The flame sputtered, sparks cascaded to the ground. The signal was returned from the far end of the lane. He handed the torch to one of his men and took in exchange his shield and baton of office.

"Let's go," he said.

With three men behind him and another three behind them, they swept forward, filling the lane so no one could slip past. The nearest pair of besotted men, both on their knees swinging ineffectual punches, glanced up and gaped. Bak relished the look of disbelief on their faces. He could imagine what they saw: a baton-wielding officer of Kemet followed by a wall of bright shields, the Medjays' legs, arms, and heads vague shadows in the dark. One of the pair bellowed like a rampaging bull, scrambled to his feet, and tried to run away from what he clearly thought were demons from the netherworld. The second man tried to rise, blundered into the first man's legs, and they fell together. Bak prodded them with his baton, forcing them forward into the mêlée.

The pair stumbled into another man, who grabbed one of them, shoved him against the wall, and slammed his head onto the plastered surface with as much force as he could muster. A Medjay broke ranks, grabbed the attacker by the hair, and pitched him into a trio wrestling on the ground.

"The Medjays!" someone shrieked. "The Medjays!"

Bak's eyes homed in on Nofery, whose hands were cupped around her mouth to form a horn.

"Don't let them take you without a fight!" she screamed. "They don't belong here! You do!"

Bak saw the closest of the brawlers stiffen, pull away from each other, stare at him and his men. He saw the besotted grins forming on their faces and knew he had just a few precious moments before every man in the lane took up the old harridan's challenge.

"Let's move!" he shouted to his men. "Quickly! Before her words give them the courage of lions!"

Irritated by her defiance, afraid of what would happen if she had her way, he swung his baton wide and whipped it down, clouting a swaying figure. Then he used it as a prod, forcing others to scramble forward. The Medjays followed, using their staffs on heads and arms and legs, their shields to squash the closest men into those farther ahead, shoving them into a helpless mass that could do nothing but retreat.

As they drew closer to the house of pleasure, Nofery's voice took on a note of urgency. "Fight, you curs! You're men of Kemet! Show the barbarians what you can do!"

The words fueled Bak's anger and his mouth hardened into a thin, tight line. With his shield clamped to his forearm, he gripped both ends of his baton, raised it horizontally at breast level, and shoved it forward, pushing the bodies ahead of him. Nofery glanced his way; her sly smile dissolved. She tried to back off, but he grabbed her upper arm. It was so fat and soft, all he caught was a wad of sagging flesh. He squeezed, forcing a groan from her lips. With the other hand, he shoved the end of the baton into the mass of fleshy wrinkles beneath her chin, forcing her head high.

"You, old woman, will be silent." He spoke with the soft hiss of a crocodile slipping into the water. "If not . . ." He nudged the baton deeper into her neck, letting the threat hang unspoken, planting a seed of anxiety he hoped would sprout and grow.

He pushed her into the building and hurried after his men, who were already two-thirds of the way along the lane. Beyond them, he heard angry shouts and ugly, resentful taunts. He cursed aloud, knowing he must resolve the situation before it developed into a pitched battle. He caught up, slipped past his men. Facing the Medjays at the far end of the lane were six or eight men who had worked themselves into a mindless fury.

A hulking dark-visaged man—a sailor, Bak thought—was standing in the center of the group, hands on hips. "Sons of whores!" he sneered. "Hairless monkeys!"

Imsiba and the Medjays with him stood stiff and mute, their muscles as taut as bowstrings, their eyes glittering with anger.

"We police ourselves!" yelled a tall, gangly man, a clerk, from the look of him. "We don't need outsiders to do it for us!"

"My father came here with the army twenty-five years ago," hissed a stocky, balding man. Bak had seen him on guard duty at the quay. "He was slain fighting your fathers. Am I supposed to submit to you now?"

Bak shoved his way around the motley group to stand with Imsiba. He whistled a long, piercing note to summon additional men. The sergeant gave him a tight but relieved smile. Some of the tension seeped from the other Medjays' faces.

"You!" Bak aimed his baton at the sailor. "And you and you!" He pointed to the guard and the clerk. "And you!" He swept his arm from right to left to indicate all those standing with them. "You will spend the night as my prisoners. Tomorrow the commandant will pass judgment."

Defiance darkened the faces of the sailor and two or three others. The less belligerent looked at one another with flagging confidence. The rabble behind them muttered and shrank back as if to distance themselves.

"We've done nothing wrong," a squat bow-legged man whined. "We were having a good time, that's all."

"Go!" Bak commanded, aiming his baton toward the intersecting lane that ran along the base of the fortress wall.

The sailor sneered. "Who are you to tell us . . . ?"

"Look!" the clerk exclaimed. "Patrol dogs!"

All eyes turned in the direction he pointed. Six Medjays had appeared in the lane behind Imsiba. Standing among them were an equal number of brindle and tan and white dogs with pointed muzzles, upright ears, and lean, powerful bodies. Each was poised for action yet ominously quiet.

The sailor's words died away; his companions' last drop of resistance dissolved. With drooping shoulders and slow, shuffling feet, they allowed themselves to be taken into custody. Well contented with the outcome, Bak ordered his men to escort all the brawlers to the commandant's residence. There, a scribe would register their names and offenses before they were taken to the barracks to sleep off the beer.

As soon as the lane was empty of humanity, Bak entered Nofery's house of pleasure, a mean and cramped space, hazy with smoke from oil lamps, though only three burned. The obese old woman was standing at the back beside a table piled high with pottery drinking bowls. A dozen low three-legged stools were scattered about, some overturned. Large pottery jars were stacked next to dirty, scarred walls. The air reeked of burned oil, sweat, and Nofery's alcoholic wares. Beyond the curtained door at the back, he had been told, lay the room where her women serviced their customers. They would have slipped away during the mêlée.

"Now, old woman," he said, "we will talk."

Rather than cringing and whining as he expected, she gave him a sly, gap-toothed smile and handed him an unplugged jar of beer. "I've heard of you, Officer Bak, and I think we can be friends, good friends."

He eyed her narrowly, sniffed the contents of the open jar, and wrinkled his nose at its sour odor. "You serve this swill to your friends?"

Cackling like a trussed guinea fowl, she pawed through a stack of jars against the rear wall. "From what I hear, you aren't always so particular, but maybe I can find something that'll please you more."

He stiffened at her words but kept his expression coolly indifferent.

She took the beer jar from him and presented a taller, slimmer vessel, this one topped with the clay seal of one of the finest breweries in Kemet. He broke the seal and removed the plug, sniffed the contents, and nodded his appreciation. Waving away the drinking bowl she offered, he sat on a stool and pulled another close to use as a table.

"What have you heard, old woman?" he asked. "Tales of vile Medjays? Savages one and all?"

Her smile was smug. "You were a charioteer, they say, a lieutenant in the regiment of Amon. They say you led the men of your company in a brawl in a house of pleasure. Not a lowly place like mine, but one in the capital itself, where the wealthy and powerful play. The scandal reached the ears of our sovereign, they say, and you were stripped of your rank and sent here with the Medjays so you could no longer embarrass your regiment and your commander."

He sipped his beer, allowing no hint of irritation to show on his face. He knew rumors flew through the land of Kemet faster than the swiftest bird, but he had not expected word of his humiliation, his disgrace, to spread through this fortress outpost so quickly.

"That makes you my friend?" he asked.

She drew a stool near his makeshift table and sank onto it, her fat haunches drooping around it. She leaned toward him, gave him a coy look. "We were molded from the same clay, Officer Bak. You enjoy the pleasures of the flesh, and I can provide them."

Bak pictured the back room, filthy, lice-infested, little better than a pig sty. He laughed. Even in Buhen he should be able to do better for himself than that. "Pleasure is not the reason I came here alone, old woman."

Her smugness faded; her voice grew defensive, plaintive. "I'm the poor slave of a business that barely keeps me in food and dress. Other than pleasure, what can I give you?"

He took another sip, set down the bowl, and tapped her fat knee. "Inciting a riot is an offense against the lady Maat." Maat was the goddess of order and truth.

She jerked away from his touch, almost toppling her stool. "You can't take me before the viceroy! No! You can't! I'd lose everything! It would kill me!" She dropped her face into her hands, moaned, and rocked back and forth on her stool as if mourning the death of a loved one.

He continued to sip the beer, allowing her to bleat on and on, giving her ample time to dwell on her fate. At last he said, "Be quiet, old woman. Listen to me."

The moaning stopped and she lowered her hands. Her face was wet, but with real tears or sham he could not tell.

"I don't like being a policeman," he said, his voice grim and hard. "I don't like this barren land of Wawat and I don't like this dreary fortress of Buhen. The only way I know of escaping, of getting back to my regiment, is to make the city within these walls a place of law and order, a city pleasing to the lady Maat. And you can help me."

She sat dead quiet, her expression a mixture of wariness and doubt.

"First," he said, "you must control your customers. I want no more complaints from your neighbors about brawls in this lane. Second, you must speak at all times with respect when you talk of my men. They're Medjays, yes—but their loyalties lie with Kemet, and you must tell your customers this truth. Third, old woman, you must tell me all you see and hear within these walls that will help me with my task."

"You'd make me your spy?" she asked, stiff with indignation.

"Would you prefer to face the viceroy?"

She studied the set of his jaw, gave a harsh but not altogether unfriendly laugh, and heaved her bulk off the stool. "You're a hard man, Officer Bak. And I like hard men. If I were twenty years younger . . ."

"Sir!"

Bak's glance swiveled toward the outer door. A slim young man stood in the portal, panting, sweat running down his bare breast. He carried the shield and spear of a fortress guard.

"You must come at once, sir. It's Commandant Nakht. He's been slain! His life taken by a hand not his own!"

Chapter Two

Nakht lay on his back in the middle of his private reception room. His eyes were closed, his face contorted in an impossible smile. Fresh blood was everywhere. It was smeared across the white-plastered floor beneath him. It stained his hands and his bare torso and his kilt. A reddish trickle ran from his mouth to the hair at the nape of his neck. A second, wider stream had flowed from the dagger imbedded in his breast and down his ribcage to a streaked puddle on the floor. His death could not have been easy, but with luck and the quick intervention of the gods, his ka, his eternal double, had slipped from his body soon after the attack.

Bak stood on the threshold, barely aware of the armed guard at his shoulder or the murmurs of disbelief and curiosity issuing from the lips of the dozen or so people clustered in the torchlit courtyard behind him. He stared with dismay at the scene. All he could think of was Nakht's reference to offenses against the gods and a burden he alone must shoulder. Had he been slain to keep secret the knowledge he had refused to share? If he, Bak, had been less concerned about himself, if he had urged the commandant to speak, would he still live and breathe?

The watch officer, Lieutenant Mery, the man who stood at the head of the fortress guard, knelt beside the bloodied form. His slim, boyish torso glistened in the light of a flaming torch mounted in a wall bracket next to the door. His face, as perfectly molded as a statue of royalty, was drawn and pale, accenting a small livid scar at the corner of his mouth.

An overturned chair lay behind Nakht's body. On a narrow cedar table standing beside it, a pair of pottery oil lamps burned with a dull glow. Several chests, low tables, and stools, all simply but beautifully crafted, were scattered around the room. A lean, hard-faced spearman was posted before a second open door. Through the portal, Bak could see part of the long mudbrick stairway that climbed the inner side of the fortress wall from the ground floor to the battlements, dark and enclosed to roof level, open to the air from the roof to the walkway atop the wall. A stairway for soldiers to use in time of battle, unlike a more formal stone stairwell in another part of the building, which rose to the private apartments on the second floor and opened onto the courtyard.

A fleeting whimper, like the mewling of a newborn kitten, drew him into the room. Standing next to the wall to his right, beside a cedar chest inlaid with ebony, was a shapely young woman of no more than twenty years. Her face, her hands, her ankle-length white sheath were smeared with blood. Her eyes, pools of amber in a rigid, stark white face, were locked on the dead man. Her red-brown hair was pulled back and braided, the thick plait hanging to her waist.

Hovering by her side, his cheeks wet with tears, was a stocky man of middle years wearing a belted white knee-length tunic. His brown braid was as thick and long as the woman's. He was the commandant's personal servant, Bak knew, a man named Lupaki, whom Nakht had brought with him from the land of Hatti. If the woman's hair and pale eyes told true, she too must have come from that distant place. Bak wondered who she was. A servant, most likely, or perhaps Nakht's concubine.

He recalled the words of Maiherperi, who had advised him at length before sending him to Buhen with the Medjays. When a man is slain in his home, the commander had said, look first to the members of his household; learn which had reason to hate him and which had the most to gain from his death and you'll very likely learn the name of the guilty man—or woman. If the burden Nakht had mentioned concerned domestic matters, Bak thought, that might well explain his reluctance to speak.

He crossed to the body, relieved this death would be so easily resolved. Kneeling beside Mery, he placed his fingertips on Nakht's neck to search for a pulse of life. As he expected, he found nothing but the chill sweat of the dead man's last fatal struggle.

"Who did this, Lieutenant? The woman?"

"No," Mery said. "No!" His dark eyes were clouded with unhappiness and something else. Uncertainty? "I saw him in her arms, Bak. I saw the pain they shared at the end. She couldn't have done this."

"You were here when he died?"

"I came as soon as I heard her scream. Too late to see the one who stabbed him, but he still lived—barely."

"Tell me what you saw."

Mery glanced toward the woman and his mouth tightened. "Her husband is dead. Must she stand there and listen? Must she be forced to relive those moments while I describe them?"

"She was his wife?" Bak asked, surprised.

Mery nodded. "Azzia, she is called."

"She speaks our tongue?"

A humorless smile formed on Mery's lips. "Better than you and me."

Bak eyed the lifeless commandant, who had been a healthy, vigorous man of at least fifty years. More than twice the age of the foreign woman. Not unusual for a man to desire a young wife, but a choice which often led to domestic troubles. Yet he saw no reason to keep her here.

He stood up and walked to her. "You may go to your chamber, mistress. I'll speak with you later."

She moved not a single muscle and her eyes never left the face of the inert form on the floor.

"You may go," he repeated, making it an order this time.

"The shock of my master's death has stolen her reason," Lupaki said, his voice husky with emotion.

He placed a brawny arm around her waist, clasped one of her blood-stained hands, and led her like an unresisting child through the door and into the courtyard. Exclamations of shock and dismay filtered through the open portal.

Bak ordered the guard posted there to stay with her. Closing the door, he turned to Mery. "Tell me what happened."

Mery stood up, his glance accusing. "Must you treat her as a prisoner in her own home?"

"For the love of Amon, Lieutenant! She's covered with his blood. What do you expect me to do?"

Mery glared at him, but his defiance quickly melted. "You're right, of course, but I can explain her appearance."

Pulling a stool away from the wall, Bak placed it a few paces from the body and motioned Mery onto it. He chose his words carefully lest he offend this officer who was his superior in rank if not in authority under the laws he had been sent to uphold.

"I see you admire her," he said, "but you must do nothing to protect her. If I'm to find the one who committed this terrible deed, I must be led along a straight and true path."

With an unhappy nod, Mery sank onto the stool and clasped his hands between his bare knees. Bak walked around the body and knelt on its opposite side so he could watch the officer's face while he talked.

"I was making my rounds," Mery said. "After checking the sentries on the battlements, I realized I'd forgotten the list of men assigned to the gates. I came here to get it. I found the audience hall filled with the rabble your Medjays had brought and your scribe Hori placing their names on a scroll. Twenty or more other men, clerks and soldiers, were standing around the chamber, watching the activity. Lupaki and Azzia's female servants were among them."

Not surprised but irritated nonetheless, Bak said, "In other words, instead of being almost empty as it would normally have been at this time of night, the building was filled with curiosity seekers as well as my own men and their prisoners."

Mery hurried on, as if anxious to get his tale over and done with. "As I crossed the audience hall, I heard a scream. I ran up the stairs. From the courtyard, I saw light flowing through the open door of this room. I looked inside." His voice thickened. "The commandant was on the floor and mistress Azzia beside him, holding him in her arms. His blood was flowing from the wound as water through an open irrigation channel. I knew no man could save him. I motioned Lupaki and all those who'd followed to stay back and I stood there, listening. I heard Nakht say, 'Don't cry, my beloved.' And she said, 'You can't go away; you can't leave me.' He replied, 'I love you more than life, my beautiful bird.' "

Mery stared at his hands. "She said, 'How will I live without you? You're my heart.' Nakht raised his hand from his breast, his bloody hand, and laid it on her face. 'I was a man when you were a babe,' he said. 'You've always known I'd die before you.' She covered her mouth to soften a moan and said, 'But not like this.' Nakht drew her face to his and their mouths met in a kiss. When she raised her head, she asked, 'Who did this to you? Why?' He shuddered as if in terrible agony and his body went limp." Mery paused, swallowed, and his eyes found Bak's. "She refused to leave him until I summoned Lupaki."

Bak was touched in spite of his better judgment. "Did she know you were standing close by when she asked who slew him?"

"I think not. She was too intent on him to see me or anyone else."

Maybe, Bak thought, and maybe not. Yet Mery's tale could not be easily dismissed. Maiherperi had said: if you have the smallest reason to suspect the members of the slain man's household are without guilt, you must cast your net wider. With a resigned sigh, he rose and walked around the room, studying the chests and stools and tables that appeared not to have been disturbed, the overturned chair, the upright table with the burning lamps, the position of Nakht's body.

"When you entered, was the table standing as it is now?" he asked. "Were the lamps alight and placed on it?"

"Everything was just as you see it."

"He was probably seated beside the table, and with two lamps so near . . ." Bak's eyes darted toward Mery. "He must've been reading, but I see no scroll."

"The one who slew him could've taken it. Does that not prove mistress Azzia innocent? She left this room empty-handed."

Unless it was a fragment, Bak thought, a piece so small she could hide it in the bosom of her dress. He examined the chair, which was free of blood, and ran his fingers over the smooth, clean surfaces of the narrow table. "If there was a struggle, it was short-lived. Otherwise, this would've fallen over, too."

"Nakht was not a man to give up without resisting. If he'd expected the attack, he'd have done all he could to protect himself."

"Therefore he was caught off guard. The blow was true to its mark, giving him no more chance than a newborn lamb facing a jackal."

Bak's glance fell to the dagger handle, slightly longer than the breadth of a hand and carved from ebony. Below the smoky gray rock crystal pommel, it was inlaid with three narrow bands of gold. An elegant weapon, the type carried by high-ranking officers and the nobility.

"Do you recognize this?" he asked.

"I do, as you would if you'd been here longer." Mery rose to stand over the body. "It was one of Nakht's most treasured possessions. He brought the blade from the land of Hatti, and our commander-in-chief, Menkhe-perre Thutmose himself, had the handle made for him." He shuddered. "For a man to use this dagger to take his life was an abomination."

Reluctant to do what he knew he must, Bak sucked in his breath, gripped the handle, and jerked the weapon out of the lifeless breast. The blade, gory with blood, made the beer churn in his stomach. Chiding himself for the weakness, he strode to the table and held the dagger close to a lamp.

The blade was twice as long as the handle and tapered to a deadly point. It was made of a dull silvery gray metal so rare he had seen it only once or twice before. Surprised, excited, he swung around to Mery. "This is iron!"

Mery nodded. "A metal as common in Hatti, Nakht told me, as is gold in our own desert wadis."

Bak gazed at the weapon with a covetous eye. "They say it's very strong and a man who owns such a blade holds the power of the gods in his hands. I wonder if . . ." He shook his head. "No! If the one who slew Nakht meant to steal this dagger, he'd have pulled it out of his breast and carried it away. His life wasn't taken for this."

More likely, he thought, it was used simply because it was here, a convenient object for a wife to lay her hands on during a heated argument. Nevertheless, he had to look elsewhere, too, if for no other reason than to satisfy himself that he had done all he should. Laying the dagger on the table, he eyed the door that opened to the dark stairway. Obviously, the woman had smeared much of the blood, but if someone else had taken Nakht's life, he might have been spattered and left some sign farther afield.

At Bak's command, a spearman brought another torch and he entered the rough-plastered, rather musty stairwell, leaving Mery and the guard behind. He wanted no one to disturb any telltale signs. He worked his way downward a step at a time to the ground floor, unable to find any fresh smudges or spots of blood. The door at the bottom was closed but not barred. He made his way upward with equal care, again finding nothing, to an open trapdoor at roof level. Had the door been left open to admit the cooler night air to the rooms below? Or to admit a man Nakht had summoned?

He stepped onto the flat, empty rooftop and took a deep breath of the clean chill air. Wondering if he should look further, he gazed at the open flight of stairs that continued up the wall to the battlements. What exactly had Nakht said? "If you'd offended the gods to the extent some men have . . ." Men. He had made no mention of a woman. The thought spurred Bak on, but the stairs above were as free of stains as those below.

After identifying himself to the sentry at the top, he climbed onto the nearest tower, which rose from the northwest corner of the inner city, the administrative sector of Buhen. From there, he could see in the waning moonlight much of the outer city, a huge rectangular area enclosed by walls as high and strong as those around the citadel. The streets were crooked, the blocks irregular in shape, the buildings thrown together in random form. Within these cramped structures were the workshops and homes of craftsmen and traders. On the outskirts lay the animal enclosures, encampments for transient soldiers, and a necropolis of the ancients. No light was visible, no human stirred. Only the creatures of the night disrupted the silence: a chorus of dogs, a howling cat, the soft tweet of birds nesting in the wall somewhere below where Bak stood.

He puzzled over Nakht's words. Had he used the word "men" as a general term, encompassing both sexes, or had he been more specific? With no ready answer, Bak watched the sentries patrolling the battlements. Besides the man who paced the sector where he stood, he could see the more distant figures of several others. They stopped at times to look over the wall and they lingered to chat when their paths happened to meet. He felt certain a cautious man could slip from one tower to the next and onto or off the stairway without their noticing.

He looked over the breastwork at the inner city, a series of grayish rectangles outlined by straight black streets and lanes infrequently traveled in the dead of night. His eyes settled on the shadowy roof of the commandant's residence, the largest house in Buhen. It nestled in a corner with two of its walls butting against the fortress wall, its facade opening to the street. Its fourth side hugged a narrow lane—bridged by a wide board, he noticed—which separated the residence from the scribal office building and the main storehouse, easily recognized by the long parallel ridges atop its barrel-vaulted ceiling. Beyond lay the treasury and the walled mansion of the lord Horus of Buhen. The scribal offices interested Bak the most. They were empty at night, as were most of the structures in the sector, and the building had a stairway to the roof. It would take but a few moments to fly from there to the stairs descending to Nakht's reception room.

He studied the dozen or more dark smudges visible in the torchlit courtyard, men who had been watching the Medjays when the woman screamed, and considered another, equally likely possibility. With so many people milling around the ground floor, a man intent on murder could easily have slipped into the dark, enclosed stairwell and later, after slaying the commandant, rejoined the crowd without being missed.

Three ways of reaching Nakht with small chance of being seen by members of the household. All possible but risky. Foolhardy, even.

No, the foreign woman Azzia must have slain her husband. Yet doubt nagged Bak like a hungry mosquito. He dreaded talking to her, dreaded having to accuse her of taking her husband's life. But if she should prove her innocence, he dreaded more the idea of having to search further. How could he, a man whose sole experience was with horses, chariots, and battle tactics, find the one guilty man in a city of nearly five hundred?

Bak crossed the courtyard with heavy feet. He had dispatched Nakht's body to the house of death and examined the slain man's personal rooms, where he found nothing of interest. He had questioned the onlookers, who all denied having seen anyone take the stairway to the second floor, and had sent them away. And he had ordered Imsiba to go with Mery to question the men patrolling the battlements as to who and what they had seen through their night's vigil.

The moon had sunk behind the fortress wall, the torches had burned low, and the stars above sparkled in an inky void. The dark forms of potted flowers and trees, which gave the courtyard the appearance of a miniature garden, scented the air with perfume. As he approached the only lighted doorway, he nodded to the Medjay he had posted there to guard the woman Azzia.

She sat on a low three-legged stool, her back straight, her hands clasped in her lap, her head held high. No bloodstains remained on her hands or her pale, oval face, and she wore a clean unadorned linen sheath. She must have heard the patter of his sandals, for her eyes were on the door when he entered.

"Have you come to accuse me of murder?" Her voice, which held no trace of an accent, was quiet and composed, with barely a hint of tension.

He stopped short on the threshold, caught by surprise. "Did you take your husband's life?"

The servant Lupaki, standing by her side, laid a protective hand on her shoulder. Seated on the floor next to a large pottery basin, a dusky, nearly naked girl of no more than ten years raised her hand to her mouth to smother a sob. Beside the child, a twig-thin, wrinkled old woman glared at Bak over an untidy pile of bloodstained linen she clutched in her arms.

"No." Azzia looked at him, her gaze steady. "Lieutenant Mery has said you believe I did."

Bak silently cursed the watch officer for saying more than he should. The female servants must have thought his scowl meant for them, for they scurried into the next room, Azzia's bedchamber.

"I've found nothing to convince me otherwise," Bak said.

"And I was there." It came out as a whisper, and for an instant she seemed close to breaking, but she stiffened her spine and tried to smile.

That smile, so fragile and filled with pain, pierced Bak through and through. He looked away, pretending to examine the room. It was half the size of Nakht's reception room and furnished much the same. Rush mats covered the floor. The lower walls were painted with unsophisticated but delicate scenes of the animals of the desert.

"I did not take his life, that I swear. He was my . . ." She paused and her thoughts turned inward. Then she shuddered as if to free herself of memories and looked directly at Bak. "Mery said that though you believe I'm guilty, you looked beyond my husband's room for signs of another person."

"That's right." Bak's tone was brisk, covering his annoyance that he had allowed her to move him. He grabbed a stool from its place near the door, set it in front of her, and sat down. "Tell me what happened this evening."

Lupaki slipped forward, dropped to his knees before Bak, raised his hands in supplication. "Don't ask this of her, sir. You must give her time to compose herself."

"Be silent, Lupaki," Azzia said firmly. "It must be now."

"Mistress . . ."

"Would you have me punished for the death of my husband? Would you allow the one who slew him to go free?"

Bak was taken aback by the blunt questions and by the depth of anger her voice betrayed. The anger of innocence, he wondered, or of guilt?

Lupaki uttered a strangled denial and hauled himself to his feet, his face flushed with shame.

Briefly, Azzia's gaze dropped to her hands, clasped so tightly together her fingers were nearly bloodless. "We took our evening meal in the courtyard where we could enjoy the breeze. While we ate, we talked about our day, as we always do." She gave an odd little laugh, or was it a cry? "As we always did."

"What exactly did you talk about?" Bak asked, hurrying her on before she had a chance to think too deeply.

"I told him about the market, the gossip I'd heard from the other women. Nothing important. He told me he'd met with several officers, Mery, Nebwa, Paser, and others, no doubt to discuss the attacks on the caravans bringing ore from the mines, the need to send out troops to hunt down the raiding tribesmen. He said he told them of suggestions you'd made based on tactics you learned with the regiment of Amon."

Bak made no comment, but he was surprised the commandant would share so much of his official day with his wife.

"He was pleased Commander Maiherperi had sent you and the Medjays." A fleeting smile touched her lips. "He felt sure your presence here would put an end to much of the wild carousing and petty crime. And then . . ." She paused, her voice trembled. "Then he looked troubled and said . . . he said, 'But they can do nothing to help me now. I must personally deal with . . . ' "

Bak leaned toward her, his pulses quickening. "Go on."

"He never finished the thought. I urged him to explain, but he said he'd do so later, after the problem was resolved." She closed her eyes tight, took a deep, ragged breath.

Bak did not know what to think. Her grief appeared genuine, but she could as easily be playing on his sympathy to learn if Nakht had confided in him.

She hurried on. "He left me soon after and went to

his bedchamber. I helped the servants take the remains
of our meal to the kitchen and spoke with them while
they cleaned the bowls. When I returned, my husband
was waiting for me in this room. He said he had something he must do and suggested I retire. He said . . ."
Her voice grew tight. "He said he would come to me
later."

With the wild panicked look of a snared fawn, she
sprang to her feet and rushed out the door. Bak hurried
after her, but stopped short when he saw her standing,
head bowed, her back to him, in the center of the courtyard. The Medjay guard, already on his feet, threw him
an uncertain look. Bak signaled him to remain where
he was and walked toward her. In the dim light, the
clinging white sheath accented every graceful curve of
her lovely body. Bak, who had known many women in
his twenty-three years, was drawn to her like a wasp to
water.

Very well aware of his weakness for an attractive
woman, he stopped a few paces away and forced himself to think of her not as a lovely young widow but as
the one most likely to have slain her husband.

She raised her head and turned to look at him.
"Nakht went to his reception room. His distress had
worried me, and I couldn't rest. I waited and waited—
too long, I thought—so I dressed and went to him."
She paused, swallowed. "He lay bleeding on the floor.
I tried to stop the flow. He said it was too late and
asked me to raise his head and shoulders. I asked who
had done this to him, but he spoke of personal matters.
Again I asked who . . ." She closed her eyes, shook her
head. "He never answered."

She turned away and walked slowly toward the
lighted door of her sitting room, where Lupaki waited.

Bak watched the two of them go inside, his mind a jumble of contradictory thoughts. Is she bravely holding her sorrow at arm's length, as she appears to be? he wondered. Or is her every word and action a lie?

"Is she telling the truth?"

The question, so closely matching his own, startled him. He swung around and spotted Imsiba emerging from the shadows of the landing atop the stairway that connected the private quarters to the audience hall. The sergeant, a dozen years older than Bak and half a head taller, walked as lithe and graceful as a leopard. His shoulders were broad, his hips narrow, his muscles solid and powerful.

"I wish I knew," Bak admitted. "Did you hear it all?"

"Merely the last few words."

Bak cursed his bad luck. Imsiba's uncanny ability to read another's thoughts might have pulled his wits from the sodden marsh they seemed to have fallen into. "What did you learn from the sentries?"

"No one saw anyone on the battlements who should not have been there, and no one noticed anyone on the roof of this house."

"None but officers and guards are allowed on the wall at night." Bak gave the Medjay a sharp look. "I know Lieutenant Mery was there. Are you saying others were, too?"

"Three men," Imsiba said. "Nebwa, the senior lieutenant in this garrison who commands the infantry, had to speak with the watch sergeant. As he was busy, Nebwa waited for some time. The second man was Paser, the lieutenant responsible for escorting the gold caravans. He climbed the stairs near the quay, walked briefly along the parapet, and returned to the ground."

"What of the third man?" Bak asked.

Imsiba looked vaguely uncomfortable. "Harmose, an archer who shares the blood of my people and yours and speaks both tongues. He translated for the commandant, who valued his judgment, so I've been told, and treated him like an officer."

"What was he doing up there?"

"He often walks the wall, looking at the ships moored at the quay, the river, and the desert sands where his mother was born. He did so tonight."

"The commandant's life was taken when the moon was at its highest point. Did the sentries notice any of the three—or Mery—near the stairway to this house at that time?"

Imsiba snorted. "They think of the moon as nothing more than a measure of the hours they must remain on watch. They know it passed overhead and they know those men were on the wall sometime during its passing. That's as specific as they can be."

Bak stared with a gloomy face at the door to Azzia's sitting room. That Nakht had spoken during the afternoon to the three officers, and possibly to his translator as well, and they had all been atop the wall near the time of his death, meant almost nothing. He had no good reason to free her from suspicion. Common sense told him she was guilty, but doubt remained in his heart. Was it because her words and behavior had played on his sympathies? Or because her youth and beauty had warped his judgment?

What he needed, he decided, was an impartial observer, and he could think of none better than a man who could sense another's thoughts.

"Come with me," he said.

Imsiba raised an eyebrow, but followed in Bak's shadow across the courtyard.

When they entered the lighted room, Azzia was standing in its center, talking rapidly in a tongue Bak did not understand, the tongue of her homeland, he assumed. Lupaki stood before his mistress, trying to speak but unable to stop her flow. Her voice and face were positive and determined, his negative and glum.

She glanced around, saw Imsiba, and stiffened. Her eyes swung toward Bak. "Are you now convinced only I could've taken my husband's life?"

"I don't know what to think," Bak admitted.

Her laugh held no humor. "My husband said you were a man who spoke his thoughts."

Bak could find no appropriate response.

"Are you as honest in deeds as words?" she asked.

"I try to be," he said stiffly.

She studied him for some time. "You were sent here in disgrace, I know, and my husband was prepared to dislike you. After he met you, talked with you, he thought you a man he could depend upon and, more important, trust." She glanced at Lupaki. "Since I have no better alternative, I must trust you, too."

Lupaki shook his head vehemently and rattled off a few unintelligible words, but Azzia ignored him. "First, lest you hear it from another's lips, I must tell you . . ." She hesitated, then took a deep breath as if to draw strength from the air. "When my husband spoke of the problem he must face, I urged him to share his burden. He refused, insisting it was his alone. I . . . I accused him of taking on all the problems of the world with no thought of those around him. And we quarreled."

A wan smile failed to steal the haunted look from her eyes. "Later, when I found him struck down, he seemed to have forgotten our harsh words, but I doubt I'll ever forget, nor forgive myself."

She turned to a small ivory inlaid chest, which had not been there earlier, and hurried on before Bak could comment or even sort out his thoughts. "I found something in my bedchamber, something my husband must've left there before . . . before his life was taken."

She raised the lid. Nesting among combs, perfume jars, cosmetic containers, and a bronze mirror were a roll of papyrus and a rectangular slab of metal. The scroll was bound with cord but its seal was broken. The rough slab was six fingers' breadth by three, and half a finger's breadth thick. Bak was sure it was gold, the flesh of the lord Re.

He stared, unable to speak. Unworked gold was the exclusive property of the royal house, of Maatkare Hatshepsut herself. In Buhen, where the precious ore was received from the mines and melted down to ingots before its shipment to the capital, where temptation was ever-present, no man, not even the commandant, had the right to possess it.

Chapter Three

"You can't keep this to yourself!" Imsiba glared at his friend. "Do you want to spend the rest of your life working in the mines? Or lose your nose and ears?"

Bak forced a semblance of a smile. "I could flee to a faraway land, as Nakht fled to Hatti when he was falsely accused of treason."

The sergeant laughed derisively. "He lived in Mennufer then, near the routes to the north, where the land is fertile and the villagers and herdsmen live and act as civilized men. You're in Buhen, with desert on all sides, a land peopled by men who live in hovels. Would you cross the barren sands by yourself? Would you choose a hovel for your home?"

Following his shadow away from the torch mounted beside the door, Bak paced the length of the small, plain whitewashed room. Imsiba dropped onto one of two low stools setting between a small table and an oblong rush basket brimming with scrolls. Shields, spears, and other weapons of war were stacked against the wall by an open stairway leading to the roof. The tools of their scribe Hori's trade—writing implements, paint and water pots, a neat stack of papyri—lay on the floor at the far end of the room. One door, closed for privacy, led outside to a narrow lane. Two others opened to Bak's bedchamber and Hori's. In addition to a sleeping pallet, Bak's room contained two plain woven reed chests, one for clothing, the other for bed linen, and a small box for toiletries. Hori's chamber was equally spare. Although modest, the house was clean and comfortable.

"No," he admitted, "a hovel would not please me at all."

"Then take the gold with you when you report to the steward Tetynefer. He holds the power in Buhen now; let him decide what to do."

"I can't throw her to the crocodiles, Imsiba!"

"You've been exiled to Buhen by no less an individual than our sovereign. Do you wish to add to your offenses in her eyes?"

A stubborn look settled on Bak's face. "She exiled me, yes, but she surely knew I did what any responsible officer would do: I stood at the head of my men when they needed me. The lieutenant who took me before the vizier, the one whose Medjay police broke up the fight, swore we were in the right and the other men had been cheating."

"The man you struck was the son of a provincial governor, his firstborn and favorite. You broke his nose and knocked out some teeth. He'll never again be thought handsome."

"Nonetheless . . ."

"You and the others in your chariotry company swept through that house of pleasure like wild bulls chased by jackals through an outdoor market. The end result was the same: total devastation. That establishment was frequented by some of the highest men in the land. The man who owns the building is a ranking priest, responsible for all food offerings in the mansion of the lord Amon. The man who pulls the strings of the old scoundrel who ran the place is one of the wealthiest merchants in Kemet."

"I know, but . . ."

"Who carries more weight with our sovereign, Bak? Men of influence who support her hold on the throne? Or you?"

"She's the earthly daughter of the lord Amon, the greatest of the gods. You'd think she'd have no need to bribe men like them for favors."

Imsiba gave him a disgusted look. "You know better than that, my friend."

Grudgingly, Bak admitted, "She wrested the power from Menkheperre Thutmose while still he was a babe. She'll not give it back until she must."

Menkheperre Thutmose was Maatkare Hatshepsut's nephew and stepson. As a small child, he had inherited the throne from his father. His aunt, acting as regent, had wrested the power from him and named herself king. Many men believed the youth, now fourteen years of age, the rightful heir to the throne. Barely a man, he was rebuilding the army into a loyal and capable fighting force. If, or more likely when, he chose to take the throne for himself alone, Maatkare Hatshepsut would fall and so would the men around her.

Bak stopped before the second stool and frowned at the thin slab of gold lying on the seat with the rolled papyrus. "If I give this ingot to Tetynefer, he'll send Azzia to Ma'am, where the viceroy will be certain to judge her guilty of murder."

"And theft."

"How would a woman who spends her days caring for a house lay her hands on unworked gold?" Bak shook his head impatiently. "No, she didn't steal it. Someone else did, someone close to her. Commandant Nakht, the viceroy will say. He'll be assumed guilty and labeled a thief in spite of the fact that this, I'm convinced, was the wrong he fully intended to right when he spoke to me."

"You'd sacrifice the rest of your life to protect Nakht's good name? You didn't even know the man." Imsiba studied Bak long and hard, as if searching deep in his soul. "Is it the woman, my friend? Has she addled your wits?"

"No, Imsiba." Bak smiled ruefully. "The fire in my groin is but a dull ember. So it will remain. I have no intention of allowing the flames of desire, and the smoke that goes with them, to cloud my judgment."

Imsiba's laugh eased the tension between them.

"Come," Bak said.

He scooped up the gold and the scroll and carried them into his bedchamber. The sergeant, looking puzzled, hauled himself off the stool and followed. Bak shoved his sleeping pallet aside. "Look at the floor near the base of the wall. What do you see?"

Imsiba studied the hard-packed earth in the swath of light falling through the doorway. "Nothing."

With a satisfied nod, Bak pulled his dagger, a plain bronze weapon of army issue, from the sheath attached to his belt. He dropped to his knees, brushed away the dust until a crack appeared, inserted the blade, and pried a carefully molded section out of the floor. Below was a hole more than half a cubit square.

"I found this by chance when we moved into this house," he said. "It smells of date wine. A previous occupant must've kept a secret supply here, I suspect to drink through the day while he performed his duties."

"It looks safe enough," Imsiba admitted, "but to keep the gold . . . it's beyond my understanding."

"Maiherperi said before we left Waset, 'If, through poor judgment, an innocent man is made to look guilty, it's as great an affront to the lady Maat as was the criminal act itself.' Since I'm not certain Azzia took her husband's life or knew before his death of this gold, I must search deeper for the truth."

Imsiba expelled a long frustrated sigh. "By all accounts, the commandant was an honorable man. If someone else—a lover, perhaps—gave the gold to her for safekeeping and Nakht found it in her possession, he would've had no choice but to take her before the viceroy. Men have been slain for lesser reasons."

"And she passed it on to me to make herself look innocent," Bak said irritably. "I know. We've been through all that before." He rammed the dagger into the sheath. "You admitted you were no more able to guess her thoughts than I was. Why do you believe she's guilty?"

"I'm not sure she is," Imsiba said with obvious reluctance.

"Hear me out." Bak paused, gathered his thoughts. "Azzia could've slain Nakht during a simple lover's quarrel, but I think it more likely his life was taken to keep him from airing his knowledge of this gold." He stared at the glittering slab, and a grim smile touched his lips. "If I give this to Tetynefer, word will spread through Buhen like dust on the wind. The man who stole it will brush away his footprints and we'll never find him. If I keep it and Azzia tells him I have it, he'll sooner or later conclude I'm as dishonest as he and will come for it."

"If no one comes?"

"I'll report it to Tetynefer."

Imsiba pursed his lips, his brow furrowed. "What if the woman is innocent? Won't she tell the steward you have it if she thinks you've kept it for yourself?"

"Yes, but by that time . . ." Bak shrugged off the doubt which threatened to swallow his confidence. "With luck, and if the lord Amon chooses to smile on us, this scroll will point to the guilty man, might even name him."

Worry clouded Imsiba's face. "You're gambling with the gods, my friend."

Bak twisted the rolled papyrus in his fingers, studying the blank surface, longing to look inside. No, he had dallied too long already. Tetynefer was expecting him. He dropped it in the hole, laid the ingot beside it, and replaced the block. Within moments, the hiding place was as invisible as it had been before, and his pallet covered it.

He stood up, smiled to reassure the sergeant. "They say the path gold takes from the mines to the royal treasury is so carefully controlled no man can lay his hands on as much as a single grain. Yet someone took that slab. When I learn how it was done, I pray my own offense will be forgiven and forgotten and Maatkare Hatshepsut herself will free me from bondage in this wretched fortress."

Hurt and disappointment settled on Imsiba's face.

A pang of conscience touched Bak's heart and he clasped the Medjay's shoulders. "You mustn't worry, Imsiba. Maiherperi will send another officer to take my place, one who'll know better than I how to convince the people of this city that you're as loyal to Kemet as they are."

The words sounded hollow in his ears. Oh, yes, he

thought, Maiherperi will send the best man available, but will he be an officer who distances himself from his men? Will he make Imsiba and the other Medjays feel utterly alone in this remote outpost where they're not wanted?

Bak hurried along a street so broad six men could walk abreast. The lord Khepre, the rising sun, had yet to climb above the eastern horizon, but traffic abounded in spite of the early hour. Yawning sentries streamed off the battlements after the changing of the guard. A column of spearmen, half-awake, grumbling, marched toward the desert gate on their way to the practice field outside the walls. Local farmers led braying donkeys laden with produce bound for the market.

Ahead, two massive towers rose into the pale dawn sky, the gate between them open and manned. Bak could not see the river beyond, but a fresh breeze smelling faintly of fish wafted through the portal and blew puffs of dust along the thoroughfare. Tired after a long night with no sleep, sticky with the previous day's sweat, he longed for a swim and his sleeping pallet. Soon, he promised himself, and headed with little enthusiasm into a narrow, less-traveled lane to his right.

Another turn, a quiet, empty lane took him to one of the larger homes in Buhen. A servant escorted him into a modest reception hall. The ceiling, supported by a central pillar, was higher than those of the adjacent rooms, allowing the faint early morning light and breeze to filter through high windows. The space was cluttered with a loom, a grindstone, pottery water jars, and a few toys. A doorway covered with a rush mat led to what Bak assumed were family rooms. Through an open portal to the right, he saw in the fluttery light of several oil lamps a heavy middle-aged man sorting through a basket filled with rolls of papyrus. He was as bald as a melon and his belly protruded like rising bread dough over the belt of his ankle-length kilt.

This was Tetynefer, the chief steward responsible for receiving and disbursing garrison supplies, collecting tolls on trade goods passing through, and recording copper and gold from the mines and tribute collected from local chieftains for the royal coffers. Thus he was the highest-ranking bureaucrat in Buhen and the man in charge until a new commandant could be appointed.

He looked up as Bak entered. "Ah, there you are, Officer Bak. Come in. Come in."

Waving his visitor onto a stool, he scooped up a scroll lying on the floor, seated himself cross-legged on a thick linen pad, and spread the papyrus across the fabric stretched tight over his thighs. Beside him lay a narrow wooden pallet in which had been cut a slot to contain reed pens and round wells that held moistened red and black ink.

"This is a serious matter, young man, very serious." With an officious scowl, Tetynefer pulled a pen from the pallet and dipped it into the black ink. "The viceroy will expect a detailed report. We must tell him exactly what happened." He glanced at Bak. "I know you're an educated man, but in a delicate situation like this, I prefer to send a document written in my own hand and impressed with my personal seal."

Tetynefer, Bak realized, could hardly wait to assume his temporary authority and gain the viceroy's personal attention. If he chose to start by taking upon himself the laborious task of writing out the official report, so much the better.

Bak told all he had seen and done, condensing the

tale to a manageable length as the steward's stubby fingers sped across the columns. When he reached the point where Azzia had given him the gold, he hesitated, reluctant to make the final irrevocable commitment. His conscience nagged him to mention the precious slab, as did his sense of self-preservation.

"Is that all?" Tetynefer prompted.

"Yes." It came out like the croak of a frog. "Yes," he repeated, his voice stronger, more firm.

Tetynefer stared at the scroll on his lap, then looked up, his chubby face as grave as any judge's. "It's clear mistress Azzia took her husband's life."

"She could be telling the truth. The room was accessible to many men."

"Come now, Officer Bak! Nakht was a tested warrior, a man who saw action many times on the field of battle. While with the army of the king of Hatti, he stood out as one among many, an officer of great valor. Would a man like that allow another to thrust a dagger into his breast without defending himself? Certainly not! On the other hand, a wife could come close and distract him with words of seduction." Tetynefer nodded, grunted his satisfaction. "Yes. That's what happened. I'm absolutely sure."

I wonder, Bak thought, if you'd be equally certain if you talked to her. "She seemed sincerely distressed by the commandant's death."

Tetynefer affected the woebegone look of the disappointed schoolmaster. "You're young, Bak, and naive. You know nothing about women."

Bak managed to keep his face blank, hiding his resentment at being treated like a child and his amazement that this fat old loaf of a man should consider himself so worldly.

"Mistress Azzia is a stranger in Kemet," Tetynefer went on. "She has no family, no one to turn to now that she has no husband. If you were she, if you'd just slain the man who provided for you—and provided quite well, as you most certainly noticed—wouldn't you be sincerely distressed?"

Bak conceded the point, but not aloud. He refused to give the steward the satisfaction.

Tetynefer dabbed the pen in the ink and poised it above the scroll. "I'll tell the viceroy you'll take her to Ma'am on the next northbound military transport. It should arrive in Buhen today and will sail away in . . . what? Three days. Yes, that should satisfy him that we're conducting ourselves efficiently."

Three days! Bak's stomach knotted. To protect himself, he had to tell Tetynefer about the gold before he set foot on that ship. Would the one who stole it screw up the courage to approach him in so short a time?

Taking care to hide his dismay, he said, "Before I left Waset, Commander Maiherperi advised me to search for the truth until I find it. In this case, I'm not sure I have. Therefore, I need more time to prove the woman's guilt or innocence."

The steward raised a disdainful eyebrow. "How do you expect to do that?"

"I'll ask questions until I'm satisfied one way or the other."

Tetynefer snorted. "You clearly have no experience in delving into the mysteries of the human heart. If you had, you'd have seen Azzia's distress for what it is: the will to live in the best and most comfortable manner possible."

Bak gritted his teeth so no words would escape. He dared not offend this man. When the time came to speak aloud of the gold, he wanted the steward to accept his reasons for keeping it, not close his ears to the truth out of spite.

Tetynefer placed pen to papyrus and scratched out a dozen more lines. When he finished, he gave Bak a complacent smile. "I pointed no finger at Azzia; however, I'm sure the viceroy will guess from the contents of this message that it was she who slew her husband."

He blotted the ink, rolled the papyrus tight, and secured it with a cord. After placing a small chunk of moist clay on the knot and pressing his seal into it, he handed it to Bak. "A courier is waiting at the quay. Tell him to take this to Ma'am immediately and to wait for the viceroy's response."

Three days, Bak thought, only three days. What could he accomplish in so short a time? He hesitated, sorely tempted to report the gold. No, he decided, not yet. He had to look at other possibilities, at other potential suspects. Where should he start? With Mery, he decided, and Nebwa and Paser, the three officers who were on the battlements near the time of Nakht's death. At the very least, one of them might have seen something suspicious.

Bak leaned against the open portal between the lane and the small walled courtyard fronting the unmarried officer's quarters, a dwelling of at least a half-dozen rooms. A mudbrick bench ran along the facade of the house and several wispy tamarisks grew along the wall to his left. The night's chill remained in the shaded court. Besides the caravan officer Paser, who was seated on the bench, the sole other occupant up and about was a reed-thin servant, a boy no more than ten years old. He squatted beside a low-rimmed pottery bowl resting on a bed of coals in a square brick hearth. The scent of onions and fish rising from the bowl made Bak's stomach ache for breakfast.

"How can you doubt Azzia took her husband's life?" Paser asked. "Have you reason to believe someone else was there?"

"No," Bak admitted, "but I hesitate to accuse her until I'm certain."

"Nakht was a true warrior, a man I admired above all others," Paser's voice hardened, "but he should never have wed a foreign woman."

Bak eyed the square-bodied lieutenant, a man in his late twenties with skin burned as dark as leather from many hours in the sun. His build, his sharp features, and a cool self-confidence bordering on arrogance testified to the fact that he was first cousin to Senenmut, chief steward of the lord Amon and Maatkare Hatshepsut's favorite. Her advisor and, if the rumors were true, her lover. Nakht had called Paser the boldest of the several officers who led the caravans back and forth between Buhen and the mines.

"I understand he lived in Hatti when they met," Bak said, "where he was the foreigner."

Paser's laugh was hard, cynical. "He was younger then."

"Are you saying he regretted the match?"

"All the world knows he couldn't bear to be away from her," Paser said scornfully. "Maybe he feared he'd lose her, maybe he could no longer please her in the privacy of his bedchamber."

Bak thought of his own father, a few years older than Nakht, who every night shared his sleeping pallet with either his matronly housekeeper or a pretty young servant girl. He knew, though, that some men lost their virility earlier than others.

"Do you believe she had a lover?" he asked.

Paser stood up and walked to the fire. "I came upon them by chance a day or two ago. They were quarreling." He knelt beside the boy, speared a fish with a pointed stick, and laid it on a small, flat loaf of bread. "Nakht made no outright accusations, but from the veiled words he used I had no doubt of his mistrust. And now . . ." He chuckled, insinuating the worst. "Well, she's free, isn't she?"

"Who's free?" Nebwa emerged from the dwelling, yawning broadly as he tried with awkward fingers to fasten his kilt. He was tall and muscular, about thirty years of age, more tanned than Paser. His hair was untidy, his coarse features puffy, as if he had just left his sleeping pallet. He was the senior lieutenant in Buhen, in charge of the garrison infantry. His men patrolled the desert and skirmished with tribesmen bent on raiding villages and farms along the sector of river for which Buhen was responsible.

"Azzia," Paser said shortly. "Nakht's widow."

Nebwa muttered a curse, glanced through the door behind him, and issued a sharp command in a tongue Bak could not understand. A slender dark-skinned woman in her late teens hurried outside to straighten his twisted belt. She wore a multicolored skirt dyed in a chevron pattern; other than a dozen or so bronze chains bearing a multitude of colorful stone amulets, her upper body was bare. She had come, Bak guessed, from one of the nearby villages.

"She's free, all right, but she's not for the likes of you and me." Nebwa wrapped a proprietary arm around the girl's waist and pulled her close. "She's a lady, unlike this one, who would lie with a monkey if it fed her."

Cupping a shapely breast in his hand, he bent to take it in his mouth. She glanced at Bak and looked away quickly as if embarrassed to be used in such a way. The boy stared at the bubbling food, his nostrils flaring, his mouth tight. Bak thanked the gods Nakht had seen fit to give him separate quarters. With only Hori sharing his house, he did not have to worry about other men's habits or tempers.

"Must you always behave like a heated ram?" Paser snarled.

Nebwa raised his head, laughed. "Isn't that why I keep her?" With another quick command and a slap on the buttocks, he sent her toward the hearth.

Scowling, Paser broke open his cooling fish, tore a piece of flesh from the bones, and ate it. "If I were you, Bak, I'd keep a close eye on Azzia."

"Why?" Nebwa sneered. "She didn't slay him. Even if she did, what do you expect her to do? Run off into the desert? Or sneak onto the first merchant ship leaving Buhen?" He flopped down on the dusty hard-packed earth. "That'd be smart, wouldn't it? It'd be an admission of guilt. All Bak would have to do is send out a courier and she'd be picked off the ship at the next port."

"For a price, half the captains on the river would hide anything or anyone among their cargo."

"Bah! A couple of soldiers can go through a ship from prow to stern in less time than it'll take you to eat that fish."

Bak would have let them squabble if he felt he was learning anything new, but he was not. "I've been told you both were on the wall last night, and I wondered if you saw . . ."

"Officer Bak!" Mery's voice, urgent, angry, interrupted, followed by the quick patter of his sandaled feet approaching along the lane.

Bak swiveled around.

Mery drew up before him, cheeks flushed, eyes blazing. "You left a Medjay in mistress Azzia's home, watching her like a common criminal. How could you do such a despicable thing?"

Bak was too tired to appease him. "What would you have me do? Call her innocent when I'm not sure she is?"

"Better that than to call her guilty when you have no proof."

"Proof!" Paser jeered. "What better proof than the blood on her hands?"

Mery swung on him, ready to strike, but a quick, hard command from Nebwa, his senior officer, broke his will to act. He slumped on the ground beside the tamarisks.

Bak's eyes narrowed on Paser. He did not remember seeing the caravan officer's name on the list of men who had swarmed upstairs from the audience hall. "You were there? In the commandant's residence?"

Paser gave him a cool look. "I wasn't, as you surely know. But I've been told how she looked. Everyone in Buhen has heard."

The woman knelt beside Nebwa with several fish. He grabbed one by the tail and tore it apart. With his mouth full, he said, "I was there. I saw the blood, and I also saw her face. I'd swear before the lord Amon himself that she didn't slay him."

Bak asked the question that had puzzled him ever

since he had seen Nebwa's name on the list. "Why didn't you take charge after Nakht was slain? You're senior in rank to Mery."

Nebwa glanced at the watch officer, shrugged. "He had the situation well in hand when I got there. I saw no reason to interfere."

"You weren't in the residence when mistress Azzia screamed?"

"I was on my way. Like everybody else, I wanted to see your Medjays bring in their prisoners. I thought they'd bring Nofery in, too, and she . . ." Nebwa looked up from the fish, grinned. "She can cause quite a stir when she wants to."

"Sorry we disappointed you," Bak said in a tone as dry as the desert sands.

"I'd have missed it anyway." Nebwa scowled at the lost opportunity. "Before I got there, I thought I heard somebody running across the roof of the scribal office building. I went up to take a look."

Bak's interest quickened. "Did you see anyone?"

"I knew it!" Mery flung a triumphant smile at Bak. "Mistress Azzia didn't slay Nakht! Someone else did. Someone who entered from the roof."

Nebwa spread his hands wide. "I saw nothing but shadows."

"How thoroughly did you search the area?" Bak asked, smothering his disappointment.

"I was a pace or two from the top of the stairs when Azzia screamed. I was pretty sure nobody was up there, but just in case, I found the guard—he was in one of the storage magazines—and sent him up to take another look. He told me later he walked the roofs from one end of the block to the other and saw nothing."

Bak muttered a frustrated curse. If anyone had been

on the roof, he'd have had plenty of time to run down the stairs and out to the street while Nebwa sought out the guard. On the other hand, it would have been an easy matter for Nebwa himself to cross from one roof to another and slip down the stairs to Nakht's reception room.

"By the time I finally got to the residence, Nakht had breathed his last." Nebwa thought a moment then, added grimly, "If I'd found anybody on that roof, he'd be a dead man, that I can tell you for a fact."

Paser helped himself to another fish and carried it to the bench, where he sat down. "From what I hear, Mery refused to let anyone near the commandant's body." He glanced at the slim young man and smirked. "For Azzia's sake, I assume."

Mery's face reddened—but whether from anger or embarrassment, Bak could not tell. "I thought Bak should see the room as I found it, not disturbed by a dozen pairs of feet and hands."

"Did he?"

"I didn't alter the scene to make mistress Azzia look innocent, if that's what you're implying," Mery snapped.

"Not at all," Paser said so smoothly it was obvious that was exactly what he meant.

Mery glared at his accuser, lips so tight the scar at the corner vanished from sight. Paser raised an eyebrow as if surprised at the younger officer's anger. Mery shot to his feet.

"Easy!" Nebwa boomed.

Mery pivoted and walked to the hearth. Bak eyed his back, wondering if his retreat was an admission of guilt. With the door closed to the men outside, he could have moved the furniture or smeared the blood or removed some object that would point to Azzia. Or he could have ended Nakht's life himself. His admiration for the woman appeared to have no bounds.

As for Paser, it seemed unwise to bait a fellow officer in a frontier garrison like Buhen, especially since they shared the same quarters. Did he know for a fact that Mery and Azzia were lovers? Or had he meant to draw Bak's attention away from his own activities?

He asked, "Where were you, Paser, when Nakht lost his life?"

Paser eyed Bak with a hint of amusement. "I believe you're actually taking this new task of yours to heart."

Bak smarted at the sarcasm, but gave no sign. "I know you were on the battlements for a time. Where did you go from there, and what did you see?"

Paser leaned back and stretched out his legs. "Are you aware that I have the ear of the chief steward Senenmut, our sovereign's right hand?"

Bak smiled. Compared to what could happen if anyone discovered he had kept the gold, the implied threat seemed insignificant. "I have the ear of the commander-in-chief of our army, Menkheperre Thutmose." It was not the truth, but Paser had no way of knowing that.

The caravan officer stared, the glint fading from his eyes. He had to know, as well if not better than most, that if Maatkare Hatshepsut lost the throne to her nephew, Senenmut would be the first among her allies to fall from power.

Nebwa slapped his thigh and laughed with delight. "What's wrong, lieutenant? Has Bak caught you with your loincloth around your ankles?"

A flush spread across Paser's cheeks, but he kept his eyes on Bak. "I don't know where I was. I walked hither and yon, thinking over Nakht's plans for providing more protection for the caravans."

"Were you near the residence at any time?"

"Probably." Paser threw the denuded fish bones into the fire. "In fact . . . yes, I saw your Medjays escorting their prisoners into the building. I had no wish to ogle a group of besotted men, so I walked on."

"Did you notice anything out of the ordinary?"

"Other than the outrageously large number of prisoners you chose to take, no."

So all three had been on the battlements during the night and, later, in or near the commandant's residence. Any of them could have sneaked into Nakht's room. Bak drew his thoughts up short. What am I doing? he wondered; I've no more reason to think these men guilty than anyone else in Buhen.

He glanced at Mery and Nebwa. "Since neither of you believe mistress Azzia took her husband's life, can you guess who did?"

"I've tried and tried," Mery said, looking up from the fish from which he was carefully stripping the bones. "I can think of no one. He was a good man, highly respected by all. Even the local people living along this stretch of the river held him in high regard."

"Deep wounds heal slowly," Bak said thoughtfully. "The army of Akheperenre Thutmose marched through this land twenty-five years ago with a vengeance. His soldiers took many lives among those involved in the uprising, and left many widows and orphan children. Do you think one among them carries sufficient hate in his heart to have slain Nakht?"

"Those savages?" Nebwa snorted, contemptuous. "There's not a man among them smart enough to slip past the guards and inside the walls."

Bak glimpsed the face of the girl, huddled within Nebwa's encircling arm, an instant before she lowered her head. He saw shame there and hurt. The boy's black eyes glittered with hate.

Mery placed a hand on the child's bony shoulder. "These people saw the might of our army and they've never ceased to fear it. None would risk having his village burned and his family and livestock carried off to the holy mansions of Kemet. The men of the desert, on the other hand, those who raid the caravans, have nothing to lose."

"The caravans are slow, our soldiers vulnerable," Nebwa explained. "Easy prey for the murderous jackals who know the best places to attack and the fastest routes to run away. But to enter Buhen to slay one man and take away no booty?" He expelled a hard, scornful laugh. "No, Bak. You must look inside the walls, not outside."

Bak nodded, certain Nebwa was right. The one who had entered Nakht's room with murder in his—or her—heart had not been a stranger. "Who do you suspect?"

Nebwa's eyes met his with no hesitation. "Those cursed Medjays you brought from Waset. Who else? The building was full of them."

Bak swallowed a curse. "No."

"They were taken to Kemet as boys. They speak like us and act like us, but their hearts belong to this vile land of Wawat. If you look at each of them in turn, you'll find one, maybe two or three, maybe all, who believe that to sever the head of the garrison is to weaken its body."

Chapter Four

"The man is abhorrent to the gods!" Imsiba growled. "For a single grain of emmer, I'd slice out his tongue and throw it to the crocodiles."

"I'd help if I thought it would do any good," Bak said grimly, "but it wouldn't. Nebwa's father soldiered in Wawat and so did his father's father. As victors, they planted contempt in his heart, and the seed has grown far out of proportion to his own experience."

He stepped out of his kilt and untied his loincloth, threw both on a black granite boulder protruding from the river's edge, and waded into the water until it lapped around his thighs. It cooled his tired legs, soothed his knotted calves.

Several hundred paces downstream, the walls of Buhen, stark white in the hot, brilliant sunlight, rose high above the river. The closest of the three stone quays jutting into the smooth brownish water was lined with small boats, the fishing fleet from nearby villages. A half dozen soldiers were carrying most of the morning's catch to the garrison cook; a few officers' wives and servants stood among the fishermen, haggling over the price of their evening meal.

"Will Nebwa go to Tetynefer with his vile accusation?" Imsiba asked.

"I think not. At least not yet." Bak splashed water
over his shoulders. "He knows he must have something
more solid than words to accuse our men of murder.
But he's a rash man, so we must be prepared in case he
does."

"What can I do, my friend?"

Bak glanced at the tall Medjay who knelt in the
shade of a row of acacias lining the riverbank. "You
must learn the location of every man in our company at
the time Nakht lost his life. Where possible, you must
find witnesses who saw them, preferably men of
Kemet."

Imsiba nodded his approval. "If we can prove they
were elsewhere, they'll be above reproach." He hesitated, asked, "Shouldn't you approach the witnesses?
They may not speak freely to me."

A broad-beamed military transport, sail lowered,
oarsmen paddling to the cadence of a drummer, swung
across the current to dock. This, Bak guessed, was the
vessel on which he and Azzia would travel to Ma'am.

"Take Hori with you. His youth and innocence can
be most disarming—and persuasive."

Imsiba smiled. "The boy could charm water from a
stone."

"He'll not like having his sleep disturbed, but when
you explain what we need, his complaints will fade
like mist in the breeze."

"Yes, he yearns to be a policeman, and he thinks of
our men as brothers."

Bak eyed a reed skiff tacking across the transport's
wake, its white sail blossoming in the morning breeze.

"He must record every word he hears, Imsiba. I want to end this matter once and for all."

"What if one or more of our men were alone, with no one to vouch for them?"

"If I must," Bak said with a faint, humorless smile, "I'll seek Nofery's help. She pledged her cooperation before I left her last night, and her women will say whatever she desires."

Imsiba chuckled. "You're a scoundrel, my friend."

Bak's laugh was hollow. "When you've learned all you can, come to my quarters. I'll not tarry here for long, for I must study the scroll mistress Azzia gave me."

Imsiba trotted away along the line of trees, heading for the fortress. Bak prayed Nofery's lies would not be needed. His decision to keep the gold weighed heavy on his shoulders; the transport's arrival and imminent departure added to his burden. Counting on the sly and no doubt greedy old woman to protect his men would add a load almost too heavy to bear.

Bak shoved his sleeping pallet back to its normal position and, scroll in hand, headed for the stairway to the roof. At the top he ran a few paces across the flat, hard surface, so hot it burned his bare feet. He ducked into the shade of a small rough pavilion, its frame made of wrist-thick bundles of reeds, its roof covered by loosely woven rush mats. A gentle breeze wafted across the rooftop to cool his naked torso. The yapping of a dog and the laughter of children drifted from the next building block. Voices of soldiers rose from nearby lanes.

Sitting beside a cold brazier, he lifted a square of

linen from the top of a round pottery bowl and peeked inside. As he had hoped, Hori had left his morning meal, a thick vegetable stew with a small loaf of bread lying on top, wrapped in leaves to keep it dry. His stomach ached from hunger; the aroma of onions and beans seemed finer than incense or myrrh. He eyed the scroll and the food with equal longing, decided to compromise. Waving off a fly, he unwrapped the bread, replaced the linen on the bowl, and broke out the plug from a beer jar. He took a long drink, praying fervently the document would name the man who stole the gold or at the very least, provide a clue to Azzia's guilt or innocence.

He tore off a piece of bread, its crust already hard from the morning heat, and began to eat. As he untied the cord around the scroll, a chunk of dried clay dropped to the floor, a fragment of a broken seal. Just a few symbols remained, but he was fairly sure it had been impressed by Nakht. Laying the binding aside, he began to unroll the papyrus. He had revealed less than two columns when he found a second scroll rolled inside. His heart soared into his throat. Two documents doubled his chance of finding what he needed.

He separated them and glanced through the outer roll. It was a list of tribute, trade items, and other products passing north through Buhen during the past two years, including gold, copper, and stone received from the desert mines and quarries. Disappointed at finding so mundane a document, he set it aside and scanned the inner scroll. It too was a scribal record, but its subject matter was far more promising. It referred to three gold mines located in the wadis, dry watercourses, of the eastern desert.

Praying this scroll would be more enlightening, Bak read the columns with a critical eye. For the past two years, for each of the cooler months when men could toil without too much loss of life, it gave the number of miners at the three locations, the amount of rock crushed and washed, and the weight of the raw gold delivered to the smelters in Buhen. All three mines, he could see, were similar in size and were worked by nearly identical numbers of men. Their yields varied slightly from one month to the next, but he suspected that was a reflection of the irregular ore content in each vein. Like the outer document, it was nothing more than a list, naming no names, pointing no fingers.

He was baffled. He doubted Nakht would have hidden the scrolls with the gold if they had no significance, but their importance eluded him. Laying the documents on the rooftop beside him, he grabbed the bowl, nested it in his lap, tore another chunk from the loaf, and dipped it in the stew.

While he ate, he glanced often at the scrolls. What if Azzia had lied? What if Nakht had not hidden them in her bedchamber, as she claimed? Had she grabbed the first two documents she could lay her hands on and included them with the gold to confuse the issue?

Far from pleased with the thought, he quickly finished the stew, stretched out full-length in the shade, hands beneath his head, and stared at the mat above him. He recalled Azzia's words and her face, pictured her lovely form as he had seen it in the torchlit courtyard, imagined her disrobed and lying naked in his arms. Feeling a growing need in his loins, he cursed aloud, told himself he had been too long without a woman, forced himself to think again of the scrolls.

The long night had exhausted him, the beer and stew had made him sleepy. His eyes closed of their own volition and he fell into a deep, dreamless sleep.

Something cool and wet touched his cheek. He jerked erect, his eyes snapped open. A lean white puppy sat on its haunches beside him, head cocked to the side, brown eyes pleading for attention. Laughing at his momentary fright, Bak pulled the dog onto his lap to scratch its broad muzzle and sagging ears. Hori had found the dirty, starving creature whining piteously on the riverbank a week or so before they had reached Buhen. The boy had washed the mud from its hair, fed it, and made it his own.

Bak eyed the shadows cast by the pavilion. He had slept the morning away. He allowed the puppy to curl up between his legs and took up the scrolls. Within moments, he knew the lady Maat, goddess of truth and order, had visited him while he slept and had removed the blindness from his eyes. They flew over the documents, picking up and registering the least discrepancy. And there was a serious discrepancy. The total amount of gold leaving Buhen had remained stable over the past twenty-four months. However, during the past twelve months, a considerably larger amount of rock had been crushed and washed at one of the three mines, called the Mountain of Re, than during the previous year. Where the yield should have increased, the weights of the shipments delivered to the smelters in Buhen had not changed. The quality of the vein could have deteriorated, but the golden slab hidden in the room beneath him convinced him otherwise.

Somehow, someone had been stealing a portion of the gold brought from the mine called the Mountain of Re.

From what he could see, far more had been taken than the single thin ingot Azzia had given him. He was awed by the brazenness of the act—and intimidated at the thought of pitting his wits against a man clever enough to steal so much and remain undetected for so long.

"You must say nothing of what I've told you, Hori. If so much as a word leaks from your mouth, the thief will wipe away all signs of himself and will never be snared." Bak gave the chubby fourteen-year-old scribe his sternest look.

"I'll not utter a word, sir, that I promise." Hori tried to look as serious as Bak, but his large black eyes glittered with excitement and his feet practically danced along the lane, almost deserted at this, the hottest time of day. "I prayed to the lord Thoth that our year in Buhen wouldn't be dull, and he's answered tenfold." Thoth was the god of writing.

Bak thought of his own, similar prayer to the lord Amon, greatest of the gods. He wished with all his heart that he'd been more specific and asked for action on the field of battle.

"What do you think we'll find in the commandant's office?" Hori asked. "The name of the one who stole the gold?"

"For that kind of luck, we'd need the prayers of every priest in Kemet, from the lowliest to the chief priest of the lord Amon himself."

His words did nothing to dampen Hori's enthusiasm. The boy chattered on, lowering his voice to a conspiratorial whisper each time they met or passed another man. His happiness, usually so infectious, did little to lighten Bak's spirits. He had decided that in all

fairness he should tell Azzia of Tetynefer's decision to
send her to the viceroy for judgment.

As they walked into the commandant's residence,
Bak placed a forefinger to his lips to silence the boy. A
vestibule and a long, rather dark hallway took them to
the audience hall, a spacious room with a high ceiling
supported by octagonal wooden pillars painted red,
and white walls decorated with bright geometrical de-
signs. Near the entrance, an archer was dictating a let-
ter to a public scribe, a tired-looking man of middle
years. Two younger scribes stood nearby, arguing with
a rotund man about the amount of the toll levied on the
trade goods he was shipping downriver. Near the portal
to the stone stairwell leading to the second floor, a fat,
older scribe was conferring with a slim gray-haired officer Bak had never seen before, a man he assumed had
come from one of the fortresses located upstream on
the long stretch of rapids called the Belly of Stones.
Several scribes and officers could be glimpsed in the
offices surrounding the hall.

Nodding to the few men he had met, Bak led Hori to
a closed door off to the side. He broke the seal he had
placed there the previous night, released the latch, and
they entered. Scattered around the office, the largest in
the building, were an armchair, several stools, and a
pair of low tables on which sat a half-dozen oil lamps.
At the rear, two wooden document chests shared a wall
with the latched and sealed door that led to the base of
the stairway to the battlements. Two more chests filled
the wall to the right. All four contained row upon row
of neatly stacked scrolls.

"For the love of Amon," Hori muttered, his spirits
flagging. "So much to read? It'll take all day and far
into the night."

Bak had to smile. "Not so long, I think. Most refer to the day-to-day administration of the garrison: assignments of men and officers, weapons disbursed from the arsenal, food and clothing handed out, quarters occupied. Those reports will tell us nothing. We need only glance through them to be sure of what they are. We'll read the rest more thoroughly, especially the entries in the garrison daybook and the reports of the caravan journeys."

"Still, it seems an endless task."

"If we're not finished by sunset, when Imsiba awakens, I'll do the rest myself. He has additional men to question, and he'll need you with him."

With an end in sight, the boy was content. He grabbed a stool, placed it in front of the nearest chest, and withdrew a scroll. Bak left him sitting there, reading, and hurried across the audience hall to the stone stairwell and the second story. Ruru, the Medjay assigned to stay with Azzia, a man so thin he looked all arms and legs, told him she and her servants were in the storeroom, gathering linen for the wrapping of Nakht's body. Bak thought of her quiet grief the previous night and could not bear to disrupt her unhappy task. He spun around and hurried back to Hori.

They were almost finished with the initial chest when Ruru tapped on the door. He said he had left the courtyard to relieve himself, and when he returned, he found the archer Harmose with Azzia. Should he send him away or let them talk?

Harmose, Bak remembered, was the half-Medjay archer whom Nakht had made his translator. One of the four men who had been on the wall during the night. A man the commandant had trusted, so Imsiba believed. Why had he come now? He had to know Azzia's usual activities had been restricted. Even her women friends had understood, sending servants with messages of sympathy rather than coming in person.

"I'll speak with him," Bak said.

Hori, unhappy at being left to toil alone, flung him an accusing glance. Paying no heed, Bak hastened upstairs. Midway across the courtyard, he had a clear view of Azzia's sitting room. She and Harmose each occupied a low stool. They were leaning toward each other, speaking so softly their words did not carry beyond the door. Her hands were clasped in his. Bak quashed a vague feeling of envy and strode to the door. If Azzia had a lover, as Paser had so sarcastically hinted, could this be the man rather than Mery?

They saw him and drew apart. Harmose stood up with an annoyed frown. He was close to Bak in age, half a hand shorter; his shoulders were broader, his wrists thicker, his upper arms heavier. His terracotta skin and oval face had been passed to him in his father's seed. His curly black hair, cropped short, had come from his mother, a woman of Wawat.

"Archer Harmose!" Bak said. "Have you not heard that mistress Azzia is to be left alone with her sorrow?"

Harmose's expression was defiant. "She should be surrounded by her friends, not held apart like this and made to weep alone. How can you be so cruel?"

Bak swore beneath his breath at this second charge in one day that he had no heart. Considering the circumstances of Nakht's death, he had been more than generous with her. Harmose knew it, he was sure. He yearned to defend his actions, but he swallowed the words. As Maiherperi had said: a policeman must look to the gods for his reward, for the men he helps thank him with curses.

Azzia touched the archer's hand. "It's all right, Harmose. I'm in my own home instead of a cell, and my servants are here to comfort me. For that I'm grateful."

"Grateful?" Harmose asked. "When you've done nothing wrong?"

She glanced at Bak and attempted a wry smile. "As you can see, my friends believe me innocent." She must have realized her voice was too brittle, for she gave up the pretense. "Have you learned anything at all that will prove I am?"

"Nothing," he admitted.

Harmose's face darkened. "You haven't tried."

"If your concern for mistress Azzia is sincere, you'll come away with me now," Bak said, refusing to be baited.

"I'll do no such thing!"

"If I'm to find the one who slew the commandant, I must learn all I can of his last hours. Would you have my questions open an unhealed wound?"

"Go with him, Harmose. Help him in every way you can." Azzia's voice grew hard, taut. "I want to know the guilty man, and I want to see him punished unto death." Her control shattered at the final word and she ran from the room.

Harmose attempted to follow, but Bak stepped into the doorway, blocking his path.

The archer glared. "All right. I'll answer your questions. But only because she asks it of me."

Bak ushered him across the courtyard to Nakht's reception room, where they would have more privacy. He motioned him onto a stool and took another for himself. The floor had been cleaned of all traces of blood. The chair had been set upright; the table beside it and the two lamps had been taken away. Bak could almost feel the murdered man's presence, as if his ka was seated in the chair, listening. Harmose must have felt it, too, for his eyes strayed in that direction.

"Where were you when Nakht's life was taken?" Bak asked.

"You suspect me?" Harmose asked, indignant.

Bak muttered a curse. He should not have begun with so tactless a question. "Other than mistress Azzia, I suspect no one." He held up his hand to stave off another spate of denials. "If she's innocent, as you say, someone else entered this room ahead of her. Someone who may've been seen coming or going, maybe by you since you spent some time on the battlements."

Harmose's expression remained wary. "I was on the wall, yes, but . . ." Bak saw the temptation to lie on the archer's face, heard the regret when he answered. "I could see nothing from where I stood. I was on the far side of the citadel, in a tower overlooking the quay."

Bak gave him a curious glance. "You remained there for some time, I've been told. What held your attention?"

"I was born in Kemet and I long for the black, fertile lands of my father's people." He flushed, as if ashamed of the admission. "The ships give me hope that one day soon I'll return."

Bak eyed him with a new interest, with the sympathy of a kindred soul. "I didn't see your name among those inside this building after Nakht was slain. Did word of his death not spread among the sentries?"

"I think by then I was in the mansion of the lord Horus of Buhen," Harmose said with some reluctance.

Bak's eyes narrowed. "What took you there? Surely no one visits the god in the middle of the night."

"I do. Often." Harmose at first appeared unwilling to explain, but finally said, "When the forecourt is cool and quiet, with no others around, I feel closer to him than at any other time. Sometimes he comes to me there in the dark to let me know he watches over me always." Harmose stared at Bak, daring him to doubt.

Bak eyed the archer with a mixture of awe and suspicion. No god had ever spoken to him, but he had heard tales of men who had been so honored. Could Harmose be one of them? "The god's mansion lies little more than a hundred paces down the street. Before you went inside, did you see anyone entering this building or leaving it?"

Harmose appeared to breathe a little easier, but not much. "As I came out of the tower, I saw your men escorting the last of the brawlers inside. Not long after, I saw Lieutenant Mery go in. A short time later, I saw Lieutenant Nebwa come out of a side lane and walk along the street in front of the storehouse."

Nothing, Bak thought. Nothing new, enlightening, or even interesting. Frustrated, he stood up and walked to the door. Across the courtyard, Ruru squatted in the shade of a potted sycamore, polishing his spear point. The old female servant bent over a loom shaded by potted trees. The peaceful domestic scene made Nakht's violent death seem unreal. What am I doing? he wondered. Asking questions that lead nowhere, hiding gold I should report, seeking a murderer when the most likely suspect is within my grasp. What folly!

Sorely tempted to give up, he turned away from the door. As he did, he noticed, standing close by, the slim inlaid cedar chest, its lid askew. Without thinking, he raised the lid to set it in its proper place. Inside he saw two empty lamps and Nakht's iron dagger lying beside a silver-inlaid leather sheath. The blade was covered with a dry brownish film, blood that had flowed through Nakht's body. Bak stared at the weapon, his skin prickling. He was certain its presence there was an omen. Arranged perhaps by Nakht's ka, urging him on.

He replaced the lid, crossed the room, and sat on a camp stool before the closed door behind which rose the stairway to the battlements. "What can you tell me of Nakht's activities on the day of his death?"

"During the morning, nothing. I was outside the wall with the other archers, practicing with the bow. He didn't summon me until early afternoon."

"After he spoke with me."

"So I believe." Harmose shifted on the hard stool; he clutched his knees. "He called me into his office. He seemed troubled, said he wanted me to stay in the audience hall. He . . . he asked me to keep my bow within easy reach."

Bak studied the archer closely, wary of his hesitant speech, his failure to make eye contact. Is he telling the truth? he wondered. Or has Azzia fed him the words to reinforce her story?

"Go on," he said, hiding his suspicions.

"He summoned the lieutenants Nebwa, Paser, and Mery, one after the other, and spoke alone with each of them." This time, Harmose's eyes met his with no hesitation. The presence of the three officers in Nakht's office had doubtless been noted by every man toiling in the building, so a lie would be foolhardy.

"Do you know what they talked about?"

"He didn't say," Harmose admitted, "but I think he

spoke of your suggestions for outwitting tribesmen who raid the caravans."

"Why talk to each man alone?"

"Men resist change, especially when it comes from the lips of an outsider." His eyes held Bak's and he went on smoothly, "Particularly an outsider who was banished from Waset at our sovereign's command."

The words pricked like a thorn, but Bak was careful to give no sign.

"When Commandant Nakht wanted a task done but knew it would meet with resistance, he separated those he needed to convince." The archer's gaze drifted toward the empty chair. "That was always his way. He spoke with one man and then another, persuaded each in turn, and in the end, the task was done as he wished."

The tactic was good and Bak vowed to use it should the occasion arise. "Who did he speak with after the officers left?"

"No one. He read the garrison daybook and the dispatches he'd received from Ma'am and from the forts along the Belly of Stones. After filing them away, he bade me and others he met in the audience hall good evening and came upstairs to his quarters."

"He never explained why he asked you to keep your weapon near to hand?"

"Never. At the time, I thought . . . well, he enjoyed using the bow and we sometimes went outside the walls late in the day to shoot at targets. Later, after he was slain, I was sure the lord Amon or another god had visited him in a dream, had warned him to take care lest someone . . ." Harmose bowed his head, stared at his clasped hands. "He should've warned me, should've allowed me to stay by his side."

Bak stood up, paced to the door and back. Nebwa, Mery, Paser—and Harmose. All in or near the building when the commandant was slain, all summoned to his office at a time when he clearly expected trouble. If Nakht had suspected one of the four of stealing gold, he could have taken advantage of the solitary interviews to confront the guilty man.

"How did Nebwa, Paser, and Mery leave Nakht's office?" he asked. "Angry? Content? Or something in between?"

"In their usual way." Harmose rubbed his hand over his face as if to wipe away his sorrow. "Nebwa growled like a lion, Paser's lips were sealed as tight as the planks in the hull of a ship, and Mery looked like a small boy who'd been spanked."

A niggling thought surfaced in Bak's heart. "Of all the officers in Buhen, why would Nakht speak of my suggestions with those three and no one else?"

"The tribesmen most often attack the gold caravans. Nebwa, Paser, and Mery have the most knowledge and experience and are the best men to judge your suggestions. Another officer, Ahmose, is equally capable, but he's away, leading a caravan across the desert from a mine farther upriver."

Bak stood quite still, his interest multiplying ten times ten. "I thought Mery had always served as watch officer and Nebwa just with the infantry."

"Before Commandant Nakht came to Buhen, Mery, Paser, Nebwa, and Ahmose took turns leading the gold caravans. The same was true of the officers who led caravans to and from the copper mines and the quarries." Harmose, noticing Bak's surprise, explained, "Our previous commandant rotated the officers because he thought the trip too strenuous for one man to make every time." His expression turned cynical. "Of course, he failed to think of the rest of us—archers, spearmen, and drovers who walked the same trail time after time with no complaint."

"You're one of the men who guards the gold caravans?"

"I am," Harmose said, nodding. "Commandant Nakht was less impressed by a man's status and rank, and more concerned with his skills. When first he came to Buhen, he watched the officers, learned each man's good points and bad. Nine or ten months ago, he gave them the more permanent assignments they now have, based on what they do best."

Bak's thoughts tumbled. Paser, Mery, Nebwa, and Harmose had all traveled to the mines. None but Paser continued to do so. Did that mean he was the guilty man? Not necessarily. Any of them could have placed an ally there to steal the gold and pass it in secret back to Buhen. And all of them spent a considerable amount of time in this building, the heart of the garrison. Azzia's home.

Irritated by the thought, he swung back to Harmose. "How long were Nakht and Azzia wed?"

"Eight years. She was fourteen when he took her as his wife, but he'd soldiered with her father for many years and watched her grow to a woman."

"Was the marriage a happy one?"

"He worshipped her. She was as the stars and the moon and the sun to him, and he the same to her."

"Yet they had no children."

Harmose's voice grew bitter, his expression filled with scorn. "In the land of Hatti, failure to please the king brings death not only to a man, but to all he holds dear. When the old king of Hatti died, the man who took the throne thought Azzia's father loyal to another man. He judged him a traitor and sent soldiers to slay the family. None lived but Azzia, who was left for dead." His glance strayed to the empty chair and his expression softened. "Nakht and his servant Lupaki found her, hid her, brought her back to life. They could do nothing to make her whole. She can have no children."

Bak's heart grew heavy with compassion. If the tale was true, Azzia had suffered more in her youth than most men or women in a lifetime. Would she, could she, have slain the man who pulled her from death? He wanted to think it impossible, but Maiherperi had said: Any man can slay another; all he needs is a weapon and the passion to strike the blow. As a child of that cruel and unforgiving court, she would have the passion.

"I've been told she has a lover," he said.

"It's not true!" Harmose sprang from his stool, his face dark with anger. "Who told you such a vile thing?"

"Do you know her so well you can say for a certainty she was never unfaithful to her husband?"

Harmose controlled his anger with a visible effort. "I've trusted her with my most secret thoughts, and she confides in me. I'd swear to the lord Horus himself that she's never looked at any man but Nakht. She loved him too much." He stared over Bak's shoulder toward the door of Azzia's empty sitting room. Worry clouded his face. "I fear for her. Without him, she has no one."

His sincerity was disquieting. So was the envy Bak felt. He quashed the unwelcome emotion. The archer's every word could be a lie, as was most certainly the case if he was the man who stole the gold and gave it to Azzia for safekeeping.

*   *   *

Bak hurried along the empty street, the rapid pat of his sandals loud and distinct on the stone pavement. Light filtered down from myriad stars spread thickly across a clear, cloudless sky. A faint glow beyond the battlements hinted of the rising moon. The aromas of fresh bread, onions and leeks, beans and lentils, fish and fowl, lingered in the air. Hushed voices drifted from the rooftops of the married officers' quarters somewhere to his left. He pictured the men lounging atop their houses, finished with their evening meal, playing with their children, lying with their wives. The air would be cooler there, fresher, not so still and heavy. He seldom regretted his unmarried state, but for an instant, he paused, listened, wished.

He stopped at the door of the commandant's residence, grasped the heavy wooden latch. His mission was simple, he told himself. All he had to do was question Azzia about her intimate life and tell her of Tetynefer's decision to send her to Ma'am.

To invade a woman's privacy was an abomination; to tell her she must stand before the viceroy, accused of slaying her husband, would take all the courage he possessed.

He raised the latch. A dog let out a long, mournful howl. He shoved the door wide and crossed the threshold. Another cur answered the first one's call. A third and a fourth joined in, and a dozen more took up the dirge, each echoing the others all across the city. He closed the door, muting their voices, and leaned back against it. He stood there for several moments, steeling himself to face her.

The vestibule and hallway were vague gray spaces, seemingly alive, otherworldly, in the light of a flickering torch mounted somewhere in the audience hall, too far away to share much light, too close to allow total darkness. The stone stairway, walled off from the light, was a series of broad shadowy lines, black and blacker alternating, steps and risers. The sole sound was the soft rustle of mice.

A scream shattered the silence. He started, stiffened. A second cry reached down the stairwell and reverberated through the empty rooms on the ground floor. A woman's voice. Azzia!

Chapter Five

Bak dashed up the stairwell, taking the invisible steps two, sometimes three at a time. He hit the upper landing, veered sharply to avoid a dozen or more porous pottery water jars stacked in a cool corner, and burst into the courtyard. The potted trees and shrubs looked like silent dark sentinels, the loom a low bier, the grindstone an offering table to the shades of night. Ruru was nowhere in sight.

Through a doorway at the back of the courtyard, he glimpsed a flickering light, heard the chitter of frightened women. To his left, from Nakht's reception room, he heard scuffling, the crash of overturned furniture, a man's curse. And Azzia half-screaming, half-yelling words he could not understand. As he ran toward the unlighted room, Lupaki raced through the rear door, followed closely by Azzia's old female servant.

"Bring a torch!" Bak yelled.

He circled a pair of acacias, whose twiggy branches raked his arm, and spotted two shadowy figures wrestling in the dark. He yelled to draw their attention. His foot hit something solid; he stumbled and fell to a knee. A quick glance told him he had fallen over Ruru, who lay sprawled in front of the door, unmoving. Bak looked up, saw the figures inside draw apart. As he scrambled to his feet, one ducked down, grabbed a spear from the floor, and threw it. The weapon struck its target but fell away. The one it hit, Azzia he felt sure, stumbled backward, bumping the wall near the darker rectangle, the open door to the mudbrick stairway leading to the roof.

A mindless fury drove Bak into the room. How could a man attempt to slay a helpless woman? He lunged at the attacker, caught an arm, and pulled him close so he could grab the other arm. Long tendrils of hair tickled his naked torso; his groping hand found a firm, round breast.

"He's getting away!" Azzia screamed, trying to jerk free of Bak's grasp.

Cursing his mistake, he pushed her roughly aside and bounded after the fleeing man, who had faded into the black stairwell, the spear in his hand. Bak leaped through the doorway, landed on the stairs. Light flooded the room behind him, Lupaki with a torch. Bak's eyes darted upward. He noted broad bare feet and thick muscular calves below a knee-length kilt. Yelling at the servant to bring the flame close, he stretched high and grabbed an ankle. The man swung around and kicked, trying to break free. Lupaki held the torch through the doorway. Bak saw in the cavorting shadows a heavy bare torso with muscles turning to fat and massive shoulders, the left dripping blood from a dark, ugly gash. The man's head was out of sight, above the opening to the roof.

The man shook his leg with the strength of a bullock. Bak's fingers slipped, held. With a furious snarl, the man swung the spear, slashing at Bak, who jerked away and lost his grip. The man leaped up the stairs and through the opening. He looked back, saw Bak pressing close, midway up the stairway. Hissing like an angered goose, he slashed with the spear. Bak dropped to his knees, and the deadly point whizzed past his head.

Before his attacker could jerk the weapon away, Bak grabbed the shaft not far above the point and pushed it hard against the frame of the rooftop opening. The man held on tight, but Bak had the advantage. Placing all his weight behind the effort, he drove the spear point forward. The shaft broke in two with a loud snap. He lost his balance, came close to tumbling down the stairway. His assailant ran.

Clutching the stub of shaft above the spear point, Bak scrambled to the top of the stairs. The fleeing man was running hard, his feet pounding across the roof toward the board that bridged the lane between the commandant's residence and the storehouse. Bak sprinted after him, praying he could catch him before he could descend the stairway in the scribal office building and get to the street. If the man was a resident of Buhen, and Bak assumed he was, he would know its streets and lanes far better than any newcomer.

The man darted across the board, pivoted, and kicked out. The bridge vanished between the buildings and crashed on the hard-packed earth below. Laughing derisively, he sped across the barrel-vaulted roof of the storehouse. Its upper surface was a series of plaster-coated half-cylinders running the width of the building, each roofing an individual storage magazine. The adjoining cylinders formed broad straight parallel ridges with narrow hollows in between. The man raced across as agile as a cat.

His laughter spurred Bak on. He ran toward the edge

of the roof where the bridge had been, uttered a brief, fervent prayer to the lord Amon, stepped onto the low parapet, and leaped through the air. The gap fell away behind him, and the impact brought him to his knees on the first ridge. As he scrambled to his feet, his sandals slid beneath him, unable to grip the sloping surface. Years of grit borne on the wind had smoothed the plaster, making it as slick as a muddy riverbank. He glared at the man ahead, nearly halfway across the storehouse roof, running easily. Bak remembered the man's bare feet, kicked off his own sandals, and left them where they fell.

His pace initially was uneven, his footing uncertain on the curved surfaces. The man pulled farther away, making no attempt to reach the stairway that descended to the scribal offices. Puzzled, Bak raced after him. As far as he knew, there was no other way off the block of buildings.

Once Bak found a pattern, four long strides, jump, four more strides, another jump, he began to close the gap. He was less than a dozen paces away when the fleeing man reached the end of the building. Bak was elated. He had him! He slowed to a trot, shifted the broken spear from left hand to right.

The man glanced over his shoulder and saw his pursuer closing in. He flung himself over the edge, legs dangling, then vanished from sight. Bak spotted the upper end of a sturdy rope tied to a heavy wooden peg embedded deep in the mudbrick ridge. His quarry had slid down to the lane below.

Spitting out a vile oath, Bak threw himself over the wall and slid down after him. As his feet touched the ground, he glimpsed the man racing around a corner, heading back the way he had come. Bak sped after him, passing the long, bare wall of the storehouse and the more impressive facade of the commandant's residence. A left turn and a burst of speed carried him along the base of the citadel wall to the unguarded twin-towered gate leading to the outer city. By the time Bak passed through, his quarry had disappeared. He searched the area as well as he could, but finally had to give up, as frustrated and confused by the man himself as by the rabbit warren of lanes. He had never gotten a good look at the man's face, but he knew for a fact he was not Nebwa or Paser or Mery or Harmose.

Bak knelt beside Ruru, his face tight with worry. The Medjay lay where he had fallen, still and silent, woolly hair matted with blood. Only the steady rise and fall of his chest gave hope he would live. Bak bowed his head and offered a silent prayer to the lord Re, the greatest of all physicians. He could do no more.

He rose to his feet and looked at Azzia. She was sitting at Ruru's head, a damp cloth in her hand, a bowl of water in her lap. The old female servant sat cross-legged beside her, mixing bits of leaves and other ingredients in a small, flat bowl.

"Who did this?" he demanded. "Did you know him?"

"I didn't see his face. How could I? You saw for yourself how dark it was." Her voice shook, and so did her hands, he noticed.

Bak had heard of men weak-kneed with fright after bravely facing the enemy on the field of battle, but to see Azzia afraid after such a valiant effort to protect her home was unsettling. Unsettling but understandable. Several angry red blotches on her bare arms and shoulders would soon turn dark, as would the slight swelling around the broken flesh at the corner of her eye. Over her shoulder, he could see Nakht's reception

room in the light of a torch Lupaki had mounted outside the door. A thin ribbon of smoke drifted from the
flame to the open stairwell door. Most of the furniture
had been overturned; a leg had been broken off one
table. The chests were open and their contents strewn
across the floor, the iron dagger among them.

"Calm yourself," he said. "He'll not come back tonight."

She dipped the cloth into the bowl, squeezed out the
excess water, and gently washed the blood from the
back of Ruru's head. "If he does?" she asked. "Will
you be here to catch him? Or will you chase him away
and return empty-handed?"

Bak flushed. He knew how close he had come to
catching his prey. The last thing he needed was this
woman's scornful reminder that he had failed.

"Here!" he said, holding out the broken spear. "You
can catch him yourself."

It was her turn to blush. "I missed, yes, because I
threw in haste." She took the bowl from the old
woman, wrinkled her nose at the gooey green mess she
withdrew on her fingers, and spread it over a linen pad.
"Next time, I'll take more care."

Her tone was matter-of-fact, but Bak heard beneath
the surface a fierce determination to do as she promised. He had never met a woman like her, so soft and
gentle and at the same time so strong and unyielding.
An intriguing mix, especially in the heat of passion.
Fearing she might guess his thoughts, he stepped over
Ruru's legs and entered Nakht's room, righted an overturned stool, and sat down to brush the dirt off the bottom of his feet.

"There'll be no next time," he said. "The wound in
his shoulder will be noted by all who see him. Word

will spread from mouth to mouth as fire spreads in a
field of dry stubble. He'll be in my hands before nightfall tomorrow."

"If he hasn't already flown from Buhen."

"No ship or skiff will sail until I have him. If he leaves
by footpath, the villagers who dwell nearby will see him,
and my sergeant, Imsiba, will hear within the hour."

Azzia raised an eyebrow, unconvinced. Bak felt like
shaking her, yet as he glanced around the disheveled
room, he had to admire her. She must have fought like a
lioness to have done so much damage in so short a time.

Lupaki hurried across the courtyard with a dozen
linen strips fluttering from his hand. Azzia took them
and said something to him in their own tongue. He
nodded, knelt beside her, and lifted Ruru's head from
the floor. She laid the medicated pad on the wound and
bound it in place, winding the strips around the Medjay's head until it looked like the head of a man
wrapped for eternity. He prayed her bandage would be
enough, that others would not be needed to bind his
body in the house of death.

"Go to the storeroom and get your master's folding
camp bed," she said to Lupaki. "We'll lift him onto it
and carry him to my sitting room. He can't lie out here
through the chill of the night."

The servant's eyes darted toward Bak, an unspoken
question formed on his face.

Her smile was fond, reassuring. "Go, Lupaki! He'll
not carry me off to the viceroy tonight."

"You've heard?" Bak asked, more disconcerted than
surprised.

Her smile vanished. She turned away to pick up the
bowl of bloody water and poured it into the dirt out of
which an acacia grew. "Tetynefer's wife, Iry, sent a

message." She passed the bowl to the old woman. "Her note said you urged her husband to wait, to give you more time."

"I reported what I saw in this room," he said unhappily. "He heard nothing more I said."

"He tells Iry all he knows, but she made no mention of the gold. Why?" Her eyes held his, probing his thoughts.

He stiffened his spine lest he wriggle like a schoolboy. "He knows nothing about it."

The old woman hissed like a cobra, spat out a dozen words in the tongue of Hatti.

Azzia's stare grew cool, distant. "I trusted you, as did my husband." She gave a hard, bitter laugh. "What innocents we were!"

The words stung, and he muttered a curse. He should have known she would learn too soon that he had kept the gold. Now he had to convince her to say nothing about it without admitting he hoped to use it as bait in a trap, a trap that might snare her along with the one who had stolen it.

He stood up, walked to the door. "I can report it tonight to Tetynefer and give him another, stronger reason to believe you took your husband's life. Or I can keep it hidden and say nothing. In the second case, you must trust me to report it when the time is right. The decision is yours."

Her disbelief evident, she drew close a clean bowl of water. With the old woman speaking to her in an urgent voice, Azzia bent over to splash her face and arms. As she dried herself with a fresh cloth, she answered with a few quick words that brought a scowl to the servant's face. A final word and a wave of her hand sent the woman scurrying across the courtyard, her back stiff with disapproval.

Azzia threw the water in a pot containing a stunted sycamore, checked Ruru's bandaged head, and stood up to face Bak. "I care nothing for the gold. Keep it, trade it for a more comfortable life if you like. But I ask this of you: find the man who took my husband's life. If you don't, if I must go to Ma'am, I'll tell the viceroy you have it."

Bak's mouth tightened. He had done all he could to help her and she not only thought him a thief, but thanked him with an ultimatum. He clutched her elbow and marched her into Nakht's reception room.

"Look at this!" He swung his arm in an arc. "The man you fought in here most likely took your husband's life."

"I know!" She jerked free of his grasp. "Why do you think I tried to slay him?"

"If you'd succeeded," he said grimly, "you'd be charged with his murder—and you'd have destroyed your sole chance to prove you had nothing to do with your husband's death."

Azzia dropped to her knees among the objects scattered on the floor, looked with moist eyes at first one and then another. When at last she spoke, her voice was barely loud enough to hear. "These things are all I have left of my husband. When I saw him here, pawing through them like a dog digs in a garbage heap, throwing them aside as if they were trash, my heart filled with rage and I took leave of my senses."

Bak wanted to hold her, to console her. He took a step toward her, backed off. She may have thrown the spear in anger, as she claimed. She could as easily have thrown it to get rid of a confederate she no longer trusted. He wished with all his heart he had Imsiba's gift for reading the thoughts of others.

He realized suddenly what she had said. "You saw him searching this room? How? The room was as black as a tomb."

"He had a lamp." She glanced up, saw how intense he was, and hastened to add, "He quenched it before I could see his face."

With a sinking heart, Bak studied the room, noting the way the objects were scattered about. The iron dagger lay in front of the inlaid cedar chest, too far away to have fallen out during the struggle. Its sheath was well off to one side. The two lamps, one broken beyond repair, were halfway across the room in the opposite direction. The lid lay near the door where the chest had originally stood. Cursing vehemently, he ran outside, grabbed the torch, and raced across the courtyard to Nakht's bedchamber. Linen, clothing, and toilet articles lay in untidy heaps around gaping storage chests. This room, like the other, had been ransacked—for the gold, he was sure, and the papyrus scrolls.

Scrolls. Nakht's office on the floor below. Swinging around, he glimpsed Azzia standing outside the door, her hand over her mouth, her eyes wide, horrified. He darted past her without a word, ran to the stairwell, and plunged downward, spreading a shower of sparks in his wake. From halfway across the pillared hall, he could see the door of the office he was aiming for. It was closed and latched but no longer sealed—as he had left it.

Though he doubted the man he had pursued would have returned to the building, he slowed, approached on silent feet, and raised the latch, careful to make no sound. He shoved the door open and held the torch high. The office was empty, the door at the rear still latched and sealed. The room looked no different than when he and Hori had left, but he had to be sure.

He mounted the torch in a wall bracket, pulled a scroll at random from a chest to his right, and looked at the date. He pulled the next one, checked the date, pulled another and checked it. As he shoved them back, he automatically aligned the ends. He repeated the process more than a dozen times and concluded they were all in the proper order. He moved on to the next chest, reached for another scroll. Its end protruded well beyond those around it. A closer look told him none was aligned. Neither were those in the top third of a chest standing before the rear wall. The scrolls had all been shoved as far back as they would go, and since none was exactly the same size as the others, some stuck out while others lay deeper in the chest. He and Hori had looked at every document in the room. He had watched with a growing impatience while the young scribe carefully aligned the ends of each and every one of them.

He took the torch, left the office, and walked slowly across the audience hall. It was apparent the intruder had spent a considerable amount of time going through Nakht's records. Bak thanked the gods that he and Hori had been before him. They had found nothing, but at least he had the satisfaction of knowing the man who followed them had been equally unsuccessful. He entered the stairwell, plodded upward. One thing was certain: the intruder was a man who could read. Bak stopped on the upper landing, nodding his satisfaction. That narrowed the field to a few officers and the scribes. All he had to do was discover which of them had a nasty wound in his shoulder.

Bak entered the courtyard with a lighter step. In the glow of a fresh torch mounted beside the reception-room door, Azzia bent over Ruru, a drinking bowl in her hand. The Medjay was sitting up unaided. Smiling with relief, Bak jammed his torch into the nearest empty bracket, trotted to them, knelt, and clasped Ruru's bony shoulders.

With mock severity, he said, "Did Imsiba never tell you to lead with your spear, not your head, when you face the enemy?"

Ruru gave him a sheepish grin. "Tonight, I should have paid no heed." He gingerly touched the bandaged wound. "The man who did this came up from behind."

"You didn't see him?"

"One moment I was standing at the reception room door, the next I woke with a bandaged and aching head."

Bak rose to his feet, frowned. "How did he get into the courtyard without your knowledge?"

Ruru stared at his feet, mumbled, "I took my evening meal in the kitchen at the back of the house."

"That was my doing," Azzia cut in quickly. "Rather than bring his food out here, I suggested he eat with my servants and me." Her voice grew cool. "Did you not tell him to watch me rather than my home?"

Much to Bak's chagrin, that was exactly the impression he had left with Ruru.

"He was meant to watch from afar," he snapped, "not share your bed." He saw with satisfaction a flush spreading across her face and was gratified he had finally stolen the gift of speech from her.

"What brought you here, to this spot where you fell?" he asked the Medjay.

"I saw a movement, the branches of the tree, I

thought. The air was still, so I walked this way to find the reason." Ruru gave Bak a shamefaced glance. "I expected to find a cat and took no care."

Bak nodded. With no forewarning of a possible break-in, he might have thought the same. Tame cats and feral prowled the city at night, hunting rats and mice, which, if not controlled, would gnaw their way into the storehouses and consume more food than the garrison troops.

"No matter," he said, clasping Ruru's shoulder. "His wound will lead us to him."

The Medjay lay back on the floor, satisfied.

Bak entered Nakht's reception room and slumped onto a stool, weary from the chase and too little sleep, but content. He had been so sure Mery, Paser, Nebwa, or Harmose had stolen the gold and taken Nakht's life, and now it seemed another man had done both. He thanked the lord Amon he had had the good sense to keep his suspicions to himself.

He hunched over, elbows on knees, chin resting on clasped hands, and stared at the overturned furniture and the objects strewn about, vaguely aware of Lupaki's arrival with the camp bed and Ruru's transfer to Azzia's sitting room. Why, he wondered, had the intruder searched less than half the documents in Nakht's office? Why was he so neat there and so disorderly here in Nakht's personal rooms? Had he grown impatient with the search below and come upstairs to ask Azzia for the gold and scrolls? Had the two of them quarreled? A man hot with anger might throw things halfway across the room.

He heard footsteps and looked up to see Azzia coming across the courtyard. She stopped on the threshold, her back rigid, her expression cool.

"May I straighten this room?" she asked.

"Yes."

She hesitated as if reluctant to begin, took a deep, ragged breath, and stepped inside. She was genuinely upset, he was sure, and had not expected her home to be violated. Maybe he was trying too hard to tie her to the break-in, the stealing of the gold.

"How did you come upon the intruder?" he asked.

She knelt beside a senet board, set it upright, and began to search for the widely scattered playing pieces. "I brought a sweet cake for Ruru. I didn't see him, but I noticed light along the edge of the closed door. I thought you'd come back and he was in here with you." Her laugh was sharp, cynical. "I knew you'd not told Tetynefer about the gold and thought you were looking for more."

Her assumption nettled, but Bak said nothing.

"No man, not you or anyone else, had a right to be here, and I meant to send you away." She moved a small table and found another playing piece, this one broken. She closed her hand tight around it. "I stumbled over Ruru and fell against the door. It flew open. I glimpsed a lighted lamp on a chest, my husband's writing implements on the floor around it, and that man." She must have heard the tremor in her voice, for she paused, spoke more calmly. "He was heavier than you, lighter skinned than a Medjay. I realized my mistake and screamed for help."

"Didn't he look around to see who you were?"

"I don't know," she admitted. "I needed a weapon, and it wasn't easy to tug Ruru's spear from beneath his shoulder. That's when the man quenched the lamp. He ran at me, knocked the spear from my hand, and grabbed me. I tried to break free, but he was very strong. What he meant to do with me . . ." She shuddered. "We heard you coming up the stairway. He flung me away. I picked up the spear and threw it."

"And I mistook you to be the aggressor."

Her eyes lifted to Bak's and she managed a crooked smile. "I don't know what he'd have done if you hadn't come when you did."

Her gratitude was disquieting. "Your screams drew Lupaki as well as me."

"I know, but . . ." She studied him briefly, shrugged, and turned away to busy herself with sorting through the objects on the floor.

Bak had the disconcerting feeling she wanted to trust him, as he wished he could open his heart to her. No, he thought, impossible! She's no more sure of me than I am of her. To ease his frustration, he left the stool and strode around the room, standing upright each piece of furniture he came to. The broken table he carried out to the courtyard. On his return, he lifted the inlaid cedar chest and stood it where it belonged beside the door. He located the iron dagger and its sheath on the floor and stooped to retrieve them.

As he stood erect, she bent to pick up Nakht's writing pallet. Her firm round breast nudged the low vee-neck of her sheath, threatened to fall free.

"Will you stay the night?" she asked.

Bak almost dropped the dagger. His eyes leaped to her face, but he saw no tenderness, no seductive smile, just anxiety.

"Or summon another Medjay?" She dropped the pallet in her lap, reached for a pen. "If that man comes back . . ." She shivered. "Ruru is ill. He could do nothing to stop him."

Bak chided himself for a fool. She was a recent

widow, mourning her husband. How could he think she would invite him into her bed? Even if she had cared nothing for Nakht, had taken his life, in fact, she would do no such thing. An offer of her body would make a lie of the sorrow, the hurt she had displayed since her husband's death. The scent of her perfume must be clouding my wits, he thought.

He shoved the dagger into its sheath and dropped them in the chest. "Summon Lupaki. I'll send him to my sergeant with a message to assign another guard. I'll stay until he comes."

Chapter Six

"We should've found him by now." Bak slapped the calf of his leg with his baton of office. "Half the morning is gone."

"With so many men helping, we'll have him before midday." Imsiba nodded toward the lane outside the door, where Hori's puppy lay sprawled and panting in a sliver of shade cast by the opposite house. The Medjay's eyes glinted with anticipation. "Thanks to the lord Re, he'll not be able to hide his wound under a tunic. It's too hot today."

"Did Nebwa resist?"

Imsiba chuckled. "I could see he wanted to, but when I reminded him that four of his men were in the brawl at Nofery's house, he could think of no excuse. I asked for thirty spearmen and I got them."

"I thought he'd help, out of curiosity if for no other reason." A smile flitted across Bak's face, but quickly gave way to worry. "If we don't find the man we seek—and get the truth from him—there are many who'll never believe he took Nakht's life."

Imsiba's good humor vanished. "Nebwa, you mean, and all those men who think Medjays the enemy."

Nodding, Bak walked to the door to look outside.

The sun, a golden ball well above the outer wall, had bleached the sky blue-white. The buildings, the lanes, the walls shimmered in the still air. No dog barked, no cat yowled, no fowl squawked. The few men he saw hurried from one spot of shade to the next. He scowled at the dreary white and dull brown world in which he had been thrown. He longed to return to the broad green valley around Waset with its bright palaces and mansions of the gods, its cooling breezes, its worldly residents. A place of fewer problems and many more pleasures. Would the lord Amon never again look upon him with favor?

He turned back to the room and eyed the Medjay. "What luck have you and Hori had in your quest to prove our men blameless?"

Imsiba laid his long spear beside the wall, dropped to the floor in front of it, and rested his shoulders and head on the cool white mudbrick. "The task you set was not an easy one, my friend."

Bak's heart became a stone in his breast. "Tell me, Imsiba. I must know the worst."

"We found witnesses, all men of Kemet, who say twenty men in our unit were nowhere near the commandant when his life was taken. We've not given up yet, but . . ." He gave a tired shrug. "From what we know so far, the remaining five were unseen."

"Five." Bak closed his eyes as if to blind himself to the truth. "I expected one or two, but so many?" His eyes popped open. "Eighteen were with us at Nofery's house, as were you and Psuro. Why were the others not in their barracks, sleeping? For the love of Amon, it was the middle of the night!"

"Ruru was there, alone. He stayed lest anyone come to report an offense. Amonemopet went to a village across the river to meet a woman. The others walked the streets, waiting to hear how the raid went. At so late an hour, they saw few men, none they recognized."

"Five men," Bak repeated in a gloomy voice. "Nofery will exact a heavy toll, I fear. She'll not only turn her heart from the bargain we made, but she'll expect many favors in return."

"When will you go to her?"

Bak's mouth set into a thin, stubborn line. "Not until I must." He crossed to the stairway and sat on the bottom step. "Where's Hori?"

"He went to the sentries' barracks to speak with the men on guard duty that night, but I believe the time he spends will be like dust thrown to the winds. When Mery and I asked what they saw, they mentioned only the brawlers and the Medjays who took them to the commandant's residence. They could see no faces from so long a distance."

Bak stared at nothing, thinking. "The three who claimed to walk the streets. Did they return to our barracks with or soon after the men who escorted the rabble?"

"They didn't come back until almost dawn."

Bak laid the baton on his lap, planted his elbows on his knees, and looked at Imsiba over clasped hands. "What does that suggest to you?"

Imsiba's eyes narrowed. "Their reason for leaving the barracks had nothing to do with the raid."

"Talk to them, Imsiba. Use a cudgel if you must. Do whatever you feel necessary to get the truth from them." Bak's expression hardened. "And pray that whatever they did that night, they were seen by other men far, far away from the commandant's residence."

*   *   *

Bak hurried outside the towered gate, where he was greeted by the laughter of five small boys playing leapfrog on the upper terrace. Shading his eyes to spare them the fierce sunlight, he studied the vessels moored at the quay, a half dozen fishing skiffs and three ships.

He eyed with loathing the largest and closest, the military transport which had docked the previous morning. The stern and prow were adorned with paintings of the lord Montu, the god of war. The large centrally located deckhouse was painted in a bright herringbone pattern of blue and green and red. The mast was bare, the rectangular sail spread across the deck while two men repaired a large, jagged tear. A sailor wearing a loincloth sat fishing at the stern, legs dangling over the side.

The other two ships were cargo vessels with heavy, rounded hulls; unadorned stern posts and stems; tall, sturdy, naked masts. One, tied across the quay from the transport, was being off-loaded and its cargo of grain carried into the fortress by an antlike line of bearers bent double beneath the heavy bags. Farther along the quay, a half-dozen gaily dressed men from the land of Kush, far to the south, stood with twenty or more long-horned pale brown cows beside a vessel on whose deck had been built the wooden stalls in which the animals would travel. From the fine appearance of men and beasts, Bak guessed a tribal chieftain was taking the cattle to Kemet as tribute for Maatkare Hatshepsut.

Bak spotted Kames, the scribe he was looking for, standing at the far end of the quay, talking with a burly man tanned the deep russet of a seaman. He gave the two of them a hostile look. He should be with his Medjays, helping with the search. Instead, thanks to Tetynefer's blind resolve that he and Azzia soon travel to Ma'am, here he was, in search of information he would badly need should they not find the man they sought.

He hastened along the smooth stone surface of the quay, passing the line of bearers. Sweat trickled down the men's near-naked bodies; their pungent odor filled his nostrils. The heavy scent of grain made him sneeze. Beyond, he wove a path through the cattle, the tribesmen, and several large malodorous mounds of manure that buzzed with flies. Hearing raised voices from the pair farther along the quay, he stopped a few paces short of them.

"I don't care what you do," the burly man shouted. "You can report me to the viceroy if you like, or to Maatkare Hatshepsut herself. But I'm the captain of that ship, and I'll not leave this quay until the hull is recaulked."

"You must!" Kames insisted. "The ore is expected in Abu by the end of next week." He was a white-haired man, half a head taller than the captain and so thin his knee-length kilt threatened to slide off his frail hips. He was the chief scribe, responsible for ore shipments entering and leaving Buhen.

"The promise was yours, not mine," the captain snarled.

"You said yourself the leak isn't serious."

"Listen to me, Kames, and listen good. The leak is small, yes, but if the wind blows like it sometimes does at this time of year, and if we're blown onto the rocks with water in the hull and a heavy load of copper, we'll lose everything: ship, cargo, and men. I won't do it!"

He swung around and strode past Bak, muttering to himself. Kames, his mouth pursed in anger, marched stiffly after him.

Bak stepped into his path. "I must speak to you, Kames."

The scribe eyed him with distaste. "You're Bak. The policeman."

"I came to Buhen with the Medjays, yes."

"I've already told that sergeant of yours that all my clerks reported for duty this morning. What more do you want?"

Bak could see he had approached Kames at the worst possible time. "I need information about the gold that passes through this city."

"What business is that of yours? You were sent here to maintain order within these walls. Nothing more, nothing less."

Bak silently cursed the man—and himself. He must learn to find reasons before wading into waters forbidden to him. He formed an impatient frown and improvised. "Commandant Nakht asked me to test the ways we protect the gold shipments. His death does not excuse me from completing this or any other task he gave me."

Kames hesitated, not entirely convinced, but finally nodded. "Come!" He turned on his heel and led Bak to the end of the quay, well out of hearing distance of the men from Kush.

The surface of the river was silvery gray, as smooth as a mirror and as reflective. The sun hung high in the sky, its white-hot image repeated on the water. Three fishing skiffs, their sails limp, drifted along the distant shore, a broad line of green separating tawny sandhills from water. Bak could barely see two tiny figures kneeling at the river's edge, women washing clothing or drawing water.

Glancing toward the Kushites as if to reassure himself he would not be heard, Kames said, "The commandant was worried about the gold, he said as much. I assured him, as I do you, that he had no reason for concern."

Bak kept his expression noncommittal, though the news that he was following Nakht's path to the stolen gold was reassuring. "Can you say with certainty that not one grain has been lost during the past . . ." He paused, pretended to pick a number from the air. "The past two years?"

Kames stared down his long, bony nose. "Surely Nakht told you about the desert raiders."

"He mentioned them, yes. He was busy, however, so he suggested I get the details from you." Bak prayed the lady Maat would forgive his lies.

"I can give you no specific weights of the gold they've taken. The records are in my office, not in my heart, but I can tell you this: none but the wildest desert tribesmen are bold enough to attack our caravans. They seldom get more than five or six donkeys, and, more often than not, the animals they take are carrying food or water rather than gold."

"What do they do with the ore?" Bak asked. "Make trinkets for themselves or use it for trade?"

"It goes through many hands, I've been told." Kames allowed himself a faint smile. "In the end it's brought back to us."

"Is its source never questioned?"

"The lord Re chose to scatter bits of his golden flesh in many of the wadis in this barren land. Most tribesmen look for it; those with the gift of patience find it. They and the raiders alike trade it for necessities. Those who receive it trade it off to other men. So it goes until ultimately it falls into the hands of the chieftains, who accept it with a smile and ask no questions. Well aware that Maatkare Hatshepsut hungers for gold, they bring it to us, either as a trade item or as tribute for the royal house in Waset."

Bak shifted uncomfortably from one foot to another. Could a local chieftain have given Nakht the ingot Azzia found? "Do you personally receive and weigh every ingot that passes through Buhen?"

"Did the commandant tell you nothing?" When Bak failed to answer, Kames expelled a long, resigned sign and spoke as if to a schoolboy. "The gold is brought to me, yes, and weighed and recorded. As for ingots . . ." His snort was sharp, cynical. "The chieftains of Kush more often than not melt the gold and form it into rings. The tribesmen of Wawat don't understand the principles of smelting nor do they bother with molds. Some bring nuggets they find in the wadis or the granules they wash from the rock. Those with larger quantities heat it, melt it, and throw it into water, where it forms rough kernels. It's easier to transport that way, with less chance of losing the smaller grains."

Bak turned away lest the sharp-eyed scribe read the satisfaction on his face. Nakht had, without doubt, gotten the ingot from someone inside Buhen. "Other than to raiders, is gold ever lost after it falls into our hands?"

"I see no way. As I told Nakht, men of proven honesty weigh it again and again, from the time it's taken from the rock until it's delivered to the royal treasury in Waset."

Bak stared across the glistening river, his eyes on the opposite bank, his thoughts on another maxim of Mai-herperi: Even an honest man will alter the balance of the scales if his hunger for wealth is great enough. "Weights can be made to lie."

Kames flung him a resentful look. "I'm responsible for those weights, young man, and I can assure you that they do not lie."

"I don't question your honor, Kames." Bak gave him a placating smile. "Merely the steps we take to ensure the gold's safety."

Not entirely mollified, Kames said, "I keep a set of master weights of proven accuracy. With them, I test all other sets at least twice a year."

"Do you go to the mines yourself?"

"I do no such thing! My responsibilities are here, not out on the burning sands." Kames unbent enough to explain, "Every few weeks or months, in no regular pattern, I send out sets of weights I know are true, and those at the mines are returned to me."

"You leave nothing to chance," Bak said, his tone admiring. The system seemed to have no fault. Nonetheless, one had to exist. How else could the gold have been stolen?

Kames's face relaxed in a modest smile. "I try to think as a thief, and then I take precautions so even I would fail."

Bak laughed, appreciative of the technique. With a fading smile, he said, "The miners are all vile criminals, men who've been convicted of offending the lady Maat. Are there no thieves among them?"

Kames's answer was lost to the angry bellow of a cow followed by laughter. Bak glanced at the cattle ship, where a lanky tribesman decked out in his traveling finery, a fringed red wrap and necklaces, bracelets, and anklets of copper, stood on the narrow wooden gangplank, trying to pull after him a cow whose hooves were planted firmly on the quay. She bawled, swept her head back and forth. A slender youth in yellow and red smacked the beast's flank with a whip. She refused to budge. Another man, older and heavier, bent low behind the cow and hissed so much like a snake that a chill ran up Bak's spine. Bellowing her alarm, the beast charged headlong up the gangplank. A lightning-quick leap to the deck saved her owner from being pitched into the river. He caught the rope, pulled her up short, and shook his fist at her in mock anger. The Kushites on the quay laughed so hard tears ran from their eyes. Their high spirits were infectious, and Bak and Kames joined in.

As the second cow walked sedately up the gangplank, Kames's smile waned. "A clever miner might take for himself a small amount of ore before it's weighed, but few try." He pointed toward the distant sandhills, where the shimmering sun-struck dunes seemed to dissolve into the molten sky. "The land you see there is baked and lifeless, the wadis where gold is found are far worse. The lord Re burns the heart from the miners, sometimes taking their wits as well, sometimes their lives. Gold loses its value when life itself is at stake."

Kames's sympathy for men forced to endure such hardships was apparent. If this man, who had insisted on sending a ship out when it needed recaulking, could feel such compassion, the miners' lives must be very hard indeed. He thought of the ingot hidden beneath his sleeping pallet and the sweat chilled on his back. Every day he kept it made any explanation he could offer more difficult to believe. If he was judged a thief, he too would be sent to the mines—or worse. He and his men had to catch the one who had ransacked Azzia's home. They had to! But what if they never found him?

His resolve to keep the ingot weakened and he fished for an opening. "If I were to tell you someone has been stealing gold for over a year, what would you say?"

"Impossible!" Kames laughed at what he took to be a joke. "For as long as I've been in Buhen, three years and two seasons, the weights of the ore leaving the mines have matched exactly the weights received at the smelters. The same is true of the ingots shipped from here to Waset."

Bak opened his mouth, quickly clamped it shut. To speak to Kames would be foolish. He must be patient. He must wait until they caught the fugitive. Or until they were certain they would never catch him. Then he would report the ingot to Tetynefer, not to this man who was responsible for the accuracy of the weights.

"Officer Bak!"

He looked down the quay, saw the husky figure of Pashenuro, one of his Medjays, burst from among the half-dozen cattle waiting to be loaded.

"You must come at once, sir!" Pashenuro's body glistened with sweat, his breath came out in short, quick gasps. "Imsiba has a message from Dedu, the headman of the village beyond the north gate. A man has been pulled from the river. He's dead. Stabbed, so Dedu says."

Bak and Imsiba paused at the top of a sloping path which cut through a low, sandy ridge lying between the river and a mudbrick village whose area was smaller than that of the dozen or more brush-enclosed donkey paddocks built off to one side. Two Medjays, one carrying a rolled-up litter on his shoulder, drew up beside them. At the far end of the slope where the water lapped the shore, thirty or more men, women, and children stared at the patch of ground they encircled, speaking in hushed voices. He could see nothing of the body in their midst.

The message had been vague, but he knew the headman would not have summoned him if a villager had been slain. The victim had to be a man of Kemet. Could Azzia's thrust with the spear have been more deadly than it appeared? He thought not. The wound had been ugly but not lethal. No brawls had been reported, no arguments between two men, and no troops had gone missing from the garrison. Maybe the body had washed downstream from one of the fortresses along the Belly of Stones.

Praying it was so, praying the fugitive they sought was in Buhen, alive and able to confess his offenses, Bak strode down the path, a track of hard-packed sand mottled with manure. Imsiba and the others followed in a ragged line. A woman spotted them and spouted a warning in the tongue of Wawat. The murmurs of the villagers tapered off. The circle parted to let a wizened old man come through.

"I am Dedu, the headman," he said. "It was I who summoned you, sir."

Before the group closed behind the old man, Bak glimpsed the waxen body. It looked intact, undamaged, not yet bloated. It had not been long in the water. He longed for a closer look, but forced himself to be patient. Headmen moved at their own speed, and he did not want to alienate a man whose goodwill might be useful, if not this day, perhaps another in the future.

He forced a genial smile and, barely aware of the curious faces behind the old man, clasped both of Dedu's gnarled hands in greeting. "Who found this man, Dedu, and where?"

Dedu spoke a command in his own tongue. A small, frail boy no more than six years of age slipped from between two older youths and came forward. He stared at his feet, too shy to speak.

The old man placed a hand on the boy's scrawny shoulder. "This child brought his father's animals to the river to drink. He saw the body caught among the reeds."

Dedu pointed downstream, where a herd of black goats nibbled, untended, at a narrow band of grass growing from the mud along the bank. A few paces farther, near a thick stand of reeds, a red bullock and five cows stood belly-deep in the water. Brown birds twittered around their heads, necks, and backs, harvesting the parasites from their hide.

"He called to his brothers," Dedu said, nodding toward the two older boys. "They waded out and brought the dead one to the shore. An hour ago. No more."

"Do you or any of your people know his name?"

"No." Dedu pulled his yellow wrap closer around his stringy arms. "Before I summoned you, I asked every man and woman. He's a stranger to them all."

"You're certain they told the truth?"

Dedu stared at Bak, measuring him as a man. Evidently deciding him worthy, he said, "If I were not, he'd be feeding the fishes far downstream from this village."

Bak had to smile at the old man's candor. "You

could've allowed the current to carry him off anyway. By doing so, you might've saved yourself and your people from suspicion."

"We trust in the laws of Kemet," the old man said, his expression grave.

When it suits your purpose, Bak thought, as it does when you know for a fact you'll not be blamed. "A messenger came to you at sunrise. He described a man we've been seeking. Could this be him?" He prayed fervently that such was not the case.

"Come see for yourself." Dedu turned on his heel and the villagers parted before him.

Bak and Imsiba knelt on the damp earth beside the body, which lay full-length on its left side, feet in the water. A spear, its shaft broken close to the point, was embedded deep in the lower rib cage. Arms, legs, and back were thick and solid; the muscles around the waist bulged with fat.

Snapping out an oath, Bak gripped the cool, clammy shoulder and shoved the body onto its back. A murmur rippled through the surrounding crowd. The dead man's neck was as thick and broad as his head; his face was square, his mouth full and coarse. A long, open gash, its lips stark white from exposure to water, bared the bone on the left shoulder.

Imsiba uttered a humorless barklike laugh. "We must call off our search, it seems."

Bak rubbed his hand across his eyes, too disappointed to respond. His instincts had warned him to expect the worst, had sent him to Kames in fact, but he had hoped for better. He had counted on taking this man alive, hearing from his own lips how he had slain Commandant Nakht. How he had managed to steal the gold and where he had hidden all he had taken through the year. Nothing was left but to learn the man's name. The rest, he feared, might forever remain a mystery.

Dedu whistled softly, as if he had noticed something that surprised him.

Alerted by the sound, Bak studied the body more closely. He noted a dozen or more spots of discolored flesh on the hands and forearms. He knew what they were; he had seen similar scars as a child. His father, a physician, had cared for a woman who had at some time in the past been badly burned by cooking oil.

His glance shifted to the spear point and what little remained of the shaft. Muttering a curse, he tugged the spear from the lifeless chest and held it out so Imsiba could see what he and the old man had spotted: the flawless edges of the bronze point, the careful sanding of the short stub of shaft. The workmanship was superb, unlike that of villagers and tribesmen, who had neither the facilities nor the skills to make so finely crafted a weapon. On the shaft close to the bronze point was a symbol that identified the spear as one from his own police arsenal.

"Have you turned your face from us?" Imsiba asked, stricken. "You stood beside us when Commandant Nakht was slain. How can you not trust us now?"

Bak followed the sergeant out of the tree-shaded courtyard of the house of death where they had taken the body. The midday heat enveloped him like a cloak, draining the sweat from his flesh.

"Can you tell me for a fact where each man was throughout the night?" he demanded.

"Not a man in our company would slay another except to protect himself. I know them!"

"This spear came from our arsenal," Bak said, holding aloft the linen-wrapped weapon.

"They're innocent, I tell you!"

Bak's eyes were drawn to two chatting women, walking across the open stretch of sand on which the house of death stood. One of the pair noticed them, murmured something to the other, and they hastened into the mouth of a narrow, crooked lane that meandered through the dwellings and workshops of the outer city. Imsiba saw nothing—his back was to them—but Bak had seen as they rounded the corner the way they stared with tight, accusing mouths. The rumors are spreading, he thought.

"Come," he said grimly, taking Imsiba by the arm. "We have much to do and not enough time."

Imsiba shook off his hand and headed across the sand to a well-worn path hugged on one side by the sunken road at the base of the citadel wall, on the other by buildings crammed together in jumbled confusion.

Bak hurried to catch up. "You misunderstand my questions, Imsiba, and the source of my anger. I don't doubt our men's innocence; I question our ability to prove it."

"Proof!" Imsiba laughed, incredulous. "Half slept through the night in the barracks, the others patrolled the streets from dusk to dawn. How can we find men who saw them?"

"It must be done. With no delay. Before every man in this garrison is blinded by suspicion." Bak's expression turned flinty. "We must not only learn their whereabouts when the commandant's house was ransacked, but we must also discover how that spear left our arsenal."

Imsiba nodded, his face glum. "Each time you give

me a task, it's ten times ten more difficult than the one before."

"Have you made any headway with the men unaccounted for when Nakht was slain?"

"The three who claimed to walk the streets went on duty at sunrise. I'll get the truth from them when they return to our barracks at sunset."

They reached the mouth of the lane where it opened onto the main thoroughfare. To the west, beyond the hodgepodge of buildings and a strip of barren sand, a long train of donkeys, their backs piled high with hay, was plodding through the great towered gate that pierced the outer wall on the desert side of Buhen. They were bound for the donkey paddocks, whose location could be pinpointed by the fine, pungent dust hanging over the southern end of the outer city. Bak and Imsiba turned east and passed through the gate into the citadel. The two Medjays who had gone with them to the village were walking along at a leisurely pace not far ahead. Three thickset men—craftsmen, from the look of their crumpled sweat-stained kilts—emerged from an intersecting lane farther along the street.

"Hori crossed the river this morning," Imsiba continued. "He should have no trouble finding the woman who shared her bed with Amonemopet. As for Ruru . . ."

He broke the thought with an angry hiss. The craftsmen were swaggering toward the Medjays on what looked like a collision course. Bak watched with a wary eye, praying his men would have the sense to avoid a confrontation. They held their ground until the last moment, finally stepping aside to let the others go by. One of the craftsmen raised his hand in an obscene gesture directed at their backs, another spat on the ground.

Imsiba growled deep in his throat. "How does word spread so fast?"

"I'd not be surprised to learn that someone is feeding the fire."

"Nebwa, you think?"

The approaching craftsmen eyed Imsiba with contempt. Bak put on his coolest, most haughty expression and raised his baton of office. They gave him an uncertain look and swung wide to pass. He turned slowly around, watching them walk on down the street. No man would spit at him and go away unscathed. They did not try.

He scowled at their backs. "From this day on, Imsiba, I want none of our men to walk the streets of Buhen alone. They must always travel in pairs, especially at night when they patrol the streets, and each pair must take a dog. They must at all times tread lightly, drawing no trouble to themselves."

"If they're forced into a corner? Can they not protect themselves?"

"If they must fight back, they should. I want none of them to look like cowards. But caution them to strike with care. The death of another man would bring a mob to our doorstep." Smiling an apology, he added, "Those rules apply to you, too, Imsiba."

The big Medjay smiled ruefully. "If Hori and I are to find witnesses for all our men throughout last night, he'll be walking by my side when my hair is white and I can no longer stand erect without the aid of a staff."

Bak's laugh held no humor, for his eyes were on the Medjays ahead. They had stopped just inside the gate that led to the quay, and two sentries had left their post to speak to them. What now? he wondered. Laughter rang out, not from one man but from four. A sentry clapped a Medjay on the shoulder, the other raised his spear in a mock salute. Bak's men ambled through the gate. The tension seeped from him, and he thanked the lord Amon that not all men in Buhen thought his Medjays guilty of murder.

The anxiety drained from Imsiba's face and he glanced at Bak. "You've said nothing about the man we took to the house of death. Was he slain by one who knew he had gold and wanted it for himself? Or was he slain at this time by chance?"

"Chance, Imsiba?" Bak shook his head. "The gods have played many cruel tricks on us since we came to Buhen, and this is the vilest of all. Chance had nothing to do with it. He was slain because of the gold, I have no doubt."

"And so our men would be blamed for murder," Imsiba said, his voice bitter. "Why? Because the guilty one hates and fears all Medjays? Or did he mean to tie our hands until he can slip away from Buhen?"

"He should not have gone so far." Bak's expression was cold and unforgiving. "We now have a personal stake in hunting him down like the animal he is."

Chapter Seven

Bak broke through the surface of the water and propelled himself into the shallows. The strip of dirt along the river was empty; no one stood among the acacias lining the bank. Relieved that Nofery had not yet come, he hauled himself to his feet and waded to the granite boulder. Grabbing his kilt and loincloth, he darted into the shade beneath the trees. A sparrow fluttered to a higher branch, twittering its displeasure at being disturbed. A lizard scurried across the ground and disappeared beneath a rustling bush. Still dripping, he hurried into his clothing. He had no wish to submit himself to Nofery's lewd comments should she find him undressed.

He lifted a fishy-smelling package wrapped in leaves from a low, flat boulder and sat down. Through the branches he could see the steep, ill-defined path rising to the top of the long stretch of sand and rock that paralleled the river south of the fortress. He flicked an ant from the bundle and unwrapped it. A dozen limp green onions lay on top of four charred fish mired in a pool of coagulated oil. As unappealing as they were, he was too hungry to care.

He broke the head off a fish, tore the body apart, and

began to eat the flesh from its bones. Am I waiting in vain? he wondered. Did Nofery laugh in Hori's face when he told her what I wanted?

No sooner had he asked himself the question than he heard querulous muttering, the swish of flowing sand, a curse. His eyes darted toward the path. Nofery was about a quarter of the way down, slightly off balance on a slope too unstable to support the weight of her heavy body. Her face was flushed, her ankle-length white sheath was stained with sweat and dust. In one hand she carried a long staff, useless in the sand. In the other, she gripped a good-sized beer jar.

"Don't sit there with your mouth agape," she shrieked. "Help me!"

Thanking the lord Amon she had come, Bak dropped the fish on the rock and raced up the slope. She grabbed him by the upper arm, clung as if her very life was at risk, took mincing steps, and whimpered. She was heavier than he had thought, and throughout the descent she did nothing to help herself. If she had not brought the beer, he would have seriously considered drowning her.

Reaching the safe, flat earth at the bottom of the slope, she spouted a flood of grievances. The heat, the long walk from the fortress, the rough desert path, the flies. Wondering how he would ever get her back up the hill, Bak ushered the bulky woman to the rock and moved his midday meal so she could sit.

"When that scribe of yours, that Hori, told me I must visit the house of death . . . well, I pledged to help you, so I was obliged to go." She rearranged her huge buttocks on the hard stone. "If he'd told me of the hardships I'd have to endure to meet you here, I'd have thrown him out on his backside."

"Come now, mistress Nofery!" Bak gave her his most boyish smile. "You wanted to know as much as I the name of the man pulled from the river."

She snorted as if indifferent, but he could see she could hardly wait to tell him what she had learned. "I care only for the living. A dead man can't buy my wares or lie with my women."

"Did you bring the beer to drown your sorrow at losing a customer?" he asked, his eyes twinkling. "Or to thank me for having the good sense to ask you to take a look before any other man or woman?"

Her laugh, coming from deep within, made her many rolls of fat shake like the gel from a well-cooked cut of meat. As the quaking subsided, she could not resist a final complaint. "I tell you this, Officer Bak. The satisfaction of being the first to lay eyes on him was in no way worth the effort it took to get here."

"Would you prefer all who live in Buhen to know you're my spy?"

"I'd have little business," she admitted. "Even my promise to speak highly of your Medjays will cost me much." Her eyes narrowed, the look on her face turned sly. "I'd be more useful to you if you released me from that vow."

Bak bent over and patted her cheek. "You must whisper their praises, old woman, not shout their merits to the world. One word spoken with subtlety is worth ten shoved down a man's throat."

Nofery's sigh was so exaggerated, so deep and long, Bak imagined her fleshy body shrinking to a twig. Shaking off the image, he sat on the ground in front of her, folded his legs, and laid his food on his crossed ankles.

"Tell me, Nofery, who was he?"

She hesitated and he saw the temptation on her face to bargain favor for favor. The stern look he gave her, along with her eagerness to relate what she knew, overcame her desire to negotiate.

"His name was Heby," she said. "He came to my place of business perhaps once a month."

"I must offer a plump goose to the lord Amon," Bak said, smiling with relief. "I feared you wouldn't know him."

"I recognized him, yes, but as for knowing him? I doubt if any man did." She unplugged the jar, took a deep drink from it, and passed it to Bak. "Most men come to relax after a long day and they wish to enjoy the company of others. He came to drink and to relieve himself with my women. He seldom spoke, never smiled, held all men at arm's length."

Bak inhaled the aroma seeping from the jar's mouth, nodded his approval, and took a healthy drink. "He had no friends?"

"Who would befriend so sullen a man?"

Bak finished the fish and began to eat another. The lord Amon had given him the wisdom to send Nofery to the house of death; why then would he not provide the answers he needed? "Did he ever say what he did to put bread in his mouth?"

"He told me nothing, but another man did. One who worked by his side day after day." She drank from the jar a second time, taking so much, Bak wondered if any remained for him. "Heby was a goldsmith, one who melted the ore brought from the mines. The scars Hori told me to look for, those on his arms, were old burns, as you thought. He'd been spattered by molten metal."

Bak pictured the ingot hidden in his bedchamber and chided himself for being so blind. Who but a goldsmith would have had the skill and the tools to melt down the ore and mold it? Who would be in a better position to steal?

"Yes," Neferperet said in a hoarse voice. "Yes, it's Heby."

He backed away from the thigh-high stone embalming table, his eyes locked on the naked body lying in the deep tray carved into its upper surface. Neferperet was a big man, heavy and muscular, a man of thirty or so years respected for his strength, but during the short time he had been in the house of death, his face had turned a sickly green. Bak suspected his own visage looked no healthier. The hot, clammy air, the suffocating odor, the eerie shadows trembling in the lamplight assaulted the senses and made him feel as if he had already set one foot in the netherworld.

Neferperet swallowed hard, swung around, and rushed past a table containing the body of an old man, stomach slit barely enough to admit a hand, innards lying in a stone bowl on the floor. He plowed through the door and vanished from sight. Bak, close behind, got no farther than the portal, where his path was barred by Min, the freckled, red-haired scribe responsible for maintaining the records in the house of death.

"We need more than his name, Officer Bak," Min said, his manner officious.

Bak edged past him into the adjoining room, crossed to the far wall, and stopped beside a deep stack of sparkling white, neatly folded linen. Even there, he could not evade the smell of death, the taste.

"I doubt Neferperet went beyond the courtyard," he

said, working hard not to show his discomfort. "He's the chief goldsmith, the man Heby toiled for."

Min screwed up his mouth in disapproval. "I've no interest in the slain man's personal habits, sir. I need to know of his family and the way they wish him to be prepared for eternity."

"Men talk of death as well as life while they toil." Bak sidled to the door that would take him out of the building. His eyes darted toward another room. On a table similar to the one Heby occupied, he saw a form cocooned in natron, the white salty substance used to dry the body. Nakht, he thought.

"We can do nothing on word of mouth alone," Min snapped. "You must go immediately to the scribal office building and return with his personal record. Only then will we know for a fact whether he's to be fully prepared for interment in a tomb in Kemet or left as he is for immediate burial here."

Bak wondered if this self-important scribe was always so impertinent or if he had heard the gossip about the Medjays and thought he could behave as he liked with their officer. "I have much to do," he said curtly. "I'll have the record brought to you when I can, possibly today, more likely tomorrow."

He pivoted and hurried along a short corridor to the exit. The courtyard, though shaded by sycamores and palms along each wall, was as hot as the inside of a cooking pot simmering on a brazier, but at least the air was free of stench. He allowed himself the luxury of several deep breaths before crossing to Neferperet, seated in the shade on a mudbrick bench beside a small fish pool. A dozen fingerling perch darted among the stems of a lotus plant beneath open white blossoms floating among the leaves on the water's surface.

The goldsmith stared at his scarred, work-hardened hands, clasped tight between his knees. "I thought myself a man, but after this . . ."

"Say no more. Those who toil here seem not to mind, but I, for one, have neither the nose nor the stomach for the house of death."

Bak sat beside Neferperet and bent over the pool, allowing the sweet scent of the flowers to drive away the odor clinging to his nostrils. He was sure Heby had stolen the gold, but he needed proof. From what he had seen of Tetynefer, the steward would prefer to believe a foreign woman guilty of murder rather than admit that gold taken from beneath his very nose had brought about two deaths. Bak was also convinced Heby had been slain because of the gold. But one who made no friends would never be tempted to confide, so who had learned his secret? This man Neferperet? Or another who toiled in the same workshop?

"What can you tell me of Heby?" he asked.

"He was a skilled craftsman and a diligent worker. He . . ." Neferperet hesitated, gave a too elaborate shrug, smiled. "He was like any other man who knows his craft well."

"He was friendly and good-humored? Well-liked and respected by all who knew him?"

The goldsmith's smile thinned. "He wasn't a man to make friends easily, but . . . yes, he was respected."

"I've heard him called sullen."

Neferperet's laugh held no humor. "I should've known you'd talk to others before me."

Bak made no comment, letting the goldsmith think what he would. A breath of warm air, the first all day, caressed his moist forehead. The leaves on the trees danced and whispered. A bee buzzed in an arc over the pool to land on a fragrant blossom and bury itself in pollen. A tiny green frog, no bigger than a thumbnail, leaped from one leaf to another and splashed into the water.

"You heard right," Neferperet admitted. "I wished many times I had ten men with his skill and none with his disposition."

"Had he no friends among the other goldsmiths?"

"They're an easygoing lot and they tried, but he'd have none of it. So they let him go his own way. None will mourn him, I can tell you."

"And you?"

Neferperet frowned at his callused hands, rubbed them together. "I'm sorry he met so violent an end and sorrier to lose so skilled a worker, but as for the man himself?" He shrugged. "He did his task well and he knew it. He wanted no other to tell him what must be done."

"Yet as his superior," Bak prompted, "you couldn't let him do as he pleased all the time."

"I put up with him for a week and then . . ." The goldsmith balled his right hand into a fist and held it up. "He was heavier than I am, but older and softer. I taught him to listen."

"How long ago was that?"

"One year, no more."

It took all Bak's will to contain his excitement. According to the scrolls Azzia had given him, the stealing had begun a year ago. He eyed Neferperet, who seemed as honest and open as Hori's puppy. As chief goldsmith, he should have noticed something amiss. Yet he had reported no thefts, no suspicions. Which meant he was not as innocent as he seemed or Heby's method of taking the gold was so clever that a master craftsman had been deceived. If so, how could he, Bak, hope to learn how it was done?

Shaking off self-doubt, he asked, "What brought Heby to Buhen? I'd think so skilled a craftsman would've toiled in Waset for the royal house."

"A man like him in so exalted a place?" Neferperet laughed, contemptuous. "He'd have lasted less than a week."

Bak heard the quick patter of approaching footsteps. Min, looking none too happy, was hurrying across the courtyard.

The scribe stopped at the edge of the pool. "Sir, will you speak without delay to the man who holds Heby's personal record?" All pretense of authority had vanished.

"I'll go when I have the time."

"Today, I beg you! If he's not to be embalmed, if he's to be laid to rest in a local cemetery . . ." Min hesitated, flushed a bright crimson. "With the days so hot . . . you must understand, sir. He cannot long be kept here."

Bak smothered a smile. "You'll have my message before the sun drops below the fortress wall."

Min thanked him profusely and hurried back inside.

He had barely vanished from sight when Neferperet began to laugh. "It seems those who toil in the house of death have no more stomach for it than we."

Bak's laughter was short-lived. A visit to the scribal offices would lead to an interview with Tetynefer, an interview he dreaded. He had reported at first light the intruder in the commandant's residence, and the steward had been none too pleased to hear a Medjay guard had failed to perform his duty. How would he react when he learned a Medjay spear had been found in Heby's breast?

Bak refused to dwell on that. "How was Heby yesterday?"

"Sullen." Neferperet appeared to like the word. "Sullen, as always."

Bak tried to imagine how he would feel if he planned to enter and search a building inhabited by four people and guarded by a policeman. "Did he act like a man afraid, or one whose thoughts were on another task or in another place?"

The goldsmith hunched over to stare at the pool. "He was sullen as usual, but . . ." Having found the words he sought, he nodded. "Yes, he was like the lions the men of Kush bring in cages from far to the south. He struck out in anger at all who came near."

A man might show anger, Bak thought, to convince himself he's not afraid.

"The rage was at himself, and with good reason," Neferperet went on. "He worked like a boy new at the furnace, and for a man like him who expected much of himself . . ." He shook his head, troubled by the memory. "Our scribe won't soon forget the tongue-lashing he got each time he told Heby the scales didn't balance."

"He poured too little in the molds?" Bak asked, taking care to show no more than average interest.

"Two molds he filled weighed light, one weighed heavy. Another he overflowed, and, I know not how, he cracked it so it can no longer be used." He shook his head in disbelief. "He dropped another and broke it to pieces. Can you imagine a man so skilled being so clumsy?"

Heby was thinking not of his day's work, Bak was sure, but of the night ahead and the danger he faced. Of a search that could stretch for hours, with so many documents to read. Read? A craftsman who could read? Bak's heart turned to stone.

"Could Heby read and write?" he asked.

Neferperet stared as if Bak had lost his senses. "Heby? Surely you tickle my feet with a feather. What need would a goldsmith have for learning?"

"Of course!" Bak smacked the palm of his hand hard against the crenelated wall. "Heby wasn't alone in taking the gold. He couldn't have been!"

Feeling somewhat foolish for speaking aloud, he glanced to right and left. No one had heard. He stood by himself atop the massive towered gate that opened onto the western desert. The nearest sentry was more than fifty paces away. Others ambled along the wall at much greater distances. Muted voices and the sound of a whiny dog drifted up from the city behind him. The odor of manure from the donkey paddocks and fowl pens came and went with the breeze.

Rubbing his stinging hand, he stared westward across the desert, an undulating landscape of sand and rocks. No creature stirred, but the earth itself appeared alive. The sand, bleached a pale beige beneath the lord Re's baleful eye, seemed to quiver around the gray-black rocks. At irregular intervals, gusts of air lifted the finer grains and sent them hurtling across the surface like a low, vaporous blanket, which fell back to rest as each gust subsided.

He should have gone directly to Tetynefer, but he had needed time to sort out his thoughts before facing the steward, and sort them out he would now that he had come to his senses.

Heby would not have been able to tell one scroll from another; therefore, he must have gone to Nakht's private rooms to look for the gold while another man, one who could read, had gone through the documents below. Since less than half had been disturbed, that second intruder must have fled from Nakht's office when Azzia screamed. Bak cursed aloud, certain he had missed him by a hair when he ran up the stairway to help her.

Obviously, she had not told Heby or his accomplice the gold and scrolls were no longer in the commandant's residence. Bak was sure she could have sent a message, even with Ruru looking on, if she had wanted to. And she had hurled the spear at Heby. Both actions proclaimed her innocence, and relief flooded through him. Another thought washed away the glow: she could have turned her back on the pair, hoping to save herself. Maybe Heby had confronted her and . . .

No more! he thought. Each time she enters my thoughts, they go around and around until I'm dizzy. I must plant my feet on firmer ground.

Heby, Neferperet had said, had been clever with his hands but none too bright, so the other man must have devised the scheme for stealing the gold. When they met after running from the commandant's residence, that man must have realized the wound in Heby's shoulder would attract too much attention, too many questions the goldsmith would sooner or later be made to answer. To protect himself, that second man had silenced Heby forever.

Using a spear from the police arsenal.

Who is he? Bak wondered. His thoughts returned to his former suspects: Nebwa, Paser, Mery, and Harmose. Which of the four—if any of them—was the guilty man, and how would he ever find proof? He stared at the desert, his expression stony. With Heby dead, the trail to his confederate was smudged, like the windswept track leading across the sands from the gate on which he stood. But wherever a man walked, traces remained through eternity. I'll follow those traces, he vowed, until I lay my hands on the second man, Heby's slayer and Nakht's. No more will I think of giving up or reporting the stolen gold to Tetynefer. This task is mine alone.

"So you've finally come!" Tetynefer said, his tone waspish. "I expected you long ago, as soon as you returned from Dedu's village."

The steward was seated on a high-backed chair, feet on a low stool, baton of office in hand, giving the appearance of a petty nobleman accepting petitions in a provincial court. Moisture dotted his forehead; a rivulet flowed down his chest between drooping pads of flesh, which, in a woman, would have swollen to breasts. His writing implements and a half-dozen scrolls lay on a table to his right.

"I had to learn who the slain man was," Bak said.

"He was a man of Kemet," Tetynefer snapped, "a man whose life and death are my responsibility. I should've sent a courier to the viceroy the instant his body was carried within these walls."

Bak's hand tightened on the door frame, but he let no hint of irritation touch his voice. "I would've thought, before you sent a message, you'd want to know as much as possible about him."

"This fortress has soldiers without number, young man, and they're all at my disposal. I can send as many couriers as I choose, one each hour of the day if necessary."

Bak pictured a line of messengers, one following another like beads on a cord, making the long voyage downriver. He was sure the viceroy, a seasoned commander in the army, would not be overjoyed at seeing so many fighting men so ill used.

The steward plucked a blank scroll from the table, spread it across his lap, and chose a reed pen from several stored in the slot of his scribal pallet. "Death is not uncommon in Buhen, as you well know, but always before, it's been the result of accident, sickness, warfare, or brawl. Now, in just three days and nights, the commandant has been slain, his residence invaded by a thief, and a valued craftsman stabbed to death by a villager, a Medjay." He aimed the tip of the pen at Bak and gave him a censorious look, as if Bak were personally responsible. "The viceroy won't be pleased, I can tell you."

Bak barely noticed. He was too surprised the steward had not heard the murder weapon had come from the police arsenal.

Tetynefer dipped his pen in the ink and poised it over the scroll. "Tell me all you know of this man and how he died. Be quick. A courier must leave before nightfall."

"His name was Heby," Bak said. "He was born in the village of Iuny. According to his personal record he, like his father before him, roamed the length of Kemet, making fine jewelry and accessories for the noble families. His skill was praised, but he was surly in temperament and not well liked. A year ago, he came here to the goldsmith's workshop."

If Tetynefer thought it strange a man would choose the tedious task of smelting ore over the far more satisfying task of creating beautiful objects, he gave no indication.

"He was close-mouthed," Bak went on, "and seldom talked about himself. When he came to Buhen he claimed to be a man alone, no mother, no father, no wife. With no one to provide for his afterlife, he'll be buried here and soon forgotten."

"So be it," Tetynefer said, shrugging.

Bak hoped when his own time came to go to the netherworld, his life would not be dismissed so easily. He turned the thought aside and went on with his report, describing where the body had been found and how.

"The one who slew him?" Tetynefer asked, looking up from the scroll. "Did he slink away to his wretched cousins in the desert, thinking to escape our justice?"

"No villager took Heby's life. He was slain upstream, well to the south of where his body was found."

The steward raised an eyebrow, chuckled. "Did you see the weapon being thrust into his breast, Officer Bak? Or have you allowed toothless old Dedu to turn your head with his lies?"

Bak struggled to suppress his resentment. "I spoke with a fisherman who knows the river and its currents. He said that at this time of year, anything dropped in the water upstream from this fortress is swept around the quay and back toward the riverbank near Dedu's village." Seeing doubt on the steward's puffy face, he added, "I've sent two of my men up the river to look for signs of a struggle. With luck, they'll find blood and the broken shaft of the spear we found in Heby's breast."

Tetynefer drew a square of linen from his belt and patted the sweat from his face. "I've been told that a Medjay spear was used. It may not be apparent to you, young man, but it's very clear to me. A villager slew the craftsman, and are not the villagers Medjays?"

"It was a spear made in Kemet," Bak said doggedly. "After I chased Heby from the commandant's residence, I believe he met another man who lives within the walls of this city, and that that man took his life."

"Heby was the man Mistress Azzia wounded?"

"Yes. His shoulder was gashed to the bone."

The steward patted his neck and his bald head, saying nothing, deep in thought. Bak shifted from foot to foot, dreading the time when he must admit the spear was from his own arsenal.

At last, Tetynefer nodded, and a smile spread across his face. His eyes found Bak's. "Good. Very good."

Bak was certain the man had lost his senses.

Tetynefer tucked a corner of the damp linen into his belt, took up his pen, and began to write. "With mistress Azzia shortly to appear before the viceroy for taking her husband's life, and with the man who broke into the commandant's residence dead at the hands of an unknown Medjay who used a spear he pilfered from . . . yes, from one of our caravans, while the men lay sleeping . . ." He paused and tilted his head to admire the wet black ink glittering on the creamy papyrus. "Yes, the viceroy will be pleased indeed at our speedy resolution of these vile crimes."

"Heby was slain," Bak said in a hard, stiff voice, "with a spear stolen from my police arsenal. A rumor is spreading through Buhen that his life was taken by one of my men."

Tetynefer sat rigid in his chair, the good humor draining from his face. A tight smile formed on his lips and he dipped the pen into the ink. "At the moment, I see no reason to distress the viceroy with petty details.

The spear was stolen; it matters not from where it was taken."

Bak felt uncomfortable with the lie, but bowed his head in acceptance. Better to let the steward make himself look good to the viceroy than to insist on the truth and put his men in jeopardy.

Tetynefer raised his pen and pointed it at Bak. "However, you must get the truth from your wretched Medjays and bring forth the one who slew Heby. Waste no time lest I be forced by circumstance to report all I know."

"None is guilty of murder, that I swear to the lord Amon."

"Hear me out!" Tetynefer snapped. "I want the guilty one's name before you take mistress Azzia to Ma'am. He must not be given time to slay half the men posted to this garrison."

Chapter Eight

Seething from his interview with Tetynefer, Bak hurried along a series of narrow, congested lanes that took him through the outer city. The gusting wind had grown stronger. Dust seeped into every nook and crevice. The thick air made it hard to breathe. The sun hanging above the western battlements was a fiery orange, its form made indistinct by the fine sand blown high into the sky. Men, women, and children scurried through the lanes, trying to finish their day's tasks and reach the shelter of their homes before the storm worsened.

Two hard-muscled, stern-faced spearmen guarded the workshop of the goldsmiths. One stood at the entrance, another rushed up when Bak appeared.

The taller of the two stepped into the portal, barring it with his bulk. "This workshop is closed to all men, sir. You cannot enter."

Bak controlled his irritation. The soldier was doing the task he had been assigned; he could not be blamed for Tetynefer's stupidity. "I'm here to see Neferperet."

"None too soon," the chief goldsmith called, hurrying to the entry with a welcoming smile. "We're almost ready to load the furnace."

The guards refused to budge until Neferperet ex-

plained Bak's mission to find the man who had slain
Heby. After stepping aside so he could enter, they continued to watch him. He felt as if he had come to steal
and would at any moment be exposed.

The workshop was rectangular in shape, open to the
sky, and surrounded by a mudbrick wall higher than
Bak's head. He thought he had never been in a place so
hot. Lean-tos covered with palm fronds ran along two
walls, providing relief from the sun but none from the
heat. Two furnaces occupied the long shelter to the
right, one stood in the shorter lean-to at the far end.
The furnaces were constructed of large round-
bottomed pottery containers held above the hard-
packed dirt floor by a ring of bricks. Four goatskin
bellows, two on either side, lay on the ground outside
each ring. Three men wearing dirty loincloths hunkered in the shade beneath the longer lean-to. They
chatted, joked, and laughed while they shared the yellow flesh of a large melon.

Bak turned his attention to a square pavilion roofed
with reed mats which stood before the long unprotected wall to the left. The light structure shaded the
scribe, a fleshy young man with thick, curly brown
hair. Seated on a stool before a low table on which
stood a bronze scale, he placed stone weights in a pan
suspended from one arm of the device to match the
weight of a pottery cone lying in the pan hanging from
the opposite arm. The cone's broad end was plugged
with dried clay. Four glittering gold ingots lay on a low
mudbrick platform beside his right leg.

Bak's eyes lingered on the ingots, the same width
and breadth of the one hidden in his bedchamber but at
least two fingers thicker. The wealth they represented
took his breath away. "Why weigh the cone?"

"It's filled with ore," Neferperet said. "It comes that way from the mines."

The scribe pointed to three identical numbers inked on the baked clay and spoke in the same offhand manner as men who weighed nothing more precious than grain or lentils or onions. "These are the weights recorded when the cone was filled, when it was handed over to the caravan officer, and when he delivered it to the treasury here in Buhen. The weight I find now should be the same."

"What of the ingots?" Bak prompted. "Have they been weighed?"

"After they cooled." The scribe waved away a fly that had settled on a pristine bar. "They'll be weighed again when we deliver them to the treasury before nightfall."

And the weight found there, Bak thought, is verified over and over until the gold is safely stored in the royal treasury in Waset. Which means these weights are accurate, just as Kames said. How then could Heby have taken gold? Minute quantities, perhaps, but not the large amount indicated in the scrolls Nakht left with Azzia. With an imperceptible sigh, he looked from one furnace to another. Maybe the answer lay in the smelting process.

"So few men work here?" he asked.

"I've three times the number," Neferperet said. "I sent the others home. After we finish today, we've nothing more to do until another caravan delivers more ore. One was expected before now but . . ."

A wind-driven cloud of dirt rolled across the workshop, catching everyone by surprise. Bak clamped his eyes shut and covered his mouth and nose. The lean-tos crackled, the scribe coughed, a craftsman swore. The finer particles clung to sweaty faces and bodies.

The air stilled. Neferperet looked up at the dull yellow sky and his expression grew worried. "I hope, for the sake of man and beast alike, the officer in charge can find a sheltered spot before this storm reaches them. If they're spread out along the trail and become separated, not one in ten will return."

Bak shuddered. He had heard of the raging sandstorms on the open desert and the dire consequences of getting lost.

One of the craftsmen swallowed the last of his melon, threw the rind aside, and wiped his hands on his loincloth. Picking up a long pair of tongs, he walked to the nearest furnace and poked the gently flaming charcoal mounded inside the container.

"It's ready," he announced.

Neferperet hurried to the lean-to to sort through a pile of rectangular baked clay molds, each slightly smaller than an outstretched hand. Finding two he liked, he set them side-by-side on a row of bricks not far from the burning furnace. The other two craftsmen stuffed the last of the melon into their mouths.

Bak looked inside the adjacent furnace. A few pieces of charcoal glowed red each time the breeze coaxed them to life, but they would soon burn out. The third furnace, located at the center of the shorter lean-to, stood well away from the others, making it an ideal workplace for a man disliked by his fellows. Bak's interest quickened and he strode across the workshop to stand before it. Unlike the other shelter, where everything had its own place, this was cluttered and messy.

"Was this Heby's place?" he asked.

"It was." Neferperet came up beside him. "He had no sense of order, as you can see." In his hand, the goldsmith carried a round spouted pottery bowl with a flat bottom, a crucible.

Bak's eyes drifted over tongs, rods, blowpipes, crucibles, and molds. They were strewn around the lean-to as if deposited by a whimsical wind. The furnace was cold, its charcoal ashy.

"Did you use this space today?"

Neferperet shook his head. "We had no need."

Bak thanked the lord Amon in one breath, prayed in the next that Heby had left some sign of how he had taken gold when, according to the weights, none could be taken. He knelt to pick up a baked clay mold, a simple affair, a rectangular dish with thicker, sturdier walls than those used for cooking. Can molds be altered with no one being the wiser? he wondered.

"The furnace awaits us," Neferperet said.

Reluctantly, Bak replaced the mold where he had found it and followed the chief goldsmith to the pavilion. He had much to learn; Heby's workplace could wait.

A guard hurried through a flurry of blowing dust to stand with Bak in front of the scale. Neferperet knelt beside the platform on which the ingots lay and set the crucible next to them. Like the scribe, he seemed indifferent to the precious metal, but Bak, who had never before seen so much wealth, felt its lure as Heby must have.

The scribe handed a cone to Neferperet. The clay plug, Bak noted, was stamped with the seal of the royal house. The goldsmith held the cone over the crucible and, with a wooden mallet, knocked off the pointed tip. A stream of golden granules looking much like coarse sand flowed into the crucible, along with larger grains up to the size of peas and a considerable number of flakes large and small. Bak smothered the urge to reach out and let the glittering particles trickle through his fingers.

The flow stopped. Neferperet tapped the cone to eject a few more bits and laid it in a bowl of water. Any gold remaining inside, he explained, would be washed out and added to the next batch to be smelted. A second cone was poured into the crucible and a third, depositing a mound of ore reaching halfway to the rim.

The chief goldsmith rose and carried the crucible to the furnace, the guard at one elbow, Bak at the other. The workman with the tongs stoked the fuel. The other two took positions atop the bellows, standing with one foot on each of a pair, and began to march in place. As each man lifted a foot, he pulled a cord attached to the upper surface of the bellows, drawing air inside as the goatskin swelled. When he dropped the foot, the air shot through a hollow reed outlet with a pottery nozzle inserted in a hole bored through the bottom of the fuel container. The charcoal glowed, the heat became intense.

Neferperet set the crucible next to the molds on the bricks. The stoker laid his tongs aside. They cradled the crucible between two flexible wooden rods and lifted it onto the charcoal.

Sweat poured from the men marching on the bellows. The stoker added charcoal, then aimed the tip of a reed blowpipe at the fresh fuel and blew long and hard, goading the heat from it. His face grew flushed; moisture dripped from his brow. Neferperet hovered like a man awaiting his firstborn son. Bak and the guard retreated to a place where the heat was not so extreme. The wind, Bak noticed, was stronger, the gusts more frequent.

The mounded ore gradually slid away and sank into the molten liquid below. The mass turned fiery. Neferperet hovered closer, studied it with a practiced eye, pronounced it ready. The pair on the bellows halted their endless march and backed off, giving their overseer and the stoker plenty of room to shift the crucible and pour the liquid gold into the molds.

Bak was stumped. From what he had seen thus far, Heby could have taken no more than a grain or two of gold without every man in the workshop being a party to the theft—a situation he could not imagine. Two men might hold a secret forever, a half-dozen for no more than a week.

"Now we let the ingots cool," Neferperet explained.

He glanced at the pavilion, which shuddered in a gust of wind, and began to issue orders to his men. The light structure must be dismantled before it blew away, the scribe's belongings moved to a more substantial shelter. Heby's place would be best, but first the tools and vessels had to be moved out of the way.

Bak muttered an oath. Heby's lean-to was his last hope of tracing a path to the stolen gold and the man who had slain to protect it. "I'll clear a space," he offered.

Ignoring the surprised look on Neferperet's face, he strode toward the shelter. A gust of sand-laden air caught him midway. He scrunched his eyes to slits, ran the last few paces, and ducked inside. The wind lashed the roof, the palm fronds crackled, but only an erratic breeze disturbed the air below.

He quickly sorted through the clutter, his thoughts

racing. A small amount of gold would be lost each time
the ore was transferred from one container to another,
and the weight would probably change—he had no
idea how much, but at least a modest amount—when
the ore was melted down. The difference between the
raw and smelted metals, he had no doubt, would be
well known, easily accounted for by the scribes. The
total loss from beginning to end would in no way
match the large amount unaccounted for in the scrolls
Azzia had given him.

He retrieved five molds, all identical in shape and
form, and examined them with care. They seemed impossible to alter in any way. Disappointed but unwilling to give up, he stacked them next to the wall and
began to separate tools from vessels, searching for the
molds Heby had broken the previous day and for anything else that might provide a lead. He glanced up
once, saw Neferperet and the stoker quenching the
smoldering fuel in the other furnaces. The pavilion
stood roofless with only its frame remaining. One of
the bellows-men, his back to the wind, was untying the
cords that bound it together. His mate was helping the
scribe gather up the scale and weights. The guards
were getting ready to move the gold. Bak's time was
running out.

Working as fast as he could, he placed like objects
together out of the way behind the furnace. Along with
the usable items, he found the spout and rim of a broken crucible, several rods and reed pipes too charred to
be of further use, and a crushed blowpipe. He found no
cracked or broken molds, not even a shard, nor anything else out of the ordinary.

Neferperet ducked into the lean-to. One arm encircled a bundle of rolled mats, the other the scribe's

stool. He eyed the neatened workspace with an appreciative smile. "To see order here is as pleasing as the sight of a well-formed woman."

Bak's smile was automatic. How, he wondered, can I learn what happened to the missing molds without asking outright? He toed the pile of broken and burned objects he had set off to the side. "Heby threw nothing away, it seems."

Neferperet glanced at the trash, shook his head in disgust. "I told him many times to let his stoker clean up at the end of each day, as the rest of us do. No man could please him, however, and he was seldom moved to do the task himself."

Bak's eyes narrowed. "How long had he refused the help?"

"Since he came a year ago." Neferperet stalked to the other side of the furnace, let the mats roll off his arm, and set the stool beside them. "Yesterday, to show you how he was, his stoker turned away to realign the molds while they were getting ready to pour. That's all he did, turn away. Heby picked up an empty crucible, the one you see there broken to pieces, and threw it at him."

"I saw no parts of the molds he broke yesterday." Bak smiled, making it a joke. "Did he throw them as well?"

Neferperet snorted. "If he had, I'd have marched him straight to the chief metalsmith for a flogging." He moved to the edge of the lean-to, ready to dart into the blowing sand. "As for the molds, I'm not surprised you didn't find them. The one he dropped couldn't be saved, so I'd guess he threw it away. The other he may've taken home, hoping to repair it."

"Can molds be repaired?" Bak asked, surprised.

"Most can't, but Heby was as clever with clay as he was with gold. He brought several vessels back I thought never to use another time."

Bak trotted down the narrow, curving lane, counting off the mat-covered doorways in the unbroken row of dwellings to his right. The wind swept him forward, released him, shoved him ahead. Sand swirled past at many times his speed, forming drifts along the walls, creeping into the smallest cracks. The tiny projectiles abraded his bare skin. He felt grit in his eyes and between his teeth, the chafing of granules in his sandals and under his kilt and loincloth. He had been equally uncomfortable in the past, but memory paled in comparison with the reality.

The seventh door, Neferperet had told him. Night had not yet fallen, but the thick brownish yellow cloud sweeping across the desert had stolen the light from Buhen. The lane was murky, the doors indistinct. Bak twice heard muffled voices within, twice saw a strip of light between a doorjamb and an ill-fitting mat.

Reaching the door he wanted, he released the bottom of the mat from the bricks holding it in place and slipped inside. The room was pitch black, stiflingly hot, and reeked of sweat, cooking oils, and musty dirt. He held the mat off to the side to get some light. Near the door were an oil-filled lamp and the tools to start a fire. Thanking the lord Amon for Heby's good sense, he dropped to his knees, set aside the mold he had brought from the workshop, and rolled the lower edge of the mat to calf height. After tying it securely, he moved the tools and lamp to the uncertain light at the threshold. Sitting with his back to the wind, he went to work. A low drift of sand had formed around his buttocks by the time he lighted the wick.

He picked up the mold and raised the lamp to look around. The light was weak but good enough for his purpose. Heby's lean-to had been cluttered and messy; the small room he had lived and slept in was filthy. Dirty, rumpled bedding covered a mudbrick sleeping platform. A charcoal- and sweat-stained loincloth lay on the hard-packed earthen floor; a kilt with red-brown blotches had been thrown across a stool. One end of a graying frayed sheet hung from the gaping mouth of a reed chest. In the corner lay a crumpled mound of cloth with heavy stains visible among the wrinkles. Bak took a closer look. The cloth, he felt certain, had been used to staunch the flow of blood.

He walked through a door at the back of the room. Beyond an open stairway leading to the roof, its woven-mat trapdoor closed, lay the kitchen. Half the depth of the first room, it was lightly roofed with branches and straw dense enough to provide shade, loose enough to allow smoke to escape. A round oven for baking bread occupied the near corner. A brazier sat beside it, its fuel burned to a powdery gray ash. Three unwashed bowls were stacked close by, the one on top lined with the thin scum of poorly strained beer. The floor at the far end of the rectangle was littered with vessels, shards, and odd-shaped lumps of dry, discarded clay. A layer of fine sand covered everything, and more was seeping through the roof.

Bak's eyes traveled back to the oven, a round mudbrick structure with an opening at the front to admit fuel and bread, and a smaller hole at the top to disgorge smoke. An irregular black stain rose up the grimy wall.

Heby had been a man alone, with no woman to cook for him—or to bake his bread. He would have traded his services or his allotment of grain for food. Bak doubted sufficient heat could be built up inside a cooking oven to melt gold, but Heby might have used it to harden the objects he molded from clay. Or he could have used it for a hiding place. For gold? Probably not. Too many people lived in the block, too many curious children, to hide something so precious in a place so easy to peek into.

Lest he err, he knelt before the oven and looked inside. Dust covered long-neglected baked clay shelves. A thick layer of ash covered the floor. He ran his fingers through the ashes, felt nothing but a few lumps of charred fuel and baked clay. He abandoned the oven with a sigh and crossed the room to kneel before the objects on the floor. Maybe here his luck would change.

Two round bowls sat off to the left. One was filled with cloudy water, the other with a partially dried lump of grayish clay, with indentations of Heby's fingers and thumb remaining on its surface. Next to the bowls, an empty cone with its tip broken off lay among several shards that had been part of a sturdy round-sided bowl. His eyes slid farther to the right and he smiled. There lay a cracked mold, the broken remains of at least one other, and a gray-black stone carved to the exact size and shape of a gold ingot. The stone, he guessed, was the form around which the wet clay was molded.

Eager to examine the molds, he shoved aside several fragments of rock-hard clay and set the lamp amid the clutter. As he made additional space for the mold he had brought with him, his eye fell on the cone. Why, he wondered, did Heby take it from the workshop? He picked it up, rotated it. He found no weight notations on its outer surface. It had never been weighed! With growing excitement, he licked a finger and ran it around the cone's interior. Holding it to the light, he looked for bits of glitter. He saw none, which was disappointing but not significant. The cone could have been washed after it was emptied.

He laid it down and took a quick look at the shards lying with it. The bowl had been thick-walled, unadorned, most likely a container Heby had used for carrying clay. A narrow gap visible at the broken edge of one piece indicated it had contained a fault when it was fired. A bubble must have formed in the wet clay.

He picked up the cracked mold. It looked no different than the others he had seen through the day, but . . . Was it a little deeper? He reached for the mold he had brought from the workshop and held the two side-by-side over the light.

He heard a sound behind him, a whisper of movement. He stiffened, every sense alert. Again he heard something; he had no idea what. He spun around, glimpsed a figure looming over him, a glittering dagger poised to strike.

Chapter Nine

Bak ducked and swung his right arm high to ward off the blow. The weapon sliced off to the side, but the force of the thrust toppled him onto the tools, shards, and bits of hardened clay. The lamp tipped over. Tongues of flaming oil flowed among the objects beneath him, licking his rib cage and arm. He dropped the molds and tried to roll away from the fire and the red-hot pain. Out of the corner of his eye, he glimpsed his assailant, arm raised, ready to strike again. Bak groped for something to throw, felt the rounded side of a bowl. He grabbed the rim and heaved it at the dark form of the other man. Water showering from the vessel hissed as it quenched the fire searing Bak's side. The bowl crashed into his assailant's shoulder, driving him backward with a grunt. Bak rolled across the sputtering fire, smothering the remaining flames. In the last flicker of light, he spotted the dagger arcing toward him.

He rolled forward, ramming his assailant's legs. The man fell heavily, cursed. Though wary of the dagger invisible in the pitchy darkness, Bak rose to a crouch and lunged. His foot slipped on the oily floor and he fell full-length on the other man, forcing the air from him. Bak found the hand clasped around the dagger's handle and tried to twist the weapon free. His own hands were so oily he could barely maintain his grip.

The man thrashed from side to side, punching Bak's lower back with his free hand, trying to shake him off. Bak swung his right fist. The blow was deflected by a hard round object, which skittered across the floor. Heby's unwashed dishes, he thought, sweeping them aside with a curse. His other hand slipped from the dagger to his opponent's wrist. He feared losing what little control he had of the weapon, but how could he prevent it?

The fist thudded against his lower back so hard it jarred his teeth. He rolled onto his side, pulling his opponent with him, pinning the flailing arm to the floor. Something solid tilted beneath his shoulder; a gritty, dusty substance poured out. The brazier, he thought, and the oven is just behind it. Holding the man close, Bak rolled hard and fast onto his back, slamming the hand holding the dagger against the oven. The blow jolted his arm to the shoulder, the man yowled, the dagger clattered to the floor.

Bak had not the leisure to feel relief. His opponent lay heavy on top of him. He tried to shove him off, but the man grabbed him around the chest. They rolled one way and another, locked so close together neither could get in a serious blow. They bumped the walls, the oven, the stairway. They smashed pottery and tumbled over shards and tools and bits of hardened clay. They spread a thin slick of oil across the floor and coated themselves with sandy particles. Bak's muscles ached, his lower back felt numb, the burns on his side and arm were fiery. Every breath was a struggle. His sole consolation was his opponent's ragged breathing.

The man suddenly relaxed his hold, twisted free, and rolled away. Bak heard him bump something, a few raspy breaths, silence. He rolled in the opposite direction to lose himself in the dark as his opponent had and hauled himself to a crouch. Hovering there, stifling his gasps, he listened for any tiny sound that would give away the other man's position. He heard nothing.

He stood up and moved his hand through the blackness, trying to find a wall, the oven, anything he could use to orient himself. His fingers slid through empty air, touched a wall not far to his right. He heard a faint scuffing noise, a sandal moving across the gritty floor. He stepped to the wall. A bit of baked clay crunched beneath his foot. Cursing mutely, he stood statue-still and listened. The silence was as thick as the darkness.

With his arm brushing the wall, he moved one foot forward, shifted his weight, and moved the other foot. The wall fell away from his upper arm, but he could feel it next to his elbow. He smothered an urge to laugh aloud. He was standing beside the open stairway, no more than two paces from the bottom step. Beyond was the door to the larger room. Once he reached the foot of the stairs, his opponent would be trapped inside the kitchen.

He took another step. His toe caught a shard and sent it rattling across the floor. A muffled curse echoed his own, the sound close in front of him. He lunged, collided with solid muscle and warm, slippery flesh. The man spun past him and began to run. Bak, a pace or two behind, glimpsed the faint light at the bottom of the mat that covered the outer door, a swath of drifted sand beneath it, and the dark figure ducking low to grab something off the floor. The mat was shoved violently forward; the cords holding it in place snapped apart. The figure darted through the portal and veered to the right. The mat blew back to slap Bak in the face. He jerked it aside and felt as if he faced a solid wall of wind and sand. He had forgotten the storm raging through Buhen.

He grabbed the sheet hanging from the reed chest. Winding it around his head and shoulders, leaving a slit so he could see, he ducked around the crazily flapping mat and pushed his way into the lane. The wind grabbed him and shoved him after the fleeing man, a vague shadow in the swirling torrent. Fine sand seeped beneath the sheet, lodged under his clothing, adhered to his oily, sweaty body. His eyes smarted, his nose was stuffed up, and his throat was clogged. The burns on his side and arm, scraped raw by the sand, stung as if still afire.

The lane ahead twisted to the left and the man disappeared from view. Bak hastened after him, made the turn. The wind caught him, threw him at the far wall. He hit it with a thud, stumbled, and would have fallen if a stronger gust had not propelled him on. The shadowy figure forged ahead. Bak plowed after him through eddying gusts which blew from all directions. Even with the sheet swaddling his head and shoulders, he felt exposed, vulnerable. He could not help but feel a grudging respect for the other man, who wore nothing but a short kilt.

He followed his quarry around another corner. A gust tore the end of the sheet from his fingers and unwrapped the section around his shoulders. He grabbed the flapping length of cloth, which caught the wind like a sail and blew him backward. He spotted a doorway, tacked toward it, and wedged himself against the jamb until he could pull the fabric around his burned side and arm. When he looked up, he glimpsed the other man much farther ahead than before, turning into an intersecting lane. Something billowed out in the wind behind him. Bak gave a hard, humorless laugh. The man had brought a cloak with him.

Bak battled the wind to the corner, made the turn, and was nearly blinded by a thick cloud of sand blowing toward him. He bent double, held his hand before his stinging eyes, and pushed his way along the lane, using all his strength to put one foot in front of the other. When he reached an intersection, the wind swirled around him, buffeting him on all sides. He stood his ground, looking down each lane in turn. The man he was pursuing had disappeared.

"So you gave up the chase."

"No, Imsiba, I did not. I'm stubborn like an ass but with less common sense. I went on and on from one lane to another, paying no heed to the turns I made." Bak was so angry with himself that he practically growled, "I lost my way."

Imsiba had the grace to make no comment.

Bak frowned at the empty sand-swept lane ahead, which was illuminated by a last faint glow of sunset and the wavering flame of Imsiba's torch. Walls hugged both sides. Dark rectangles marked doors whose mats had been removed to allow inside the clean, fresh air. At the gradual bend ahead, the light dwindled, faded to blackness. Murmuring voices, a baby's whimper, the smell of burning oil, onions, and fish filtered down from rooftops cooled by a soft, gentle breeze. High overhead, the stars were brightening as the barque of the lord Re sailed deeper into the netherworld and the last bits of dust drifted back to earth. Bak found it impossible to appreciate the peace of the moment. His battered muscles ached, his side and arm burned. He could not remember a time when he had felt so grimy.

"He knew every lane, every whim of the wind. As for me . . ." Bak's laugh was bitter. "With the sand so thick, I couldn't see the battlements; I didn't know north from south, east from west. When I finally stopped to ask, those who lived in the block were traders. They had no idea who Heby was or where he lived. I was lucky they could direct me to the citadel."

They stepped over a low drift running diagonally across an intersection and turned into another, similar lane. The rippled sand covering its surface was scarred by the footprints of a man and a dog.

Bak pointed at the shadows ahead. "The seventh door on the right."

"You're certain he came back?"

"With so much to lose, wouldn't you?"

Imsiba's smile was rueful. "I'd think it a fearsome thing to do, but if my life depended on it, yes."

A thick-chested brindle bitch loped past them. Spotting a striped cat sniffing a doorjamb, the dog barked and raced at the smaller animal. It shot through the darkened doorway with the dog in hot pursuit. A man yelled, let out a string of curses; children laughed with delight. The dog scooted out the door, its tail between its legs, and ran on up the street. Imsiba chuckled.

Bak was too irritated to see humor anywhere. "If only I'd seen his face!"

"He had no scars; no marks to tell you who he was?"

"I glimpsed the dagger, nothing more." Bak grimaced at the crude bandage wrapped around his fiery side and arm. "And the flames spreading beneath me." He stopped in front of Heby's door, where the mat hung askew, its lower end torn and tattered. "One thing I know. His body is hard, not soft with age or inactivity, and he thrusts the weapon like a man trained to use it."

"He's a soldier."

"He can read, Imsiba. He's an officer." Or a translator, Bak thought.

Pushing the mat aside, he stepped across a calf-high drift unmarked by footprints and stopped a couple of paces inside the room. Imsiba followed with the torch. The chest and stool were overturned; sheets, sleeping mat, and clothing were strewn over the floor. Fine sand blanketed every surface, but all footprints that might have been left had been erased by the wind blowing under the mat. Scalding the air with a string of curses, Bak led the way to the kitchen. The floor was littered with tools and with bits of pottery crushed beyond recognition. Like everything else, the brazier had been smashed, its ashes smeared across the gritty oil-stained floor. Bak had expected the worst, but was disappointed nonetheless. From the look on Imsiba's face, he was not alone in the feeling.

The big Medjay prodded the ingot-shaped stone with the point of his spear. "We'll find no gold here."

"If Heby kept it in this house, its hiding place will remain."

"Is that all we look for? An empty hole?"

"The cone I saw had never been weighed." Bak glanced toward the top of the stairway, where the exit to the roof was blocked. "I doubt Heby brought it here empty, meaning to repair it. I'd bet a month's ration of beer that it was brought to him by the man who attacked me and it was, at that time, filled with gold. We must search for a trace of that second man."

"If we find none?"

Scowling, Bak uttered the unthinkable. "We start again at the beginning and pray to all the gods in the ennead we'll have better luck the next time around."

"You fill my heart with joy, my friend . . ." Imsiba eyed the room, his expression glum. ". . . and a wish to forget this hopeless search you plan and return to our men's barracks. They're cooking a feast, pigeons and lentils. Would you not like to eat while they're hot?"

Bak was so hungry he could almost smell the birds roasting on the brazier. He shook off the temptation to leave at once and returned to the larger room. Imsiba followed and mounted the torch in a bracket by the door.

As Bak began to examine the bare sleeping platform, he asked, "What of the tasks I set you this morning?"

"I spoke to our men of the need to patrol in pairs and to walk around those who seek trouble." Picking up a dirty sheet, Imsiba wrinkled his nose in distaste. "They vowed to do as you asked, for one of the watch sergeants had already warned them of the gossip and most had seen for themselves the fear and mistrust in other men's eyes." He set the chest upright and dropped the sheet inside. "That vow tasted bitter on their tongues, my friend. They came to this city, proud to be chosen above all others to police its streets, and now . . ." He gave a hard, cynical laugh. "Your order that they fight when they must took some of the sting from their mouths, and won their loyalty like nothing else could."

"No man who serves me will ever act the coward," Bak said grimly.

"That knowledge eased my other tasks. As did the fact that you've never questioned their innocence in the slaying of Commandant Nakht or the goldsmith."

"Tell me . . ." Bak broke off abruptly, feeling a mud-brick in the corner jiggle beneath his fingers.

Imsiba dropped a stained kilt into the chest and hurried to his side. "You've found something?"

"We'll soon know." Bak knew better than to expect success in so short a time, but his voice was tinged with hope.

He hurried into the kitchen, scanned the clutter on the floor until he spotted a chisel, and hastened back with it to pry up the brick. Both men peered into the hole he'd made, saw nothing behind but another brick. Bak probed with the tool, but the surrounding bricks were firmly anchored to those around them.

Muttering an oath, he continued his examination of the platform. "What luck have you had in placing our men elsewhere when Nakht and Heby were slain?"

Imsiba swept a second kilt from the floor and flung it at the chest. "I know where every man was at the time the commandant's life was taken. One man, Ruru, was alone and unseen. In the barracks he was, sleeping. As for last night with so many hours to account for, all in the dead of night when most men slept . . ." He expelled a mirthless laugh. "That task is more hopeless than looking for gold in this house where none remains."

"You must not give up, Imsiba!" Bak's voice was sharper than the chisel in his hand. "To ask Nofery to lie for five men was a task I dreaded. To ask for more is a thing I won't do. She'd make me her slave—and you and all our company. That's too high a price to pay."

Imsiba knelt beside the sleeping mat, his expression bleak. "I'd not like to kiss her dirty feet for the rest of my life, but I see no other way."

Bak regretted his outburst, backed off enough to ask, "How many men do you speak of?"

"Ten. All those assigned to patrol through the night."

Bak had to laugh. "If you were the viceroy, Imsiba,

what would you do if you learned ten Medjays, police-men of Buhen whose duty it was to walk the streets from sunset to sunrise, had spent all the night taking their pleasure with Nofery's women?"

Imsiba's shoulders sagged. "The storm must've carried my wits far into the desert."

Leaving the sleeping area, Bak gave the glum-faced Medjay an understanding pat on the shoulder. He stopped before a wall niche containing a crude baked clay image of the squat, ugly household deity Bes. From the dusty cobwebs draped around the figure, he guessed no offering had been made for many weeks. Unpromising though it seemed, he swept the webs away to examine the niche.

"I should've reported the gold the moment I laid eyes on it," he said unhappily. "Heby and his confeder-ate would've retreated to the shadows, fearing discov-ery, and they'd have done nothing more. Because I made it my secret, I left them free to act. I alone set off this chain of events which led to Heby's murder and the vile rumors holding our men responsible."

Imsiba finished with the mat, threw it on the plat-form, and surprised Bak with a smile. It was stiff and too hearty, but a smile nonetheless. "We'll find that other man, my friend, and the gold he's stolen as well. We'll be looked upon as men of valor, and we'll grow fat and lazy with nothing to do day after day but watch the lord Re sail across the sky."

"Boredom seems a small price to pay for the an-swers I long to find."

Bak examined an empty niche and each of the four walls. Imsiba cleared the floor, throwing Heby's mea-ger possessions on the sleeping platform, and swept the sand out the door. They both got down on hands and knees to inspect the dry, hard-packed earth.

"You spoke of those men on patrol last night," Bak said, brushing away pieces of grit embedded in his knee. "What of the others?"

"Except for Ruru and Pashenuro, who stayed with mistress Azzia in the commandant's residence and are still there, all were in the barracks from dusk to dawn."

"Unseen by any but themselves and you."

"You err, my friend. One other man was there, a man of Kemet."

Bak's head popped up, a query on his face.

Imsiba busied himself with a crack so thin and snake-like that a blind man would know it had no depth. "The scribe Ptahsoker, he is. The steward Tetynefer's right hand. He came while we ate our evening meal and stayed through the night, playing the game of knuckle-bones with Amonemopet and the men on watch."

Bak wanted to believe, but suspicion lurked in his heart. "You said nothing about him this morning."

Imsiba gave an elaborate shrug.

It's not the truth, Bak thought, or is it? Would a man so close to Tetynefer risk such a lie? Prudence dictated he let the matter drop. "What of the three who claimed to wander the city when Nakht was slain?"

Imsiba rocked back on his heels, frowned. "As you thought, they had better things to do than await the re-sults of our raid on Nofery's house. They were at the quay, gambling with some sailors. They feared to ad-mit as much, for they lost much of their portion of our monthly rations."

Bak's expression hardened. "And now the other men will have to share with them, leaving less for them-selves through no fault of their own."

"They'll not soon make the same mistake, I promise you. I ordered the stick, thinking a firm reminder will long remain in their thoughts."

Bak nodded his approval. The punishment was just.

A short time later, he hauled his weary, aching body off the floor and walked into the kitchen. He prayed they would find something, anything. Imsiba brought the torch, which flickered and sputtered, the fuel nearly burned away. With the uneven light urging them to hurry, they continued the search. Bak concentrated on the stairway; Imsiba took the floor.

"Where was Amonemopet when Nakht's life was taken?" Bak asked. "Across the river, as he said?"

"With a village woman, yes. He shared a skiff with three other men of Buhen, scribes they were. They went over for the date wine, which is sweet and very strong." Imsiba chuckled. "It crept upon them in the night and stole their senses. If he hadn't come back with them, the current would've carried their vessel downriver and they'd be well on their way to Ma'am."

Pausing on the seventh step, Bak eyed the big sergeant. "Would one of the scribes you speak of be Ptahsoker, the man who spent last night in our barracks?"

"I failed to ask," Imsiba said, his expression bland.

Bak thought of pledging a goose to the lord Amon in thanks for the debt Ptahsoker had incurred to Amonemopet, but he decided to wait. Wait for a greater gift from the god, one far more substantial than a lie.

He reached the top of the stairway, finding nothing, and raised the trapdoor over his head. As it tilted up, sand showered down through the poorly woven mat. The rooftop was stark and empty beneath the starlit sky. If Heby had left anything there, the wind had swept it away. Two glinting yellow eyes—those of a cat, he thought—stared from a roof across the lane. A donkey brayed somewhere in the distance.

He ducked back inside and let the trapdoor fall in place. Kneeling on a step, his shoulders hunched beneath the mat, he studied the room. His eyes came to rest on the oven. When he had looked inside before, he had retrieved nothing from the ashes. Maybe he should take a closer look.

He descended the steps, cursing the man who had reduced his lower back to a nagging ache. Retrieving the torch from the bracket, he scrambled over Imsiba's long legs, knelt in front of the oven, and peered in through the lower hole. It looked no more promising than before. He fished through the ashes and withdrew every solid object he found. Finished with his own task, Imsiba hunkered beside him. Bak balanced the torch in the oven door and set about examining his finds: a few good-sized lumps of charred fuel and several pieces of baked clay. The largest was a hard ring-like object, the top quarter of a pottery cone. Another was a dried clay plug.

Not enough of the cone remained to say with certainty whether or not it had been weighed, but not so much as an inkblot marred the small amount of surface that was left. The plug, which had never been stamped with a seal, fit so well Bak was sure the clay had dried inside the cone. The objects appeared to verify his theory that gold was being brought to Buhen outside the normal channels; they did nothing to help identify the man who was bypassing those channels.

Imsiba spoke aloud Bak's thoughts. "To find so small a thing when we need so much . . . I fear the gods have turned their backs to us."

All Bak could think of was Maiherperi's final warning: most men do wrong without thought, and you'll bring them to justice with no great effort. But a time may come when the man you seek is so clever at hiding his actions that you'll never find him. Bak prayed this was not the case, for if so, how could he hope to wipe away the doubt and suspicion which had fallen on his men?

"You lost it?" Bak asked, incredulous. "You lost your spear three days ago and you said nothing?"

Kasaya, his eyes glued to his feet, seemed to shrink within his hulking body. "Yes, sir."

"Why did you not report it?"

Beads of sweat glistened on the young policeman's broad forehead. "I thought . . ." His voice dropped to a low mumble. "I thought I'd find it and there'd be no need."

"I pray to the lord Amon you'll never be moved to use your wits again!" Bak jerked his arm from Hori's grasp to aim an accusing finger at the biggest, strongest, youngest, and, he was convinced, the most stupid man in his company. "You and you alone are responsible for the rumors which say one of us took the goldsmith's life."

Kasaya shifted his weight, swallowed hard.

"Sir!" Hori said, dismayed. "If you don't sit still, I'll not finish tonight."

Bak reined in his temper. Open anger was unseemly in an officer and would gain him nothing. The damage caused by the loss could not be undone. He lowered his arm and held it out to Hori, who began to spread a thick brown salve smelling of mold over the scorched flesh.

They were in their quarters, Bak seated on a stool and Hori on his knees in front of him. A neat white bandage, wound around Bak's torso, covered the burn on his side. Strips of linen, a pottery water basin, and a bowl containing the salve were scattered around them. Imsiba glared at Kasaya from beside the stairway leading to the roof.

"Tell me," Bak said in a more rational tone. "Where and how did you lose it?"

"I left it at the place where Lieutenant Nebwa trains his spearmen." Kasaya's eyes flitted toward Bak, back to his feet. "Outside the walls of this city."

Bak checked the impulse to be sarcastic. "Go on."

"I went there to watch them practice, sir. Hoping to see better, I thought to climb a rocky mound. I couldn't go up so steep a place with one hand, so I . . ." Kasaya's voice wavered. "I laid my spear on the ground, out of sight between two boulders."

"You forgot it," Imsiba growled.

Kasaya stiffened as if slapped. "Yes, sir."

Bak wanted to wring the young Medjay's neck and hang him up like a goose awaiting the cooking pot. "Were you seen by anyone, or were you alone?"

"I kept to myself, but other men stood above me on top of the mound. Officers, they were, and four sergeants and two of lesser rank."

Bak's eyes darted toward Imsiba. Had the gods looked on them with favor after all? Imsiba met his glance, raised the butt of his spear a hand's breadth off the floor, and squeezed the shaft for luck.

"Sir!" Hori exclaimed.

Bak glanced down, saw salve smeared across his leg, ribbons of linen dangling from the half-bandaged arm. He had pulled it from Hori's grasp without noticing. Offering the arm to the scribe, he asked Kasaya, "Did you know the men atop the mound?"

"Commandant Nakht was there. The others I didn't know."

"Did I not tell you and all the men in our company, long before we reached Buhen, that you must learn before all other things the names and faces of the officers in this garrison?"

Kasaya croaked a word or two, cleared his throat, said, "I know them now."

Bak thought he had never met a man so aggravating. "Can you tell me which men stood atop that mound?"

Kasaya wriggled in place, nodded.

"Speak!" Imsiba commanded. "This instant!"

"The commandant was there." Kasaya glanced at Imsiba, whose scowl grew murderous, and the rest came tumbling out. "The man who translated for him, Harmose, was with him. Lieutenant Nebwa was there with his sergeants and a herald who signaled his commands on the trumpet. Lieutenant Paser was there and so was another lieutenant—Mery he's called."

"I see no other way." Imsiba's voice rang with conviction. "You must go to mistress Azzia and question her. If she refuses to speak, she must be made to tell the truth."

He and Bak sat cross-legged on the roof, filling themselves with cold roasted pigeon and the thick lentil soup Hori had warmed on the brazier. Familiar clusters of stars glittered bright and strong in the inky sky. Moonlight seeped over the dark shadowy battlements at the far end of the block. Rooftops spread out around them like a flat plain, lumpy with the bodies of men, women, children, and animals who had abandoned the hot, cramped houses to sleep in the cool, gentle breeze wafting across the city. The night sounds were muted, the usual chorus of howling dogs was silent.

"If she's innocent of wrongdoing?" Bak asked, trying to sound reasonable, certain he failed.

"The wounds will heal, the bruises fade."

Bak pictured her as he had last seen her, sitting on the floor among her husband's possessions, head bowed, the light glinting on her lovely smooth shoulders. "No."

"You vowed she'd not turn your head!"

"She was the commandant's wife, Imsiba! A foreign woman, yes, but a woman of quality. Only at the viceroy's command can she be dealt with so harshly."

Imsiba retreated into silence, allowing the truth of Bak's words to hang between them like a vaporous cloud.

Bak set his bowl on the rooftop, placed his hand on the Medjay's knee. "Listen to what I believe, and judge my words fairly."

Imsiba's nod could barely be seen in the darkness.

"If Azzia knows the man we wish to snare and if she truly loves him, I doubt the most strenuous beating would bring his name to her lips. She seems a gentle woman and vulnerable, but I saw the will of a lioness when she threw the spear at Heby. On the other hand, if she cares nothing for him and points a finger his way, he'll deny his guilt. To admit the truth would be to forfeit his life. Am I not right?"

Imsiba let out a long sigh. "Yes, my friend, you are. I've no doubt which of the two the viceroy would believe. The words of any woman found with her husband's blood on her hands would carry little weight."

"We need proof the one we seek is guilty," Bak said, pressing his advantage. "I know of no other way to be certain his denials will go unheeded."

"Proof!" Imsiba's laugh was bitter. "We don't even know his name."

"No, but the lady Maat may well have guided the hand of that witless Kasaya. Thanks to him, we've more reason than before to suspect the four who were on the battlements the night Nakht was slain."

"You speak of the lieutenants Mery, Nebwa, and Paser . . ." Imsiba hesitated, then added reluctantly, ". . . and Harmose."

Bak dipped his drinking bowl into the larger bowl nested in the brazier, wiped away the soup dripping down the side, and licked his finger clean. "All who stood atop the mound could've seen Kasaya place his spear between the boulders. Nakht has gone to the netherworld. Of the others, I doubt any but those four can read."

"Another man, perhaps one of Nebwa's spearmen, might've found the weapon later."

"Or a villager?" Bak asked in a wry voice.

The reminder of Tetynefer's message to the viceroy brought a grim smile to Imsiba's lips. "I think both unlikely," he conceded.

Bak hunched forward. "According to Harmose, Nakht spoke with Mery, Paser, and Nebwa, each man alone, a few hours before he was slain. I think it safe to assume he also spoke alone with Harmose. They were all four near the residence when Nakht was slain, and all have traveled to the mines."

"Harmose would slay no man off the field of battle, my friend," Imsiba said with conviction, "nor would he steal."

"Have I pleaded my case to deaf ears? He looks no less suspicious than the other three."

"I've talked with him several times. He'd do no wrong."

"Mery, too, appears to be a man of honor, but I'll not proclaim him innocent until I know for a fact he's the man he seems."

Imsiba spat the tiny bones of a pigeon wing into his hand and threw them into a bowl containing other discarded bones. "What of Mistress Azzia? You've never proclaimed her innocence, that I grant you, but neither have you looked for proof of her guilt."

The accusation stung. It was true and Bak knew it. He had not approached her friends, women in whom she might have confided, nor had he searched for hints of a liaison which might have reached the ears of officers and men other than Paser. Now his time was running out; he had but a single day left before he must take her to Ma'am. Worse yet, with him away from Buhen the growing hatred of his men might well reach a climax, and he would not be here to help them.

Hori could go from house to house and from barracks to barracks, using his youthful candor to pry the truth from women and men alike. So extensive a task would take longer than one day, far longer. Another, faster way must be found.

He thought long and hard, wrapped in darkness, enveloped by Imsiba's reproachful silence. When the answer came, the food in his stomach hardened to stone. If Azzia knew nothing, as she claimed, she would never forgive him. If she was injured, he would never forgive himself. However, if he learned the name of the man he searched for, if his Medjays could be freed of blame for the wretched goldsmith's death, would it not be worth the sacrifice?

"I think I know a way to find the guilty man." Bak glanced across the rooftops, saw the rising moon fully visible above the battlements. "Before I explain, we must go to the commandant's residence—and we must waste no time."

Imsiba looked up, startled. "You expect . . . what?"

"If Azzia is innocent, nothing. But if the man we wish to snare gave the gold to her . . ." Bak swabbed the last of his soup from the inside of the bowl with a chunk of bread, set the bowl aside, and stood up. "He took Heby's life to silence him and he tried to slay me when he feared I'd find whatever was hidden in the goldsmith's house. Will he not try to slay her if he thinks she might speak his name?"

Imsiba cursed his dull wits. "She'll not remain silent if the viceroy judges her guilty of murder." He jerked the bowl off the brazier and turned another bowl over the smoldering fuel to quench it.

Bak swallowed the bread, swept up the leaf-lined basket containing the remaining pigeons, and folded the leaves over the top. "If he tries to reach her tonight, you and I, with Pashenuro and Ruru, must be prepared to catch him."

"If he stays far away?"

"We'll make sure he approaches her tomorrow."

Imsiba stared, surprised. "You'd use her as the bait in a trap?"

"Do I have a choice?" The words echoed through Bak's heart, mocked him.

Chapter Ten

"To find me in Heby's kitchen, looking at molds, must've been quite a shock," Bak said, stifling a yawn. "If he thought before that I knew nothing of the stolen gold, he knows now for a fact that I do."

"I hope he spent as sleepless a night as we did," Imsiba grumbled.

A worried frown darkened Hori's usually carefree visage. "I think you must walk the streets of this city with great care, sir."

"He's surely guessed I didn't see his face. If I had, we'd have made him our prisoner many hours ago."

They stood on the roof of the scribal office building, waiting for the lord Khepre, the rising sun, to show his face above the battlements. The city lay in the deep shadow cast by the towered wall. The sky above was a cloudless azure streaked with gold. Good-natured banter rose and ebbed around them. Twenty or more soldiers were spread across the storehouse roof, removing the sand left by the storm between the long cylindrical ridges. A second group was clearing away deep drifts which had collected on the roof of the commandant's residence along the fortress walls. The scribal office building and the stairway rising to the battlements had been swept clean at first light.

"What if he believes you're closer on his heels than you are?" Hori asked, his worry unabated. "Will he not try again to slay you?"

Bak gave the boy a reassuring smile. "He had every chance when I lost my way in the storm, yet he chose to return to Heby's house. He cares more for covering his tracks, I think, than for taking a life before he feels he must."

"He carried no weapon then, my friend," Imsiba pointed out. "I doubt he'll try to slay you at close quarters, but if I were wearing your sandals, I'd look to the distance and be wary of men who carry bows and arrows."

"I pray this trap you plan will snare him," Hori said.

Imsiba flung him a censorious scowl. "For it to work, you must wipe the cloud from your face. All those you speak with today must think you gossip with a light and innocent heart."

Hori's eyes widened. "I'm to have a part in this hunt?"

"You'll lay the scent that will guide him to us."

"I no longer have to walk through this city, asking endless questions about our own men?" As Hori spoke, his boyish face lit up as if touched by the sun. He stiffened his spine and sucked in his plump stomach. "I can lay aside my writing pallet to take up the arms of a policeman?"

Bak wished with all his heart his own worries could be so easily set aside. "You'll use guile, not a spear. With luck your well-placed words will be far more deadly."

Disappointment flickered across Hori's face, replaced by curiosity and a cautious interest. "What must I do?"

Bak related his interview with Kasaya and the conclusions he had drawn. Spotting Imsiba's grimace when he included Harmose with the other three, he thanked the lord Amon that Hori had made no special friendships among the quartet.

"I think it fair to assume that the man we seek has guessed I know of the stolen gold, but he can't be certain how I learned of it. You must make him believe I was set on its trail before we left the capital. Speak of the royal treasury and its overseer, Sennefer. Say nothing of gold and always talk in circles, letting him guess your meaning by what you fail to say. As if an afterthought, tell him Mistress Azzia may see her friends today, and let him know I mean to thoroughly search the commandant's residence after her guests are gone. He must be made to think I've just begun to connect Nakht's death with the gold."

Hori's eyes twinkled; he uttered a mischievous laugh. "I'll chatter like a monkey, leaving those who are innocent with a pounding head and the guilty man sick with fear."

"Don't make him so afraid he'll run away," Bak cautioned. "He must be drawn to the residence, thinking to remove all signs of his theft."

"The gold and scrolls, you mean," Hori said.

Imsiba opened his mouth to speak, glanced at Bak, changed his mind. The risk to Azzia hung in the air between them.

Bak tried to shake off his fear for her. An unreasonable fear, he told himself. For if she knew nothing about the thefts, the man who had taken the gold had no reason to hurt her. On the other hand, if she knew of his crime and shared his guilt, her fate was already in the hands of the gods. Somehow that was no consolation.

"I may receive anyone who wishes to see me?" Azzia asked, surprised and a bit puzzled.

"As the translator Harmose said, to hold you apart from those who can comfort you is cruel and unfeeling, especially today when . . ." Bak paused, cursed his clumsy mouth. The last thing he wanted was to remind her of the next day's voyage to Ma'am. ". . . When you need your friends, those who can share the sorrow of your husband's death."

Her dark eyes leveled on his and a hint of a smile flitted across her face. "Can I go to them if I so desire?"

Is she teasing me, he wondered, or testing me? "You must remain here."

She turned away and crossed her sitting room to stand in the courtyard door, her back to him, her face and thoughts hidden from him. The sun touched her shapely legs, visible to the thighs below the short belted white tunic common to her homeland. Her ivory flesh, her slender waist, the thick reddish braid hanging down her back made her seem to Bak like an exotic bird. A bird torn from faraway Hatti, pushed ever farther south by the winds of fate, and dropped finally in this vile desert of Wawat.

He prayed with all his heart that she was free of guilt. He could not bear to think of so lovely a creature ending her life in this barren, unforgiving land.

"May I send Lupaki with a message?" she asked, pivoting to face him.

"A message?" Had his thoughts drifted so far away he had missed something? Had she threatened to tell Tetynefer about the slab of gold she had given him?

"How else can my friends know they may come?"

"My scribe Hori has too few tasks to fill his days," he managed. "He'll spread the news."

A spot of pink colored each of her cheeks. "While they're here, sharing my sorrow, will your Medjays be stationed in every corner to remind them I'm soon to stand before the viceroy, accused of taking the life of the man I mourn?"

Bak felt his own face color. He yearned to set her free, to leave her in peace. But he had to go on with his deceitful game and play it through to the end. "Ruru and Pashenuro will remain. As will I."

She studied his face for so long he feared she was reading his thoughts. "I see."

Swinging away, she passed through the door and crossed the courtyard to sit on the floor before her loom. He followed with hesitant feet, like Hori's puppy, he thought, when it had not yet learned to trust, and feared a harsh word. The dusky servant girl was sweeping sand across the floor. The cloud of dust she raised billowed around Pashenuro, who sat with his back to the wall, forehead resting on his knees, sound asleep. Ruru sprawled in front of Nakht's reception room, his bandaged head bowed over the blade of his spear, which he was honing to a fine point.

"We'll not hover," he said, kneeling beside the loom. "Only Ruru need remain in the courtyard. With his head swathed in linen, none will take his presence to heart."

She glanced up from the shuttle flying back and

forth through the threads stretched taut across the frame. "For that I thank you."

Rebuffed by the stiffness in her voice, he rose to his feet.

With a rigid back, her eyes locked on her work, she said, "Yesterday you brought the body of a man from Dedu's village, I heard, a goldsmith called Heby. I understand he was slain with a Medjay spear, but had another wound in his shoulder."

"Yes." He was relieved the news had reached her. If she had allied herself with the thief, at least now she knew to what lengths the vile criminal would go to protect himself. "He was the man you found searching this house. The wound was the mark of the weapon you threw."

"The man you vowed you'd find with little difficulty."

Bak's laugh was cynical. "I thought not to find him the way I did, with his lips sealed forever."

She let the shuttle slide to a stop and gave him an odd, rather chilly look. "You guessed right away he'd come for the gold my husband hid. Is that not true?"

"I did," he admitted, wondering what she was getting at.

"And did you guess at that time he was a goldsmith? One of the few men in this city who could've molded the bar you've hidden away?"

He eyed her warily. "Not then, no."

"When did you guess his craft?"

"I had no need to guess." He heard a tinge of irritation in his voice, moderated it. "I learned his name and the way he earned his bread from one who saw him in the house of death."

She tamped the threads tight and went back to her

task, but her attention was far away, her face clouded by her thoughts. The shuttle raced across the loom, its whisper inaudible beneath the swish of the broom and the rasp of the stone grating across Ruru's spear point.

"What of the spear in his breast?" she asked. "They say it came from your police arsenal."

"Mistress!" He shook his head in disgust. "If all those who speak with so much wind were to open their mouths at one time, the desert sands would blow to the farthest ends of the earth."

"I learned the weapon was yours from the steward Tetynefer's wife. How can you deny it?"

Suddenly he understood. Appalled, he knelt and slammed his widespread hand down on the shuttle, jamming it midway across the loom. "You think I took Heby's life!"

She stared straight ahead. "Did you?"

He grabbed her chin and pulled her face around so she had to look at him. "I've slain no man, mistress Azzia, nor will I ever without good reason. To my way of thinking, that thin bar of gold you gave me is not reason enough."

"What of the bandages you wear?"

He barked out a disbelieving laugh, jerked his hand away, and stood up. "They cover burns, not the slashes of a weapon, and it happened during the storm, many hours after Heby was slain."

Azzia's eyes never wavered from his face, but for the first time since Nakht's death, she seemed unsure of herself. Does she still doubt me, he wondered glumly, or is she thinking of the man I seek?

Bak would always remember that afternoon as one of the most disagreeable in his life. Partly because he hated himself for using Azzia, partly because he felt like a common eavesdropper, listening to private, sometimes intimate conversations he had no right to hear.

Azzia's servants had bustled about, overjoyed with their mistress's release from loneliness, temporary though it was. The women prepared fruit, sweet cakes, and bowls of fragrant flowers. Lupaki, with Pashenuro's help, built a reed pavilion in the courtyard and furnished it with stools and small tables. Azzia received her friends in its shade, where a lazy breeze wafted down from the rooftop. Wearing the long, unadorned white shift popular in the capital, no jewelry, and her hair braided as always, she seemed to Bak more gracious and elegant than any woman he had ever known.

Tetynefer's wife Iry, a woman as plump as her husband, arrived ahead of the rest. Kames's spouse came shortly after with two other women, officers' wives, Bak gathered. All four wore long shifts and were decked out with multicolored bead collars, armlets, and bracelets. Iry's hair was pulled back in a linen bag. Kames's wife sweated under a heavy wig. The others wore their natural hair straight, clipped horizontally across the shoulders. A trio of senior scribes and an elderly priest appeared, the latter's shaven head as shiny as a mirror.

Although good-natured, Bak soon realized mistress Iry had a will of iron. She appeared genuinely fond of Azzia—motherly, in fact—and guided the conversation like a commander might guide his battalion through a narrow, treacherous valley. Not a word was uttered about Ma'am or Azzia's precarious future. No one mentioned Ruru, sitting in a shady out-of-the way corner near the stairwell leading up from the audience hall. Pashenuro they could not see in Nakht's reception room.

While they chatted, Bak prowled the rooms behind the courtyard, glimpsing the guests from shadowed doorways, catching snatches of conversation. No matter where he went, he seemed always to be in the way of the servants hurrying to the pavilion, carrying bowls piled high with food or vessels filled with drink. His presence was a constant reminder that their mistress was not free. Their cheerful smiles faded, the looks they gave him grew tight-lipped and resentful.

Azzia was quick to notice their flagging spirits. She excused herself from her guests, hurried inside, and found him watching Lupaki pour a deep red wine from a heavy storage jar into a smaller long-necked, blue-glazed vessel. Lupaki rolled his eyes toward Bak, grimaced. She nodded her understanding, caught Bak's arm, and aimed him toward the courtyard.

"I'll not let you steal my happiness this day," she said, her voice grim and resolute, "nor will I allow you to rob my servants of joy."

He hung back, thinking she meant to usher him to the pavilion, to embarrass him before her guests. To place him there before he chose to show himself. Instead she drew him into Nakht's bedchamber. Bed, chests, and stools had been set upright and tidied since Heby's invasion. The room looked much as it had when Bak had searched it after the commandant's death. Long, thin shafts of sunlight filtered in through slits in the woven reed mat covering the courtyard door. The voices outside were clearly audible.

"I've no intention of running away." Azzia spoke slightly above a whisper so those in the courtyard could not hear, but with grim intensity. "I'm not so foolish as to make myself look guilty of a crime I didn't commit."

She had never before touched him, and all he could think about was her hand, so warm and firm, clutching his arm. "I can't leave you unguarded. You know that."

"Are you so certain I took my husband's life?"

"I've tried to find proof of your innocence, that I swear." It came out too loud, too defensive. "I've run out of time, as you well know."

Her hand dropped to her side; she turned away and walked to Nakht's bed. Beyond, through the doorway to her bedchamber, he saw a rush basket half full of clothing and linen standing beside an open, empty chest, mute reminders that she had been packing for her trip to Ma'am.

She picked up a folded camp stool leaning against the wall and faced him. Holding the stool before her like a shield, she said, "I no longer know what to think of you, Officer Bak. Sometimes I believe all you say. At other times I feel your words have no more substance than the mist that drifts over the river each morning."

"Go back to your friends." His tone was harsh, his dismay well hidden. She had every right to mistrust him, if not for the reason she thought.

Crossing the room, she pulled the stool open and set it in front of the mat. "If it pleases you to watch me through the day, sit here. I'll have Lupaki bring you food and drink."

She slipped out the door without another word. Bak slumped onto the stool, humiliated and depressed. The lady Hathor, goddess of happiness, had to be playing a game with him. She had dangled Azzia before him and

teased him with her beauty, but made it impossible for
him to reach out to her.

The minutes stretched to hours. Except for Iry, who
remained through the afternoon, Azzia's friends came
and went: women and their offspring, scribes, officers,
chief craftsmen. A few seemed merely curious, but
most paid their respects and offered their support with
a sincerity that made Bak's suspicions seem petty and
unfounded. Azzia rarely glanced his way, but when she
did, he felt his stomach knot with guilt.

Not one of the four men he hoped to attract had
come. He knew if he were the guilty one he would wait
until late in the day in hopes of finding Azzia alone, but
he could not understand why the innocent among
them, men who professed to care for her, had not
rushed to her side.

The voices droned on and on. Bak's sleepless night
began to catch up with him and he reached a point
where he could barely hold his eyes open. He stood up,
stretched, flexed his muscles. The activity helped, but
not much. He wandered around, looking for something
to keep him awake, finally stopping in front of a reddish hardwood chest. It had held, he remembered, several personal documents, all related to Nakht's tomb
and some land in the north of Kemet. Before, he had
read a few words, enough to dismiss them as unimportant. But now . . .

Curious to know more, especially since Azzia had
no doubt inherited Nakht's estate, he removed the lid,
took the scrolls, and carried them to his stool by the
door.

As he sat down, he heard her say, "I don't fear death,
for only then can I walk beside my husband through

eternity, but to think I might die accused of taking his life is an abomination."

Mistress Iry, Bak thought, must have lost control of the conversation.

"The viceroy is a fair man, my dear, and wiser than most," a deep-voiced man assured her. "He'll judge you innocent, I know."

"What can that young officer, that Bak, be thinking of?" The voice was Iry's.

Bak dropped the scrolls in his lap and peeked through a slit in the mat. Iry's face wore a disparaging scowl, as did most of the others'. Azzia looked straight ahead, taking care not to glance his way.

"He's a soldier." This from a thin, stooped man with the white cloud of blindness in one eye. "They're taught to obey orders, not to use their wits."

The man must be a scribe, Bak thought, one who knows nothing of the art of war.

Iry patted Azzia's hand. "No one with good sense could think you guilty of taking another's life. Certainly not Nakht, whom you loved so long and so well."

"Kames told me he was sent here in disgrace," said a distinguished-looking man of middle years who wore a calf-length kilt. "Something to do with a house of pleasure. A brawl, I believe."

"A fight over a loose woman, I heard," a full-figured, bewigged matron said, sniffing her disapproval.

"From what I heard, his archer wagered away his weapons of war in a game of chance and Officer Bak took exception." The deep-voiced man sipped from his drinking bowl. "You know how those chariotry officers are: as protective of their archers as a goose is of her goslings."

"You'd be protective, too, if your life depended

upon the one man riding in the chariot with you." The speaker was a large, muscular man of military bearing. "Without his archer, a charioteer wouldn't last through a single assault."

"That doesn't excuse his involving the rest of the men in his company," the deep-voiced man said.

"I'd guess they involved themselves. Those charioteers are a close-knit bunch of men."

Azzia reached out to pluck a date from a greenish glazed bowl sitting on the low table in front of her. "My husband thought him an honorable man in spite of his rash behavior in Waset." She raised her eyes from the bowl and looked straight at Bak's hiding-place. "I pray he judged him right."

Bak squirmed on his stool, spilling the scrolls to the floor.

"Honor is one thing," the stooped man said. "Good common sense is quite different. And that he seems not to have."

"My husband's equally witless," Iry said, disgusted. "He won't listen to one word from me."

A plump young woman of about fourteen years giggled. "Officer Bak is very handsome and well formed. To share a sleeping pallet with a man so favored . . ." She shivered with ecstasy.

The matron gave her a scathing look. "You'd do well to covet a man who thinks with his wits, not with his male parts."

Bak cursed beneath his breath. Did Azzia also think him such a fool? Her face was turned away, so he could not see her expression. Beyond her he glimpsed Ruru, whose head was bowed, his shoulders shaking with laughter.

Bak snatched the scrolls from the floor and marched

into Azzia's bedchamber. Rejecting her sleeping pallet for a stool, he spread the first document across his lap. It proved to be a legal agreement between Nakht and a cousin who lived near Mennufer. In exchange for a parcel of farmland Nakht had been given as a reward for exemplary military service, the cousin had agreed to have Nakht's tomb excavated and its walls painted. The next four scrolls, all from the cousin, discussed the progress of the construction. In each, he complained bitterly about the cost, airing his grievances to a point where Bak could almost hear him whine.

The final scroll was another legal document, written after the tomb was finished. To repay his cousin for the unexpectedly high costs, Nakht had given him the remainder of his estate: a second, adjoining piece of land. As a condition of the transfer, the cousin would take Azzia into his household if anything should happen to Nakht.

Bak rolled up the scrolls with a heavy heart. Such a nebulous position would not please any woman. Had she become involved with the man who was stealing the gold to save herself from such a fate?

Chapter Eleven

The shadows lengthened across the courtyard; the sun nudged the western battlements. A stiffening breeze cooled the air, drying the moisture on faces and backs and arms. The reeds atop the pavilion rustled as if inhabited by mice. The leaves on the potted trees danced. Azzia's guests departed in ones and twos until none but Iry remained. She was on her feet, preparing to leave.

Bak could hardly wait for her departure and the chance to escape from this room in which Azzia had condemned him. The longer he remained alone and inactive, half-listening to the chatter in the pavilion, the more doubts he had that his plan would succeed. He knew he had no talent for subterfuge, and this plan, so fraught with opportunities for failure, seemed destined to prove it. Not one of his four suspects had come.

He paced the floor, fretting like a dog waiting for its master to throw a bone. What would he do if his plan failed? He paused at the door to Azzia's bedchamber and scowled at the half-full chest of clothing. Maiherperi's words came to him unbidden: If you've done all you can to reach the truth but have failed to grasp it, you must trust to the lady Maat to place wisdom in the heart of the man who metes out justice.

He turned his back to the room—and the thought. The day was not yet over.

"I dislike leaving you, my dear, but I must," he heard Iry say. "You've no idea how irritable Tetynefer gets when his stomach is empty."

"I thank you for staying through the day." Azzia's voice grew softer, wavered. "And for agreeing to care for my servants if I cannot return from Ma'am."

"You'll come back to us. The viceroy has but to look at you and he'll read the truth in your face."

"I'd rather he listened to my plea and found the truth in my words," Azzia said, her tone wry.

"Ah, look who's come." Iry laughed, pleased. "I knew he wouldn't disappoint us."

Bak lunged toward the mat, praying the newcomer was one of his suspects. Through a slit, he saw Lieutenant Mery striding toward the two women. Bak breathed a heartfelt sigh of relief, although he had to admit the watch officer did not look like a man intent on saving his skin. His smile was broad and open. He was spotlessly clean, freshly shaven. His jet-black hair was shiny and neat, and his lithe body glistened with the oil he had used after bathing. He carried his baton of office and wore a bronze dagger on his hip, its wooden handle polished to a high sheen.

Bak studied the officer, looking for signs of the struggle in Heby's dwelling. Mery's knee was bruised, his right hand abraded. The ruddy stain of sandburn on face and limbs betrayed his exposure to the storm, his body protected by a cloak. The injuries were minor but promising. Other than the burns and an ugly bruise on his lower back, Bak himself had come away unmarked.

Mery glanced at Ruru, sprawled in front of the wall, eyes closed, breathing slow and deep. Dismissing the Medjay with a grin, he entered the pavilion. Ruru's eyes flickered open, snapped shut; his fingers inched toward his spear.

Greeting Iry, Mery showed not only the respect due a mature woman of her station but also a genuine affection. From her fond smile and the way she patted the young officer's arm, Bak could tell the feeling was mutual. Mery took Azzia's hands and, holding them far longer than necessary, offered his sympathy and loyalty. Iry looked on with so obvious a satisfaction Bak was certain she would have tried to make a match if Azzia had not been so recently widowed. The thought rankled.

The sun dipped behind the fortress wall, enveloping the courtyard in shadow. Iry embraced Azzia, and the two women bade a sorrowful good-bye. As soon as the older woman departed, Mery reached out to Azzia as if to clasp her hands—or more. She turned away. Brushing a tear from her cheek, she suggested he take a stool.

Bak, eager to get on with his plan, hastened to a deep reed chest filled with neatly folded bed linen. Sliding his hand inside, he withdrew the items he had hidden there earlier in the day: a papyrus scroll and a linen-wrapped object the size of the thin gold ingot Azzia had given him. Each was bound with cord, its knot secured with a flat lump of dried clay stamped with Nakht's seal. The pretense of a search was not necessary, he rationalized. All he had to do was display the objects and wait for developments.

He returned to the door and raised his hand to sweep

the mat aside, but a quick peek outside changed his mind. Azzia, seated on a stool facing her guest, was pouring wine into a drinking bowl while Mery watched her with the adoring look of a lovesick puppy. Was he, after all, nothing more than an admirer, with no knowledge of stolen gold? Smothering his impatience, Bak sat down, laid the objects in his lap, and pressed his forehead to the mat.

"I yearned to come to you before today, as you must know," Mery said, accepting the bowl, "but I could think of no way to break the wall of solitude Officer Bak raised around you."

"The days were long and empty, yes." A sad, rather ironic smile touched her lips. "But even loneliness can have some value. With so much time to myself, I've learned to accept my fate as a woman alone."

Mery reached toward her as if to caress her cheek. She recoiled, a tiny frown touching her face, and she swung away to lift a shallow bowl of deep purple grapes from a nearby stool.

He flushed, withdrew his hand.

She looked directly into his eyes. "A woman who must go on by herself, with no man to walk beside her or share her burdens."

Bak was confused. Was she telling a confederate their relationship was over? Or was she reminding a would-be suitor that her widowhood had just begun? As far as he could tell, she had not warned Mery they had an eavesdropper.

The watch officer's flush deepened. "Your sorrow at what has passed is great, I know, but one day . . ."

"I'll wipe this nightmare from my memory and go on as if nothing had happened?" Her voice cracked on the last few words. Visibly controlling herself, she pulled a low, baked-clay table close to Mery's thigh and sat the bowl on it. "My husband has been torn from my arms. In one week, two at the most, I must stand before the viceroy in place of the man who took his life. Judged innocent or guilty, I'll never forget. How can I?"

Bak was so distressed by the pain he heard that he almost missed the anger boiling close below the surface.

"You must forget!"

"My husband was life itself to me and now he's gone." She shook her head. "No, I'll not forget. Nor will I ever forgive the man responsible."

Her face, her words were filled with loathing. Bak had no doubt she spoke from deep within her heart. She had not taken Nakht's life. He was relieved, but also troubled. She might be guilty by association.

Mery's eyes slipped away from hers; he shifted uncomfortably on his stool. Exactly as a disheartened suitor would behave, Bak thought, or a man with a guilty conscience.

With his eyes locked on his drinking bowl, Mery asked, "When you go before the viceroy, what will you tell him?"

An odd question, Bak thought, for a man blinded by love. He shifted closer to the mat, torn between his wish to know the truth and his dread that Azzia would incriminate herself.

"What can she say?" a male voice demanded.

Mery jumped, startled. Azzia looked toward the stairwell and smiled a warm, relieved welcome at Harmose, the archer. Cursing the untimely interruption, Bak stared hard at the newcomer, who came striding

across the courtyard, his powerful muscles accented by
the deepening shadow, his entire being bristling with
indignation. Had he barged in so abruptly because he
was the guilty man instead of Mery?

Like the watch lieutenant, Harmose was neat, clean,
and freshly shaven. Much of his body had been chafed
by blowing sand, he walked with the heavy step of
weariness, and his torso and limbs wore the fresh abrasions and bruises of a long day on the practice field. If
he had been Bak's opponent in Heby's house, fresh
marks of battle covered the old.

He knelt before Azzia to take her hands. "For you to
be dragged off to Ma'am and humiliated . . . it's . . .
it's indecent!" He released her and flung himself onto a
stool. "Say the word and I'll carry you away tonight."

She gave him a wan smile. "I fear the desert more
than the viceroy, my brother."

Mery glared at the archer, resentful of the mild en-
dearment—or, more likely, the offer.

"They say there are large and fertile oases many
days' journey to the south," Harmose said. "The land is
so rich it repays a man tenfold for the effort it takes to
plant the fields. You've seen for yourself the fine cattle
the people of Kush bring as tribute from far upriver."

Azzia raised her hand to silence the dream. Or was it
a dream? Bak wondered. Could Harmose seriously be
thinking of fleeing with Azzia? And the gold?

"What of the Belly of Stones and the garrisons along
its length?" Mery scoffed. "The soldiers who man
them would stop your flight within hours, and Azzia's
guilt would be taken as fact."

"I'm going to Ma'am," Azzia said in a firm voice. "I
must convince the viceroy I'm innocent. Only then can

I journey to Mennufer with my husband and see him placed in his tomb with the honor and dignity he earned through his life."

"How will you convince him?" Harmose asked irritably. "By naming the guilty man?"

"All I can do is tell the truth."

Neither Mery nor Harmose looked happy with her answer. Bak did not know what to think. Her simple, straightforward statement could have been a subtle threat. On the other hand, if she knew nothing of the stolen gold, she might truly believe veracity would set her free. A faith that might well be misplaced.

With the thought goading him on, Bak decided to show himself—and the package and scroll. The time had come to bait his trap. At the same time, he could learn the whereabouts of Mery and Harmose during the storm. If either was in the company of others, he could be eliminated as a suspect.

He slipped out a side door and followed the servant girl along the passage connecting the kitchen to the courtyard. She carried a delicate long-necked wine jar. The octopus-and-vine design told him the vessel had been imported from the faraway island kingdom of Keftiu.

He paused at the exit and eyed the two men with Azzia. Neither Mery nor Harmose looked capable of offending the gods in any way. The watch officer appeared too ineffectual, the archer too open. Nebwa he would have thought a more likely man to steal and slay without hesitation—or Paser. Yet both men had failed to come. He doubted they would at so late an hour. Already the sky had turned from blue to pale gold, heralding the sun's disappearance beyond the horizon.

"I know well the kind of justice meted out in the

land of my birth," Azzia said. "All my family was destroyed at the whim of a king. At least here, with the lady Maat balancing the scales of justice, I can be sure the viceroy will hear me out and judge me fairly."

As the servant walked into the courtyard, Azzia spotted Bak at the door. Her eyes darted to the objects in his hand. Surprise, followed an instant later by bewilderment, registered on her face. She covered her reaction with a quick smile at the girl.

"Our sovereign, Maatkare Hatshepsut, can be as whimsical as the king of Hatti," Harmose said. "As for the viceroy . . ." His expression darkened and he shook his head to show how hopeless he thought her situation. "He'll hear none but Officer Bak, who'll stand beside you, describing the blood he saw on your hands. At best, he'll offer no word in your favor. At worst . . ."

Azzia flashed him a warning glance.

He swiveled on his stool, saw Bak, and went on, ". . . He'll twist his words to hide his own ineptness."

Glimpsing Azzia's distraught face, Bak gave the archer his best smile and dropped onto the nearest stool. Harmose glowered. Mery nodded an unenthusiastic greeting. If either noticed the objects Bak carried, or cared about them, they gave no hint. He pulled the baked-clay table close, shifted the bowl of grapes, and laid the scroll and package beside it. Azzia watched his performance, looking more mystified than ever. She caught his eye, probing for an answer to her unspoken question.

Mery glanced at the scrolls, at Azzia, at Bak. His mouth tightened; the small scar at the corner of his lip turned fiery.

Harmose eyed the objects with contempt. "I heard you planned to search this house. Was this the second

time? The third? Can you think of no better way to
spend your days?"

The serving girl, pouring wine into drinking bowls
for him and Bak, smirked her agreement.

"What would you suggest I do?" Bak asked.

"The rumors fly that one of your Medjays took the
commandant's life and that of the goldsmith. Are you
so blind you can't see the fear and hatred growing
within this city?"

"I'm neither blind nor deaf. I know very well the
situation."

"You do nothing to stop it! While your men patrol
the streets of this city, risking an attack around every
corner, you waste your hours here, allowing the slayer
to walk free while you treat mistress Azzia as a common criminal."

Bak let a touch of insolence creep into his voice.
"Do you, a man who shares my Medjays' blood, believe one of them would slay for no good reason?"

Harmose's expression was cool, disdainful. "I believe an officer should stand beside his men in the heat
of battle, not run away to a safe haven like Ma'am
when he sees the enemy approaching from all sides."

Bak contained his resentment. The words echoed his
own thoughts. "I've no choice in the matter, as you
well know. The chief steward, Tetynefer, has given the
order."

"No man or woman can change his mind," Mery
said bitterly. "I've tried."

The archer's eyes flashed anger. "How can you, a
man who looks at Azzia with sheep's eyes, speak up
for this . . . this cur who spits dirt on her good name?"

"Enough, Harmose!" Azzia raised her bowl, smiled.

"This wine is the finest I have. Will you allow harsh words to turn it sour?"

Harmose was too angry to heed her plea. "Has Bak told you he believes you have a secret lover and you took your husband's life to gain your freedom?"

Mery gasped. Azzia stared at Bak, appalled.

Bak wanted to throttle the archer. "You exaggerate. I merely asked the question."

"Since all who know you believe you'd never look at another man . . ." Harmose's eyes shifted from Azzia to Bak. ". . . His own men must shoulder the blame."

A new, deeper voice said, "No man of Kemet would take the life of Commandant Nakht. Who does that leave but a Medjay?"

Bak recognized the voice and the accusation before he glanced toward the stairwell. Lieutenant Nebwa was leaning on the doorjamb, his coarse features leaving no doubt as to the strength of his conviction. A second figure, Lieutenant Paser, stood in the shadows behind him. Bak was so surprised at seeing them both that his exasperation at Nebwa's unfounded charge fled. He had expected the man who had taken the gold to come late in the day, but to have all his suspects here at one time was incredible.

Harmose's curse was long and vehement. Mery muttered beneath his breath. Azzia closed her eyes and rested her forehead on her fingertips. She took a deep breath, lowered her hand, and smiled at the newcomers. Bak noticed in the fading light how drawn her face was, how tired she looked.

Nebwa strolled to the pavilion, indifferent to the furor he had raised. His hair was rumpled, his kilt askew, his sandals worn and dusty. Of far more interest

to Bak were his swollen blackening eye, and arms and
torso dappled with livid scratches and grayish bruises.
All looked fresh in the uncertain light. Nebwa had
probably spent the day training his spearmen in the art
of hand-to-hand combat, a necessary task for a man
who led troops on skirmishes outside the fortress, but
would an experienced officer allow his men to punish
him so badly?

Bak shifted his attention to Paser, trailing a pace or
two behind, eyeing with distaste his companion's back.
The caravan officer was as clean and tidy as Mery and
Harmose—and displayed as many signs of bodily
abuse. His legs and arms were rough and chapped. He
wore a linen bandage on his right hand and wrist. The
arm and shoulder were badly bruised.

Sipping the heady wine in his drinking bowl, Bak
eyed the four men. He felt certain that each of them,
especially the one he had fought in Heby's dwelling,
had a fine tale to tell about the way he had come by his
injuries.

Nebwa, looking like an unkempt bull, knelt before
Azzia and took her hands. She accepted his rather
clumsy offer of sympathy with her customary grace
and charm. Bak could detect no special feeling between them. Paser stood while greeting her and gave
her the careful smile a palace courtier might give a
woman in Maatkare Hatshepsut's retinue when unsure
of her status. His words were proper, correct. Her response was as gracious as before but a shade cooler, a
touch more distant. Bak wondered if they had always
disliked each other or if Nakht's death had torn asun-
der a close alliance.

The stool beside Bak was unoccupied, so Nebwa sat
there. Watching Paser's greeting, he raised his chin to

look down his nose and made a prissy face meant as a parody of a courtier in the royal house. Mery smiled, his irritation no match for such childish humor. Bak concealed his own smile with an effort. When Paser swung around to find a place to sit, Nebwa's face wore the innocence of a child. Neither man appeared to notice the scroll and package.

Nebwa's glance slid past the still-fuming Harmose and came to rest on the bandages around Bak's arm and waist. "The storm found you outside, I see."

"I was caught in the wind, yes, but these . . ." Bak touched the bandages. "Oil spilled from a lamp and I was burned." He eyed the officer's black eye. "I see you were injured, too."

"As were half the men in Buhen," Paser said, reaching out with his left, uninjured hand to take a drinking bowl from the servant girl. She poured his wine and moved on to Nebwa.

Azzia said to Mery, "Iry told us a sentry atop the outer wall was blown into a gate tower and fell at least halfway to the ground. Is it true his leg is broken?"

"His leg, an arm, and some ribs." Worry darkened the watch officer's face. "The physician bound the bones straight and offered the necessary spells. With luck he'll walk again."

"With luck he'll live, you mean," Nebwa muttered.

"Were you on the wall when it happened?" Bak asked Mery. Nebwa's whereabouts remained a mystery, but the watch lieutenant's location was no less important.

"I tripped and fell not long after the wind stiffened, so I went to my quarters." Mery's eyes darted toward Azzia, fell away. He stared shamefaced into his drinking bowl. "I thought, since my men have been through many storms, they needed no guiding hand to keep them safe. I judged them wrong, it seems."

Bak cautioned himself not to leap to any conclusions. Mery had been alone, yes, but what of the other three?

"Soldiers are soldiers," Nebwa said. "Good, brave men, but they need the same attention and care you'd give a child."

The servant girl slipped among them with a plate of sweet cakes. Bak could not resist their yeasty aroma though he had eaten well while imprisoned in Nakht's bedchamber. As she moved on around the circle, he eyed Harmose. The archer's scowl was directed at Nebwa, whose blanket accusation of the Medjays, had drawn his anger away from Bak.

Paser accepted a cake and took a bite from it. He favored the right arm, Bak noted, but the injury was not so serious that it crippled him.

"How did you happen to be caught in the storm?" he asked.

"I set out to inspect a new herd of donkeys. That old thief Dedu delivered them yesterday morning and I thought to use them in the next caravan I lead into the desert. I didn't want to learn the morning we leave that half were too old or too infirm to make the journey."

"Old and infirm!" Nebwa guffawed. "If the drovers you chose for the journey hadn't slipped off for home as soon as the wind came up, they'd have set you straight in a hurry." He threw a sly grin at Azzia. "Those animals are so young and frisky one of them butted him and knocked him into a wall. That's the truth of the matter."

Bak's smile was automatic—and stingy. Another man alone with a tale that may or may not be true.

Paser threw Nebwa a look that would have shriveled a man less thick-skinned. "At least I had the good sense to stay inside the fortress. Unlike you, who walked into the desert and lost your way."

"You didn't have a company of fighting men outside the walls like I did," Nebwa retorted. "I've never lost a man in a storm, nor will I ever if I can help it."

Evidently thinking of his own failure to remain on duty, Mery flushed and stared glumly at his hands.

Oblivious, Nebwa gave Paser an insolent look, daring him to contradict. "I didn't lose my way, merely my sense of direction for a moment or two."

Paser raised a skeptical eyebrow. "An hour or two, I'd say."

Bak felt better about his own experience with the storm. At least he had the consolation that he had not been the sole individual to get lost. If Nebwa had indeed been lost.

Nebwa's eyes narrowed, his expression turned belligerent.

"How can you two share the same quarters?" Azzia's tone was light, teasing, designed to sap the tension between them. "You bicker like a pair of old women with nothing better to occupy your time."

"I thank the lord Amon I'll be free of him soon!" Nebwa winked, as if he had been joking all along. "Ahmose's caravan, the one we feared was lost, straggled in this morning. Paser will leave in two days' time with fresh supplies for the miners."

Paser looked at Harmose. "You'll lead the archers who come with us, I've been told."

"Is this true, Harmose?" Azzia asked, surprised.

"Tetynefer, it seems, has no need for a man who speaks the tongue of this land." Harmose did not

bother to hide his disgust. "He believes all who enter
this garrison should know the words of Kemet."

Nebwa twisted around and spat his contempt in the
dirt of the potted plant behind him. "That overripe
melon has no more sense than a stone. Only a witless
civilian would place a Medjay over a unit of archers
guarding a caravan."

Harmose glared. Mery frowned. Paser rolled his
eyes skyward. Azzia, looking like a woman who had
had about all she could take, told her servant to clear
away the empty bowls and dishes.

Bak wanted information, not a quarrel. With dusk
turning to darkness, with Azzia's patience coming to
an end, he had no time to waste. "Harmose, I see you
survived the storm unscathed."

The archer tore his smoldering eyes off Nebwa, saw
Azzia's pleading look, managed a stiff smile. "A
mighty falcon—the lord Horus himself, I'm convinced—saved me from certain death."

Nebwa sputtered, but a sharp look from Azzia kept
him mute.

"To be blessed by a god is an honor above all others." Bak hoped he sounded impressed rather than suspicious. "Where were you? In the desert, hunting?"

Azzia's quick smile of gratitude was tempered
by . . . what? speculation? Had she realized his questions concerning their whereabouts held a purpose?

"I was far out on the river," Harmose said, "fishing
from a skiff. I saw the storm approaching and sailed
back this way, but too late. The river came to life, the
waves washed over me." A note of awe entered his
voice. "The lord Horus swooped down and flew low
overhead, guiding me to the shore. He left me there,
safe, and flew away."

Could the tale be true? Bak wondered. Why would the lord Horus favor this half-Medjay archer when not a single god in the pantheon had lifted a finger to help identify a man who had stolen the flesh of the lord Re and taken two lives? They would not, it seemed, even bother to help eliminate any of the suspects.

He made himself smile and congratulated Harmose on his good fortune, as did Azzia, Mery, and Paser with varying degrees of astonishment.

Nebwa looked thoughtful. "With the lord Horus watching over you, maybe . . ." He scowled, shook his head. "No. Another man should lead the archers who guard the caravan. One who shares no blood with those vile savages who took Nakht's life."

Leaping to his feet, Harmose balled his hands into fists. The infantry officer stared at him with the irritating innocence of a man whose thoughts were engraved in granite.

"Enough!" Bak snarled at the incensed archer, who reluctantly returned to his stool. "Much blame has been laid at the feet of the Medjays these past few days. Ill feeling has grown like scum on a stagnant pool. I know little of the local villagers and less of the desert tribesmen, but one thing I do know: my Medjays have done no wrong."

Gripping Bak's shoulder, Nebwa spoke as one comrade to another. "I don't fault you for standing beside your men. I'd do the same if my troops were in trouble. But to allow an innocent woman to stand accused of their vile crime?" He shook his head, his fingers clamped tight. "No, in that you go too far."

Bak shook off the offending hand, the grinding pain in his shoulder. The irony of the situation did not escape him. First, Harmose charged him with abandoning his men; now Nebwa was accusing him of protecting them at the expense of the truth. "Not one man in my company could've taken Nakht's life. That I know for a fact."

"Is that what they told you?" Nebwa asked, giving Mery a knowing wink.

"Bak might well be speaking the truth," Mery said. "I heard his scribe, the boy Hori, asking for men who saw them elsewhere that night."

"He found them," Bak growled, rubbing his shoulder.

He saw no need to mention Ruru, the one man who had been alone in the barracks. Except for the white bandage on the tall Medjay's head, he was almost invisible in the deepening darkness. A reminder that night was almost upon them and he had no more time to waste listening to these men squabble.

As if to stress the need for haste, Lupaki emerged from the house carrying two brightly flaming torches. He mounted one on the wall beside the rear door and the other at the head of the stairwell. After collecting two unoccupied stools and a table, he left as silently as he had come. In the better light, Bak saw Harmose eyeing him with a new appreciation. Azzia's thoughts were hidden in shadow. Nebwa remained unconvinced.

"What of the time the goldsmith was slain?" Paser asked. "Have you proven your men innocent of his death, too?"

Thanking the lord Amon for giving him the opening he needed, Bak smiled. "Most are accounted for through the night. As for the rest . . ." He picked up the scroll and package and held them out so everyone could see the seal securing the knotted cords. His voice took on a note of grim expectancy. "With luck and the favor of the gods, their whereabouts will be of no importance."

"You can name the one who took the goldsmith's life?" Mery asked, his eyes locked on the objects.

"Not yet, but maybe . . ." Bak cut himself short, letting them assume what they liked.

All four men and the one woman stared at the objects. Mery looked bemused. Nebwa's eyes were as narrow as Azzia's were wide. The rise and fall of Harmose's breast ceased. Paser set his drinking bowl on the table, so unaware of his action it landed with a thud.

Nebwa jerked the scroll from Bak's hand, glanced at the seal, and snorted. "Nakht sealed this document, and he was slain long before the goldsmith." With a scornful smile, he tossed the scroll back. Bak barely had time to catch it.

"When I find a thing in a secret place," he said grimly, "I must believe it contains a secret."

"How could you . . . ?" A startled look flitted across Azzia's face, she clamped a hand over her mouth and stared at him, her shock apparent.

She had realized, Bak felt sure, that he suspected one of these four men of slaying her husband and was using the objects as bait in a trap. It was time to end his game. He rose from his stool, walked to the edge of the pavilion, and looked up at the stars filling the sky with a milky white brilliance. "The hour is late. I must go."

The trill of a nightbird rang out, the sound so clear and pure the creature might have been perched directly above the courtyard. Another answered from farther away and a third from a greater distance.

He looked at Azzia. Her face was pale and drawn but composed, her glance a query. In spite of the fact that she had to know he had used her, had to despise him for it, she appeared to be waiting for his next move. His admiration increased tenfold, as did his guilt. "I suggest you all come with me. After so long a day, mistress Azzia must be tired."

"Yes," she said, following his lead. "I am weary, that I admit." She offered them all a wan smile. "To be with my friends today has been a gift I value above all else, but I've much left to do this night."

Bak waited at the stairwell door while they said their good-byes. Mery prolonged his farewell. Harmose hovered. Nebwa poked among the remaining dishes, collecting a handful of grapes, figs, and dates. Paser's parting was as stiff and proper as his greeting.

They were halfway down the stairs with Bak in the rear when Hori burst through the ground-floor doorway. His face looked pale in the light of the guttering torch shining from above.

"Sir!" he shouted. "You must go to the quay at once. Two of our men have been drawn into a fight."

Bak muttered an oath and plunged past the others down the stairs. They followed close behind, curious to know what had happened.

"Tell me!" he demanded.

"They were patrolling the harbor." Hori's words tumbled out in frantic excitement. "Four men, sailors I think, blocked their path. They had knives and were taunting our men. A sentry atop the fortress wall saw them clash and sent word to me."

"I knew this would happen," Bak snarled. He shoved the scroll and package into Hori's hand. "Give these to Ruru. Tell him to take them to my quarters and wait for me there. Then go to the barracks, rouse Imsiba and a dozen men, and send them to me at the harbor." Swinging around, he rushed to the outer door and the street.

Bak raced across the rooftops of the housing block where his quarters were located. Four times he had to stop to silence and reassure uneasy neighbors who had taken their sleeping pallets to the roof when darkness fell. As he approached his own building, he spotted Imsiba's dark figure, lying on the roof, peering over the low parapet at the gray-black lane below. He scuttled to the Medjay, crouching lower with each step, and dropped down to lay prone beside him.

Imsiba flashed a quick, tense smile. "I thought never to hear Ruru's signal. What took so long?" He spoke in a whisper but with the urgency born of anticipation.

"None of our suspects came until the sun fell below the battlements."

"Which man walked into your snare?"

"All of them." Bak smiled at the surprise on Imsiba's face, but quickly sobered. "As we feared, the man we seek gave nothing away. I've no better idea now than I did before who he is."

"They all heard Hori's tale?"

"Yes, and my order that Ruru bring the scroll and package here." Bak gave no hint of the worry crowding his thoughts. "The guilty man should follow him from the commandant's residence. He'll wish to strike while he thinks me at the harbor and no threat to his safety."

The thin whistle of a nightbird sounded in the distance. A second, closer song rang out.

"Ruru's signal! And Woser's." Imsiba scrambled to a sitting position. "He's on his way, my friend." He answered the call with a slightly different birdsong. As the last note died away, he lay back with smile. "Our wait will seem shorter if you tell me of mistress Azzia's gathering."

The air was still and balmy, the roof hard and unyielding. Barking dogs and a tomcat yowling for a mate disrupted the quiet, abated, began all over again. Bak spoke quickly, skimming over much of the afternoon, leaving out nothing important.

At the end, Imsiba asked, "You're certain mistress Azzia didn't take her husband's life?"

"No man or woman could pretend so much hate, Imsiba."

"She placed you in Nakht's bedchamber. Could she not have been speaking for your ears rather than those of Lieutenant Mery?"

"Possibly," Bak admitted, "but it matters not. If you'd seen and heard her, you'd be as convinced as I am."

Imsiba grunted.

Bak hesitated to say more lest he reinforce the Medjay's conviction that Azzia had addled his wits, but silence was not his way. "Later, when she realized I believe one of the four took Nakht's life, she was not just surprised. She was shocked."

"As I would be if I feared my secrets were known."

"Hear me out! We've not much time."

Imsiba's sigh was long and exaggerated.

"She may've been disturbed because she thought I knew more than I did. I think, and here I admit I walk on marshy ground . . . I think she had no idea who slew her husband, and to learn that one of those four might be the guilty man was a new and shocking thought."

Imsiba eyed him for some time. When he finally spoke, his voice reflected a deep concern. "For your sake, my friend, I pray she's as innocent of all guile as you hope she is."

Bak appreciated the Medjay's solicitude, but resented the assumption that emotion controlled his thoughts. "Should not Ruru have come before now?" he asked irritably.

"He was to walk, not run as you did, but . . ." Imsiba looked along the dark, narrow, empty lane, and concern deepened to worry. "Yes, we should've heard another signal."

A cool breeze, the breath of the lord Amon, Bak was sure, touched his back, sending chills up his spine. From the look on Imsiba's face, he knew the Medjay had felt it, too. As if to affirm their worst fears, the frantic kew-kew-kew of a snared falcon carried through the air, the call so faint they barely heard it. A second call was stronger but no less frenzied. Imsiba shot to his feet to answer the summons. Azzia's wine rose to Bak's throat, soured by the knowledge that his plan had gone awry.

Bak knelt beside the dark form crumpled at the base of the single pillar in the vestibule of the commandant's residence. In the light of the flaming torch Pashenuro held above them, Ruru's eyes, wide open, sightless, stared at him, accused him. Unshed tears burned the backs of his eyelids, guilt ate at his heart. He was as much to blame for Ruru's death as the man who had thrust the dagger into his heart. He had told Hori to make sure the four suspects left the building before Ruru's departure. Never dreaming the guilty man would dare to slip back inside, he had posted no Medjays in the offices surrounding the hall.

Imsiba squatted next to him, examining the long,

bronze blade he had pulled from Ruru's breast. A pool of fresh blood painted the floor beneath the body a bright, glittery red. Kasaya stood in the shadows by the door, his back to them, his head bowed between hunched shoulders. He had found the body. As the first of a dozen Medjays hidden along the path Ruru should have taken, he had been the first to suspect something was wrong. He had heard Ruru's signal, waited, realized too much time had gone by, and hurried to the residence.

Imsiba, who looked as defeated as Bak felt, pointed to the symbol close to the handle. "The mark of the garrison arsenal. Every spearman and archer in Buhen carries a weapon like this."

"The scroll and package are gone, Imsiba. No ordinary soldier did this." Bak stood up abruptly, made a fist, and slammed it against the pillar. "We must not let him outwit us again. He must pay for this death."

Imsiba hauled himself to his feet and stared at Ruru with a dismal face. He transferred his gaze to Bak, and worry overshadowed unhappiness. "When he sees the scroll is blank and finds a bar of lead rather than gold, he'll fear you greatly, I think—and hate you. If we don't snare him soon, my friend, he may well snare you instead."

Chapter Twelve

"Why did you not summon me to the river?" Nofery complained. "Why come here where all the world can see?"

She swung the rush broom, driving a roiling cloud of dust across the hard-packed earthen floor. The flesh hanging from her upper arms swayed, her sagging breasts rolled from side to side beneath her sweat-damp white shift.

Bak, standing at the open door of her house of plea-sure, filled his voice with honey. "You said my swim-ming place was too far away, too long and hot a walk. Can I never please you, old woman?"

"Some can; some can't." Her tight-lipped scowl told him he fell in the latter group.

He had no time to spar, so caught the broom handle in midswing, forcing her to be still, and added a woe-begone smile. "I thought to find a friend when I passed through your door, not one so heartless she'd sweep me out with the dust."

"I welcome no man into my house whose presence could lead to the end of my business."

She sounded gruff, too gruff. His smile broadened and soon a twitch at the corner of her mouth betrayed her enjoyment of the banter. She jerked the broom from his hand and propped it across the doorway, barring entry. Pulling a stool out of a corner so he could sit, she placed it well off to the side where he would not be seen from the lane.

Ignoring the seat, he walked deeper into the room, which looked bleak and shabby in the dim early morning light. The stench of beer and sweat lingered; dust hung in the air. The large beer jars stacked against the scarred walls, the stools and tables shoved together in the corner, the chipped and stained drinking bowls, gave the place a look of abandonment. At the rear door, he brushed the curtain aside and peered into the back room. Three naked young women, two light-skinned, the other dark, lay curled together on a lumpy sleeping mat. One snored so softly the sound was like a whisper. Their satiny flesh glowed with youth; their faces in repose looked childlike, innocent. The delight their comely bodies promised threatened to rob him of his purpose.

"So it's pleasure you came for," Nofery said, sidling up to him with a knowing smirk.

Her words snapped him back to reality. He let the curtain fall, put a finger to his lips to soften her voice, and drew her away from the door. "Not today, old woman." He cleared his throat, cleared away a last image of those three inviting bodies. "The steward Tetynefer has summoned me. I must know the latest rumors before I cross his threshold."

She tilted her head and gave him a crafty smile. "You're to leave at midday for Ma'am, I hear, with the commandant's widow, mistress Azzia."

"I've no time to haggle," he said impatiently. "I must convince the steward we can't go now. I must stay in Buhen until the threat to my Medjays is resolved." And until the man who took Ruru's life is within my grasp, he thought. "What have you heard?"

She gave an elaborate shrug. "Why should I speak, when by saying nothing, I could be free of you?"

He wanted to shake her. Instead he let out a sigh as exaggerated as her shrug. "I've grown fond of you, old woman. To take you before the viceroy for inciting a riot will pain me deeply. But if I must, I must." He glanced around the room, his lips drooping as if he were looking at a favorite haunt for the last time. "You'll like mistress Azzia. She'll be a pleasant companion on the long voyage we face."

Nofery had the temerity to laugh. A forced laugh to be sure, but a laugh nonetheless. "Many men in Buhen believe death walks in your shadow. Though I think they err, I must admit I'd not like to be on a ship for days on end with you as my companion."

Bak did not think her words funny. "Tell me what you've heard. Make haste, for Tetynefer is not a man of patience."

The old woman sobered. Her face, her voice reflected a worry unlike her in its depth. "The rumors are multiplying ten times ten that your Medjays took the lives of Commandant Nakht and that sullen goldsmith Heby. There's much wild talk, with one man's anger building on that of another. They say your Medjay Ruru was slain as an act of vengeance for the commandant's death, and other acts of violence are sure to follow."

Bak shifted from one foot to another, moving into the sunlight that flooded the forecourt of the mansion of the lord Horus of Buhen and back to the shadow of a fluted column. Muted voices and, when the breeze was right, the faint musty odor of the river drifted over the high walls enclosing the god's mansion. He shifted his weight, frowned at the small stone building and the bright painted reliefs of Maatkare Hatshepsut marching with the god across its facade. Tetynefer was inside, assisting the priest with the morning ritual in the dimly lit, probably cool sanctuary. If Bak had known the steward was serving as a web priest through the month he would have found a more worthwhile task than lingering in the hot, stifling courtyard.

At first, the time had seemed like a gift from the lord Horus himself, for it had given Bak a chance to rehearse his plea. However, as the minutes dragged and doubts assailed him, his argument seemed shallow, unconvincing. What could he say? The rumors about the Medjay police were multiplying; further trouble was inevitable. All of which Tetynefer must already know.

Too fretful to stay motionless for long, Bak left the shade to pace the open court, his path parallel to the colonnade running along the precinct wall. He searched his memory, trying to recall any appropriate words of wisdom Maiherperi might have uttered. He could think of none. Even worse, as if to emphasize the fact that he stood alone with no one to share his burdens, he could barely remember the timbre of the commander's voice, and his dark, well-formed features had faded to a blur.

The squeak of a door and murmuring voices tore his thoughts from the morass in which they had sunk. Tetynefer and an aging priest, a slight man with a shaven head, emerged from the god's dwelling. The faint aroma of incense drifted across the court, tickling Bak's nostrils. The steward bade good-bye with a promise of returning for the evening ritual and strolled toward the outer portal, enveloped in an aura of piety. The priest slipped back inside the stone building.

Bak cut diagonally across the court to catch Tetyne-fer, who offered an indifferent nod and walked on. Bak muttered an oath, certain the steward had forgotten his summons.

"You wished to see me, sir?" he asked.

Tetynefer stopped, managed somehow to look surprised and blank at the same time. His eyes narrowed and he pursed his mouth. "I summoned you at first light, Officer Bak, and I expected you then. Do you never come when bidden?"

Bak tried to look contrite.

"To waylay me here, to rob me of my moment of peace . . ." Tetynefer sniffed. "I suppose I shouldn't be surprised by your lack of good judgment. You'd not have been sent to Buhen if you behaved judiciously."

"Another man has been slain, this time one of my own, and rumors about my Medjays are fouling the air." Bak's voice was stiff, bordering on insolent. "I thought, before you sent word to the viceroy about Ruru's death, you'd want to know the direction of the wind and how strong it is, for no man wants to be blown away in a gale."

"Well!" Tetynefer said, surprised. "It seems you're not as indifferent to political necessities as I thought."

"I fear for my men." The steward's half-formed smile froze, and Bak hastened to add, "Their well-being reflects on all of us—you, me, the other officers in this garrison. If they're forced to run before an angry mob, word of our failure to keep order will go far beyond the viceroy. Maiherperi will hear without doubt, as will our sovereign, Maatkare Hatshepsut herself."

Tetynefer's eyes darted around the forecourt as if searching for an eavesdropper. The mansion door remained closed and no one had come through the portal

in the enclosure wall. With a satisfied grunt, he drew
Bak well away from the entry and into a narrowing
strip of shade cast by the wall.

"How any man can believe those rumors is beyond
me!" Tetynefer said irritably. "No one but the widow
Azzia could've taken Nakht's life and a villager slew
the goldsmith, as we both know."

The steward had obviously convinced himself the
tale he had concocted for the viceroy was true. Bak
could not hope to dissuade him without speaking of the
gold. To do so before he laid his hands on the thief
would be a mistake. At best, Tetynefer would choose to
believe he had an over-fertile imagination. At worst, he
would consider the thin bar of gold an additional reason
to take Azzia before the viceroy as soon as possible.

Bak could not let that happen. "Mistress Azzia is
well-liked, greatly admired in fact. Most men find it
easier to blame a Medjay for her husband's death than
to think she slew him. As for the goldsmith Heby, I told
you before: the spear found in his breast came from my
police arsenal."

Tetynefer tugged a square of linen from his belt,
shook out the folds, and scrubbed the sweat from his
face, bald head, and the roll of fat around his neck.
"Are you saying, after all, that your Medjays were responsible?"

"No!" Bak tamped down his exasperation. "Men's
thoughts follow the shortest path to the thing they wish
to believe, sir. They say Ruru's life was taken to
avenge Nakht's death. Untrue, I know for a fact, but a
logical step along the path of self-deception."

"You know who slew the commandant?"

Cursing his slip of the tongue, Bak went on as if he
had not heard. "If the rumors continue to grow, and

I've no doubt they will if left unchecked, an attack will be made on my Medjays. For that reason, I must not take mistress Azzia on the ship scheduled to leave today. I must be seen to stand beside my men, and I must do all I can to prove their innocence and their worth to this garrison."

A smile spread across Tetynefer's face. "You've been thinking much as I have, it seems."

Bak had no idea what the steward was talking about, but he doubted their thoughts ever coincided. "I can stay?"

"You'll not be separated from your Medjays, and you'll have every opportunity to prove their worth."

Bak eyed him with suspicion. He was not at all reassured by the steward's self-satisfied expression.

Tetynefer refolded the linen and tucked it into his belt. "Ahmose . . . I doubt you know him; his caravan returned yesterday from the desert." He clasped his hands behind his ample buttocks and paced the length of the shade in a parody of every military officer of high rank Bak had ever seen. "Several days ago, Ahmose was warned by a wandering shepherd that the next caravan bringing gold from the mine called the Mountain of Re will be attacked by a large and well-armed contingent of tribesmen. The caravan, as you surely know, will leave Buhen tomorrow." Facing Bak once again, he added, "Every fighting man who can be spared will go with it."

Bak was appalled. How could a man wise enough, or wily enough, to rise to the high scribal rank of steward presume to take the authority of a military commander? To make so rash a decision based on the word of a shepherd was beyond belief.

"That, young man, is why I summoned you," Tetynefer said. "You're an officer trained in the art of war, and I've heard you yearn for battle. Now you'll have your wish. Your Medjays will accompany the caravan, and you, their commanding officer, will go with them." He glanced around and lowered his voice, as if taking Bak into his confidence. "With your men away in the desert, far from Buhen, neither of us need worry further about trouble brewing within these walls."

Bak was so disgusted, he was robbed of speech. Tetynefer might be stupid enough to accept the word of a lowly shepherd, but he was smart enough to shift potentially embarrassing problems onto the shoulders of the officer in charge of the caravan. To Paser, a man equally watchful of his own interests. Which left no one but Bak to take the blame if the fear and mistrust of his Medjays came to a boil while they were in the desert.

"What of mistress Azzia?" he asked. "What will happen to her?"

"She'll remain here until I find a suitable escort."

"Only I know all the facts about Nakht's death. How can any other man present her case fairly to the viceroy?"

Tetynefer scowled. "You came to me, young man, saying you wanted to stay with your Medjays, to stand beside them. Have you altered your thoughts? Have you decided you prefer the safety of this fortress instead?"

So sour was the taste of bile in Bak's throat that he paid no heed to the implication that he might be a coward. "I'll go with my men into the desert."

Bak hurried along the narrow, sun-drenched lanes, his thoughts in too much of a turmoil to notice the people he passed, the donkey train, the dogs fighting over the torn body of a rat. As much as he had hoped to face

an enemy on the field of battle, he found scant consolation in the thought that at last he might have the opportunity. Tetynefer had left him no option, but even if he
had, Bak would have chosen to go with his men. In
spite of the fact that by doing so, he was turning his
back on Azzia in her time of need. He would be gone
for many days; she would reach Ma'am long before his
return. She might somehow convince the viceroy of
her innocence, but with no one there to cast doubt on
her guilt, he thought it unlikely.

Even if she were allowed to remain in Buhen until
Bak's return, he might well lose any chance he had of
proving her innocence beyond a doubt, of laying his
hands on the man who had stolen the gold and had
slain Nakht, Heby, and Ruru. True, he would be crossing the desert with two of his suspects, Paser and
Harmose. Mery would certainly stay in Buhen to command his sentries, and Nebwa, the senior and most experienced infantry officer, would have to remain to
oversee the more junior officers who patrolled the
desert around Buhen. If either of the pair had taken the
gold, the respite would give him time to bury his tracks
much deeper—or to escape if he felt he must.

Bak could see a single glimmer of light. The Mountain of Re, Tetynefer had said. The mine from which
the gold had been stolen. He would be able to see for
himself how the ore was handled, might learn—should
the gods choose to smile on him—how a portion could
have been stolen undetected, and by whom. He let out
a cynical laugh. The knowledge would be of little use
if the man behind the thefts got away. Nor would it
bring Ruru back to life or save Azzia if Tetynefer sent
her to Ma'am as planned.

Despair hounded him all the way to the unmarried

officers' quarters. Paser stood ramrod stiff at the far
end of the courtyard, his face stormy. Nebwa paced
back and forth, slapping his thigh with his baton of office. Mery slouched on the mudbrick bench, hair rumpled, expression morose. The servant boy huddled in a
corner, his eyes darting from one officer to another
while he scrubbed out the eating bowls with dry sand.

"That old fool must be mad!" Nebwa snarled. He
spotted Bak, nodded a perfunctory greeting. "To strip
this fortress of half its men is folly."

Mery raised a hand to Bak. "Buhen hasn't been attacked for many years. He must believe the walls alone
have kept it safe."

"You can be sure Senenmut, my cousin, will hear of
this," Paser promised with a cruel sneer. "He'll not
keep silent before our sovereign. And she listens when
he speaks!"

Nebwa turned his back on him, hiding his contempt
for a back-stabber, and eyed Bak. "I see by your face
you've talked to Tetynefer." His voice took on a jeering
note. "Did he let you convince him you must go with
Azzia to Ma'am?"

"I'm staying where I belong, with my men."

"I thank the lord Amon! I feared they'd be left in my
charge."

"Tetynefer said nothing about placing them in your
command. He's sending them to the mine with . . ."
Bak realized the implication of Nebwa's statement,
gaped. "You're going with the caravan?"

"We're all going," Mery said bitterly. "Nebwa with
an entire company, a hundred spearmen and archers.
Me with half my sentries, fifty spearmen who should
remain on duty atop the walls of this fortress. Paser,
who must take twice the number of donkeys to supply

us with food and water, and twice the number of drovers to care for the animals."

"Not to mention your wretched Medjays," Paser said. "Twenty-four men whose very presence among the rest bodes trouble."

Bak barely heard him. If all his suspects went to the mine, his search for the murderer would not be disrupted. "What of Harmose?" he asked, as casually as he could. "Will he also go?"

"You don't think that dolt Tetynefer would fail to include the regular caravan guards, do you?" Nebwa snarled.

Bak's relief at the news was tempered by sadness. He might catch his prey, but too late to help Azzia.

"He's halving the forces in this garrison!" Mery was so distraught he ran his fingers through his hair, making it stand on end. He had never looked so untidy.

"Only a civilian would make so stupid a decision," Nebwa snarled.

"I've led more caravans to the mines than any other man in Buhen." Paser was stiff with indignation. "I've lost no more than fifteen donkeys at the hands of raiding tribesmen, and just six men have died. Six! Yet he treats me as a new and untried officer, one who needs help to do a task I've done well for many months."

"You've no need to worry, Paser." Nebwa reached over his shoulder with his baton to scratch his back. "I'll not usurp your authority. I'll be off in the desert much of the time, looking for that ass Tetynefer's great army of tribesmen."

"If you hope to see an army," Paser scoffed, "you'll have to stand atop a hill and look down upon your own infantry."

Even Mery smiled at that.

"Will my Medjays and I go with you, Nebwa, or remain with the caravan?" Bak asked.

"I'll not have those savages with me! I want no trouble between my men and yours." Nebwa's harsh growl faded to a grumble. "Besides, you'll be of more use with the caravan. I've always thought Harmose sends word to his desert cousins before the raids. With you keeping watch, he'll not have the chance this time."

"Bak has trained with the regiment of Amon," Paser said, "and he's practiced warfare with men numbered in the thousands. If by chance the tribesmen have formed into an army, you'll need him with you as a leader of men, not with me as a spy."

"I sorrow for you, Paser," Nebwa said, "but with Mery by my side, I'll have all the officers I need. No, Bak and his Medjays will stay with the caravan."

For the first time in his life, Bak knew how a pariah must feel.

"Can I not go with you?" Hori asked for perhaps the tenth time in half that number of hours.

Imsiba rolled his eyes skyward. "You're like a gnat, Hori, buzzing and buzzing around our heads. Will you never give up and fly away?"

Bak ran his finger along the bright, freshly honed edges of the spear point. Satisfied with the way they bit his flesh, he laid the weapon on the rooftop beside his thigh and reached for his battle ax, which lay outside the shadow of the pavilion. The bronze blade was almost too hot to touch. He placed the handle between his knees and began to rasp the whetstone across the cutting edge.

Hori fussed with the ears of his puppy, lying half-

asleep in his lap. "What if you don't return?" he
blurted.

Imsiba made a rude sound with his mouth. "If you
wanted to be a soldier, you should've learned the arts
of war."

Bak shook his head in exasperation. "How many
times must I tell you? Your task here is more important
than ours by far."

"To watch over this house and our barracks?" Hori
scoffed. "To look out for Mistress Azzia for the short
time she'll remain?"

"Caring for our storage magazine and arsenal is no
light burden." Imsiba plucked a fish from the bowl sitting on the cold brazier. "Seeing that our stores are re-
filled when next month's rations are issued is more
important yet." He broke the fish apart and peeled the
spine away. "We'll eat poorly while we're gone and
suffer from a lack of water. We'll return with our clothing in shreds and our weapons broken or lost."

Hori's mouth continued to droop.

Bak understood the boy's yearning for adventure,
and he sympathized. So he glanced around, examining
the rooftops spreading out in all directions. Two
women, a mother and daughter, he thought, were laying linen out to dry across the lane. Though they were
too far away to hear, he leaned close to Hori and lowered his voice to a conspiratorial whisper. "Do you
think I'd dare leave the gold and scrolls behind if you
weren't here to keep them safe?"

Hori stared wide-eyed. "You're leaving them here?
With me?"

"Who else can I trust?"

Hori sucked in his breath. He glanced from Bak to

Imsiba and back again, the desire to go with them vying on his face with the need to feel important. The latter won and he grinned. "I've heard mistress Azzia's servants prepare food fit for the gods. I'll go there now and offer my services." He moved the puppy from his lap to Imsiba's, stood up, and nudged the brazier with his toe. "With luck and if the gods choose to smile on me, I'll not cook another fish until you return."

As their laughter died away, Hori disappeared down the stairway. Bak went back to work, tightening the leather thongs binding the ax blade to the handle.

Imsiba swallowed a final bite of fish and let the puppy lick the juice from his fingers. "You'll think it unwise, I know, but I spoke with Harmose this morning."

Bak glanced up from his task. "Did he ask for my thoughts about mistress Azzia?"

"He talked of our journey and the trouble our presence may cause. He's very uneasy, as you can well imagine."

"Does he fear for us? Or does he fear our presence will remind those men who don't trust us that he shares the blood of a Medjay?"

"Must you always think the worst of him?" Imsiba grabbed another fish, tore it apart. "You said something yesterday—I know not what—that gained his respect. He believes you'll do all you can to keep us safe. He said that if we must fight to protect ourselves, he and his archers will stand beside us."

Guilt flooded Bak's thoughts, swept away an instant later by suspicion. Harmose's offer might indeed be sincere, but could as easily be a ploy to lower Bak's defenses. The barren desert would be an ideal place to slay a man, especially one too quick to trust.

Chapter Thirteen

"The lord Re must think man a toy." Imsiba scowled at the dry, eroded watercourse below. "To spread bits of his golden flesh through these vile desert wadis, then tempt man with the metal's perfection, was an act of cruelty beyond measure."

Bak headed across a steep slope covered with loose, broken rocks, taking care where he placed his feet. "You've lived in the land of Kemet too long," he teased. "You've been spoiled by a life of ease and comfort."

"Humph!" Not long after midday, the caravan had entered the wadi where the mine called the Mountain of Re was located. Bak and his Medjays had left the long line of men and donkeys before it reached its destination. While they had set up camp on a rocky shelf some distance above the wadi floor, the sturdy beasts had been led farther up the dry watercourse to the miners' camp, where food, water, tools, and other supplies had been unloaded. After an hour's rest, the animals had been laden with empty water jars, and the drovers, under the watchful eyes of Harmose and his archers, had led them off to a spring a few hours' walk away.

Dust hung in the air along the path they had taken. Nebwa's troops had camped lower down the wadi, Mery's men with them.

Imsiba laid his bow and quiver beside a cracked, rough-surfaced boulder and removed a sandal to brush a rock fragment from the sole of his foot. "My own sweat has washed the dust of travel from my body, and I feel like a man cooking in his own juice."

Bak's smile broadened. "I heard no complaints from the nomad shepherds we passed along the trail." He had no need to remind the sergeant that the nomads were Medjays, just as he was.

"They know no better way of life. If they did, my friend, they, too, would find fault with their lot."

Bak eyed the surrounding terrain, and his smile faltered. Like the sergeant, he thought the land foul, a place forsaken by the gods. The wadi was narrow, the dun-colored peaks to either side harsh, ragged, and barren of life. The heat was intense, the sun blinding. Sweat trickled down his face, breast, back, and thighs. Thirst parched his mouth. He longed to taste the waters of the river and to feel its soothing current the length of his body.

He shook off the dream and spoke with reluctance. "Nebwa drew me aside this morning. He complained of the many times you stand apart with Harmose and speak of things no other men can hear."

Imsiba's mouth tightened. "Who I make my friend is no business of his."

"He thinks the two of you plot against the caravan. He fears for its safety and for the safety of the gold we'll carry when we return to Buhen."

"Surely you don't believe him!"

"You know I don't!" Bak wiped the sweat from his

face and spoke in a more reasonable voice. "No man is more loyal to the land of Kemet than you, Imsiba. But I must admit I feel no better about your friendship than Nebwa does."

"Because you suspect Harmose of murder and theft?" Imsiba's laugh was hard, cynical. "You err! He's as eager to find the man who slew Commandant Nakht as you are, and as worried for mistress Azzia."

Bak tried to swallow the lump rising in his throat, a lump which formed each time he thought of Azzia. Where is she? he wondered. Safe in Buhen? Or has she gone to Ma'am and is she standing even now before the viceroy? Could she already be dead, unjustly punished?

Shoving away so fearsome a thought, Bak forced an apologetic smile. "I worry at seeing you befriend a man who might be less than he seems, that's all."

The Medjay did not return the smile. "I accept your belief in the woman's innocence. Can you not accept mine that Harmose is without guilt?"

"I'd like to, yes, but I dare not."

Stiff with wounded pride, Imsiba shouldered his quiver and picked up his bow. "That boulder overlooks the mine." He pointed to a wind-gouged lump of stone protruding from the hillside farther along their path. "I'll watch you from there. Should any man approach you with a dagger in his hand or a spear or any other weapon, my arrows will fly true."

Bak muttered an oath at his friend's obstinacy. He glanced along the slope in the direction from which they had come, squinting to lessen the glare. A craggy outcrop hid their campsite, but two of his men, both fully armed, were traversing the hillside at a higher level, ensuring his safety. If the man he hoped to catch meant to slay him, he had made no attempt during the long trek from Buhen. Imsiba and the other Medjays were as concerned for his welfare as he was for theirs, and as careful to guard his back. This his adversary doubtless knew.

"The men who follow us can use the bow as well as you." Bak clasped his friend's shoulder, determined to mend the rift between them. "You must come with me to the mine. We'll be here only a few days, and I'll need your eyes and ears If I'm to learn how gold is stolen."

The invitation was a declaration of trust and the big Medjay accepted it as such. His gloomy expression dissolved, and a smile formed on his lips, a twinkle in his eye. "You err, my friend. My skill with the bow is unmatched. But if you wish to place your life in the hands of lesser men, so be it."

Bak and Imsiba stood among a cluster of jagged, broken boulders lying alongside a stream of loose sand and rocks, the rubble left by water which had rushed down the hillside many months, maybe years in the past. They stared across the wadi, taking their first good look at the mine, a gaping hole in the opposite slope fifteen or so paces above the dry watercourse. The peak towered above the hole, its face harsh and precipitous, its summit capped by boulders.

The tunnel opened onto a shelf formed from the refuse of the mining process. A chain of nearly naked men, all burned by the sun, plodded along the shelf, carrying rush baskets filled with rocks. They were hauling their heavy burden from the mine to a dozen or so lean-tos built on a mound of refuse that filled the base of a short, steep subsidiary wadi. A foreman stood on the slope above them, his stubby leather whip held in the crook of his arm. Shadowy figures labored inside the shelters, rickety affairs made of piled stones and twisted branches covered with cloth, rushes, brush, whatever came to hand to stave off the sun. At least a dozen guards, hard-looking men armed with spears, kept a wary eye on the activity.

Paser and Nebwa stood on the wadi floor below the mine, talking to a hulking man with a neck so thick it seemed a part of his head. His left shoulder sagged, the arm hung useless and wasted. Bak saw that he carried a baton of office.

"The man with Paser and Nebwa must be Wadjet-Renput, overseer of this mine."

"So I assume," Imsiba said. "A good man, Harmose told me. He once oversaw a gang of stonemasons building our sovereign's new memorial temple across the river from the capital."

Bak chose to ignore the reference to the archer. He wanted no further argument. "What of his arm?"

"A column toppled, with him beneath." Imsiba's voice grew sad, pitying. "It took him many months to heal and when he did he was sent here."

So terrible a reward after so dreadful a misfortune might make a man bitter, Bak thought, bitter enough to seek revenge. "How long ago did he come?"

"Five months, no more."

The gold had been taken over the course of a year, starting long before Wadjet-Renput's time. True, he could have been made a party to the thefts upon his arrival, but it was equally possible that he, a man with no experience of mining, could be blinded by a clever deception.

"Our sovereign thought him bad luck," Imsiba added.

Bak tore his thoughts from the gold. He wanted no talk of bad luck. "More likely," he scoffed, "she wanted no man there to remind the others of the danger they faced when raising those huge blocks of stone."

His words failed to erase the uneasy look from Imsiba's face. "Bad luck and danger make an uneasy partnership, my friend. This Mountain of Re strikes a fear in my heart like few other places I've been."

Like most individuals isolated from their equals, Wadjet-Renput proved to be a garrulous man. He greeted Imsiba with as much enthusiasm as he did Bak and, starved for news of the capital, questioned them both at length. Paser made a pretense of being aloof, but Bak noticed he paid particular attention to the sometimes spectacular rise in positions of men close to his cousin Senenmut. Nebwa shuffled from foot to foot, bored with talk of a world he had never known, and scowled his disapproval at the Medjay's inclusion in the group.

Aware of the time slipping away, Bak took advantage of a break in the conversation. "How many men toil here?" he asked, eyeing the mine-mouth, the line of filthy, sweating men laden with baskets, and the lean-tos.

Wadjet-Renput's gaze traveled from one end of the shelf to the other, and his chest swelled with pride. "Eighty prisoners and half as many guards. The miners work in gangs of ten, which I rotate from one task to another each week. Half the guards stay here, the rest keep watch from the heights around us."

Bak could not understand how any man could hold his head high with so cruel an assignment, but he thanked the lord Amon it was so, for it would make his own task easier. "Neither Imsiba nor I have seen gold taken from stone. Will you show us?"

The overseer's face lit up like a lamp. "Come!" He plunged up a path worn smooth by many feet, as quick and agile as a gazelle in spite of his useless arm, and stopped on the shelf not far from the lean-tos.

Bak exchanged a quick glance with Imsiba and they hastened after him. Nebwa looked down the wadi as if his camp beckoned, but decided to follow. Paser frowned, evidently preferring gossip to a tour of a mine he had visited often, and plodded up the slope behind them.

Wadjet-Renput glanced at the sky, where the sun hugged the weathered peaks to the west. "It's too late to enter the mine; no man stays inside after dusk." Shaking off an obvious disappointment, he smiled. "That you can see tomorrow, the rest I'll show you now."

A bearer trudged past, reeking of sweat. He stopped at a knee-high pile of broken rock near the lean-tos, swung the heavy basket from his shoulder, and dumped his load. A fine pale dust rose in the air, coating his already grimy body. As he turned back to retrace his path, he looked neither right nor left, merely plodded past the onlookers like an ox across a field. Bak gave silent thanks to the lord Amon that he was not that man.

Wadjet-Renput plucked a rock from the pile, held it out so they could see the glittering flecks in the quartz, and began to talk. He moved on to the nearest lean-to and the next and the next, explaining, elaborating, adding anecdotes of success and disappointment as the miners had followed the vein deeper into the mountain. They watched nearly naked men huddled beneath the lean-tos, crushing the rocks to the size of peas in large mortars. Others ground the ground stone in hand mills to the consistency of coarse sand. A third group washed the powder in a sloping stone basin, using precious water to separate out the heavier gold.

Prisoner-miners they were, men who had killed or stolen or cheated or committed some other serious offense against their fellow man, offending the gods by their behavior. A few went mad in the heat, Bak knew; others died of exposure or in accidents, or their hearts stopped beating when they could take no more. None who returned to Kemet ever forgot the mine; none repeated his offense. And no wonder, Bak thought, for he could think of no greater punishment than drawing the precious flesh of the lord Re from stone.

He watched and listened intently, seeing many points in the process where gold could be stolen, but never more than a few grains at a time. At that rate, it would take months to collect a large enough amount to make a bar the size of the one hidden in his bedchamber in Buhen. Yet if he had interpreted Nakht's scroll correctly, enough gold had disappeared in one year to make a dozen or more similar bars. One glance at Imsiba told him his friend was equally puzzled.

As they watched a prisoner pick golden granules from the bottom of a basin, Bak asked Wadjet-Renput, "How much gold is lost to theft?"

"You jest!" The overseer swept his baton in an arc, drawing all eyes to the dry and rock-strewn land around them. "What man with good sense would try such a thing?"

"Greed sometimes makes men foolish—and desperate."

"Bah!" Nebwa spat on the earth by his feet. "These

men have been reduced to animals. What use can a wit-less beast make of so precious a metal?"

"They watch each other, Bak." Paser spoke as if to a child with an overactive imagination. "None is willing to share the blame for another man's folly, and such would be the case if gold were found missing."

They walked to the final lean-to, built on the hillside three or four paces above the others. Wadjet-Renput beamed at the man inside. He was scrawny, about thirty years of age, with short curly hair and hands so delicate Maatkare Hatshepsut herself would have envied him. He wore a long kilt and sat behind a scale and a set of weights. A pile of pottery cones lay beside one hip, writing implements by the other. He was a scribe, not a prisoner.

"This is Roy," the overseer said, "the foremost teller of obscene jokes in the land of Kemet."

A shrill whistle pierced the air, cutting short the introduction.

"The day has ended," Wadjet-Renput explained and added with a contented smile, "Shall we see what our labor has brought forth for our divine sovereign?"

Bak was surprised at how much time had passed. The sun had slipped beyond the horizon. The wadi lay in shadow, and the peaks to either side were bathed in an orange-gold afterglow. He had been so intent on learning all he could that he had forgotten his thirst and the heat enveloping the land.

The bearers made a final trip across the shelf to empty their baskets. A gang of naked men snaked out of the mine, so covered with dust they looked as if the lord Khnum had molded them on his potter's wheel from the earth itself. The men who crushed the stone and those who ground it up abandoned their lean-tos.

A dozen guards shepherded the lot off the shelf and up the wadi toward their camp.

Those who remained, the men who washed the gold from the rock, carried small pottery bowls to the lean-to and handed them to the scribe. Inside each bowl were the glittering grains so painstakingly collected through the long, sweltering day. Bak's pulse quickened. This lean-to, with so much of the precious metal in the hands of one man, seemed a likely place for theft. Except two guards stood close by, watching the exchange.

As the prisoners hurried away, Roy poured all the gold into a single round-bottomed spouted bowl about the size of his cupped hand. He then weighed it. While he toiled, he chattered to those watching, relating one tale after another, all funny, all vividly obscene. Bak laughed with the rest, but kept a surreptitious eye on those delicate fingers, intrigued by their deft manipulation of the bowls and the weights. The guards, he noticed, were too distracted by the talk of women and pleasure to pay attention to Roy's supple hands.

Bak caught Imsiba's eye. The Medjay was laughing along with the rest, but his brief nod said that he, too, thought the scribe a likely source of the stolen gold.

How could one be sure?

Reaching into the lean-to, Bak grasped the spouted bowl. Shocked, the scribe stopped his patter in midsentence. The guards stiffened, looked to a gaping Wadjet-Renput for guidance. Paser sucked in his breath. Nebwa took a quick step back, his eyes darted from Bak to Imsiba, his hand clutched his dagger. Whether he meant to protect the gold from men he thought thieves or whether Roy was his confederate and he feared discovery, Bak could not tell.

Bak took a generous pinch of the ore between his fingers, careful to hold it over the bowl so none would be lost. "Could a man not take this much gold every day and carry away a handful at the end of a year with no one the wiser?"

"By all the gods in the ennead!" Nebwa exclaimed. "Are we back to that?" His hand remained on his dagger.

"You take your task as a policeman too seriously," Paser said in a tight voice.

Roy's face blanched to a waxy white.

Bak dared not look at Imsiba for fear his elation would show. He had seen few men look guiltier or more afraid. As casually as he could, he let the brilliant flecks trickle into the bowl and handed it back. Muttering a disgusted curse, Nebwa let his hand swing away from the dagger. Wadjet-Renput, Paser, and the guards relaxed.

Roy went on with his task, his tongue less glib, his hands no longer so quick and sure. He pried the plug off a partially filled cone, poured in gold nearly to the top, and plugged it with wet clay, which he impressed with the royal seal. Placing it on the scale, he noted its weight and scribbled it on the baked clay surface. The remainder of the ore he poured into an empty cone and repeated each step though the vessel was less than a quarter full. He turned both sealed containers over to Wadjet-Renput.

As at the goldsmiths' workshop and at every other step of the process, there seemed no way to steal the gold in any significant quantity. Yet Bak was certain the scribe was taking a part of each day's proceeds. His impulse was to accuse then and there, but common sense prevailed and he elected to wait. Wadjet-Renput would not take kindly to having his scribe charged with a serious offense simply because he looked and acted like a guilty man.

Bak had to find proof. He had to examine the tools of Roy's trade. There, he felt sure, lay the secret of the thefts. To do so he needed the bright light of day, not the deepening shadows of evening already filling the lean-to. He muttered a frustrated curse at the need to wait and vowed to return at first light. In the meantime, his Medjays would have to watch Roy, to protect him from the same fate Nakht, Heby, and Ruru had suffered. If the scribe were to die, the trail to the man who had slain the three might forever be lost.

"Bak!" A hand clasped his shoulder and shook him awake. Nebwa was bending over him, his face dark, grim. "One of my sentries saw a man leave this campsite last night. He slipped away in the dark, but we caught him this morning, hiding in a crevice above the miners' camp."

Bak sat up and blinked the sleep from his eyes. The wadi below was dark, the hillside gray and featureless. The pink glow of dawn had just begun to wash over the eastern peaks. His Medjays lay scattered around him, a few sleeping or pretending to sleep, most raising their heads to peer at the intruder.

"You've not harmed him!" Bak's voice was sharp-edged, concerned.

"Not yet." Nebwa spat on the ground by his feet. "I thought to hear your explanation first—if you have one."

Bak rose from his thin sleeping mat and urged Nebwa along the slope away from the camp. "Like you, I think Tetynefer wrong in believing the tribes-

men have formed an army. However, should he prove
to be right, they might believe this mine vulnerable, the
place to start a war. I'll not let my men fight blind if
fight they must. I sent them out to study the ground on
which they'd have to stand."

Nebwa nodded a grudging approval. "You think like
a soldier." His eyes narrowed and he muttered a curse.
"We caught one man. How many others slipped past
my sentries unseen?"

"Three," Bak said, careful to give no hint of the grat-
ification he felt. "They'll describe all they saw to those
who remained behind."

Nebwa's dour face promised trouble for the negli-
gent sentries.

Bak pressed his advantage. "You've had men
watching us from the time we left Buhen. Is their task
to ensure our safety? Or to protect your army of almost two hundred men from my small company of
twenty-four?"

"I want no blame attached to my name if trouble
arises, nor do I want to lose men I might someday
need."

"Need? My Medjays?" Bak asked, incredulous.

"Tetynefer is a great fool but, should his prediction
come true, I'll need every man I can get—including
your wretched Medjays."

"Men you don't trust."

"If they're as loyal to Kemet as you claim, let them
prove it. If not, no man among them will return to
Buhen."

Bak somehow managed to control his anger. "I want
the man you hold. Where is he?"

"My sentries took him to our camp." Nebwa's expression soured. "They spoke long and loud of seeing

him skulking about the wadi. Those who think the
worst have visions of being slain in their sleep by Medjays who steal upon them in the night."

"You've no one to blame but yourself. You've said
time and time again you think my men traitors and
murderers. What can you expect of those who follow
you?"

Nebwa's voice hardened. "I'll deal with my men, of
that you can be sure. To ease my path, you must leave
this wadi. I want you gone before the lord Khepre rises
above the eastern horizon."

Bak stepped back a pace, stunned. "What are we to
do? Camp alone in the desert, far from food and water?"

"You'll hunt for game," Nebwa snarled. "The miners need fresh meat. They've had none in more than a
month. By the time you return, I'll have set my men's
thoughts on a proper course."

He's done nothing before to quell his men's fear and
hatred, Bak thought. Why is he sending us away now?
Is he giving himself time to silence the scribe Roy? An
accusation formed on his lips and died unspoken. He
could say nothing without proof. He tried to make ex-
cuses, but Nebwa was adamant: the meat was needed
and men spawned in the desert were the logical choice
to hunt it down. It mattered not that none of them had
lived in Wawat since they were children. As Nebwa
was in command until their return to Buhen, Bak had
no choice but to agree.

"We'll go," he said, "but Imsiba and three other men
must stay. I'll not leave my campsite untended." Nor
will I leave Roy unprotected, he thought.

Nebwa's mouth tightened. "You must all go together."

"You take many men into the desert each day, Nebwa, to sweep the land for raiders. The mine could be attacked while you're gone. If that should happen, only my Medjays can slip through the enemy lines undetected."

Nebwa thought it over, said grudgingly, "Leave them here if you must."

He plunged diagonally down the slope in the direction of his camp, heedless of the rocks and sand his feet set in motion. Bak picked up a palm-sized stone, glared at Nebwa's back, and turned away to throw it as hard as he could across the hillside. He could not remember a time he had been so outraged. At least with Imsiba staying behind he had no need to worry about Roy's safety. Or did he?

". . . So all is well, my friend," Imsiba said, summing up the events of the past three days. "The miners toiled from dawn to dusk and Roy weighed the gold as before. No attempt was made on his life. His good spirits have returned as if he has no worry or guilt."

Bak felt like a man reprieved. "I knew not what I'd find on my return, but I feared the worst." He gave his friend a weary smile. "I prayed with each step I took that no harm would come to him. Or to you, Imsiba, and the men who stayed with you."

They stood at a bend in the wadi, looking back at the miners' camp, a dozen squalid stone hovels joined together with common walls. The shelters clung to the hillside well above the level of the deadly flash floods which sometimes thundered through the narrow valley with no warning. In the dry watercourse below the structures, a gang of men was butchering the four gazelles Bak and his Medjays had delivered at midday.

Vultures soared overhead and a jackal barked, birds and beast alike alerted by the metallic stench of blood carried aloft by the gentle breeze.

"I, too, prayed," Imsiba said grimly. "Each time Nebwa took men from his camp to search the wadis for tribesmen, I feared they'd stumble on you and only the carrion creatures would know what fate befell you."

"Not a man among us failed to think a similar thought," Bak admitted. "We marched many long hours before we began the hunt." He turned away from the camp and headed down the wadi toward the mine. "Tell me, Imsiba. What brought happiness back to Roy's heart?"

The Medjay's expression grew perplexed. "Initially I thought him relieved because you'd gone. But later, when he heard you'd returned, he seemed not to care."

"Who spoke with him? Which of our suspects could've set his heart at ease?"

Imsiba snorted his disgust. "All of them. He hasn't enough to do through much of the day and he's not a man to gladly spend time alone. He searched out all those who had the leisure to listen to his jokes." He plodded on a dozen paces, added, "Nebwa spoke with him more often than most. He enjoys that kind of humor and can listen to Roy's tales well beyond a time when any other man would fall asleep from boredom."

"All four?" Bak queried Imsiba with a glance. "Harmose returned from the well with the donkeys?"

"Two days ago," Imsiba admitted. "As he and his fellow archers have had no rest since leaving Buhen, they remained behind while other guards went with the drovers to fill the jars another time."

Bak sighed. Once more the gods had conspired against him. He knew no more now than he had before.

True, he suspected Nebwa more than the others, but to discount any of them would be folly.

A short time later they reached the wadi floor below the mine, too close to the sharp eyes and ears of other men to speak further.

Wadjet-Renput, standing near the clustered lean-tos, shouted a welcome and beckoned them to his side. "You've done well, my young friend," he boomed, clapping Bak on the shoulder. "We'll make an offering to the lord Re in your favor tonight, of that you can be sure."

"To hunt in the desert is always a joy." As indeed it would have been, Bak thought, if he had had no other cares.

The overseer's expression turned rueful and his good hand moved as if of its own volition to his wasted arm. "I can no longer use the bow, but I well remember the pleasure of the hunt." Shrugging off regrets, he smiled. "Now that you've come back safe and well, the caravan will return to Buhen. If you're to go inside the mine, I suggest it be today."

"I'd like to see it, yes," Bak said, smiling. Imsiba looked less certain, but nodded.

Wadjet-Renput swung around, bellowed, "Roy!"

The scribe popped out of his lean-to and hurried to them. He greeted them effusively, his smile so broad and sly a blind man would have grown suspicious.

"My scribe will guide you." The overseer grinned at the scrawny clerk, teasing him. "He grows bored with so little to do, and his small size allows him to pass through the tunnels with no trouble. He's volunteered to go in my place."

The smile froze on Bak's face. He thought of Roy's renewed good spirits and wondered if this was the reason. Had the scribe and his confederate planned a fatal accident in the mine, with Bak as the victim? He had to take the risk. He doubted gold could be stolen before leaving the tunnel, but he must see for himself. Surely the miners, hapless prisoners though they were, would let no man be slain inside when they themselves would be blamed.

He sucked in his breath, heard himself say, "Your offer is most generous, Roy. I thank you." He glanced at Imsiba, who looked appalled. "I alone will go, Imsiba. You'll remain here to await our return."

"You'll not go without me!"

"What if a tunnel should collapse?" Bak asked, making it a joke, sneaking a look at the scribe. Roy gave no outward sign that such might be the case, but . . . "Our men would have no shepherd to care for their safety, and the knowledge we share would be lost to other men."

Imsiba took the hint and said no more. As he walked to the mouth of the mine with Bak and Roy, his face was grim and disapproving.

When they reached the gaping hole into the earth, the foreman whistled a signal. The sound was repeated by a bearer inside and by another and another until it faded away deep within the mine. The signal warned bearers and miners alike, Roy explained, that free men, not prisoners, were entering and would pass through to the end.

Bak gave Imsiba a reassuring smile, uttered a brief but fervent prayer to the lord Amon, and strode into the tunnel behind the scribe. His heart was pounding so loud he failed to hear the Medjay's farewell. A polished bronze mirror at the entrance caught the sun and threw it deeper into the passage, where it struck another mirror to light the next segment of tunnel. Each time they passed through the beam, a blackness deeper than the darkest night filled the passage ahead. Bak thanked the gods that Roy walked ahead of him instead of behind.

The tunnel began to slope upward and narrowed to the width of Bak's shoulders. The ceiling dropped so low in places he had to hunch over. Small pottery lamps replaced the mirrors as sources of light, their soft flames filling the passages with an eerie yellow glow. Bak bumped his head, scraped an arm, stumbled over the rough floor. With the space so cramped, the bearers had to relay the rock-filled baskets from one man to the next. They toiled like oxen, communicated with grunts. They were coated with yellowish grime, a mixture of dust and bitter-smelling sweat. When Bak and Roy passed, they shrank back into shallow alcoves or the pitch black mouths of old, abandoned secondary tunnels.

This mine, Roy told him, was deeper than most and more spacious, a better place for a prisoner to fulfill his sentence. If so, Bak thought, edging past an outcropping rock, he hated to think what the other mines were like.

They plodded on, veering slightly to right or left, following the vein of gold-bearing quartz. The tunnel shrank further, forcing them at times to bend at the waist or to sidle through spaces so narrow Bak feared he would get stuck. Sweat rolled off his body, as much from nervous strain as from the heat. He yearned to escape this nightmare place, but his mission drove him forward. As did the desire to face the trap he was certain the scribe meant to spring.

The heat grew more intense, the air more suffocat-

ing. The light ahead seemed brighter but cloudier.
They heard the rhythmic thunk of mallets on chisels,
which accounted for the dust floating around them.
They had reached the end of the tunnel.

Roy knelt so Bak could see beyond him. One begrimed man tended a fire, which blazed before the wall
at the head of the passage, heating the rock so it would
fracture and break. Three others knocked away flame-
blackened sections of wall, using wooden mallets and
heavy bronze chisels. Another smashed the fallen sections into smaller pieces to fill baskets setting at his
feet. Secondary tunnels, none more than a dozen paces
long, opened to right and left, where equal numbers of
begrimed men performed identical tasks. They worked
like wooden dolls with jointed legs and arms, expres-
sionless faces.

Bak watched as long as he could stand it, absorbing
every detail. He did not know which was worse: the
thick air, the reek of sweat, or the revulsion he felt for
men whose excessive greed or anger or licentious behavior had set them apart from their kind and, in the
end, had brought them lower than beasts of burden.
Yielding at last to the urge to flee, he tapped Roy's
shoulder to let him know he had seen enough and
headed back the way he had come. The nape of his
neck prickled with awareness of the scribe behind him,
and he slipped into the first secondary passage he came
to, more relieved than he cared to admit.

With a sly smile, the scribe hurried on ahead, barely
giving the bearers he met time to get out of the way.
His sudden haste worried Bak, who stumbled after him
as fast as he could, determined not to let him out of
sight. He wanted no surprises, such as Roy slipping

unseen into a secondary tunnel and leaping out with a weapon to strike him down from behind.

The tunnel broadened, the floor leveled out. The scribe strode past one mirror and the other, with Bak closing the distance between them. Ahead he saw an irregular oval of natural light, the mouth of the mine. He hastened on, drawn by the bright glow and the clean, pure air he longed for. Roy's speed slackened midway along the final passage. He clutched his side and grimaced as if a stitch had developed. Bak was suspicious; his instincts cried out for caution. He saw Imsiba, standing with the foreman a dozen paces beyond the exit, a relieved smile on his face. All was well outside, it seemed. The scribe walked on, holding his side. Bak followed close behind. A bearer entered the mine with an empty basket and stepped aside to let them pass. The foreman whistled, signaling the men deeper in the mine that they had the tunnel to themselves.

Throwing caution aside, Bak slipped past Roy and the bearer and hurried out through the mouth of the tunnel. As he stepped from shadow to sunlight, he heard the rumble of falling rock. Imsiba and the foreman looked upward; their faces froze. The Medjay yelled. Bak swung around, saw the hillside above collapsing. Sand, rocks of all sizes, and boulders were sliding, tumbling, bouncing toward the wadi floor, and he was directly in their path.

Imsiba hit him, the full weight of his body knocking Bak off his feet and away from the mouth of the mine. The force of the impact carried them off the shelf and they tumbled together to the wadi floor, bombarded by sand and rocks falling from above, enveloped in a cloud of dust. They scrambled to their feet and ducked

off to the side, away from the fall. The rumble subsided. A few isolated rocks continued to clatter downward, hidden within the cloud of dust billowing out
from the hillside. The cloud quickly broke up in the
breeze and drifted away, revealing the sloping mass of
rocks, boulders, and sand under which the mine entrance was buried.

Bak was appalled. Thirty, maybe more, prisoners
were trapped inside. "Summon our men!" he yelled,
scrambling up the slope.

Imsiba's whistle carried above the horrified murmurs of prisoners stumbling out of the lean-tos to
gather on the shelf near the base of the slide. The two
Medjays stationed on the slope opposite the mine relayed the signal, dropped their weapons, and half-ran,
half-slid down to the wadi floor. The rest of the men
appeared within moments and followed suit.

Standing on the shelf, Bak studied the fall and the
scarred hillside above. The shape of the summit had
changed. At least one large boulder no longer stood
where it had before. Below, other boulders had been
swept away as if by a torrential flood.

"That slide was no accident, my friend," Imsiba said
in a grim voice. "You were meant to die."

Bak tore his eyes from the peak and stared at the
mass covering the mine-mouth. "Did Roy follow me
out, Imsiba? Or did he step back to save himself?"

The question hung between them unanswered.

Chapter Fourteen

"Dig them out!" Wadjet-Renput yelled.

Prisoners and guards alike gawked at the slide, too stunned to think or act.

"Move, you vermin!" he bellowed. "Would you want to be buried alive?"

The men dived at the slide, frantically scrabbling at rocks and sand. They made almost no headway, merely shifted the debris from one place to another. Shouting a string of curses, the overseer grabbed a basket of gold-bearing rocks abandoned by a bearer, tipped its contents onto the ground, and shoved it into the hands of the closest man. Imsiba ran along the shelf, collecting more baskets. Bak organized the newly arrived Medjays and set all but two to work. Those two he sent to Roy's lean-to with orders to protect its contents with their lives. If the scribe no longer lived, his belongings might speak for him.

Wadjet-Renput quelled the miners' frenzy and split them into gangs, appointing guards and Medjays to lead them. Soldiers drawn by the shouts pitched in to help. The mound of fallen stone was soon covered with men toiling under Bak's sharp eyes, and the overseer was shouting commands at lines of men hauling away the debris.

The mound was bathed in heat. Dust clouded the air. The vultures widened their circle as if they sensed death within the mine. Empty baskets were filled to the brim and carried away. Sand and rocks slid beneath bare feet, sometimes carrying the men above into the arms of those below. Dislodged rocks clattered downward amid warning yells and nervous laughter. Smaller debris was scooped from around boulders that Imsiba prised loose with a lever and allowed, when all was clear, to roll into the wadi. Several times, the hulking young Medjay Kasaya shifted a boulder by brute force alone.

When the slide had been cleared to a quarter of its former size, a gap opened at the top, allowing fresh air to enter the tunnel. The men outside heard a muffled cheer from within. Buzzing with excitement, they labored on with renewed energy. The hole grew steadily larger until the trapped men were able to crawl out one at a time. Roy was not among them. A head count of bearers came up two short. After much hugging and thanking men and gods alike, the released miners, too shaken to toil on what remained of the slide, stumbled down to the wadi floor to await news of the missing trio.

The rescuers, grim-faced, fearful of what they might find, dug away more of the mound, levered away a boulder, and went to work on the rubble inside. A low moan led them to a man buried in loose sand and rocks, a bearer covered with bruises and groggy from a bump on the head, but otherwise unhurt. The second bearer, they found buried under the rubble beside a blood-stained boulder. He was breathing, but would

not long survive the great ugly gash that bared the
bones of his chest and shoulder.

They found Roy crushed beneath another boulder.
He would never speak again. Bak knelt beside the torn
and bloody form, half sick with horror and disappointment. The scribe, like Heby, had been doomed the
moment he had taken for himself the flesh of the lord
Re, but why, Bak wondered, did he have to die like
this, before he named the man who had planned the
thefts?

Roy's lean-to was bathed in sunlight. It's contents
looked no different than they had the day Bak had
watched the scribe receive the gold and weigh it. He
prayed to the lord Amon that in the ensuing days Roy
had not substituted one weight for another, or one bowl
or anything else. He sat on a flat stone the scribe had
used as a stool and inspected the scale, the weights,
and the baked clay cones, moving from one object to
another, studying each intently. On the hillside behind
him, the Medjays he had assigned to guard the lean-to
chatted in their own tongue. A tiny brown bird twittered atop a nearby lean-to while it searched for insects
among the twigs and rushes. The men at the mine,
clearing away the last of the slide debris, spoke with
voices muted by the deaths of their fellows.

Bak picked up one of three round-bottomed spouted
bowls Roy had used to collect the golden ore for
weighing. He noticed a slight discoloration on its
lower surface, both inside and out, but thought nothing
of it. The second bowl was a consistent reddish-brown.
The bottom of the third, like the first, was a shade
darker. This time the stain aroused his suspicions.
Praying that he held in his hand a key to the thefts, he

scratched the discolored interior surface with his fingernail. Bits of dried mud flaked off the baked clay.

Practically holding his breath, he scraped away the remainder of the thin mud veneer. A single flat bead remained in the center of the bowl. He wiped the sweat from his brow and, fairly certain of what lay beneath, pried it up. It plugged a hole, small enough to escape notice, large enough for small granules of gold to seep through. He turned the bowl over. The hole did not penetrate the discolored bottom surface. He was not disappointed; he had expected as much. With trembling fingers, he scraped off the dry mud skin, disclosing another small hole. He raised the bowl toward the sun, twisted it around a bit, and laughed aloud as he matched up the inner and outer holes. The bottom of the bowl was hollow.

He felt like shouting his joy to all the world. He knew at last how the gold was taken. Roy would coat the outer surface with mud and let it dry. The next time he used the bowl, bits of gold would trickle into the cavity from above. Later, alone and unseen, he would open the bottom hole and let the gold flow into a cone, which he would later hide on one of the donkeys bound for Buhen.

Bak resisted the urge to break the bowl and look at the cavity or to tamper with the second mud-coated bowl. He would save them until later, until the time came when he had to demonstrate to Tetynefer how the gold had been stolen before the eyes of many unsuspecting men. Of course, he had yet to identify the man responsible for the thefts and for Roy's death and the others, but he felt more certain of success than he had for many days.

He wrapped his trophies in the dirty cloth Roy had

used to erase his scribal mistakes. Heby must have made the bowls, forming the wet clay around molded lumps of wax that melted away when they were fired. He had seen no spouted bowls in Heby's house, but . . . the crucible shard! Yes, he had noticed a hollow at the bottom, a fault, he had assumed. Heby had used exactly the same method to melt the gold that Roy had used to steal it, forming the thin slabs in the false bottom of a crucible while a dozen or so coworkers toiled around him.

Bak clambered up the final steep, rocky incline and stood amid the jumble of outcropping stone and boulders that capped the summit above the mine. From high above the wadi, he watched the two Medjays return to their camp, one carrying the bundle containing the false-bottomed bowls. He was delighted at having found them, but could not help but castigate himself for his failure to question Roy the instant his suspicions were aroused. If he had not been so set on finding proof before he acted, the scribe would still be alive and he would know the name of the man responsible for murder and theft.

While Imsiba ascended the last few paces, Bak wiped the sweat from his face, the self-blame from his thoughts. At least he knew how the gold had been stolen, and with Roy dead, no more would be taken. He gazed down the hillside to the wadi floor below. Miners, guards, soldiers, and Medjays, all so filthy it was hard to tell them apart, were standing or sitting or squatting, their arms around each other's shoulders, their voices loud and raucous.

"Look at them," he said with a bemused smile. "Yesterday misery filled the miners' hearts; they walked like wooden dolls and none thought of any man but himself. Our men stood alone, with few soldiers willing to befriend them. Today they celebrate life together, sharing their small rations of beer with men they feel closer to than brothers."

Imsiba chuckled. "I think we Medjays have proved our worth today."

"Maybe not to Nebwa's satisfaction, but the miners won't forget." Bak clasped his sergeant's shoulder, teased, "If one among them is a teller of tall tales, you may someday be spoken of as heroes, men who sit among the gods."

Imsiba's cynical snort failed to hide the pleasure the thought gave him.

Bak sobered, eyed the boulder-strewn summit. "Come. Let's look for proof of what we suspect."

They sidled between two boulders and worked their way around a jagged slab of rock to the topmost point of the landslide. There they found two stone fangs the height of a man and, between them, a depression partially filled with sand. Both fangs showed signs of recent damage on the sides facing the shallow hole. The fresh abrasions and places where the stone had broken away were paler than the rock, which had been long exposed to the weather. The fangs had supported another tooth, which would ultimately have fallen through the natural process of erosion, but probably not for many years without help.

Bak knelt beside the depression and picked up a chunk of broken rock as thick as the palm of his hand. The boulder had been well-supported and could not have been easy to dislodge. Rocking forward, he dug through the sand. He found several bits of wood and a splinter half the length of his lower arm, rounded on one side as if torn from a pole. Someone had levered the boulder off the summit.

"I doubt the man who did this carried his lever back to camp," he said, holding up the splinter. "He'd not risk someone noticing."

Imsiba glanced toward the west, where the sun hung low over the horizon. "We'll soon be robbed of daylight, my friend. We must hurry if we're to find it."

They examined every square cubit of the summit, working as quickly and thoroughly as possible. They found nothing but a few indentations in the soft sand that might have been footprints.

Assuming the man who had set off the slide had intended to destroy the bowls in Roy's lean-to, they worked their way down the back side of a steep, irregular shoulder that dropped to the floor of the secondary wadi behind the shelters. Rocks and boulders of all sizes cluttered the slope, cracks and crevices abounded. Sharp, broken stone scraped their sandaled feet. The hot still air caked the dust on their sweaty bodies. They found no sign that another man had preceded them until, halfway to the wadi floor, the last lingering rays of the setting sun touched an object jammed into a narrow fissure, making it shine. Hurrying to it, they saw the tip of a polished bronze spear point.

"Will you bet a good, long drink of water that this isn't the lever we've been seeking?" Bak asked.

"You think me so foolish, my friend?"

Bak tugged the weapon free. The end of the shaft was broken, jagged. The splinter he had found on the summit fit snugly within a long gouge that followed the grain of the wood. The identifying symbol, much to his relief and Imsiba's, told them the weapon had come from the garrison arsenal rather than their own. Bak murmured a prayer of thanks to the lord Re and another to the lord Amon for good measure. The Medjay's long silence testified to the fervor with which he gave thanks.

The two men descended a mass of tumbled rocks and came upon a narrow trail which followed the contour of the hillside. Bak thought it a wild animal track, but a closer look told him many human feet had smoothed its surface.

"While you were hunting in the desert, Pashenuro came upon a shrine near the upper end of this wadi," Imsiba said. "This must be the path to reach it."

"A shrine?" Bak's eyes narrowed. "Let's take a look."

"Even if the man we hope to find went that way, he'd have gone long ago."

"True, but he may have left an offering to appease the god for the destruction he wrought on the mine and those trapped within. We might learn who he is by what he left."

The path rose steadily, taking them up the rough, narrow watercourse. Soon they saw, a hundred or so paces ahead, an uneven rock-hewn stairway rising to a deep semicircular bay atop a ledge. A movement caught Bak's eye, a bit of white. Someone was up there. The man who had hidden the spear? Would he have remained for so long?

Bak and Imsiba forgot their thirst, their bruised and aching feet. They raced along the path through the deepening shadow of evening. Gripping the damaged spear, Bak took the stairs two at a time and, with the Medjay at his side, burst onto the ledge. The archer

Harmose was there, kneeling at the rear of the bay, his head bowed. Imsiba pulled up short, his sandal skidding on the gritty floor. Harmose swung around, startled, and clutched the dagger at his waist. He saw who they were, his hand fell from the weapon, and he rose to his feet.

"I thought no one near," he said with a sheepish smile. "I should've known I'd not be alone for long."

Imsiba stared, looking surprised and rather confused.

"How long have you been here?" Bak demanded. "Why have you come?"

Harmose frowned, puzzled by the brusque questions. "I came to give thanks for the men whose lives were spared."

Bak walked deeper into the bay. Boulders lay on the slopes to right and left, most of them etched with graffiti left by men who had toiled in the mine through the passing years. In the center, behind the archer, he saw a small shrine carved in the living rock. The gray-brown body of a dead hare lay in the deep niche. Bak lifted it's head. It was limp, not long dead.

Imsiba relaxed, smiled at the archer. "We thought . . ."

"How long ago did you come?" Bak cut in, glaring a warning at the sergeant.

Harmose shrugged. "Not long. I knew nothing of the accident until after the tunnel had been opened. I saw the men come out and thought, while I was close by, to bend a knee in gratitude for their safety. Why do you ask?"

Bak scowled at the offering. Would the man who had caused the landslide have had the time to flush a hare? "Accident?" He shifted the spear so the archer could see the damaged end. "A man used this to unseat a boulder high above the mine-mouth. Now two men are dead."

Harmose's horrified eyes darted to Imsiba and back. "You think the slide deliberate? Surely you know not what you say!"

Could anyone pretend such shock, such revulsion? Bak glanced at Imsiba, who gave him an I-told-you-so look. The big Medjay obviously had no reservations about the man he had so recently made his friend.

"Imsiba and I have been high above this wadi since the slide was cleared. How did you get here unseen by either of us?"

Harmose could not help but realize the import of the question. He spoke in a voice tight with suppressed anger. "I came over that ridge." He pointed west, toward a point from which he could have seen the mine, but Bak and Imsiba could not have seen him. Clamping his mouth shut, he pivoted on his heel and strode to a boulder near the shrine. From a space alongside, he withdrew his bow and quiver and the limp bodies of five hares. He held the creatures up by the thong binding their rear legs together. "I spent much of the day hunting in the wadi west of here."

Bak knew from his own hunting excursion that to find six hares and slay them took much patience and many hours, especially in the heat of the day when small creatures hid from the sun and from birds of prey.

"I've taken no human lives," Harmose snapped. "Nor will I ever except on the field of battle."

"You must forgive the questions," Imsiba said quietly. "We had to ask, as you must know."

Bak left Imsiba to placate the archer and wandered

around the arc of boulders. He looked at the words scratched into the rocks but his thoughts were on Harmose, a man who had volunteered to help his Medjays should trouble arise with Nebwa's men. The archer behaved like an innocent man. The hares were newly slain. And Imsiba, usually a good judge of men, trusted him.

Bak stopped before a text so worn he had trouble reading it in the deepening twilight: "I came in year eleven of the reign of Khakaure Senusret to take the flesh of Re from this mine." The simple message, scratched on the stone in the far distant past, had been signed by a man called Nakht. The written name jarred Bak's memory, reminding him for the first time in many days of Commandant Nakht's office and the scrolls that had been disturbed by a man who could read. Harmose had been Nakht's translator, which made him seem an educated man. But basically he was an archer, and few archers knew how to read even the simplest words. Could Harmose?

He uttered a brief prayer to the ancient king Senusret, who had long ago joined the company of gods, then called to Imsiba and Harmose "This text must've been written when the mine was first worked." His excitement was real, but it had nothing to do with the ancient message. "Come, let me show you!"

Imsiba headed his way, openly puzzled by the odd summons. Harmose trailed behind as if suspicious.

Bak touched the faint symbols contained in an oval. "I think this reads Khakaure Senusret." He moved his finger to the right. "This could be year ten. And this . . ." He hesitated, glanced at the archer. "Can you make it out, Harmose?"

The archer flushed. "What kind of man are you? First you accuse me of wanton murder. Now you make light of me because I can't read. Why do you treat me so?"

Bak was certain no man could pretend so great a hurt and frustration. His suspicions vanished once and for all and he started to laugh. The gods had torn that wretched scribe Roy from his grasp, but they had given much in return. He had survived the landslide, he had the false-bottomed bowls, and he had at long last eliminated one of his four suspects.

He clasped the startled archer's shoulders. "Come back with us to our camp and share our evening meal. I've a tale to tell, and then you'll understand."

A delighted smile brightened Imsiba's face.

The long line of men and donkeys plodded across a broad, flat, dun-colored plain which simmered in the heat. Fine sand, disturbed by hooves and feet, rose around the caravan to smudge the clear blue sky. The hot erratic breeze licked up funnels of sand and sent them scudding across the valley floor. Vague images of water and trees and animals, floating near enough to the earth to seem real, tantalized the eye with promises of life where none existed.

Bak and Kasaya walked parallel to the column, well off to the side where the air was clean. They moved faster than the weary, dust-stained men and animals, overtaking one after another on their way to the head of the caravan. They had been on the trail for four days, rising before dawn to travel through the cooler hours of early morning, resting in the midday heat, and traveling again late into the night. From the start, Bak had made a practice of walking the length of the caravan each time they set out, morning and evening. He assumed Roy had passed on at least one cone of stolen gold before his death and that it had been hidden in one of the donkeys' loads for transport to Buhen. He hoped to find it.

"Kasaya!" a spearman yelled. "Come take this beast on your shoulders. We'd move twice as fast if you carried him."

The soldier was trudging along beside a black donkey laden with heavy jars filled with water. He and the rest of Mery's men had been spread out along the caravan by Nebwa to guard the animals and their cargo.

"Why don't you carry the water for him?" Kasaya retorted with an easy grin. "Give him a chance to complain of your slow pace." The young Medjay had become a favorite among the soldiers who had toiled alongside him on the landslide.

The good-natured banter continued as they walked along the column, relayed by men who had helped at the mine and many others as well, men who had remained neutral before, waiting to see which way the wind blew. Bak listened to the jokes and laughter as if they were music, paying little attention to the words but enjoying every note of the tune. His eyes were on the donkeys, his thoughts on the loads he had seen placed on their backs before daylight.

The rangy gray beast with an ugly gall on its shoulder carried food in its baskets: onions, lentils, dried fish. Slung from the back of the next in line, a dainty creature more black than gray, were two equally balanced bundles of spears, a portion of the arsenal. Three spearmen walking alongside joshed Kasaya. A sergeant tried half-heartedly to silence them with a scowl, but failed to do so.

Bak eyed the next donkey, a sullen creature laden

with the officers' tents. He knew from experience it nipped any man or beast who came near its vicious mouth. Mery was walking beside the fat, bow-legged drover. Bak nudged Kasaya and they veered toward the column.

"Mery!" Bak called. "I thought I'd find you at the head of the caravan with Paser and Nebwa."

The watch lieutenant grimaced. "When those two are together, I prefer the company of animals."

His hair was tousled and dusty, his well-formed body coated with sweat-streaked dirt. Bak took a perverse delight in Mery's disheveled appearance. He knew he looked no better, but if Azzia were to see them like this, she would not be comparing a fine-feathered oriole with an ordinary sparrow.

If she was alive and well.

He quashed the thought, refusing to allow his fear for her to distract him from his mission. "They're still bickering over the disposition of men?"

"That and everything else. Nebwa yearns to take his company into the desert in search of an enemy, and I pray each day he will. Paser gives an order, he countermands it. If we were raided we'd face disaster."

Kasaya, who had struck up a conversation with the drover, dropped back to walk alongside the plodding donkey. Crooning to it as if to a baby, he ran his hands over its shoulder and flank. By the time he left the animal, he would know every solid object it carried. The method was imperfect. He could not probe deep within the larger bundles and baskets without being noticed. It did, however, narrow the number of possible hiding places.

"And you?" Bak asked. "How do you fare?"

Mery shrugged. "I resent seeing my sentries turned

into caretakers of animals, but it does no good to complain."

"You must be proud of those who helped clear the mine. Did you see the mountain fall and the way they toiled to free the men inside?"

"I'd walked far down the wadi, so I knew not what had happened until later." Mery stared at an undulating row of hills on the distant horizon. His voice grew thick with emotion. "I mourned mistress Azzia and felt the need to be alone. I loved her, you see, and I'd hoped one day to make her my wife."

Bak's usual compassion failed him. He, too, feared the worst, but to take for granted that Azzia's fate was already sealed was unthinkable. Had Mery simply given up hope as his appearance suggested? Or was his conscience eating away at his heart because he had allowed the woman he loved to shoulder the blame for one of five deaths he had brought about?

"You must forgive me for speaking my thoughts," Bak said in a tone of friendly concern, "but mistress Azzia has traveled with her husband through many lands. She knows much of the world and can even read and write. Do you think she'd be content as the wife of an ordinary officer, a man whose skills are limited to the arts of war?"

"Except for this vile place, I've not been beyond the borders of Kemet," Mery admitted, "but I am a reasonably learned man. I used to write poetry for her." He glanced at Bak, flushed. "I dared not show it to her when she was wed to another, but I'd hoped, with Nakht no longer living . . ." His words tailed off, he sighed. "Now she's rejoined him in the netherworld— or soon will—and all my dreams have gone with her."

Bak wanted to silence the young officer with a blow.

Instead, he muttered an excuse and hurried on up the column, leaving Kasaya behind. He did not know which he thought more offensive: pessimism or misery born of selfishness. After he cooled down, after he convinced himself that Azzia might well be safe, he thought about what he had learned. Mery could read; therefore, he might be the man who had been stealing the gold. He seemed too weak, too easily broken by adversity, but his appearance could be feigned. A man so selfish would most certainly sacrifice his love to save himself.

"I find Buhen to be an interesting place," Bak said. "It's a city but not a city. A place where villagers from far and wide come for all the good things in life, yet the objects they consider desirable would be less than ordinary to those who dwell within the land of Kemet."

Nebwa dismissed the observation with a shrug. "Other than the fact that we're the largest garrison in Wawat, and Buhen's commandant administers all the fortresses along the Belly of Stones, it's no different than any other in this land."

"Commandant Nakht told me he thought to tame its frontier demeanor, to make it a city of women and children in addition to soldiers."

"I knew of his dream and wished him well."

Bak eyed the long stretch of desert ahead of them. Low, gently rounded ridges of sand punctuated by solitary blackish rock formations and, on the horizon, long table-like mounds that probably rose no more than ten paces above the surrounding landscape, offered a minimum of relief from the monotony. Some men might think the prospect dreary, but Bak rather liked its sparse beauty.

"If you were to become commandant, Nebwa, would you follow that dream?"

"Me? Commandant?" Nebwa's laugh boomed out. "I was born in this land and grew to manhood here. I've served in the army on the southern frontier from the age of fourteen. I've had neither the opportunity nor the desire to make friends in high places. Nor do I have the talent, if the truth be told."

Bak smothered a smile. No truer statement had he ever heard than the last one. "Come now, Nebwa. Don't you believe that you rather than Tetynefer should stand at the head of this garrison?"

Nebwa's eyes narrowed. "What are you doing, Bak? Are you trying to make a case against me as the slayer of Commandant Nakht?"

"I'm trying to learn who slew him, yes, but I can do that as easily by eliminating a man from suspicion as by pointing a finger at him."

Nebwa stopped, planted his hands on his hips, and glowered at his interrogator. "Make no mistake about it: never did I think to step into his sandals. He was one of the finest men I've ever known."

"Did he ever say he wished you to inherit his position?"

"No." Nebwa glanced back toward the unit of spearmen walking at the head of the caravan, saw how close they were, and stepped out of their path. "He said I might in time make a good garrison commander, but he believed the commandant of an administrative center like Buhen should be an educated man."

Bak gave him a sharp look. "Educated? What exactly did he mean by that?"

"I never had the time or the inclination to learn to

read and write. How could I? I've lived my life as a soldier, with no leisure for scholarly pursuits."

Bak chose not to enlighten the infantry officer, but if he was telling the truth—and who would lie about an inability to read?—he had just eliminated another man from his list of suspects.

"This desert is home to many men," Paser said, "yet we've trekked more than half the distance to Buhen and we've met no one. Where are they? Why have they not come to trade with us as they always do when we travel this path?"

"Men don't change their ways for no good reason." Harmose's face was dark with foreboding.

Bak sipped from the communal goatskin waterbag and let the warm, stale water roll around in his mouth. It barely moistened his tongue and failed altogether to quench his thirst. "My men believe the nomad shepherds have taken their flocks deep into the wadis behind us to a place where they'll be safe from theft and destruction."

Paser accepted the waterbag with a worried frown. "They either fear a tribe that preys on less warlike peoples or an army that must live off the land through which it passes."

All Paser's usual petty pretensions had vanished, erased by his concern for the welfare of the caravan. Bak liked him better for it. The thought was fleeting, swept away by a futile impatience. They could do nothing but watch and wait.

He stood up and climbed the rocky outcrop beside which the three of them had sought shelter from the midday heat. It provided a minimum of shade, but was better than the broad sand-swept plain where the men and donkeys were resting. From the top, he could see the entire camp rather than the small portion visible from their resting place. Drovers and soldiers alike lay in the shade of any object they could find: a shield, a swath of heavy cloth, a mat, anything to shelter them from the sun's heat. A dozen sentries walked the periphery, their feet and their spears dragging.

His glance shifted to an irregular, haze-shrouded escarpment far to the west. It rose from the valley floor like an impregnable wall, spreading to right and left as far as the eye could see. An ancient watercourse, invisible from so far away, cut through the plateau beyond. If they continued at their current pace, they would sleep at its mouth and pass through the next day. Deep and gorgelike in places, shallow with gently sloping walls at other locations, he thought it a perfect place for an ambush.

"If only Nebwa would trust my men!" His voice rang with frustration. "They should be scouting the land ahead, not plodding along behind the caravan, smothered by dust."

Paser's laugh was hard, cynical. "I've told him as much, and so has Mery. Like the rest of us, he senses mischief in the air, but he'll listen to no man but himself."

"He clings to his beliefs like plaster to a wall," Harmose added bitterly.

Bak eyed a thin smudge of dust dissolving in the air beyond the caravan. The cloud raised during the morning march had long since dissipated, so something more recent had disturbed the sand while he and the others had shared their skimpy meal. He was about to clamber down the outcrop to investigate when Imsiba broke out of a group of perhaps twenty men standing at the far edge of the encampment and beckoned frantically.

Certain something was amiss, Bak hastened through the mass of resting men and animals to the sergeant's side.

Imsiba flung him a quick but very troubled look and shouldered his way into the cluster of men, mostly soldiers, and two or three drovers. Bak followed close behind. The focus of attention was Nebwa, who stood with a grim-faced Mery and two nomad shepherds, tall rangy men sparsely clad in rags, powdered with the dust of travel. Nebwa was speaking with them in their own tongue. Bak knew no more than a dozen words that his men had taught him, but he could tell Nebwa was interrogating the pair. His tone was brisk, theirs reticent, the answers not easily drawn from them.

Bak saw none of the sly humor on their faces that he had found in Dedu and had learned to expect from the men of Wawat who dwelt near the river and Buhen. Maybe men of the desert were different than those who lived in villages, but he thought not. He glanced around, searching for the scraggly dogs that always trotted at the heels of shepherds. He saw none, nor did he see any sheep or goats they would have brought if they had come to trade. The scene did not ring true. Imsiba's dubious expression did nothing to allay his suspicions.

Nebwa gave a final nod of satisfaction and spoke to a sergeant standing nearby. "Bring them water. Four skins' full. They've earned that and more." His eyes darted toward Paser, who had hurried after Bak, and a broad smile settled on his face. "That old fool Tety-nefer was right after all! Can you believe it?"

"What are you saying?" Paser demanded. "What did they tell you?"

Nebwa, his eyes glittering with excitement, raised his baton in a gesture of jubilation. "The tribes have come together! They've formed an army! They're camped at a well a day's march south of here. If we leave right away, we'll have them within our grasp before sunset tomorrow."

Bak knew Nebwa longed for action, but to leave with that treacherous watercourse a mere half day's march ahead was absurd. "How can you be sure these men have told the truth? This could be a ruse to draw your infantry away."

"We've two times the number of donkeys we usually bring and many times the number of weapons." Paser's eyes flashed anger. "Not to mention the gold. I can think of no more desirable a prize to men like these."

Mery nodded vehemently. "You call Tetynefer a fool, but you propose to leave this caravan unprotected after hearing a tale no more credible than the one he heard."

"That was different," Nebwa said. "I had to pry the news from these men's lips. If they'd not been desperate for water, they'd have said nothing."

"Where are their flocks?" Bak asked. "Why did they not bring at least one ram to trade for what they need?"

"Did I not say they were desperate for water? They had to leave behind all they own so they could travel fast enough to intercept us."

"A nomad's life depends on his flock," Paser said. "He cares for it above all things. If this tale were true, one man would've come, not two. The other would've remained behind to see to the animals."

Nebwa waved off the objection. "You know as well as I that the women and children tend the animals."

He beckoned two approaching soldiers. Each had a wooden yoke balanced on his shoulders, with full waterbags suspended from either end. A drover helped transfer the yokes to the waiting shepherds, who strode off across the sandy plain, heading in a westerly direction.

"Rouse the men and arm them," Nebwa ordered his sergeant. "We leave within the hour."

Bak glared. "You can't leave this caravan unprotected!"

"It's folly!" Paser exclaimed.

Nebwa swung on Mery. "You and your men will stay here." His eyes slid toward Bak. "You'll stay, too, you and your wretched Medjays. Does that satisfy you?"

"How can you divide our forces like this?" Mery demanded.

"The tribesmen want a battle and I mean to give them one." Nebwa wheeled around, cutting off further argument, and strode away.

No, Bak thought, *you* want a battle and you fully intend to have one.

As the foremost rank of infantrymen marched out of the camp and Nebwa disappeared in a cloud of dust at their head, Bak drew his sergeant aside. "Those nomad shepherds lied, Imsiba."

"They are no more shepherds than I am. They live off the toil of others—stealing, burning, killing." Imsiba's voice grew harsh with anger. "Men like them came to my village when I was a child. Well I remember the death and ruin they left behind. They burned our fields and gardens, carried off our flocks and all our young women, my sister among them."

"How would you like to balance the scales of justice?"

Imsiba eyed him with uncommon interest. "The thought pleases me exceedingly, my friend."

"I believe those so-called shepherds are part of a band of raiders." Bak glanced at Imsiba for confirmation, received a nod of agreement. "I'd guess their numbers are too small to risk an attack when Nebwa's infantry was with us, but are large enough to feel they can succeed with our forces weakened. I think we should give them the chance to try."

A hint of a smile touched the corners of Imsiba's mouth. "You mean to catch them in a snare while they try to snare us?"

"You must leave now, taking two other men with you, and follow them. Stay close on their heels, learn all you can, then come back to us with what you know. We must not go headlong into battle with no knowledge of what we face."

Chapter Fifteen

"Where are they?" Mery fretted. "Should not they have returned by now?"

"They'll come." Bak's voice betrayed no hint of his own worry.

"You don't think they've been captured, do you?"

Bak scowled at the young officer, whose anxiety had begun to wear on everyone around him. "Imsiba is too clever by far to allow himself and the others to be caught."

A donkey brayed as if mocking his words.

Cursing the beast, he pulled his wrap closer around himself and stepped out of the black shadow of the escarpment into the lesser darkness filling the mouth of the dry watercourse. The night was cold, the air so clear the stars seemed close enough to touch. The indistinct figures of men and animals bobbed and shifted in the eerie light before daybreak. The drovers swore at the fractious donkeys, their voices rising above the thunk of hooves on sand, the blowing and squealing and braying. Paser walked among them, overseeing the loading for the morning march. Harmose had drawn his archers aside to issue last-minute orders.

"What if we've guessed wrong?" Mery asked.

"What if the raiders plan to attack at the first bend in the wadi?"

"What if the lord Khepre fails to rise above the horizon?" Bak snapped. "What if the world is shrouded in darkness forever more?"

Mery recoiled at the sarcasm. "It's the waiting," he mumbled. "The thought of battle, the anticipation, makes me babble."

A sharp whistle pierced the night. Silence enveloped the camp, then the sounds of men and animals gradually resumed. The voices had changed pitch, quickened with tension.

"They've come!" Bak let the wrap fall from his shoulders and sprinted up the wadi in the direction from which the whistle had sounded.

Mery raced after him. Paser and Harmose broke away from their duties to join them. As they neared the apex of the wadi mouth, Imsiba emerged from the shadows. The two Medjays he had taken with him straggled behind, each holding a rope looped around the neck of a nearly naked tribesman with his hands bound behind his back. One prisoner grimaced with every wheezing breath; ribbons of torn flesh crisscrossed his back. The other walked with a limp, and dried blood coated the side of his face. They stood as erect as their injuries would allow, their pride damaged but apparently not crushed. They were not the pair who had prompted Nebwa and his infantry to go into the desert, but they were as tall and rangy, as caked with dust.

Bak clasped Imsiba's shoulders. "We expected you long ago. What kept you?"

Imsiba smiled. "We let the men we followed lead us to their camp, as you suggested. It was farther than we thought, but well worth the patience it took to get there."

"And you found . . . ?"

"Many men, not an honest shepherd among them. They were resting amid a scattering of boulders about three-fourths of the way along this wadi but to the north. Far enough from our path so any scouts we might send ahead would fail to find them." In a more ominous tone, he added, "Thirsty men they were. They drank all the water Nebwa sent, saving none for later."

"Which leaves no doubt of their intent," Harmose said grimly. "They expect to drink from the jars we carry."

"Did you get close enough to hear what they plan?" Paser asked. "Could you understand their words?"

"We understood enough." Imsiba nodded toward the prisoners. "With a small amount of persuasion, those two told us the rest."

"Why did you bring them here?" Mery's voice was taut, anxious. "Their companions will miss them, will come looking for them."

"They were sent to watch us"—Imsiba gave Bak a quick smile—"so I thought to give them a firsthand look."

"But what if . . . ?"

Bak raised a hand for silence. "We've not much time, Imsiba."

The big Medjay glanced around, spotted a patch of drifted sand a half-dozen paces away. He knelt beside it and the others hunkered around him. With a few deft strokes of his finger, he drew a rough map of the wadi, identifying verbally the landmarks they had passed on the journey from Buhen.

"Here," he said, driving his finger into the sand, "is

the place where the wadi narrows to pass through a granite inclusion. We should reach it by late afternoon." He broadened the line, forming an oval. "Beyond, the wadi opens into a bowl longer than its width. This wider place is where the boulders have rolled down from above, with no clear path for the donkeys and walls difficult if not impossible to climb. Farther on, the wadi narrows again and turns to the right." He glanced at Bak. "There they mean to block our path with sand and rocks."

"And while we take the time to clear it," Bak said in a grim voice, "they'll close the path behind us."

"Trapping every man among us, every donkey, in their snare," Paser added, though the conclusion was obvious.

Bak cursed beneath his breath. He had spent much of the night working out various schemes designed to capture a band of unruly tribesmen, men of action rather than thought. He had, it seemed, underestimated them.

He glanced at Imsiba. "Many men, you said. How many?"

"They outnumber us, I think, but not by much. In the dark, with most of them lying among the boulders and others scattered as sentries, it was impossible to count their numbers." Imsiba eyed the prisoners. "Those two claim they've two men to our one. I think they lie."

"A number we can't ignore," Bak said, thinking aloud, "a formidable force, but with our superior weapons and discipline . . ."

"Must we face them?" Mery asked.

"If we evade them now, they'll attack us somewhere else. With so large and ungainly a caravan . . ." Paser shook his head, cursed. "I fear many of us will be slain or injured and we'll lose many animals."

"I say we wait here for Nebwa," Mery said. "He'll not be gone for long. He took only enough water for two days."

Paser snorted. "Each day we wait, our supplies dwindle. Would you have us cower here, and march on to Buhen with no food or water?"

"I'd rather die in an honest battle," Harmose said.

While they argued, Bak stared at Imsiba's map, letting their words drift around him. He visualized the wadi from end to end as he remembered it from their outbound journey. A clever man, he thought, should be able to turn the situation to the caravan's advantage. Yet try as he might he could think of no way to do so. He had no training in this type of warfare, no concept of fighting with so few spearmen and archers and no chariotry, no knowledge of battling the enemy in a confined space with limited means of escape. Should he try to draw the tribesmen into the open, where he could plan a battle in the manner he knew? No. As Paser had said, too many lives would be lost and there'd be no way to protect the donkeys.

He thought of the raiders' chieftain, a man he felt sure was very clever indeed. What would he do if he walked in their sandals? Attack from a secret place. What secret place? Bak turned his thoughts upside down, shoved aside his knowledge of conventional warfare. The voices ebbed and flowed around him, with only Imsiba sitting silent and expectant.

"We must walk into their trap." Bak's eyes, glinting with conviction, swept around the ring of men. "They'll attack, intent on their prize, and give us the chance to take them, each and every one."

"Have you gone mad?" Paser exclaimed. "The instant they close the wadi behind us, we'll be as helpless as ants in a bowl of honey."

"I know of what I speak. Have you forgotten? I trained as a soldier, not a policeman."

Paser arched an eyebrow. "You learned the arts of war with the regiment of Amon, where five thousand men fought mock battles in the open desert. In these wadis, warfare is reduced to little more than brawls. More deadly, to be sure, and with more to lose, but all the training in the world can't take the place of experience."

"Hear me out," Bak insisted. "If you think I err, we'll work out another way."

"There's no other way," Mery said. "We must stay here and wait for Nebwa."

"We can't stay," Paser snapped. "We've just enough supplies to get us back to Buhen with no days wasted. We'd do better to climb out of this wadi and follow its course well to the south across the plateau. We'd have a battle, I've no doubt, but at least we'd be out in the open and they'd not be able to approach by stealth."

"We'd lose half the donkeys and supplies in the dunes and wadis we must cross." Harmose shook his head. "I say we listen to Bak. We've nothing to lose, maybe much to gain."

"To deliberately walk into a trap?" Paser barked out a cynical laugh. "It makes no sense."

"Both your plan and Mery's would be costly, too costly," Bak said. "My plan, should we carry it through to success, would save the caravan and would also gain us prisoners, men we can send to Waset to serve our sovereign and the lord Amon."

"Nebwa thinks us poor soldiers." Imsiba spoke to

Harmose, but Bak was sure his words were meant for
Paser. "To win a battle and take prisoners while he fol-
lows the wind would fill my heart with joy."

Paser eyed the Medjay a moment and a smile spread
across his face. "All right, Bak. Let's hear what you
have to say."

Bak glanced to the east, where a faint glow in the sky
announced the coming of day. He swept his hand across
Imsiba's map and in its place began to draw another.

A man coughed, a tribesman hidden on the clifftop
fifteen or so paces above Bak. The man's proximity
worried him. As long as he remained where he was,
crouched in a cleft of the broken wall of rock, he could
not be seen. Later, when he had to leave his hiding-
place, he would be an easy target for a man with a bow
looking down upon him.

Sweat poured from Bak's dirt-stained body. His
mouth was so dry not even the stone he held on his
tongue could slake his thirst. His over-taxed muscles
knotted each time he sat still for any length of time. Yet
as he eyed the wadi below, his discomfort seemed a
small price to pay for the sense of satisfaction he felt.

From his perch high above the elongated bowl,
he could see to his left the place where the ancient
channel sliced through the granite inclusion. Paser
would soon lead the caravan through the narrow cut.
To the west, below the glaring orange sun, he could see
the mouth of the outgoing trail, which vanished at the
right-hand bend. He and his men had found it blocked
when they arrived.

The bowl itself, three hundred paces long and half as
wide, was ringed by sandstone cliffs. Their high rock
faces, battered by sun and wind, had broken away

through the ages, forming huge solidified piles of debris which sloped diagonally to the wadi floor. Sharp, treacherous shards of stone paved the incline on the side of the bowl where Bak waited. Fine sand blanketed most of the opposite slope. Recently fallen rocks and boulders dotted the surfaces of both. The wadi floor was a maze of boulders, many larger than a man. A dozen pale, snake-like fingers of sand marked the course of the water that surged through the boulder field on the rare occasions when rain pelted the surrounding plateau.

The wadi was empty, silent except for the sporadic chirping of a kite. No creature moved. No breath of air rippled the sand on the opposite slope, which was unmarked by feet or hooves.

The quiet, the serenity were a sham. The raiders had gathered at the top of an ancient landslide which broke through the cliff not far from the outgoing, westbound trail. From there, they could swoop down on the caravan, protected by the glare of the sun at their backs. Others, armed with bows like the man above, were scattered along the clifftops.

The bowman coughed as loud as before, affirming the raiders' confidence that they alone occupied the area. The sound, worrisome as it was, brought a smile to Bak's face. His Medjays and most of Harmose's archers, forty-five men in all, were concealed in the cracks and crevices along the base of the cliffs. Pashenuro and another man were hidden on the plateau above, serving as lookouts.

Each time he thought of the day's effort, his heart swelled with pride. The men had outdone themselves, as he was sure they would in the heat of battle. He, Imsiba, Harmose, and the others had left the caravan at daybreak. With no animals to slow their pace, they had reached the bowl before midday. A thorough search had revealed no tribesmen near the wadi. They had gone back to their camp, confident the caravan would walk into their trap.

Bak had sent a couple of his Medjays to keep an eye on that camp, a couple more to make sure no other tribesmen came to relieve the men Imsiba had captured, and two others to search out hiding places along the cliffs. The rest of the men had toiled in the boulder field, shifting the heavy stones a quarter-cubit here, a cubit there, making enough space among the boulders to admit all the laden donkeys, taking care that the wadi floor appeared undisturbed from above. Rocks of a more manageable size had been stowed near the periphery, where they could be quickly lifted in place to form a breastwork. Bak's final act when he learned the raiders had left their camp had been to send his men to their battle stations and dispatch a messenger to Paser.

A large rock fell from the cliff somewhere to the left and clattered down to the slope below. The sound was followed by the quick chirp of a startled kite. Pashenuro's signal. The caravan was approaching. Grabbing his spear and cowhide shield, Bak scrambled to his feet. He leaned forward, careful to keep his head in the shadow, and peered toward the cut through the granite inclusion. The time crawled. He shifted his weight, wiped the sweat from his face. The man above him coughed. How, he wondered, am I going to get out of here?

Paser strode into the sunny bowl and followed the broadest stream of sand into the boulder field. A couple of soldiers, a drover, and a gray-black donkey followed close behind. The men were talking among themselves, laughing. Other men and animals appeared, Mery among them, forming a procession behind the caravan officer. Paser walked tall and straight, chatting with the men at his heels. He never hesitated, never gave a hint he expected an attack. Nor did Mery or any of the other men. Bak watched their performance with admiration. For so many to knowingly walk into danger and give no sign of the fear they undoubtedly felt touched him deeply. He offered a fervent prayer to the lord Amon that their faith in his plan would not lead one man among them to the netherworld.

Paser disappeared in the mouth of the outgoing trail. More than half the column was plodding across the boulder field; the remainder had yet to pass through the cut. Bak willed them to hurry, prayed the raiders would not attack until every man and animal had entered the bowl. So intent was he on the scene below, he barely noticed the pebbles rattling down the cliff face from above.

The drover who had followed Paser led the gray-black donkey back into the bowl. Mery intercepted him at the base of the landslide where the raiders were waiting. The watch lieutenant may have felt fear, but he played his part to perfection. He stood with his back to the tribal army, heard the drover out, issued orders. His words were lost in the distance, but his gestures were clear: the trail ahead was blocked; the members of the caravan should disperse among the boulders and rest.

The message was passed on, rippling along the length of the procession. Those at the front turned around, forming a knot of men and animals among the boulders. Bak held his breath, expecting the tribesmen to recognize their vulnerability and take advantage.

Mery, standing firm, bawled an order that quickly untied the knot and spread the men out, making room for the rest entering the bowl. Releasing the air in his breast, Bak eyed the young officer with a new respect.

The caravan broke apart. The men with laden donkeys drifted toward the center of the boulder field. Those entering the bowl through the incoming cut joined them one after another. Mery's spearmen and the few archers Harmose had left with the caravan flopped down in whatever patch of shade they could find. As if by chance, most collected at the end closest to the concealed raiders.

Bak forgot his physical discomfort, the bowman above him, everything but the upcoming attack. Though he had never engaged in actual combat, he was not afraid. Rather, he felt the same sense of anticipation, the same excitement he had felt each time the regiment of Amon had practiced the arts of war. Those mock battles had been as hard and dangerous, as deadly to careless men, as facing a real enemy.

A white jenny cleared the cut. Her color signaled to the men concealed around the bowl that she was the last animal in the procession. A half-dozen men brought up the rear, all of them dark skinned. Bak smothered his laughter. One was a Medjay, the man he had sent with the message. The others were men of Kemet, their bodies smeared with charcoal. He wondered who had thought of that. Paser, most likely.

A muffled cough swept the smile from his face. He had told the men to remain hidden until he emerged from the cleft. But as soon as he stepped out where they could see him, the man atop the cliff would sink an arrow into his back. He hefted his spear, testing its balance. To drop an enemy on level ground was easy, to heave the weapon fifteen paces at a man almost directly above was an impossible feat.

A single blood-curdling yell ruptured the quiet.

The raiders swept down the landslide, dark silhouettes pouring forth from the glare. They screamed like wild men to make themselves seem fiercer. Ten or more broke to their right to seal Paser's small band in the narrow, outgoing trail. The rest raced at the boulder field. Dust rose around their pelting feet, enveloping all but the leaders in a pale roiling cloud. Donkeys brayed, terrified by the clamor.

Bak had to show himself. He shifted the spear to his left hand and scooped up a rock bigger than his fist. Muttering a hasty prayer to the lord Amon, he dove out of the cleft and swung around, raising his shield against the arrow he expected. He spotted the tribesman above, could see the surprise on his face as he realized Bak had been below him all along. The man swung his bow down and pulled the string taut. Bak heaved the rock, striking the bowman's chest. The arrow flew wide. The raider jerked another missile from his quiver, recoiled, and collapsed on the rim. Bow and arrow fell from his hand and clattered down the cliff-face. Bak gaped at the man, who was trying to scramble away. An ax was embedded in his shoulder. Pashenuro peered over the edge, waved, and grabbed the injured man's wrist to pull him out of sight.

Bak pivoted to face the bowl. The men he commanded had left their hiding places. A few archers had taken a stand to pick off bowmen who dared show themselves on the rim above. The rest were working their way down the slopes all around the bowl, darting from one bit of cover to another. Each time they stopped, they fired arrows into the cloud rising around the raiders, who were trying to penetrate the western edge of the boulder field, their wild shouts spreading terror among the donkeys. The creatures screamed, reared, fought to break free.

Fine sand whirled around the men on the opposite slope, making them hard to see. The incline where Bak stood was a mixed blessing. No dust filled the air to offer cover, but at least the descending men could see and breathe.

He dashed toward the wadi floor, setting off a miniature slide of loose, chattering stones. More than a dozen archers were spread across the slope, racing downhill, ducking into shelter, firing their weapons. Bak thought he saw arrows strike home, but the whirling dust made it impossible to be sure. About halfway down the incline, a shower of missiles rose from the enemy ranks, pelting the slopes around Bak and his men. He threw himself behind a thick stone slab. The archer to his left fell beside an outcropping rock, moaned. Other men dropped, whether to save themselves or from injury, Bak could not tell.

Across the bowl, he identified Harmose, zigzagging through the sand, raising a vaporous trail behind him. An archer flopped onto the sand, which erupted around him, and dug himself in behind an outcrop too small to shelter a hare. Kasaya darted to a fallen man, grabbed his arm, and pulled him to safety. A cloud rising at the west end of the bowl signaled heavy fighting. Bak assumed Imsiba and a handful of men were trying to relieve Paser.

In the dry streambed below, the tribesmen's charge had been halted by the spearmen who stood behind the crude, hastily constructed breastwork. The yelling had ceased with the need to save every breath for the labor of combat, but the donkeys, terrified by the clash of weapons and the smell of blood, refused to be quieted.

Bak doubted the raiders would stand and fight for long at a location impossible to breach. They would spread out, working their way around the boulder field in search of another, weaker point to attack. He was certain they would find one. He had been an officer long enough to guess that, soldiers being soldiers, many of the men assigned to guard the flanks had been drawn by excitement to the forefront of the battle.

He no sooner had the thought than a stream of tribesmen emerged from the cloud and began to work their way along the outermost boulders under cover of their shields. He glanced toward the outgoing trail. The sun lay squashed on the horizon, its orange glow veiled by the rising dust. The mouth of the trail was shadowed, almost lost in the haze. Imsiba, he prayed, had relieved Paser, and their men had entered the fray.

Bak stood up and gave a piercing whistle to attract the attention of the men he commanded. Arrows flew from below, one nicking the edge of his shield. Those who heard his signal passed it on from one man to the next around the bowl. Harmose, half enveloped by dust, waved an acknowledgment. Bak raised an arm and swept it in a semicircle, motioning the men to his left to move down the slope. They ran in fits and starts from one stony refuge to another, forming an arc across the hillside with Bak at one end, the man farthest to the left at a point near the boulder field. Harmose's force on the opposite incline performed the same maneuver.

Bak whistled a second time, and, as the sun shrunk to a sliver, he swept both arms forward, ordering an advance along all fronts. He and his men began to move, closing on their foes. The men across the wadi did the same. Forced to make a stand on the lower slopes, the raiders were caught between Mery's spearmen inside the breastwork and the archers on the slopes above. Abandoning their offense, they turned around to retreat. They had nowhere to go. The route they had used to enter the bowl, the landslide, was blocked by Paser and Imsiba with their joined forces.

Some of the tribesmen surrendered, a few lay where they had fallen. The rest broke ranks and took off in all directions. Mery's spearmen scrambled over the breastwork to give chase. The line of archers swept friend and foe alike toward Imsiba and Paser. The battle deteriorated to a free-for-all, with pockets of men battling face-to-face.

Bak raced toward them, infected by excitement, drawn by the clatter of weapons striking shields, the grunts of fighting men, the cries of the wounded. A spear-wielding tribesman streaked with sweat and dust broke away from his fellows and charged him. Bak sidestepped and deflected the deadly point with his shield. Too close together to thrust their weapons effectively, they leaped forward, shields clashing. Bak pressed his assailant backward with the strength of a victor. The tribesman, with the desperate tenacity of the vanquished, twisted away and leaped to the side, ready to drive his spear home.

Bak raised his shield to ward off the thrust. An arrow sped from out of nowhere and lodged in the wooden frame. His assailant's spear splintered the shaft, driving the arrowhead deeper. The tribesman, looking as startled as Bak, jerked his weapon back to strike again. Bak danced half around, feinted with his spear. A second arrow flew over his shoulder and lodged in his opponent's upper arm. The tribesman gave a strangled curse; the spear slid from his hand and rolled downhill out of his reach. He let his shield fall and slumped to his knees in a gesture of surrender.

Bak dropped to a crouch beside the man and swung his shield around to protect them both should another missile fly their way. None came. The battle was over, the dust settling, the donkeys quieting down.

Clusters of men were descending the slopes, soldiers bringing in tribesmen who had tried to run away. The men in and around the boulder field were disarming captives and binding their arms. Others had begun to collect the weapons strewn across the battleground. A few soldiers, a far greater number of raiders, sat on the ground, trying to staunch the flow of blood. The more badly injured lay among them, moaning for relief from their pain. A dozen or more lay motionless, enveloped in the silence of death. Bak saw a couple of his Medjays among the wounded, but neither looked badly hurt.

Imsiba, standing low on the opposite slope, waved to attract Bak's attention, then clasped his hands high above his head in celebration of victory. From his broad grin, Bak guessed the men in their company had suffered no serious casualties.

Delighted with their good fortune, he stood erect, let his shield slip to the ground, and raised his spear high, acknowledging their triumph. His prisoner yelled and lunged toward the shield, plowing into Bak and knocking him off his feet. As he toppled, something scraped his shoulder blade and he lost his spear. He rolled away from the tribesman, grabbed the weapon close to the point, and scrambled to his knees, ready to brain the man should he attack again.

He glimpsed Imsiba, running toward them through

the boulder field. He waved the sergeant off, for the man posed no threat. He lay sprawled on the ground, holding his right shoulder. Blood flowed between his fingers. The impact of his fall had torn the arrow from his flesh. The man spoke a few urgent words in his native tongue, his voice choked with pain, and stretched an arm toward the shield.

He wants the shield! Bak thought, and something struck me as I fell!

Cursing his slow wits, he spun around, caught the edge of the shield with one hand, and reached back with the other to touch his shoulder blade. His fingers came away bloody. The sweat from his hand made the open wound sting.

A cold chill raced up Bak's spine. If this man had not knocked him over . . . he dropped low beside his prisoner and held the shield upright in front of them both. Tense, wary, he glanced at the spent arrow and followed the course it must have traveled from the western end of the bowl. The dust was slow to settle there, making it difficult to see. A large group of men were milling around the wadi floor, too many for one among them to use a bow without being seen. He concentrated on the higher elevations, staring so hard his eyes watered. His patience was rewarded. A figure emerged from a clump of rocks near the landslide and scuttled through the haze to the denser cloud below. The grunt of his prisoner indicated that he, too, had seen the bowman.

Bak sucked in his breath and let it out in a long, slow hiss. The figure had been clad as a man of Kemet, not wearing the colorful leather kilt of a tribesman. The man who had stolen the gold had tried once more to take his life.

Harmose, whom he had already concluded was innocent, stood in the boulder field, supervising the men who were tying up the captives. Nebwa was far away in the desert. Which left Paser and Mery.

Not until he was sure the danger had passed did he stand up and help his prisoner to his feet. He placed a hand on the man's shoulder and smiled to reassure him. The look he got in return was wary and a bit puzzled. Bak wished with all his heart he could speak the man's tongue, could thank him properly.

As he led his prisoner to the boulder field, he examined the dry watercourse below, looking for Mery and Paser. He spotted them both in the thinning dust near the mouth of the outgoing trail. Neither held a bow, but such a weapon could have been easily enough disposed of. One of them, he was convinced, was the murderer he sought.

Chapter Sixteen

The caravan emerged from the wadi at daybreak the following morning. The plateau receded behind. An endless surface of golden sand spread out before them, broken at intervals by isolated, flat-topped rocky formations and crosscut by broad, shallow watercourses as dry as the desert through which they ran. This was the dreariest portion of the journey, yet men and donkeys alike walked with a lighter spirit than they had for many days. The animals sensed water ahead; the warriors, flushed with victory, knew the tall gates of Buhen lay less than two days' march away. Only the prisoners trod with little enthusiasm.

Not long after they stopped for their midday rest, they spotted a faint smudge in the sun-bleached sky far behind them. By the time they finished eating, the stain had grown larger, turned yellow like the sand from which it rose. They were being pursued by a fast-moving column of men. Maybe Nebwa and his infantry. Maybe another contingent of raiders. Tension spread through the camp. The men prepared for battle.

The cloud drew closer, expanded. Officers and men alike stood ready, their attention divided between the approaching force and a lookout posted atop an eroded rock monolith several hundred paces to their rear. When at last his mirror flashed an all-clear signal, apprehension melted away and good humor took its place. The men broke ranks and hurried back to their makeshift shelters, not to rest but to busy themselves with unnecessary tasks, to exchange delighted quips and grins. Not a man among them wanted to miss the look on Nebwa's face when he laid eyes on their many prisoners.

Bak slipped away to climb the low escarpment beside which they were camped. Imsiba, Harmose, and twenty archers were strung out along the rocky rim. In case of attack, they would have been in a perfect position to pick off enemy troops. Though no longer needed for its strategic position, it offered a panoramic view of the expanse of sand where Paser, Mery, and a dozen others awaited Nebwa's arrival.

"I'd not like to be in Nebwa's sandals today," Bak said, sitting on the rough, weathered stone beside Imsiba. He flexed his wounded shoulder, grimaced. The injury stung; the bandage wrapped around his upper torso, glued by grit and sweat to his flesh, itched.

"You should be among the men who greet him. If not for you, the caravan would've suffered a horrific loss. He should be made to know that."

"He'll know soon enough." Bak smiled a bit sheepishly. "The truth is that I wished to distance myself from Mery and Paser. Each time I'm with them, my thoughts go round in circles until I'm dizzy. One has done nothing; the other has slain five men." He expelled a derisive laugh. "Before yesterday's battle, I'd have sworn Paser the one and Mery too weak. When

facing the enemy, however, Mery stood up well, with
no lack of courage." He stared out over the camp, his
expression glum. "I don't know what to think, Imsiba."

They sat in silence, watching the dust-shrouded column. It passed the towering chunk of rock where the
lookout was posted, floundered across a broad, shallow
wadi, and advanced along the final stretch of sand, the
men marching at a killing pace. Bak identified Nebwa
in the lead, followed by a sergeant and the foremost
unit of spearmen. Those behind were enveloped in the
yellowish haze, their spear points glinting dully
through the dust.

"Do you think an army of tribesmen is hot on their
heels?" he asked in a wry voice.

Imsiba snorted. "I think, as they passed through the
place where we fought, they saw many signs of battle
and they mean to rescue us from the fierce tribesmen
they believe hold us captive."

As if to verify his guess, the column slowed to a
stumbling walk about two hundred paces away and
spread out across the sand, the men positioning themselves for battle. Paser waited. Not until Nebwa raised
his arm, preparing to signal his troops to attack, did he
lead the welcoming party out to meet the column. The
infantry officer hesitated for a long time, evidently sus-
pecting a ruse, but finally signaled his men to halt and
strode forward with a small party of his own. Imsiba
watched him with the expression of a man who had bit-
ten into something sour.

Bracing himself for an argument, Bak said, "I mean
to tell Nebwa about the gold, Imsiba, and all we've
learned since Nakht's death."

The Medjay's head swung around, his expression

incredulous. "You would take that one into your confidence? Him, of all people?"

"He's a good officer. A bit foolhardy, but . . ."

"Bah!" Imsiba's eyes burned with contempt. "His idea of soldiering is to charge at the enemy like a wild bullock gone mad with the pain of an arrow in its haunch."

Bak agreed—to a point. "I can well understand how you feel. I, too, hold him responsible for the mistrust and hatred our men have had to face. But this is not the time to harbor a grudge. We need the kind of help he alone can give."

"What of Harmose? Could he not help as much?"

Bak made no effort to hide his irritation. "We've looked for many days and have found no stolen gold among the supplies the donkeys carry. Either the scribe Roy passed on none this time—which I doubt—or it's hidden too deeply within a basket or bundle for us to lay our hands on easily. Can Harmose order a more thorough search?"

Imsiba gave a noncommittal grunt. Whether it denoted acquiescence or was intended to draw attention to the scene playing out below, Bak had no idea.

Nebwa, a dozen paces short of Paser's small band, was staring toward the camp. The men assigned to guard duty, a dozen of Bak's Medjays among them, were urging the captive tribesmen onto their feet. They stood up a few at a time, unwilling objects of a joke they well understood.

Bak thought the jest cruel, but would not have interfered even if he had been forewarned. Every man in the caravan had to share his precious food and water with the prisoners, tend their wounds, and help carry

the badly injured on litters. True, they would be rewarded later, when the captives were sent north to
Waset to serve Maatkare Hatshepsut and the lord
Amon. But now they had the right to celebrate their
victory in any way they chose short of slaying or
maiming the prisoners.

Nebwa stood dead still, apparently too stunned to
speak. Suddenly he began to laugh. The welcoming
party and the men in the camp added their voices to a
rising chorus. The good humor was infectious, prompt-
ing even Imsiba to join in. The men in Nebwa's company, drawn by curiosity, broke ranks to swarm toward
the source of the merriment. Their laughter was slower
to come, somewhat chagrined, but ultimately just as
hearty.

"Nebwa takes the joke well," Imsiba said.

Recognizing the words as a tacit admission that the
infantry officer might have a few worthy traits, Bak
smothered a smile.

After a long silence, Imsiba asked, "What task am I
to do that I must overlook his faults?"

"Once I convince him of the truth of my tale, I'm
certain he'll agree that we must search the caravan far
more thoroughly than we've been able to so far. I want
our men to conduct that search and I want you to lead
them."

Imsiba uttered a short, sharp laugh. "You expect the
gods to hand you a miracle, my friend. Nebwa would
never lay so much temptation before men he believes
dishonest at birth."

"I hope to make it his idea."

Imsiba's smile died before it was fully formed.
"What of Paser? Will he not interfere?"

"He must be drawn away. And Mery as well." Bak

eyed the pair walking with Nebwa toward the prisoners. "An archery contest might be a good way. I'd like to learn how skilled they are with the bow and how they react when hard pressed."

"You have the audacity of a priest," Nebwa growled.

In one fluid motion, he pulled an arrow from his quiver, seated it, drew the bowstring taut, and sent the missile hurtling through the air. Shouts of approval burst from the onlookers and competing archers. Harmose stood among the men who meant to compete, mostly archers and sergeants. The lieutenants Mery and Paser stood with them.

"You drag me into your dangerous game and only then do you admit . . ." Nebwa's eyes narrowed. "What else have you failed to tell me?"

Bak frowned at the black cowhide shield propped against a low hump of sand one hundred paces away. The arrow had struck dead center, joining four others Nebwa had fired off before them. All were buried so close together and so deep that they looked, from so far away, like a white flower in the center of the shield. Like all senior officers at Buhen, Nebwa used a composite bow, which was considerably more powerful than the ordinary bow used by lesser men. Except for Harmose and a couple of other worthy men who also carried the composite bow, the latter would compete in another match, facing no competition from the much better weapon.

Unlike most charioteers, who depended on the archers riding with them to strike down the enemy, Bak had some skill with the bow. Not nearly enough, however, to outshoot a man as talented as Nebwa. "I've held nothing back."

"How could you think me capable of so vile a deed?" Nebwa asked indignantly. "The goldsmith and your Medjay were names without faces; the scribe at the mine was of no account. But Commandant Nakht? I thought him the finest man who lived."

Bak glanced toward the camp, a sea of shelters touched with the golden glow of the late afternoon sun. Most had been abandoned by men who preferred the distraction of the contest over rest. The sole activity was at the far side, where the drovers were working among the donkeys. He itched to walk among them, but he could not be in two places at once. To display too much interest would make a lie of Nebwa's tale of redistributing the remaining food, water, and supplies so the weaker donkeys carried less weight. Imsiba was there with the other Medjays, helping, watching. None but them knew of the stolen gold, and it had been an easy matter to convince Nebwa that the secret should go no further.

Bak shook off his impatience. If there was any gold to find—and he prayed there was—Imsiba or one of the others would recover it. "Four men were in mistress Azzia's courtyard the evening I gave Ruru the package and the scroll. You were among them. I assumed, when you recognized Nakht's seal, that you knew how to read."

"I make no secret of my lack of learning."

"I've not been long in Wawat," Bak reminded him.

"Long enough," Nebwa said, scowling at the many prisoners confined between the escarpment and the camp.

Bak suspected any comment he made would be unwelcome, so he readied his weapon and released the arrow too quickly. It thunked into the shield a hand's length above Nebwa's arrows. He muttered an oath,

waited for the good-natured jeers he well deserved.
The spectators made no sound, disappointed, he
guessed, at so poor a showing from the man who had
planned their victory. He raised his bow, determined to
live up to their expectations, and fired the next missile,
taking greater care than before. It plowed through the
hide a hair's breadth above the clustered feathers. He
shot off three more in rapid succession, placing them
so close together they formed a bud atop Nebwa's
flower. The watching men shouted, not as loud as they
had for his opponent but with enough enthusiasm to let
him know he had redeemed himself.

"You seem not to have made too big a fool of yourself," Nebwa said, his good humor restored.

"I'll never have your skill," Bak admitted ruefully.

Nebwa laughed. "After you found the target, you
performed well enough. Not bad at all for a charioteer."

"A policeman," Bak said, laughing. He realized this
was the first time he had used the word to describe
himself, and, much to his surprise, it bothered him not
at all.

He had no time to dwell on the thought. The next
pair of archers, men who served as caravan guards,
were approaching to take his and Nebwa's places.
Mery's match with Harmose would follow. Before
their turn, Bak had to plant in the watch lieutenant's
heart, with Harmose's help, the seed of competition
and a desperate need to win.

As he and Nebwa rejoined the spectators, a youthful
soldier with a bandaged arm hurried to the target. He
pulled out the arrows and threw aside the shield, whose
center had been riddled by the sharp, pointed missiles.
After smoothing the disturbed sand, he set up a new
target, this one a deep reddish brown.

Contestants and onlookers alike took barely a moment to praise Nebwa and commiserate with Bak. Their thoughts were on the next contest, the archers' prowess, how the long, arduous journey might have affected their strength and accuracy. Bets were offered, negotiated, settled on. Nebwa dropped his bow and quiver on the sand and hastened away to stake a bronze dagger and a dozen other objects he had won by betting on himself to win his match with Bak. Paser, who had again usurped his authority, glared at the more senior officer each time he crossed his path. Mery made a few bets and wished competing archers luck with a slap on the back, but his smile was fixed, his voice too hearty.

Are his thoughts on stolen gold hidden among the supplies? Bak wondered. Is he thinking of Azzia and guilt-ridden for what he's done to her? He swallowed the anger rising in his throat and the fear for her safety that clutched his heart. Mery might not be the guilty man, he cautioned himself. He might simply be one who bends beneath the weight of misfortune, who loses hope too easily, who needs others close by to stiffen his spine. A man unworthy of so strong yet gentle a woman.

Harmose approached the young watch officer, a few words passed between them, and they slipped out of the crowd. Uttering a silent prayer to the lord Amon that the charade he and the archer had planned would reveal the truth, Bak laid his bow and quiver next to Nebwa's and strode toward the pair.

"It was an omen, Lieutenant Mery," he heard Harmose say. "I know it!"

Mery's face registered a confused wonder, doubt mixed with hope. "Can it be true?"

An arrow whished through the air and rammed into the target. The second contest had begun.

Harmose saw Bak approaching and smiled a greeting. "The lord Horus came to me in a dream last night, sir." His words were quick, excited. "I was telling Lieutenant Mery. It bodes well for mistress Azzia."

Bak feigned surprise, curiosity.

"He gave me wings," Harmose went on. "We soared together, the good god and I, across the sky to the west."

"He must favor you exceedingly," Bak said, acting suitably impressed.

"He must." Harmose paused as if the thought overwhelmed him. "We flew to Buhen. From high above I saw mistress Azzia, standing atop the wall, welcoming this caravan as it passed through the gate." He laughed, delighted. "She's not yet gone to Ma'am, sir!"

Bak wished with all his being that the tale were true. "Could the man who slew Commandant Nakht have been found?"

"No." Harmose looked deep within his memory and let the words tumble out. "When next I saw her, she was with a man, a bowman, a renowned warrior he was. This man, whose face I couldn't see, stood with her before the viceroy. He cared for her above all others, his love so strong and true the viceroy knew she must be innocent." Another pause and he added, "I saw her a third time, in the courtyard of the commandant's residence. She was weaving a swath of fine cloth for a man's tunic, her body heavy with his child."

Bak prayed Harmose had not gone too far, prayed the watch officer did not know Azzia was barren.

"Who was this warrior?" Mery demanded. "Bak?"

"He was there, I think, but . . ." Harmose shook his head. "No, he stood apart."

"Who could he have been?"

Bak relaxed. From the wistful look on Mery's face, he had no doubt the officer believed every word and wanted above all things to be identified as Azzia's lover.

Shouts, whistles, and clapping announced the end of the match. The bowmen, Bak saw, had planted every arrow inside a circle the size of a clenched fist. "You both value mistress Azzia over all other women. You're both reputed to be excellent marksmen, and you're next to compete with the bow. Could not the dream have meant that the better man will be the one to save her?"

Harmose's eyes widened. "Of course! Why did I not see so obvious a truth?"

"Who's next?" Nebwa yelled.

Harmose raised his bow and waved it. "We are. Lieutenant Mery and I."

"I'd wager my best pair of sandals that the man who saves her will be the one to win her heart," Bak said.

Mery paled, the scar at the corner of his lip flamed.

Harmose appeared eager but practical. "You'll take along the winner when you sail with her to Ma'am?"

Bak looked from one man to the other, his own face solemn. "I cannot change the fate the lord Horus has revealed."

The archer flashed a broad grin and strode away to face the target, walking with a brisk, confident step. Mery produced a distracted smile, stiffened his spine, and hurried after him.

Relieved the pretense was over, Bak glanced toward the camp, seeking reassurance that all was as it should be. Imsiba stood facing the archery field, talking across the back of a donkey to another man. Several Medjays were standing guard, the rest were helping the drovers. He could not see what they were doing, but Nebwa had told them to pour foodstuffs from one basket to another, water and wine from jar to jar. To rebundle extra weapons, clothing, and the officers' tents. Nothing would escape their sharp eyes, he knew, but would they find stolen gold?

Nebwa hastily settled on one last bet and rushed to Bak's side. "All went well?"

"Harmose could make a man believe night is day and day is night."

"That's the Medjay half of him." Nebwa's expression turned sour and he glanced toward the donkeys. "I know you trust your men, but . . ."

Will the poison never drain from his heart? Bak wondered. "If my Medjays find stolen gold, Nebwa, you'll hold it in your hands before darkness falls."

"Will I?"

An angry retort rose to Bak's lips, but he swallowed it. He had no wish to quarrel with the one man who could help him get under Paser's skin. Especially now, for the caravan officer was next in line to compete. He, like Mery, must be stretched as tight as his bowstring before he fired his first arrow.

An image of Mery's handsome face, drawn and tense, flashed before Bak's eyes. He felt a momentary guilt, which he quashed with a vision of Azzia standing before the viceroy and Nakht and Ruru lying lifeless on the floor of the commandant's residence. The thought strengthened his resolve to do whatever he had to do, no matter how distasteful.

He looked at Paser, standing among the wagering

men, speaking with a gangly archer whose skin was mottled by a peeling sunburn. "If he doesn't soon come to us, we must go to him."

"He'll come. I've trod too hard on his toes for him to register no complaint. My order to consolidate the supplies without so much as telling him I intended to do so should be the tiny flame that sets the village afire."

Bak detected a surprising lack of enthusiasm. "I thought you enjoyed baiting him."

"Baiting is one thing. The possibility that I might doom him is another."

Bak could think of nothing to say. He well understood Nebwa's qualms.

The caravan officer must have felt their gaze. He glanced toward them, and a ruddy flush spread across his face. Has nothing more than anger at Nebwa sent the blood to his cheeks? Bak wondered. Or is his anger mixed with fear that stolen gold will be discovered? That he himself will be named a thief and murderer?

Paser abandoned the archer without a word and wove a path through the betting men, his expression dark, smoldering. He stopped squarely in front of Nebwa. "I hope you're satisfied. Our food and supplies must now be scattered to the four winds. We'll not be on our way before dawn tomorrow."

"So be it," Nebwa said, shrugging.

"If we lose one man or donkey for lack of water, I'll take you before the new commandant and see you broken."

Nebwa spat on the ground near Paser's left foot. "Tired men fall away from a column, too. And my men need rest."

The bettors' voices ebbed to whispers. Harmose

stood facing the new target, bow poised, string taut. His arrow took wing and slashed through the center of the pale brown hide, burying itself to the feathers.

"They'd be no more weary than mine if you'd been less gullible," Paser snapped, "if you'd not marched them off to chase tribesmen who didn't exist."

Nebwa's expression turned stormy. "They grew tired when I hurried after you, thinking you needed help."

"How many are here, watching this match when they should be sleeping?"

"An hour or so of amusement never hurt anyone."

A second arrow slammed home and a third, peeling the feathers from the first, littering the sand with bits of white. Awed murmurs burst from the onlookers, silencing Nebwa and Paser, drawing their eyes to the match. Mery stood stiff and silent, his face unreadable from so far away. Bak prayed he had not already convinced himself he had no chance to win.

Harmose let fly his next arrow, which began to flutter the instant it left the bow. It thunked into the target a hand's breadth below the other three. Many of the onlookers, men who had bet on his skill, groaned. The archer scowled, fussed with the bowstring wound around the end of the weapon. Bak suppressed a smile. Harmose, he was sure, had planted the arrow exactly where he intended.

"After a few hours' sleep," he said, "I see no reason why Nebwa's men can't march throughout the night."

Paser's eyes raked him from head to toe. "You know nothing of the desert, Bak. We could at any time be overtaken by a storm or our water could go foul and the donkeys die of its poison."

"You worry like an old woman," Nebwa said, dis-

missing the possibility of catastrophe with a wave of
his hand.

Paser's cheeks turned fiery. "I see why Nakht no
longer allowed you to lead the caravans. He looked
into your heart and found you irresponsible."

Harmose sent his final arrow hurtling through the
air. It plowed into the shield within a hair's breadth of
the first three. The men who had backed him shouted
with glee; the rest yelled encouragement at Mery.

"If you think me so reckless in my duty," Nebwa
sneered, "why do you not write the worst to your
cousin, the high and mighty Senenmut? As our sovereign's toady, he commands far more power than any
fortress commandant—or viceroy, for that matter."

"Don't press me too hard, Nebwa. I'm loathe to use
my influence, but I will if I must."

Mery moved into position. The timing could not
have been better. Bak placed a hand on Paser's broad
shoulder, ushered him a few paces away from Nebwa,
and spoke as one friend to another. "Make no threats,
Paser, I beg you. You're a fine officer, brave beyond all
others. I'd not like to see you . . ."

He stopped deliberately, watched Mery pull back
the bowstring and release it. The missile flew straight
and true, sending more bits of feather raining down on
the sand.

Bak lowered his voice to a confidential murmur.
"The regiment of Amon stands at full strength an
hour's march from Waset and the royal house. The regiment of Ptah, they say, could take the northern capital
of Mennufer within a day." He paused, watched
Mery's second arrow take wing, cut through the shield
next to the first. "As you know perhaps better than

most, both regiments are commanded by Menkheperre Thutmose, whom many believe the rightful, sole heir to the throne." Mery pulled the bowstring taut. "I know nothing for a fact, but . . ."

A shrill, tooth-jarring whistle pierced the air. Paser's shoulder twitched beneath Bak's hand. Mery's bow jumped, sending the arrow high and wide to bury itself in the sand behind the target. One of the bettors moaned as if the missile had penetrated him instead. Bak swung away from Paser. He saw Imsiba weave a path through the mounds of supplies and drop from sight behind a donkey. He doubted gold had been found. The signal was intended to harry, not pass on information. With a noncommittal grunt, he turned back to the caravan officer.

"What I'm trying to say is this," he said. "Hold yourself far away from Senenmut. If what I've heard is true, he'll not long be the most powerful man in Kemet."

Paser's eyes were on Mery, his face impossible to read. "I'm not a blind man, Bak."

What does that mean? Bak wondered.

Mery wiped his brow with his hand and elevated his bow. His stance was wrong. All who watched could see he had given up the struggle. The arrow thudded into the target three fingers' breadth above those he had shot off before. He seated his final missile, raised the bow, and stood as if immobilized. Slowly he lowered his weapon, said something to Harmose, and clapped the archer on the shoulder. The winning gamblers laughed and shouted. The losers grumbled about the fool whose whistle had ruined Mery's concentration.

Paser pivoted on his heel and hastened to join the

sergeant with whom he would compete. Mery and Harmose walked back together, the former with a set smile in a haggard face.

Nebwa hurried to Bak's side. "Well? How did it go with Paser?"

Bak tore his gaze from Mery, spread his hands wide, shrugged. "If my words troubled him, he gave no sign."

Nebwa grunted, apparently not surprised.

The betting dragged on. The orange-red orb of the lord Re hugged the horizon, casting long shadows across the sand. Bak and Nebwa stood shoulder to shoulder, studying the two suspects. Paser chatted with the sergeant as if he had not a care in the world. Mery quickly withdrew from the onlookers to stand alone with his unhappiness. Nebwa shook his head, unable to decide which man might be guilty. Bak refused to speculate.

The sergeant raised his weapon. The bettors' voices tailed off. One arrow followed another, forming a tight knot at the center of a reddish shield. As he released the fourth missile, Imsiba let loose another ear-splitting whistle. The sergeant started, sending the arrow a finger's breadth too high. Bellowing a curse, he threw a murderous look toward the camp. Angry murmurs burst from the men who had bet on his skill. The sergeant jerked a final arrow from his quiver and drove it deep into the center of the feathery mass. Those who had backed him shouted with delight; the remainder yelled at Paser, urging him to win.

Bak closed his eyes and promised a host of offerings to the lord Amon if he allowed him to learn before the match ended what he needed to know. Deep down his suspicions were focusing on one man, and he wondered if the prayer should be more specific. No, he decided, for if I err, the god might give me no answer at all.

Paser lifted his bow. The instant before the arrow took flight, Imsiba's whistle tore through the still, calm air. As far as Bak could tell, Paser never flinched. The missile flew high nonetheless, slicing through the shield four fingers above those the sergeant had bunched together. Paser readied the weapon a second time. He hesitated as if awaiting another whistle, but finally let the arrow go. It plowed into the hide lower than the first, but still too high. The third shaved the edge of the sergeant's cluster. He steadied the bow for his next attempt. Bak had no doubt the arrow would fly true. He had seen men before who shot well enough to wound a creature of flesh and blood but had to find by trial and error the heart of the beast.

"Bak!" Imsiba's shout.

Paser, his arms steadier than the branches of a tree, sent the arrow straight and true. It thunked into the shield among those the sergeant had let fly. One or two onlookers grumbled at the distraction, the rest howled their approval of Paser.

Bak pivoted, saw Imsiba loping toward him and Nebwa. He prayed the big Medjay was bringing stolen gold and not merely pretending for the suspects' benefit.

"You found it?" Nebwa called.

Imsiba slid to a stop before them and, with a soft, deep-throated chuckle, grabbed Bak's wrist and dropped two pottery cones into his hand. Neither was impressed with the royal seal, nor had their weights been noted by the scribe Roy as they should have been. Nebwa gave an ecstatic yowl and clapped the Medjay on the back so hard he almost lost his balance. Bak laughed, partly because they had found the gold, partly because Nebwa had forgotten, temporarily if not for long, his dislike and mistrust of at least one Medjay.

Reminding himself that all was not yet over, he wheeled to watch the end of the match. Paser's weapon was armed and ready, his stance good, his arms steady. The arrow sped through the air and smashed into the target's heart. Paser said something to the sergeant, laughed.

Bak could not be sure and he had no proof, but he thought he knew the name of the guilty man. Curbing his elation lest he be premature, he beckoned his companions and headed back toward the camp.

"Where did you find the cones?" he asked Imsiba.

"Deep inside two baked clay images covered with written words to protect the men from serpents and scorpions, sickness, and dangerous wounds. The statues were hollow. The cones fit snug inside. A layer of dried clay smeared over the holes hid their contents."

"There must be a dozen or more of those things scattered through the caravan." Nebwa eyed the Medjay with a new respect. "I take them for granted, as do all the men. Never would I have thought to look inside."

"Nor would I," Imsiba admitted. "If Bak hadn't told us to look hardest at objects the goldsmith Heby could've molded or altered, I doubt we'd have found them."

Wheeling toward Bak, Nebwa swung a thumb in the general direction of the target. "Tell me. What did you learn from that?"

Bak looked for men close enough to eavesdrop. He found none. At least half the contestants and onlookers, including Mery and Paser, had gathered around the target. A bowman held it up so all could see and inspect the damage. From the heated words erupting from the group, Bak guessed they were settling a dispute over a wager. The remaining onlookers were standing as before, awaiting a new match.

"I believe Paser to be the man we've been seeking," Bak replied.

Nebwa stared at the men grouped around the target, his expression uncertain. "What did he do or say that I missed?"

"You watched both him and Mery, as I did. Of the two, who showed the greater strength of will? Who allowed nothing to move him from the task he had set himself?"

Imsiba nodded his understanding. "Lieutenant Mery is like a dry twig, easily broken. He might've slain Commandant Nakht and the goldsmith in fits of desperation, but he'd not have returned a second time to Heby's house. To find you there once would've torn the heart from him."

"I doubt he'd have hidden in the commandant's residence, laying in wait for Ruru," Bak said grimly. "Nor would he have climbed to the summit above the mine, where he could've been seen at any time. Or slipped away to fire arrows at me with half the men in the caravan looking on."

"A desperate man might find such courage," Nebwa said.

"He showed no fear when he walked into the trap the tribesmen set," Imsiba reminded them.

"He couldn't even summon the nerve to win a contest he thought would give him Azzia!" Bak said bitterly.

Nebwa drew back, surprised at the outburst. His

eyes narrowed and he seemed about to comment, but thought better of it. "When will we make Paser our prisoner?"

"We've no hard proof of his guilt."

"A good beating should start his tongue wagging."

Bak's laugh held no humor whatsoever. "Have you forgotten his cousin Senenmut? The man who stands close to Maatkare Hatshepsut by day and probably shares her bed at night?"

Nebwa muttered a curse. Imsiba gave an uncomfortable grunt.

Bak surprised them with a wry, almost modest smile. "I feared many times through the past weeks that I would never learn the name of the man we sought. Now that I know it—at least I believe I do—cannot the three of us, working together as we did today, conceive a way of establishing his guilt beyond doubt?"

Chapter Seventeen

Bak watched Paser, a dozen paces ahead, walk into the passageway through the towered gate that would take him inside the walls of Buhen. For the first time in two days, much of the tension drained from him.

Although the discovery of the unmarked cones had not been made public, Paser must have ascertained that the statues were missing. He was astute enough to realize he might soon be accused of murder and theft. Bak had thought him too bold and self-confident to abandon the gold he had slain for, the gold he had undoubtedly hidden somewhere inside the city. He had worried anyway. Especially when the caravan neared the river, the only practical escape route through the barren, wasted land.

With Paser safe inside Buhen and a half-dozen Medjay policemen dispersing around the fortress to close off the exits, he could set in motion a chain of events that would demonstrate once and for all that Paser rather than Mery was guilty of theft and murder. He hoped also to satisfy Senenmut that his cousin had been stealing gold and had slain five men to protect his secret.

Nodding to the sentry on duty, he paused at the base

of the tower and waited for the heavily guarded string
of donkeys carrying the marked cones of gold to follow Paser through the gate. He looked back at the harbor and the three quays jutting into the river like long
white fingers pointing toward the opposite shore and
the desert through which he hoped never again to
march. The naked masts of two broad-beamed cargo
ships rose above more than a dozen small vessels bob-
bing against the quay, disgorging soldiers, captives,
drovers, and donkeys. Nebwa's commands, the men's
good-natured curses, and the braying of nervous animals were lost in the excited clamor of garrison troops
and civilians flocking out of the city to watch the spec-
tacle. Word had spread quickly that a large number of
prisoners had been taken.

Bak knew he should be well-satisfied. He had
planned and won a battle. His Medjays had been accepted by almost every man who had journeyed with
the caravan. He had put an end to the thefts at the mine
and identified the man responsible. And, with the help
of the gods and a handful of mortals, he should be able
to prove Paser's guilt. Yet his sense of accomplishment
was blunted by concern for Azzia.

Cursing Hori for failing to meet his boat at the quay,
Bak plunged into the passage behind the last donkey.
After so many days on the burning desert, the dim corridor felt cool and soothing to his roughened, weathered skin. He strode on to the bright, hot, dusty street
beyond. The clean white buildings; the odors of fish,
cooking fuel, smoke, and sweat; the sharp yips of
scrapping dogs were a welcome relief after so many
endless days and nights of heat and dust and thirst. It
was good to be home. Home? he thought. Buhen? He
dismissed the idea as a flight of fancy and turned his

thoughts to the tasks ahead. He must learn Azzia's fate, lure Paser into his net, and when that was done, hold a council of war with his allies.

As he followed the gold laden donkeys up the street to the treasury, a stream of people hurried in the opposite direction, eager to see the soldiers and their human trophies. He was about to stop a man to ask about Azzia when he saw Paser enter the treasury, the domain of the chief scribe Kames. Gold and all other objects of value were stored there until a ship arrived to carry them downriver to Kemet.

Kames would know where Azzia was. Bak hastened along the line of donkeys, reaching the treasury door as Paser returned to the street.

"What are you doing here?" Paser asked, slapping the lead animal's gray flank, making it sidle around so he could get to the load it carried. "Should you not be preparing to march through the gate at the head of our victorious troops?"

Bak eyed the drover and guards, all close enough to hear. "Like you, I had another, more pressing task."

"So Nebwa alone will lead the procession." Paser expelled a contemptuous snort. "Does that not bother you?"

"Our archers and spearmen won the battle. I did nothing but point the way."

Paser gave him a long, thoughtful look. "I've known few men so modest." He burrowed deep inside a bundle tied to the donkey's back. Withdrawing two gold-filled cones, he held them out to Bak. A smile played at the corners of his lips. "Do you not trust me, Bak? Do you fear I'll keep a portion of this precious cargo for myself?"

He's taunting me! Bak thought, and produced a

smile of his own. "To take gold impressed with the royal seal would be foolhardy. You're not a foolish man."

"Why come to the treasury? Did you recover something of value during our journey that you mean to send on to the capital?"

Bak was amazed at the man's nerve. "I've nothing for Kames."

The two men stared at each other, Paser's expression speculative, Bak's as bland as bread without honey or oil or fruit to give it flavor.

"Paser!" Kames called. "Must I wait until day turns to night?"

The caravan officer jerked his eyes from Bak's, spun around, and carried the cones inside. Bak drew in a long breath, let it out slow and easy. He was sure Paser understood that he did not intend to turn the unmarked cones into the treasury. Did he believe the lie? Did he think all men as dishonest as he?

Bak followed him as far as the threshold. The treasury antechamber was small, cluttered with writing paraphernalia, a scale and weights, and baskets heaped with scrolls. Kames, lean and gray, presided from a low stool. He accepted one cone at a time and weighed it, his face grave, his demeanor so formal he turned the simple task into a ritual. A solemn young man seated on the floor, legs folded in front of him, scribbled the information Kames dictated. A beefy guard stood straddle-legged before a rear door which led to the valuable objects stored beyond.

Bak held his tongue until Paser edged past to collect another pair of cones. "Can you tell me, Kames, if Commandant Nakht's widow, mistress Azzia, is still within the walls of this city?"

Kames scowled. "You're the policeman, aren't you?"

Bak remembered the same tone of mild distaste the last time they had talked. "Will you tell me . . ."

"I'll be happy to answer your questions later. Tomorrow." Kames flicked his hand through the air as if brushing away a fly. "Leave us, sir. You're blocking the doorway."

Any other day, Bak would have laughed. Instead he muttered an oath beneath his breath, spun away, tapped Paser on the shoulder, and beckoned. "We must speak further. I've something in my possession that will be of interest to you."

Paser's eyes flitted to the treasury door. Bak thought he was going to refuse, but indecision turned to calculation and he said, "I must take these cones inside. Then we can talk."

With a curt nod, Bak slipped past the drover and lead donkey, and strode up the street, stopping well out of earshot of the men tending the animals and their cargo. His eyes were drawn to the commandant's residence, and his heart as well, but he had teased Paser and had to follow through without delay.

Leaning a shoulder against a wall, which was hot to the touch, he glanced at the western sky. The lord Re peered over the battlements, his long arms angling into the street as if to touch for one last time the golden bits of his divine flesh that the donkeys carried. The animals swished their tails and flung their heads around to nip at swarming flies.

The trickle of people hurrying to the quay had ceased. A few soldiers and scribes had begun to gather on the rooftops to watch the caravan's triumphant passage along this, the main thoroughfare. Three soldiers were chatting before the doorway of the commandant's residence. He saw no one on the roof, no sign of Azzia or her servants.

Paser emerged from the treasury and hurried to Bak's side. "Kames agreed to wait, but not for long. If you've something to say, say it."

"I'll come straight to the point." Glancing at the men on the nearby roofs, Bak lowered his voice and spoke with care so no eavesdropper would understand his meaning. "Before Nakht was slain, he left Mistress Azzia a legacy. In her confusion and grief, she gave it to me. It included three objects which, through much diligent effort, led me to a man of courage and guile."

Other than a slight flicker of the eyelids, Paser's face remained impassive.

"One object is of value for itself alone," Bak said. "The others, two scrolls, are not in themselves precious, but could be of worth to a man who wishes to lead a long life free of worry and fear."

"You were fortunate indeed to receive so generous a gift." Paser's tone was smooth, his dark eyes wary.

"In the beginning, I was content with my prize. Not for long, however. A diligent study of those scrolls suggested a path that, when once I set foot on it, proved to be long and arduous." Bak's voice turned flinty. "Five men died, one of my Medjays among them, and three attempts were made on my life." He nodded as if to himself. "At last I came upon a legacy of my own, two images containing, not merely spells to protect men from illness and physical harm, but a modest wealth that I must share with those who helped me find it."

"You sound like a man sorely used."

Bak bared his teeth in a humorless smile. "Given the proper incentive, I could forgive and forget."

Paser gave him a shrewd look. "What of the many men whose help you enlisted? Are their memories as faulty as yours?"

He's nibbling at the bait! Bak thought. "They believe the scribe Roy—and no other man or woman—knew of the objects they now share," he lied. "I alone know the full significance of Nakht's legacy, and I mean to keep it that way."

"I see."

Something about the way he spoke sent a chill up Bak's spine. "I'll be atop the outer wall tonight, on the tower overlooking the center quay. I'll have the scrolls with me. If you'd like to meet me there, I'm certain we can agree on a mutually advantageous exchange."

"So public and well-guarded a place?" Paser laughed. "I think not. If we're to meet at all . . ." He appeared to puzzle over his answer. "Somewhere along the river where no man will see us together. Upstream would be best, where the rocks reach into the water."

Where the goldsmith Heby was slain, Bak guessed. "So private and empty a place? Do you think I care so little for life?" He shook his head. "No! We'll meet . . ." He knew full well where he wanted to face Paser, but he frowned as if searching for an idea. "There," he pointed, "on the roof of the commandant's residence. When the moon reaches its highest point and the sentries can look down upon us."

Paser studied the building, suspicious. "How can I be sure you'll not have men hidden close by?"

"Darkness will have fallen long before we meet and most of the garrison will be fast asleep. You'll have plenty of time to inspect the surrounding streets and buildings should you feel the need."

Paser eyed him thoughtfully, letting the silence grow.

"One thing you should know," Bak said. "I've posted my Medjays at all the gates leading out of Buhen. I've instructed them to intercept everyone—officer, soldier, or civilian; man or woman—and examine each bundle and basket they carry, no matter how small or large. They're looking for weapons or any of the other garrison supplies so often taken outside these walls and traded to nearby villagers. If there's anything of value to be found, they'll find it."

"You've left me no option, it seems." Paser pivoted on his heel and walked toward the line of donkeys.

Bak had caught no more than a glimpse of the officer's face and the fierce defiance of a creature at bay, willing to fight to the death rather than let its captor snare it. I've hooked a crocodile, he thought, not a great fish that's helpless out of the water. He had expected no less, but the thought of confronting Paser in the dead of night sent another chill up his spine, this one radiating across his bandaged shoulders and around his rib cage.

Bak hurried along the street to the commandant's residence. Keeping himself alive was just one of his problems. He also had to convince Paser to go to his cache of gold and bring a portion back, and he had to wring a confession from his lips.

"Officer Bak!" Hori shouted from the rooftop.

He looked upward, as did the soldiers standing before the door. The scribe knelt at the edge of the roof, his youthful face aglow with excitement. Standing beside him were the three servants of the household: Lupaki, the old woman, the girl. And Azzia.

Bak's worries and fears melted away in the warmth of her smile. "You're here!"

"I owe much to mistress Iry." Azzia's voice was as soft and gentle as he remembered it. "She persuaded her husband to let me stay."

Bak glanced at the soldiers, who had begun to edge out into the street so they could see the roof and its occupants. He waved them back to the doorway, but was too happy at finding Azzia alive and well to notice their failure to obey.

"She convinced Tetynefer of your innocence?" he asked.

Hori's smile stretched all the way across his face. "She threatened him with divorce!"

A smile fluttered across Azzia's face, vanished. "If the breeze is fair, the viceroy will sail into Buhen before nightfall tomorrow. I'm to stand before him the moment he sees fit, probably the following day."

"He's bringing the new commandant," Hori explained.

Bak thanked the lord Amon for his good fortune. If the steward's wife had not intervened, if a storm had blown the caravan apart on the desert, if another group of tribesmen had attacked, he would not have arrived in time to save her.

Azzia knelt beside Hori. Her long reddish braid snaked over her shoulder and fell between her breasts. "We've heard many rumors since word came that you were waiting to be ferried across the river. We heard of the accident at the mine and the fierce battle you fought. So I know you've had much to think about since you left Buhen, but did you now and again give thought to the man who took my husband's life?"

"I believe I know his name."

Before she could question him further, Bak shot a warning glance at the listening men. Her nod told him she understood he could not speak freely.

Lupaki grabbed Hori and hugged him. The female servants fell on their knees and wept with joy.

"I thank your gods and mine," Azzia said. "And I thank you more than all of them." Her final words were muffled by tears, making a lie of the smile she tried to show him.

He did not know what to do or say. He longed to hold her close, to console her with his love, as he had done with many other women through the years. She would not welcome his embrace. She was too recent a widow, too fine a woman. He could not take advantage of the gift of life he hoped soon to give her.

The buzz of voices drew his eyes to the rooftops paralleling the street. Soldiers and civilians, men, women, and children were jostling for the best positions from which to watch the triumphant army and their prisoners enter the city. Paser, he saw, was removing the gold from the next to last donkey.

"You'd better go, sir." Hori was practically dancing with excitement. "After all the vile things that have been said about our Medjays, I can't wait to see you and Imsiba and all the others march at the head of the prisoners you took."

"I thought to let Nebwa . . ."

"You can't!" Hori exclaimed. "You won the battle. They say he wasn't even there!"

"You must enter this city with your men, Officer Bak." Azzia cleared the tears from her throat, brushed a hand across a wet cheek. "They've earned the right to walk tall and proud, all together, behind the man who led them to victory."

One of the soldiers who had been listening piped up, "I've followed Lieutenant Nebwa into the desert a dozen times. We've brought back prisoners—though not so many," he added ruefully. "Half the fun was marching behind him through that gate when we had something to show for our trouble."

Bak remembered the grueling practice sessions with the regiment of Amon and the joy he had shared with his men whether they won or lost. How could he have forgotten? To march past the residence, knowing Azzia was standing on the roof, watching, smiling at him, would increase that pleasure tenfold.

He grinned. "I'll return the instant the donkeys are inside their paddocks. We must talk."

He headed back toward the quay and his men. As he approached the donkeys in front of the treasury, he thought of Paser and the fearless way he had walked into the tribesmen's trap. He, too, had earned the right to march at the head of the procession, to have his brief moment of glory before being brought to his knees.

Bak checked, not for the first time, the dagger at his waist. The weapon slid easily into its sheath. His belt and kilt were too snug for it to catch on a stray bit of fabric should he need it quickly. Realizing he was fidgeting, he forced himself to sit still. He wanted to appear wary, not eager to do battle or fearful.

He sat midway on the open flight of stairs which rose from the commandant's residence to the walkway atop the battlements. He was clearly visible in the moonlight to the patrolling sentries—and would soon be to Paser, lurking somewhere in the building below.

For almost an hour, he had heard the infrequent signals his Medjays had given while they stalked the car-

avan officer: the call of a nightbird, the whine of a lost
puppy, the harsh yowl of a tomcat prowling for a mate.
The sounds had begun not long after their quarry had
slipped out of his quarters. They had signaled his as-
cent to the battlements, where he had stood for a long
time, studying the rooftops and lanes within the
citadel. They had marked his descent and followed his
slow progress as he made a careful and painstaking examination of the dark, deserted buildings in the vicin-
ity of the commandant's residence. The shriek of a
female cat mounted by a tom had warned Bak that the
man he awaited had entered the antechamber below.
Since then, time had dragged.

Bak scanned the roof—flat, ghostly white, empty.
His eyes probed the dark rectangular opening where
the stairway descended past Nakht's reception room to
the ground floor. He studied the larger, dimly lit square
of the courtyard. Paser could be watching him from the
stairwell or hiding among the potted trees and shrubs,
one shadow among many. Bak pictured Azzia and her
servants, lying awake and fearful, listening to the
stealthy footsteps of the man who had taken the life
most dear to them. He had wanted to move them elsewhere, but their absence would have aroused Paser's
suspicions. In fact, Azzia, brave beyond all other
women, had insisted he let her stay.

He surveyed the rooftops of the nearby blocks of
buildings. He saw no movement, heard only the usual
chorus of barking dogs. The bird, the puppy, the tomcat were silent. His hand inched toward his dagger. He
jerked it away and wiped the sweat from his face, cool
sweat in a chilly night. Will Paser never convince himself I'm here alone? he wondered.

A soft thud, the sound of baked clay bumping mudbrick. He started, almost laughed aloud. Paser was coming, climbing the stairs. He had caught his toe on the string Bak had stretched along a step, setting in motion a stemmed bowl.

Paser's head and shoulders burst out of the black stairwell. With barely a glance at Bak, he pivoted, making a fast but thorough inspection of the rooftop. Satisfied they were alone, he ascended to the open trapdoor and stepped onto the roof. He carried a spear. A sheathed dagger hung from his waist. Bak rose to his feet to give himself greater mobility.

Paser looked up at his adversary, safely out of reach of a quick thrust. "You're a careful man, Bak."

"I've underestimated you before. I know better now."

Paser eyed him with open curiosity. "Why did you have me march with you and Nebwa when the victorious troops entered these walls?" He tilted the spearpoint toward Bak, drawing attention to the sharp, deadly weapon. "Did you believe so generous an act would lower my defenses?"

"I doubt much of anything could weaken your instincts to survive, Paser." Bak kept a cautious eye on the spear. "You didn't hesitate to slay your accomplices Heby and Roy even though, without them, you no longer had any way of laying your hands on the precious ore from the mine. It's clear you value your life above all things."

Paser's laugh was as brittle as poorly made glass. "You understand me better than I thought."

"A man who hunts a dangerous beast must learn its habits."

"Is that meant to be a compliment?"

It depends on the beast, Bak thought, but the glittering spear point warned him not to press his luck. "If I thought you like the lowly jackal, a creature that slinks among the tombs, waiting to tear the flesh from the un- resisting dead, would I have taken such care to protect myself?"

Paser opened his mouth to respond, but Bak hurried on, "The night is growing short. I think it time we dis- cuss the scrolls mistress Azzia gave me."

"I can make no bargains until I see them." Paser held out his free hand. "Since you refuse to trust me, I sug- gest you throw them to me."

"I didn't bring them."

Paser tensed; he hefted his spear as if making ready to throw it.

Bak's hand flew to his dagger. "Think, Paser! Would I offer up the very objects that serve me as a shield?"

"You're despicable!"

"Fine words from one who's slain five men."

Bak slid his weapon from its sheath and raised it slowly, letting his opponent know he would use it if he must. Both men knew who held the advantage. A man could throw a lightweight dagger faster and truer from a hilltop than hurl a heavy spear from the valley below with the force and accuracy necessary to take a life.

"Set your spear at ease, Paser."

The caravan officer muttered an oath beneath his breath, swung the spear point high, and rammed the butt of the shaft on the rooftop with a solid thud. "What do you want from me?"

Bak let himself relax, but not too much. "Did Nakht let you read the scrolls when he called you into his of- fice the day of his death?"

"Do you jest? He told me of their existence, but left no doubt as to their contents."

"Good! We've no need to haggle over their worth."

"What do you want?" Paser repeated through gritted teeth.

"I'm not a greedy man." Bak's voice was smooth, generous. "For each scroll, I wish to receive a single bar of gold. I'll need a third bar for the document I prepared that relates in detail the path I took that led me to you."

"You swine!"

Bak made a tut-tut sound with his tongue. "I suggest we meet again within the hour. Here on this roof. I'll have the scrolls with me, that I promise, and I expect you to bring the gold. After the exchange is made, I'll withdraw my Medjays from the gates. If you choose to remain in Buhen, your life and mine will go on as before and I'll make no further demands. If you flee with the remainder of your prize, I'll do no more than go through the motions of tracking you down."

"If I fail to meet you here?"

"You'll not survive the night."

Paser glared, stretching the silence and the tension gripping Bak's heart. "All right." He swung away to plunge down the stairs.

"Leave your weapons behind," Bak called to the back of his head. "I'll make no trade with a man I can't safely approach."

Paser lost himself in the darkness. The baked clay bowl made no noise. He must have torn it from the step.

Bak stood quite still, alert to every sound no matter how ordinary: the hoot of an owl, barking dogs, the faint squeak of a rat. At last the tomcat yowled. Paser had left the building. Bak rammed his dagger into its sheath and slumped onto the step. He thanked the lord Amon for his help so far and prayed for additional favors. Only the god could allow the Medjays to blend into the dark and follow Paser unseen to the place where he had hidden the stolen gold. Only the god could lead Paser back to the rooftop and give him enough self-confidence to loosen his tongue.

Not until later did it occur to him that Paser had never once mentioned his powerful cousin, the high and mighty chief steward Senenmut.

Chapter Eighteen

The moon had passed over the battlements and the open stairway lay in shadow when next Bak heard the caterwauling tomcat. Relief flooded through him. He had told the Medjays who had been following Paser to give no signals after the caravan officer left the building, preferring to remain ignorant of his movements rather than risk raising his suspicions. The long silence had threatened to erode his confidence.

He had recovered the scrolls from their hiding place in the courtyard, grabbed a plugged jar filled with wheat he had found by the grindstone, and raced back to the roof. After mounding a portion of the grain near the stairwell opening, he had left the container on a lower step and climbed back up to his previous perch. Then he had waited, so still and silent that eight or nine rats had crept across the rooftop to devour the feast he had provided them.

Taking care not to frighten away the rodents, he shifted from one buttock to the other, touched for reassurance the scrolls on the step beside him, and fingered the handle of his dagger. Miniature rivers of sweat, cold and reeking of tension, trickled from beneath the bandage around his shoulder and upper chest. He

imagined Paser hidden in the shadows of the courtyard, studying him, searching for a sign of danger—or
an indication of weakness.

One of the feasting rats, the largest, lifted its head
and stared toward the stairwell. Bak sucked in his
breath, held it. The creature remained motionless, listening. Abruptly it let out a shrill squeak and shot
across the roof, away from the opening. Its mates
scampered in all directions, leaving nothing behind but
a scattered pile of grain. Paser's dark head rose to the
level of the rooftop.

Bak scrambled to his feet, vowing to thank his un-
witting allies with the wheat he had held in reserve.

If Paser noticed the grain, he gave no sign. As cautious as before, he climbed out of the stairwell and
stepped onto the roof. He carried no spear and the
sheath tied to his belt was empty. The absence of
weapons surprised Bak, troubled him.

"Have you brought the gold?" he asked.

"Here." Paser held out his right hand, displaying a
small, neat parcel wrapped in linen. "Where are the
scrolls?"

Bak nudged the three cylinders with his toe, shifting
them on the step so Paser could see them. "Unwrap the
package."

Paser folded back the corners of the fabric to display
three thin bars of dully gleaming metal, exactly like the
bar Nakht had left for Azzia to find. "Let me see the
scrolls. I must be sure they're what you say they are."

"You don't trust me, lieutenant?" Bak asked, forcing
a smile to hide his own mistrust. Buying time.

"No more than you do me, policeman."

Bak eyed the officer's short white kilt, so smooth
around the waist and hips he could conceal nothing in-

side bigger than a battle scar. "Lay your package on the stairway, on the highest step you can reach. I must be sure you've brought the flesh of the lord Re, not a lesser metal."

"I'll not walk to a place where you can jump me. We meet on level ground or not at all."

The demand was reasonable, but Bak hesitated. His instincts cried out, warning him to take care. Unfortunately, he could see no other way of making the exchange. "Stand away from the stairs. I've no more wish to be attacked than you do."

Paser backed away as directed, but stayed close enough to the opening to leap into the stairwell if threatened. Bak scooped up the scrolls with his left hand, leaving his right hand free to draw his dagger. Paser's failure to comment on the weapon added to his sense of unease.

They met near the trapdoor, two arms' length apart, close enough to trade one object for another, far enough to duck away from a sudden attack. Bak laid two scrolls on the step beside him and held out the third, the record of precious objects which had passed through Buhen on their way north to the capital. Paser took the document and handed over one golden bar.

"Tell me . . ." Bak eyed the ingot, caressed it with his fingertips to convince Paser of his greed. ". . . Did you set out to blame my Medjays when you used a spear from the police arsenal to slay your ally Heby?"

Paser glanced up from the scroll he had begun to unroll, raised an eyebrow. "Is that why you went to such effort to track me down?"

"Nakht's legacy to mistress Azzia prompted me to act." Bak formed a wry smile. "I must admit the trouble the spear brought about goaded me to a greater effort."

"I didn't plan on laying the blame at your men's feet." A note of bitterness crept into Paser's voice. "I thought, when I shoved him into the water, the current would carry him far away, not deposit him on a river-bank an easy walk from Buhen."

"You must've known him well to enlist him in your dangerous game—and to trust him to handle so much gold without being tempted."

"We played together as children, grew to manhood in the same village." Paser's voice softened. "No two men could've been closer."

"Yet you took his life."

"Not without regret, believe me." Paser sounded truly remorseful. "Heby knew the wound in his shoulder would lead you to him, and he wanted his share so he could flee. However, he didn't know this barren land as I do. He could never have survived the desert and he would've been snared within a day or two if he'd traveled by boat. What could I do but slay him?"

Bak was too aware of the careless way Paser had admitted to murder to think up an appropriate reply. It was obvious the officer had no intention of letting him live to repeat his words. When would he strike? With what? He remembered how evenly matched they had been when fighting in the goldsmith's house. If they were to clash here, and he suspected they would, the weapon Paser used might well give him the advantage.

Keeping a wary eye on his adversary, Bak examined the ingot he held. The weight, the color, the softness of the metal told him it was indeed gold. A faint, satisfied smile touched his lips. If Paser had taken it from his cache, he had led the Medjays who had been following him to all he had stolen through the year.

"This document, by itself, is worth nothing." Paser

rolled the scroll into a thin cylinder and tossed it toward the stairwell opening.

Dropping the golden bar beside the container of grain, Bak picked up the second scroll, which listed the amounts of ore recovered at the mines, and held it up with a wry smile. "If it has no value, I doubt you'll want this one."

Paser offered an ingot without a word. While he studied the document, Bak inspected his prize. His thoughts, however, were on the scroll so carelessly thrown aside. Though the action had appeared casual, it was as ominous as Paser's easy admission of guilt.

"What of the scribe Roy?" he asked. "Was he also a childhood friend?"

"He was Heby's friend, not mine, but I knew him well enough." Paser's laugh overflowed with scorn. "His greed was immense, but his fear of the desert knew no bounds. I knew he'd not run from the mine with what belonged to me."

Bak did not choose to remind him that the gold belonged to the royal house, not mortal men. "I feared you'd slay him while I was away in the desert, hunting for game. Were you not afraid I'd get to him before you could silence him forever?"

"I'd guessed by then how close you were to the truth, and I knew that to take his life alone would be futile. Later, after I decided how best to slay you, I needed him to lure you into the mine."

Bak's blood chilled at the matter-of-fact way he spoke. Laying the ingot on the step, he picked up the third and final scroll. It took all the patience he could muster to stand there, doing nothing to protect himself, while he waited to hand over the document.

Paser rolled up the second papyrus. As before, he

flung the cylinder toward the stairwell, not bothering to watch where it fell. Bak eyed the scroll teetering on the edge of the opening and the other document lying on the roof a half pace away. He could think of but one reason for so cavalier an action. Paser was freeing his hands, preparing to make his move. Since he had not once turned around, he must have a weapon concealed at his spine, something small, probably a dagger.

Paser held out the third golden bar, his expression open, sincere, trustworthy.

Bak ignored the offering. He had more to learn. "When you took the commandant's life, did you mean for mistress Azzia to shoulder the blame? Or was that, like the Medjay spear you used on Heby, a quirk of fate?"

"I've no love for the foreign woman," Paser admitted, tearing his eyes from the scroll. "She's always been too much the grand lady for my taste. But at the time, I thought only to slay him, to save myself from disgrace and death. Later, when I learned she was found with blood on her hands, I thought to cast doubt on her honor."

For that alone you deserve a slow, cruel death, Bak thought. "Nakht expected you that night?"

Paser's mouth twisted with contempt. "I was to bring all the gold we'd collected through the year and a written admission of guilt, then fall on my dagger. If I failed to obey, he vowed to take me before the viceroy and make my shame public before I suffered an official death."

"So you gave him no chance, no opportunity to defend himself."

"I offered to share with him. He refused. He was so smug, so convinced I'd bow to his demands, he even provided me with the weapon I used, the iron dagger. It lay on the table by his elbow. I snatched it up and thrust it into his breast."

Bak started to hand over the scroll, pulled it back. "What of my Medjay, Ruru? Did you have to take his life? Could you not have stolen up behind him and knocked him senseless?"

"With what?" Paser snorted. "I carried nothing but a dagger."

Bak had heard enough. Letting his long-dormant anger bubble to the surface, he threw the scroll as hard as he could. It struck Paser on the cheek, startling him, sending him back a pace. Drawing his dagger, Bak prepared to lunge. His opponent dropped the ingot and reached back, grabbing the weapon Bak expected. They stood three paces apart, knees bent to spring, daggers poised to strike. Paser, Bak noticed, had smeared a dark substance on the deadly blade so the glint of bronze would not be seen by a sentry on the wall above.

"You spawn of a snake!" Paser snarled. "You never meant me to leave this roof alive."

Bak sidled to his left, away from the zigzag shadow cast by the steps, and held his dagger higher so it could be seen from atop the wall. "You brought the hidden weapon, Paser. Why if not to slay me?"

"I knew you'd not be satisfied with three ingots. What was I to do? Let you bleed me dry, leaving me with nothing?"

As he spoke, he shifted to his right and a pace forward. His intention was clear. He meant to press Bak close to the rising stairway, gradually herding him backward into the corner, deep in the shadows where the sentries could not see.

"Surely the cousin of a man as lofty and influential as Senenmut has no need for gold." Bak spoke with a biting sarcasm. "Or does the chief steward think too little of you to raise you to the position of wealth and power you feel you deserve?"

"Senenmut cares for no one but himself." Paser edged closer, narrowing the distance another half-pace.

Bak held his ground. "You took the gold in a fit of pique?"

Paser expelled a sharp, bark-like laugh. "You said one time that you had the ear of Menkheperre Thutmose. You know better than I that one day his regiments will march on the great cities of Kemet and he'll take the throne for himself alone. You said as much the day of the archery contest."

Bak had forgotten the long ago lie, his claim of knowing the young king who stood in the shadow of his powerful co-ruler. He thanked the lord Amon that Paser had believed the tale. It had made him more cautious, had forced him to contrive ways of slaying Bak that would be accepted as the will of the gods. At least until now.

"My dear cousin will fall with our sovereign, and all those close to him will fall as well." Paser took another tentative step, bringing him dangerously close. "Senenmut has had no thoughts to spare for me. I see no reason why I should share his fate. The gold will give me a new life of ease and luxury in a place far to the north of Kemet. Perhaps in the land of Mitanni, or Keftiu, or far-off . . ."

He stopped, listened. Bak heard it, too. The soft whisper of sand falling on the roof from somewhere above. Paser's eyes darted upward. His face turned

ugly, mean. Bak dared not look up, but he was sure the
officer had spotted Imsiba in the deep shadow cast by
the wall, slipping down the stairs from the battlements.
Paser lunged. Bak ducked into the shadow, felt the
blade shave his left arm. Paser's momentum drove him
on and he slammed into Bak, shoving him against the
stairway, pinning his right arm and dagger between his
body and the mudbrick.

The quick kew-kew-kew of a falcon carried across
the rooftops, Imsiba warning the Medjays who had
encircled the building after Paser's return that the fish
they had caught might soon attempt to break out of
the net.

Bak tried to twist away, to release his dagger. Paser
caught him by the throat, shoved his head hard against
the stairway, and dug his fingers into the vulnerable
flesh, stealing the breath from Bak's lungs. As the caravan officer pulled back his weapon to strike, Bak
grabbed his wrist with his free hand to stave off the
thrust and at the same time rammed a knee upward,
aiming for Paser's crotch. Clamping Bak's neck with
the strength of a madman, Paser jerked aside, saving
his private parts but giving Bak the room he needed to
extricate the hand holding his dagger. Paser twisted his
own weapon and raked the point across Bak's left
wrist, forcing him to relax his grip. Bak, his vision
blurring from lack of air, shoved his dagger at his captor's middle. Paser slashed his weapon downward to
parry the blow. The dagger spun from Bak's numbing
fingers and clattered across the roof.

Imsiba had to be close by on the stairs, but Bak
doubted the Medjay could help. With him and Paser
pressed so tight together, limbs entwined, one looking

much like the other in the shadow, none but a creature of the night could tell them apart. He had to help himself—and soon—before he had no strength left.

He let himself go limp. His knees buckled. Paser clutched his neck tighter but, unable to support his weight, let him slide down the wall. Suddenly, before the caravan officer could drive his weapon home, Bak shot upward, smashing the top of his head into his captor's chin. Paser grunted and staggered back. His fingers slid from Bak's neck.

Gasping for air, Bak stumbled a couple of steps along the stairway, stretching the distance between them. He heard the rustle of sandals on the stairs and glimpsed through a blurred halo the point of Imsiba's spear above him. Common sense told him Paser would accept his fate and give up. Instinct told him to breathe as deeply as he could, to stiffen his wobbly knees with air.

Paser shook his head to clear it. His eyes darted upward. He bared his teeth and uttered a sound somewhere between a moan and a growl. His arm shot up and back, ready to heave his weapon.

"Do you want to die?" Imsiba spoke in so ordinary a manner he could have been asking about the weather.

Paser hesitated, neither lowering his arm nor throwing the dagger.

"I suggest you look behind you." Imsiba nodded toward the stairwell opening.

The caravan officer glanced over his shoulder and spat out a curse.

Nebwa, armed with a heavy spear, emerged from the stairwell and stepped onto the roof. "A dozen Medjays are scattered around this building. If you use that dagger on any one of us, their dogs will tear you to pieces."

Releasing a hard, bitter laugh, Paser slowly lowered his weapon. "When first I laid eyes on you, Bak, I thought you a simple soldier. Never would I have guessed you'd make a fool of me."

"Drop your dagger, Paser." Bak's voice was hoarse, lacking the authority he intended. "We want you living, but we'll take your life if we must."

Paser charged at Nebwa. Swinging his spear to impale the approaching man, Nebwa stepped sideways so the impact would not drive him through the opening behind him. His sandal skidded on the grain, and the spear point leaped upward. Before he could regain his balance, Paser rammed into him, knocking him off his feet, and grabbed the weapon. The burly officer fell with a solid thud, but had the presence of mind to seize Paser's leg.

A light flickered in the stairwell and brightened to cast a golden glow over the pair. Paser shoved his dagger into the sheath he pulled around to his hip and raised the spear to plunge it into the man who held him. Bak grabbed the only object close by, the jar of grain. Not much of a weapon, but all he had.

A torch followed by a head and shoulders appeared in the opening. Bak stared, appalled, at Kames, the highly placed civilian he had recruited to hear Paser's admission of guilt. The chief scribe had been told to stay in the courtyard until all danger was past, yet here he was.

"You've got him!" Kames said. "I heard every . . ." The torch wavered and the reedy old man gaped at the spear suspended over Nebwa's chest.

Bak threw the jar. Imsiba hurled his spear an instant later. The jar hit the butt of Paser's weapon and burst apart, spraying shards and grain over his head and shoulders. The weapon was torn from his hand and its deadly point slid past Nebwa. Imsiba's spear, its path deflected by a shard, sliced through the flesh of Paser's right shoulder and struck the edge of the opening where Kames stood. The old man cringed, wrapped his arms around his head. Nebwa released Paser's leg and tried to grab the weapon, but it slid down Kames's back and clattered to the steps below. The old man ducked out of sight.

Bak, running toward them, saw Paser glance at the lighted stairwell which promised a way out. "Stop!" he croaked. "My men surround this building. You've nowhere to go."

Paser leaped past Nebwa's grasping hands, through the opening, and down the stairs. Cursing the villain's obstinacy, Bak raced into the swath of light. He heard Kames cry out, the thud of a fallen body, and Azzia shrieking angry words in her own tongue. Bak turned his curses on himself. She had vowed to remain in her bedchamber with her servants. He should have realized she would do no such thing with her husband's slayer close by.

Dreading what he would find, he plunged down the stairs. The old man lay crumpled in the doorway of Nakht's reception room, his long white kilt bunched around his knees, the torch lying on the floor, sputtering. As Bak leaped over him, he saw Paser just outside the courtyard door, struggling with Azzia for possession of Imsiba's spear. The caravan officer spotted Bak. He jerked the spear, and her with it, out of sight. Her screams ended abruptly.

A frigid hand clutched Bak's heart. "Azzia!"

No answer.

He ran to the door and peered around the jamb.

Azzia stood chalky-faced midway across the courtyard. Paser stood behind her, his left arm holding her
close, the dagger in his bloody right hand much too
near her white throat. The blood dripping from his
wound was smeared across her bare shoulder. Smoke
drifted over them from a torch mounted beside the
door leading to the stairway and the audience hall below. Imsiba's spear was nowhere to be seen.

A soft moan drew Bak back away from the door.
Kames had regained his senses. Bak thanked the gods
that at least his witness was all right. Imsiba mounted
the torch in a bracket by the door, preventing a dreaded
fire, and was raising the old man to a sitting position.

"Come out where I can see you, Bak," Paser called.
"Bring no weapon. I'll not take her life or yours, that I
promise. I need you to clear my path to the river, and
she's my guarantee that you'll cooperate."

"No, Bak!" Azzia cried. "I'd rather die than see the
swine go free."

"Silence! Do you want me to run my blade down
your pretty face?"

Imsiba spat out an oath in his own tongue.

"May all the gods of the ennead lay misfortune on
his shoulders," Kames muttered bitterly.

Bak's thoughts tumbled over each other. He dared
not help Paser leave Buhen. Once outside the walls, the
officer would take a skiff from the quay and sail off
with Azzia. The moment he no longer needed her, he
would slay her. She had to be torn from his grasp.

He glanced around, seeking a weapon. Something
small, something he could somehow conceal while he
waited for Paser to lower his guard.

"I know you're there, Bak," Paser called. "Show
yourself!"

Nakht's iron dagger! Bak swung toward the inlaid cedar chest, where he had placed the weapon the night Heby had ransacked the room. Praying Azzia had not moved it, he lifted the lid. The dagger lay exactly as he had left it. Withdrawing it from the sheath, he noticed for the first time the blood coagulating on his left hand, more than he would have thought possible from a wound that barely stung. An idea took form, a way of concealing the weapon.

"Nebwa is on the roof above us, Bak." Paser sounded grim and a bit desperate. "If you don't call him off, this foreign bitch will never again look in a mirror without shedding tears for her lost beauty."

Bak dropped the dagger where he had found it, squeezed the cut to make it bleed more, and smeared his chest. Praying he could deceive Paser, he held the injured wrist in front of the stain, making the wound appear far more serious than it was, and stepped into the courtyard. Azzia gasped at the sight of him. Nebwa, peering down from the roof, expelled a breastful of air and a curse.

Paser, who had taken shelter among the potted plants, his back to the wall, pressed his blade to Azzia's cheek. "Call off your dog. Now!"

Bak hesitated, his unwillingness to obey not a sham. "Drop the weapon, Nebwa, and back off. He's won the game, I fear."

The infantry officer's face reflected indecision, dismay, and when he looked at Azzia, helplessness. He laid the spear on the rooftop and backed far enough away that he could not easily reach it.

"Good." Paser's gaze dropped from the roof to Bak. "Let's go."

"I'll do all you say, but first I must stop the bleeding." Bak was glad his voice was so rough, making it easier to pretend weakness. "Give me time to bind my arm. I can tear the cloth from Kames's kilt."

Paser studied him with narrowed eyes, nodded. "Go, but waste no time. And bring bandages back for me."

Bak retreated into the reception room, his relief tempered by fear for Azzia. Kames and Imsiba had begun to tear strips of cloth from the bottom of the old man's kilt. Bak grabbed the sheathed iron dagger and a piece of linen. Working as fast as he could, he tied the sheath upside down to his bloody wrist, inserted the dagger, and wrapped a loose bandage around wrist, dagger handle, and hand.

Imsiba offered him several additional lengths of fabric and squeezed his shoulder. "Good luck, my friend."

Bak returned a tight smile and hastened to the courtyard. Arms spread wide, he pivoted to show Paser he carried no weapon. Azzia bit her lip, disappointed at how readily he had complied with her captor's orders.

"Go to the stairwell," Paser commanded. "I want you in front of me, not behind when we descend."

Bak made a wide circle around the officer and his captive, praying all the while to the lord Amon that he would have a chance to strike before Azzia was hurt. Paser edged sideways in the same direction, hugging the wall, where necessary shoving the heavy pots out of the way with a foot. Bak yearned to signal Azzia that he had a weapon, but the risk was too great.

When Bak reached the exit, Paser shifted the blade to her neck. "Enter the stairwell. Slowly. Or I'll bleed Azzia before your eyes."

Bak backed one careful step at a time onto the dim,

enclosed landing at the top of the stairs. The tall, heavy
water jars were stacked along the wall like ghostly sentinels. "It's blacker than night below. We'll need the
torch."

"Go to the far wall and feel your way down."

Bak bumped into the wall behind him. Paser pushed
Azzia across the threshold. She jerked to her right,
slamming his injured shoulder into the doorjamb. He
grunted, the dagger twisted away from her neck, but
still he clung to her waist. Taken by surprise, with no
time to think, Bak caught the neck of a jar, tipped it
onto its side, and shoved it hard. It rolled forward and
struck Azzia's legs and Paser's, sending them stagger-
ing backward, and smashed into the jamb. The neck
snapped off and water gushed across the landing. Paser
lost his balance and fell backward into a potted acacia,
pulling Azzia with him. The limbs of the tree, too
spindly to support their weight, collapsed beneath
them, spilling them onto the floor. Paser landed hard
on his wounded right shoulder.

Bak jerked the iron dagger from its bandage and
splashed across the puddle. Paser, grimacing with pain,
managed to keep Azzia on top of him. Bak halted in
mid-stride, as helpless to come to her aid as before.
She gave him a quick, desperate look and, like a wild
creature, began to twist and turn, to kick Paser's legs.
She tugged an arm free, clawed his thigh, the arm
around her waist, his bleeding shoulder. His face contorted with rage. He loosened his grip on her waist,
grabbed her flailing arm, and pinned it to the floor. He
flung his other arm wide to drive the dagger into her
side. She jerked away, exposing his chest. Bak threw
the iron dagger, burying it to the hilt. Paser stared at the

weapon, fashioned a smile of sorts, and tried to sit up.
He coughed, gagged. Blood dribbled from his mouth.
His dagger clattered to the floor and he crumpled life-
less alongside Azzia.

She lay as still as Paser, staring at him, horrified.
Bak wiped the sweat from his face and strode toward
her. She gave a strangled cry, rolled away from the
dead man, and began to sob. Bak knelt, drew her into
his arms. She clung to him, trembling, sobbing, laughing, half hysterical with relief. He lay his cheek on her
head and murmured words of comfort.

Imsiba, Nebwa, and Kames streamed out of Nakht's
reception room, the excitement in their voices muted
by death. Kasaya and Pashenuro came with them, the
latter carrying a small rush basket. The golden ingots
inside glittered in the torchlight.

Bak looked beyond Azzia's head to Paser's pros-
trate form. He did not regret the officer's death, nor
did he rejoice in his own victory. Paser must have
known he was doomed the day he decided to take the
flesh of the lord Re as his own, yet in the end he had
fought like a demon to escape. Had he, Bak wondered,
chosen the more valiant death over the harsh justice
meted out by man?

Chapter Nineteen

Bak entered the commandant's residence, hurried up the stairway, and burst into the courtyard, which was bathed in a clear morning sunlight so bright it made him blink. The change he found, the disarray, brought a lump to his throat, a sense of impending loss. A husky male servant he had never seen before trod back and forth, moving furniture and storage baskets to rooms the new commandant, Nakht's successor, was taking as his own. Two rectangular baskets, their lids tied and sealed for travel, sat outside the door of Azzia's sitting room. The rest of her belongings, he had seen Lupaki stow safely aboard the ship that would carry her away.

She had to go, he knew. Though she had been born and reared in a land whose customs were far different than those of Kemet, she had vowed to respect her husband's beliefs and wishes. She would travel for many days down the river and place him in his tomb near Mennufer with all the pomp and ritual due a man of his rank. Bak had no quarrel with that. But what of later?

He had seen her every day since Paser's death more than a month ago, usually early in the morning before her friends came to call. His love had deepened until the merest glimpse of her lovely face and graceful body took his breath away. Those few weeks, which had passed much too quickly, he had respected her recent widowhood. He had never touched her, nor had he uttered a word of what lay in his heart. He knew he must speak— and had come to do so—before she sailed out of his life forever. He could only pray she would understand that necessity drove him to act sooner than he should.

He walked to her sitting room, a barren space devoid of furniture and personal possessions. She sat on the floor, her eyes overflowing, draping a long string of blue and red beads around the young servant girl's neck. The child sobbed as if her life were ending. The older female servant knelt nearby, letting tears travel down her wrinkled face while she folded a dress into a travel basket. She, too, wore a necklace, a parting gift. Only Lupaki would travel north with his mistress. The women would stay behind to care for the new commandant and the wife and children who had arrived on the ship that would carry Azzia away.

Azzia drew the child into her arms to comfort her. He retreated, giving them the time they needed. The aromas of fresh bread and roasting duck, the sound of a woman's laughter, filtered into the courtyard from the rear of the house. A new mistress had taken charge of Azzia's kitchen. The thought drove him on to Nakht's reception room, empty except for memories.

Azzia found him there, sitting on a low bench he had borrowed from the husky manservant. "I hoped you'd come. To say good-bye at the quay . . ." She gave him a crooked smile, shook her head. "Better here where I can speak what's in my heart."

He did not delude himself that she meant to talk of love. "You can say anything you like other than words of thanks. First, however, you must promise to hear me out." He tried to keep his voice light, teasing; the words came out strained, too intense.

Her smile faded. A touch of pink colored her cheeks. She half-turned and he feared she would flee. She caught herself and her eyes met his straight on. "No, Bak. Some things are better left unsaid."

Blood rushed into his face.

"My heart is heavy at having to leave a home I've learned to love. A place of sorrow now, but of many happy memories. A place of friends I hold dear." She tried a smile that failed dismally. "Speak of something joyful, Bak. Tell me of the message the courier brought from the royal house. For you alone, I've heard."

He scolded himself for being so thoughtless. She had just bade her private good-bye to two servants who had been closer to her than any friend. He, like a clumsy fool, had been so intent on his own purpose that he had given her no time to collect herself.

"I was given two scrolls. One from our sovereign, Maatkare Hatshepsut herself, and another from Commander Maiherperi, the man who sent me to Buhen."

"You received much praise, I've been told." Her voice was tense but steadier.

He produced a smile, even managed to tease. "If you know their contents, why ask me to repeat what they said?"

"The tale is yours, not that of any other man."

Her smile, though tentative, was so warm and sincere he wanted to reach out and draw her into his arms. Resisting the urge, he kept what he was sure was a silly grin plastered on his face, shifted to the end of the bench, and patted the space beside him.

She hesitated, but finally sat down and folded her hands primly in her lap. "Tell me."

"The brief message from our sovereign recognized a task well done. She—or more likely the vizier or one of his scribes—made no mention of Paser or of the stolen gold or of any death except Nakht's." He had a hard time balancing pride, modesty, and cynicism.

"Has the truth been kept from her?" she asked, surprised.

"I've no doubt Maiherperi told her all that happened, but in private so no other man would hear. He values his position too much to air in public a tale she'll keep to herself as long as Senenmut remains her favorite."

"I suppose it's natural that she'd want to protect him and his family, and therefore herself, but with so many here in Buhen knowing the truth, will word not spread? What if the tale should reach the ears of Menkheperre Thutmose?"

Bak leaned toward her, letting his shoulder touch hers, and murmured, "Can you keep a secret?"

She could not help but see beyond his mischievous smile. "He knows already?"

"A scroll went north to him on the same ship as the message to her. The man who sent it—I'll not repeat his name—believes he'll say nothing until he's ready to take the throne for himself alone."

"And I thought those who live in the palace of my homeland were masters of intrigue!"

He laughed.

The last bit of tension vanished from her and she offered him an affectionate smile. He basked in its glow.

The old woman came through the door, carrying a small leaf-lined basket of sweet cakes, an unplugged wine jar, and two stemmed drinking bowls. Without a word, giving no hint of what she thought, she set the cakes at their feet, handed over the bowls, and filled

them with the pungent red liquid. Bak sensed disapproval. Or was his conscience nagging him for wanting
to speak before Nakht was laid to rest through eternity?

"Maiherperi's message was not so formal," he said,
watching the servant leave the room. "He was free with
his praise and, better yet . . ." He raised his bowl toward far-off Waset, offering a toast to the commander of
the royal guard. "He gave me back the rank I lost. I'm
once again a lieutenant, Azzia, and free to rise through
the ranks with no black mark to besmirch my name."

Her smile was lovely, as grand a reward as any he had
been given. "I'm pleased, Bak, and very happy for you."

"Azzia . . ." He reached for her hand.

Her fingers slipped away and she bent to take a cake
from the bowl at her feet. "I was told that Maatkare
Hatshepsut rewarded you, but not with the gold of
valor you earned."

"So conspicuous a recognition would've raised too
many questions."

Azzia handed him a sweet cake—in the hope that it
and the wine would keep both of his hands busy, he felt
sure. "You aren't disappointed?"

"She gave me land, a small farm across the river
from the capital. My father's home is close by and I
know it well. It has a house, small to be sure, but it can
be made larger, and the soil is dark and fertile."

"You plan to keep it for your own?"

He caught her eye, held it. "With a good man to tend
the fields—a servant like Lupaki, for example—it
would be an ideal place for a woman alone to live."

She flushed to the roots of her hair.

He set his cake and drinking bowl on the floor and, to
make sure he had her undivided attention, took the bowl
from her hand and set it with them. "Azzia, I know you

must take Osiris Nakht to Mennufer, and that I respect. Later, after he's resting peacefully in his tomb, I'd like you to go to my farm and make it your home. While you're there, think of me. Here in Buhen, also alone."

"You're staying? I assumed . . ."

"That I'd been given permission to return to the land of Kemet? Someday perhaps, but not now." He laughed, surprising her and himself. "I thought never to say this, but I've grown used to Buhen and the way of life in this garrison. I've learned I like being a policeman. The freedom, the excitement of the chase, the problems I must think out and resolve. And the very thought of leaving Imsiba and all my Medjays, of parting from Hori, Nebwa, Kames, even pompous old Tetynefer . . ." He shook his head. "I don't regret remaining here. If the truth be told, I'd hate to leave."

"My husband would be pleased. He thought you'd . . ."

He caught her chin and forced her to look at him. "Will you do as I ask, my sister? Will you go to my farm? Then later, when the time is right . . ."

"I owe you my life, Bak, and for that I'll never forget you. As for anything more . . ." She gave him the tenderest smile he had ever seen. "I'm sorry."

"Azzia! I know about Nakht's cousin. I read the scrolls he sent when he was overseeing construction of the tomb. He's a mean and petty man. He'll take you in; by contract he must. As soon as you're a part of his household, he'll claim all you have as his. Your few belongings. Lupaki. Maybe even your body. You'll become his servant, Azzia, a woman with nothing of her own and nowhere to go. I would spare you that."

"I appreciate your concern more than you'll ever know." She took his hand and pressed it to her warm cheek. "Have you not learned that, short of being accused of taking a life, I can protect myself almost as well as any man?"

He forced a smile. "You've a tendency to let your opponent get too close and take your weapon from you."

"As a young man, Lupaki was a fine soldier. He'll hone his skills and mine." Her soft lips brushed his fingers, making every nerve in his body tingle.

"I love you, Azzia."

She pushed his hand firmly into his lap. "I loved my husband, Bak, more than life itself. I still love him. How can I give myself to any other man? Or think of it?"

"In time . . . ?"

"If I could love another, it would be you. But today I cannot. Nor can I make any promises or look to the future, for who can say what fate the gods plan for us?"

He could see that any further plea would turn her from him. "I'll say no more," he said, making no effort to mask his disappointment. "You must never forget that my farm is yours should you change your mind."

She released a long, slow breath and smiled a heartfelt thank-you. Biting back a fresh entreaty, he returned her wine bowl and took up his. They sat together, sipping the heady liquid in a silence strangely companionable after so unsatisfactory a resolution, at least as far as he was concerned.

Too soon the wine was finished.

"I must leave you, but first . . ." She bent over the basket of cakes, withdrew Nakht's sheathed iron dagger from beneath the leaves, and held it out to him. "I want you to have this weapon."

He gaped. "You can't give it away! It's value is too great, both for the memories it holds and for the objects it could buy should you be in need."

"I know of no other man who has more right to it."

"Are you sure, Azzia? I was told Nakht kept it with him always."

"It took his life, Bak."

"It saved yours."

"For both those reasons, you must have it." She placed the dagger in his hand and gave him a quick, soft kiss on the lips. He reached out to her, but too late. She stood up and ran from the courtyard.

He longed to follow her, but he knew full well that to draw out their parting would hurt her as much as him. He slid the dagger from its sheath and stared at the long, tapered blade of iron. He had coveted it exceedingly when first he had laid eyes on it; now he would give it up without a moment's thought if he could have Azzia instead.

Bak stood alone atop the towered gate, intent on the harbor below and the river flowing north to Kemet. The sun beat down on his shoulders, draining the moisture from his body. The city behind him lazed in the midday heat, its streets still and silent except for the sporadic barking of dogs, their naps disturbed by the wailing of the hired mourners standing on the terrace that ran along the base of the fortress wall facing the harbor.

He leaned farther over the crenel, his eyes glued to the sleek traveling ship swinging away from its mooring. The mast and rigging had been lowered, the sail stowed away. The current would carry the vessel downstream. It's prow, on which had been painted the half-open blossom of a blue lotus, rose high and proud above the sun-dappled river. The captain bellowed orders from the low forecastle. A man at the stern worked the rudder. To the beat of a drum, the other sailors, twenty in all, dipped

long oars into the water, maneuvering the ship toward
the stronger midstream current.

Baskets, bundles, and furniture were stowed in and
around the yellow-and-blue checked deckhouse. Lupaki stood beside Nakht's shrouded coffin, waving to
Imsiba and Nebwa on the quay. Bak could not see
Azzia, who had disappeared beneath a woven reed
awning attached to the rear of the deckhouse.

Earlier, he had been one of many in the long procession of mourners who had accompanied the coffin
from the house of death to the quay, the women moaning and keening and throwing dirt in their hair, the men
marching with tears in their eyes. Almost every man
and woman in Buhen had come to display grief for a
commandant they had loved and respected. With the
coffin safely on board the ship, all except the ululating
women had gone on about their business.

The vessel cleared the quays and began to gather
speed. The oars rose and fell in unison to the rhythmic
cadence of the drummer. Imsiba and Nebwa waved a
last farewell to Lupaki and turned back toward the
gate, walking close and easy together, chatting like
brothers. A smile flitted across Bak's face as he
thought of the mutual dislike and mistrust they had
held for each other a few short weeks before.

He looked back at the ship and his heart twisted.
Azzia had come out from beneath the awning. She
stood beside Lupaki as if saying a final good-bye to a
place she had thought of as her home. Raising her arm
high, she waved. Bak scanned the harbor but saw no
one there paying the slightest bit of attention. He returned the signal. Her good-bye was for him alone.

With luck and the favor of the gods, he would one
day see her again.